the song reader

A NOVEL

lisa tucker

DOWNTOWN PRESS

New York   London   Toronto   Sydney

An *Original* Publication of POCKET BOOKS

 DOWNTOWN PRESS
A Division of Simon & Schuster, Inc.
1230 Avenue of the Americas
New York, NY 10020

Copyright © 2003 by Lisa Tucker

ISBN-13: 978-0-7434-6445-1
ISBN-10: 0-7434-6445-1

First Downtown Press trade paperback edition May 2003

10 9 8 7

DOWNTOWN PRESS and colophon are trademarks of
Simon & Schuster, Inc.

For information regarding special discounts for bulk purchases,
please contact Simon & Schuster Special Sales at 1-800-456-6798 or
business@simonandschuster.com

Book design by Jaime Putorti

Manufactured in the United States of America

Critical acclaim for Lisa Tucker's novels

The Song Reader

"An achingly tender narrative about grief, love, madness, and crippling family secrets."

—Publishers Weekly (starred review)

"Engaging and bittersweet. . . ."

—Booklist

"A good old-fashioned story . . . that people can't stop talking about."

—Philadelphia Weekly

"A clear winner. . . ."

—Albuquerque Tribune

Shout Down the Moon

"The situations Tucker describes here in starkly lyrical prose are as chilling as if they were all derived from her own experiences."

—People

"Tucker's portrayal is refreshingly real."

—The Philadelphia Inquirer

"Well-drawn, emotionally nuanced characters. . . . This compulsively readable tale deftly moves over the literary landscape, avoiding genre classification; it succeeds as a subtle romance, an incisive character study, and compelling women-in-peril noir fiction."

—Publishers Weekly

"Tucker's straight from the heart narration is instantly gripping."

—Booklist

"Tucker excels at setting her young protagonists in the heart of complex, often damaging familial relationships."

—St. Louis Post Dispatch

Once Upon a Day

"Tucker's graceful prose and well-crafted characters create a compelling odyssey of transfiguration."

—People (Critic's Choice)

"Lisa Tucker's third novel is her most ambitious yet. It's a tragedy, a mystery, a romance, a twisted family story about loss, violence, obsession, and forgiveness. . . . Tucker is a graceful writer with an ability to create characters whose flaws help make them sympathetic and believably human."

—The Boston Globe

"Tucker's new fable is self-consciously the stuff of fairy tales. . . . The book is charged with the sense that life is charmed, that chance encounters can change fates and remake them for the better."

—*San Francisco Chronicle*

"The title of Tucker's third novel sounds like a Nora Ephron movie, and on the surface the fanciful plots seems to play right along. . . . [But] another narrative strand casts a welcome emotional shadow . . . lifting *Once Upon a Day* out of the realm of romantic comedy and into the darker territory of an Old World fairy tale."

—*The New York Times*

The Cure for Modern Life

"An enjoyable literary page-turner that also explores serious social issues. In crisp, lively prose, Tucker cleverly executes a series of surprising twists that make the novel as fast-paced as a thriller, but with astute and often humorous observations about the shifting morality of twenty-first-century America."

—*Publishers Weekly* (starred review)

"A touching and very modern relationship story with some compelling social issues [and] a multi-faceted analysis of what it means to be a good person in the twenty-first century. . . . This fast-paced, funny, and smart novel is a sure bet for book clubs."

—*Booklist*

"*The Cure for Modern Life* is so inviting because it's about people we all know, or at least think we know. . . . Tucker deftly forces us to ponder what we'd do in this exploration of the complexity of human nature and our relationships with one another."

—*The Salt Lake Tribune*

"Lisa Tucker, once again, brings a fresh view to the intricacies of relationships in *The Cure for Modern Life*. . . . Tucker continues to grow as a writer, and *The Cure for Modern Life* gives readers some ethical questions to ponder. It's an approach that has long been Jodi Picoult territory, but Tucker comes at it from a different direction. The questions aren't the source of the plot, but they drive the relationships among central characters. It's a structure that should make the novel attractive to book groups who've enjoyed Picoult's work."

—*The Denver Post*

For Laura Ward, beautiful sister,
best friend, and true believer.

chapter
one

My sister Mary Beth was a song reader. Song reading was her term for it and she invented the art as far as I know. It was kind of like palm reading, she said, but instead of using hands, she used music to read people's lives. Their music. The songs that were important to them from as far back as they could remember. The ones they turned up loud on their car radios and found themselves driving a little faster to. The ones they sang in the shower and loved the sound of their own voice singing. And of course, the songs that always made them cry on that one line nobody else even thought was sad.

Her customers adored her. They took her advice—to marry, to break it off with the low-life jerk, to take the new job, to confront their supervisor with how unfair he was—and raved about how much better off they were. They said she was gifted. They swore she could see right into their hearts.

From the beginning, my sister took it so seriously. She'd been doing readings less than a month when she had those cards printed up. Each one said in bold black letters:

Mary Beth Norris
Song Reader/Life Healer
Let me help you make sense of the music in your head.
[Family problems a specialty.]
Leave a message at 372-1891. Payment negotiable.

She had to work double shifts at the restaurant to pay for the cards and the answering machine, but she said it was just part of her responsibilities now. "I have a calling in life," she told me, "and I've got to act like it."

I wish I'd saved one of those cards, but I wasn't there the night she buried them at the bottom of the garbage can. It was after Ben left, and after I discovered she'd lied to me about my father. It was when the trouble with Holly Kramer was just beginning, and I still thought—like most of the town—that her talent was undeniable.

Some people even claimed she had to be psychic. After all, no one else knew that Rose was in trouble except Mary Beth; no one even suspected that Rose would take Clyde's car on that sun-blind Saturday morning and drive it right over the sidewalk and through the glass wall of his News and Tobacco Mart except my sister, who told Rose two months before that she'd better stop seeing Clyde. From the song chart, Mary Beth knew Clyde had to be bad news. She shook her head when Rose got stuck on "Lucille" for five weeks and warned her a life can't hold this much sadness for long. When Rose started humming "Hungry Heart," Mary Beth knew the lid was about to blow off Rose and Clyde's relationship. But she didn't tell Rose I told you so when we went with Rose's mother to bail her out of jail. She wasn't that way with her advice, not at all.

My sister kept file cards on her customers, "song charts" neatly alphabetized in a large green Rubbermaid box in the corner of our kitchen. On Saturdays she would meet with new customers in the little room downstairs our landlady Agnes had donated to the cause—as long as Mary Beth kept the room clean and didn't disturb Agnes's husband's sketches and charcoal pencils still sitting on the desk exactly as he left them when he died eighteen years before. Sometimes she gave advice at these first meetings, but usually she waited until she'd kept the chart for at least a few weeks before she gave them a reading.

They were instructed to call twice each week, on Sunday and Wednesday, and leave a short message telling her the songs and the particularly important lines they had hummed for the last few days. She had to rewind the cassette on the Phonemate back to the beginning to fit all the messages that would come in. I helped her update the charts. (It was a lot of work, especially when they reported country and western songs, which I hated.) I wrote down the titles and lines exactly as they said, even if they got it wrong, for what's important, Mary Beth said, is how *they* hear the words. But if they were off on the lines, we would make a little star on their chart since Mary Beth said they might be hearing them wrong for a reason. We also made an "S" if they'd sung the lines on the machine, and a "C" if they'd sounded like they were crying or struggling not to.

Mary Beth was proud of this organized system. It allowed her to just glance at an entry and know quite a bit. For example, one of the entries on Dorothea Lanigan's chart was the last two lines of "Yesterday." Dorothea had changed only a word and a tense, but Mary Beth had nodded when she looked at the chart later that night and said, "Well, that's that."

Even I thought this one was obvious. After all, the song was about lost love, wasn't it? "It's too bad Dorothea and Wayne are splitting," I said. "She must be miserable."

Mary Beth looked up at me from the floor where she was sitting surrounded by charts and burst out in a laugh. "Leeann, they are going to be engaged by the end of the month. You mark my words." And of course, it turned out to be true. They had their wedding the next summer. Mary Beth was the maid of honor, since Dorothea said it was all thanks to her.

It was a gift, everybody said so. Sometimes I wished I had the gift, too, but I knew I didn't; I'd tried and failed too many times with my friends to believe otherwise. I asked them about their music and I gave them my theories, but I was always way off, and Mary Beth finally told me I was dangerous. "You can't mess around with something like this. What if somebody believes you?"

I knew, though, there was little chance of that. Mary Beth was the kind of person you take seriously; I had never been. Only my sister saw me as the thoughtful, intense person I felt I really was; my friends and acquaintances looked at me as a sweet, happy-go-lucky, go-along-with-anything kind of person. And I knew that was a side of me, too, but I was more comfortable at home, always had been, even though I didn't have parents.

Sure, we were a small family after Mom died, but it wasn't lonely. We had the endless stream of my sister's customers and of course the music. Every day, all day, our stereo would play and Mary Beth would talk about the lyrics, what they really meant. Even when we got Tommy, she kept it up, because she said babies could adjust to noise just fine, as long as you gave them the chance.

When Tommy first came to us, Mary Beth wasn't even all that surprised. She was only twenty-three, but she'd wanted a child as long as she could remember, and she was a big believer in things working out, no matter how improbable the odds. "It was meant to be," she concluded. "It's a sign that I've waited long enough."

At first, I didn't see it that way. I was eleven then; I knew you couldn't just hand over a living, breathing baby as payment for services rendered. Of course Mary Beth insisted Tommy wasn't payment, but I didn't see the distinction. After all, a customer had given him to my sister after the song reading was over, the same way they gave her cakes and stews and afghans and even cash occasionally.

Her name was Linda, but she called herself Chamomile, like the tea. She had a garden of red and purple flowers tattooed on her back, a string of boyfriends back in Los Angeles, and a fourteen-month-old son with big black eyes and curly black hair that she hadn't even bothered to name.

She called him the blob, because she was so sure he was retarded. He couldn't walk or crawl; he didn't talk or coo or even cry much. Nobody wanted that baby: not Linda, not her parents, and not any of the families on Missouri's waiting list for perfect, white infants. Mary Beth took this as another sign that she was supposed to have him. She didn't care if his daddy was black or brown or from Mars, because the first time she picked him up, he held on to her hair with his fist like he was afraid she'd disappear. When she curled up next to him at night, he breathed a fluttering little sigh of what she swore was pure happiness.

Linda was back in Los Angeles and the adoption was already final when the doctor confirmed what Mary Beth had been saying all along: the only thing wrong with Tommy was the way Linda had been treating him. He turned into a chubby-legged toddler who giggled as he followed us all over the apartment. He called me "E-ann" in the sweetest little voice. He called Mary Beth, Mama.

Sometimes I thought Mary Beth's gift would bring us everything.

My sister Mary Beth was a song reader. Nobody else in the whole world can say that, as far as I know. And even after everything that happened, I still find myself wishing I could go back to when the music was like a spirit moving through our town, giving words to what we felt, connecting us all.

chapter
two

It started when we tried to find our father, once, a long time ago. Mom had just died and we were reeling from the loss of our normal life.

Tracking him down was my idea, although I thought it was the obvious thing to do under the circumstances. My sister didn't agree. At Mom's funeral, when people asked if we were going to contact our father now, she stared right through them. Later she said she couldn't believe such a rude question. How could it matter after this? How could anything matter after this?

Mom had been on her way home from the July sale at Venture department store when she pulled out in front of an eighteen wheeler on Highway 61. Her car was cut in two, but when the insurance adjuster pried open the trunk, the bag from the sale was still intact. A green and pink striped bath towel, two packages of girls' size 10 underwear for me, and the album *Plastic Letters* for Mary Beth. Mom didn't know anything about

Debby Harry or punk, but she'd always called Mary Beth her "blondie."

What I remember about that time is how tired I was. I would go to bed so sleepy that I felt like I'd be out for hours, only to startle awake and realize again what had happened. Mary Beth had the same problem, but when the doctor at the hospital had offered her sleeping pills, she'd said no. "Doctors try to cure everything with pills," she told me, "even feelings."

I would have gladly taken them but nobody offered. I was just a kid.

We waited weeks to clean out Mom's bedroom. We bagged up the clothes first, to give to the needy. It was what Mom would have wanted. Mary Beth was almost six feet tall; Mom had been five-three at best, and I had no immediate plans to wear polyester pant suits and stiff-collared shirtdresses.

Dad had been gone five years by then, and the room seemed like it had always been only Mom's. There was no aftershave stain on the dresser, no tie collecting dust in the bottom of the closet, no flattened, laceless wing tip under the bed. It was just luck that I found his ring under Mom's cedar chest—luck in the form of an old vacuum cleaner that balked and spit the silver circle back at my ankle hard enough to make me bend down and take a look.

It took me a minute to realize that the ring must have been Dad's. It was engraved with his initials, HN, Henry Norris, but it was so small it fit me. I found out later that he'd worn it as a little boy, a gift from his mother. Dad adored his mother. This was one of the few facts I had about him.

He grew up in Tennessee. His father died when he fell off a train, drunk, when Dad was seven. His mother had to support them with her sewing, "piecework" they called it, since she was paid only when she finished a piece of clothing, getting nothing if she was too sick or tired to turn in anything at the end of a day. But when Dad was seventeen, she, too, died suddenly. She had a stroke of some kind, quite rare for as young as she was, and I'd heard whispers between cousins I barely knew about Dad's reaction: how he had a kind of nervous breakdown and great-aunt somebody had to take him to her house to recover, and how after that he, the brightest-smartest-could-have-made-something-of-himself boy you ever saw, never even finished high school.

Mary Beth told me once it takes guts to go nuts, and he must have had guts. "Most people," she said, "ignore the wound, put a Band-Aid on it, and forget it. Only the gutsy ones can look right at the blood, stare into the pain, and risk losing their minds to know what's what."

I didn't think she was talking about Dad, though. She almost never did. Even when the social worker assigned to my "case" asked about our father, Mary Beth just said he was "out of the picture." (The social worker was supposed to figure out where to put me after my mom died, but her job didn't make a whole lot of sense. Mary Beth was twenty-two and perfectly responsible; then too, my sister was the only person who wanted the job of caring for me. What was there to decide?)

I wore the ring for several weeks, thinking it would tell me something about him. I'd had a dream he was standing on a boat wearing a skipper's cap, holding a compass, issuing directions to unseen sailors. Later I realized I'd seen a picture of him on a boat, taken when he and Mom were on their honeymoon at the Lake of the Ozarks, but this didn't shake my feeling that he had crossed the sea and was thousands of miles from Tainer, Missouri.

When Mary Beth saw the ring on my finger, she said, "How

cute," as though I was a little kid playing dress-up, as though this ring was as meaningless to me as the ones that shot out in colorful plastic orbs from the gumball machine.

She knew I didn't really remember Dad. I was five when he left us; she was seventeen. One of the only discussions we'd ever had about him was when she realized I was making up things, telling my friends whatever came to mind, from a secret government assignment that called him to Venezuela, to a job in Hollywood, behind the camera for *Eight is Enough*.

I think she felt sorry for me, because she gave me two true stories instead. When he worked for Hedley's Auto Parts and Tires, she said, he made a jungle gym out of junk parts and old tires that had a ten-foot-tall hideout that was the favorite of all the kids in the neighborhood. And once, he won a contest at the civic club downtown. It was like *Name That Tune* and he could name them faster than anyone. He always loved music, especially show tunes like "Oklahoma" and "Camelot" and classical stuff.

Neither of these things helped. The jungle gym had nothing to do with me; I'd never even seen it. (We'd moved into our apartment on the second floor of Agnes's house when I was just a baby; Mary Beth said the gym would have been impossible to move even if we'd had the yard space.) And the contest business was just another connection between Dad and my sister that I didn't share. She was the musical one, the one who'd had the largest record collection in the senior class.

Maybe I wanted to know something about him that she didn't. Maybe that's why I started writing to his relatives to locate him, without mentioning what I was doing to her or anyone.

Mom had kept some of their addresses in her blue phone book. I began with the N page, for Norris, and just kept going, writing one a day every afternoon, before Mary Beth came home from her waitress job. I knew it was a long shot, but Mom always said hard work would pay off in the long run.

And it turned out to be true. After a few months of writing, I got the information I was waiting for. Joseph Morgan, from Kansas City, a second cousin of Dad's whom I'd met only once long ago at a family reunion in Boonville, had seen Dad. His letter went on for two pages, updating me about people and things I'd never heard of, but it ended with the news that Dad had given him an address. No phone, not even an unlisted one, but a street and an apartment number and even a zip code.

I folded the letter carefully and stuck it in my dresser, under my pajamas. I intended to keep it a secret from Mary Beth for at least a few days, but I barely lasted through dinner.

She didn't speak for a full minute after reading the letter. I thought for sure she was upset, but then she smiled. "You did it, honey. Good for you."

It crossed my mind that she'd known all along I'd been trying to find him, but I was too happy to care. When I told her I was going to write him that night, she nodded. "Of course you are."

It wasn't a long letter. I told him we were doing fine, that I was in the fifth grade and my favorite subject was history. In the last paragraph, I told him about Mom. I almost didn't, figuring it would come as such a shock, but I worried that if I didn't, he might not write back. I signed my letter, "All my love. Your daughter, Leeann."

I circled the date I mailed the letter on the calendar, Tuesday, December 5, and calculated how long I would have to wait for a response. I figured for sure I would hear something by the fifteenth, but when the fifteenth came and went, I decided he hadn't written because he was going to just show up for the holidays and surprise us. I wished I'd asked him what he wanted for Christmas. I had to get him something, but I didn't know what he liked or his size or even his favorite color. I settled on a one-size-fits-all acrylic sweater from The Men's Place in bright blue and violet stripes. My favorite color was blue, Mary Beth's was violet. I figured our father had to like one of those colors at least a little.

Mary Beth knew I was buying Dad a present and she didn't try to talk me out of it. "It's sweet of you. If he doesn't come here for Christmas, we can always mail it to him. But what's really important is what you want for Christmas. You haven't told me yet, you know." She sighed. "I want to make this holiday as normal as possible. I think it's what Mom would want for us."

I didn't really care about presents, but I made a short list. On Christmas morning, it was all there: a pair of jeans, a Sony portable radio, and a set of fancy drawing pencils. But Dad didn't come. Of course. His sweater, wrapped in green and yellow snowmen, stayed under the tree in the back, almost out of sight, until New Year's Day when Mary Beth and I packed up the ornaments and put the tree out in the street with the trash.

I stuffed the present under my bed, where it was safe, and where I wouldn't have to see it every day. I stopped thinking about Dad. I knew I'd have to keep trying, but I didn't know where to begin. But about a month and a half later, I came up with a plan. I would go to Kansas City to deliver the sweater myself.

This time when I told my sister there was no smile. She was watching *One Day at a Time* and filing her nails. She said it wasn't a good idea, and turned up the volume on the TV.

"Come on, Mary Beth," I said. "I'm sure we could get there in a few hours. It's not that far."

"It takes about five hours, but that's not the problem." Her voice was flat; she was concentrating on the edge of her thumb. "Think about it. He knows exactly where we are, and he hasn't ever come back to see us. There has to be a reason for that."

When I pressured her to tell me what that reason could be, she shook her head. "I'm not up to discussing this right now. Please, Leeann, just leave it alone."

But I couldn't do that. Every night that week after she got home from work, I begged her to change her mind, and every night, she told me to drop the subject. I tried everything, from promises of good behavior to persuading her latest boyfriend, Nick, to take my side. Nothing helped. My promises were sweet, she said, but they didn't change the situation. And Nick's advice was meaningless. What would he know about *her* family and *her* life?

He wasn't the first guy to hear that from my sister, and he wasn't the first (or last) to be dumped when he tried to interfere. She told him not to call anymore after she found out that he'd offered to take me to Kansas City himself one Sunday when she had to work. I felt bad for him, but I had to tell her. I knew it would be just the thing to make her realize she had no choice in the matter.

I didn't want to go with Nick; I wanted to go with her.

And it worked. She said we could leave in a few weeks, as soon as she could arrange a weekend off. I hugged her and thanked her. I said it would be an adventure, a real-life long-lost-loved-one kind of meeting like the ones in the movies.

"Maybe," was all she said.

When the Friday evening finally arrived, I packed up the present and my nicest skirt and knitted beige sweater while Mary Beth threw together some of her stuff. The drive took almost exactly five hours, and I was so tired when she pulled into a Travel Lodge motel in Independence that I fell asleep immediately, with my clothes still on, when I lay down on the stiff motel bed.

The next morning we had to get our bearings in Kansas City and find the downtown area, and then go south, like the map Mary Beth bought at the motel told us to do. When we finally got close to Dad's, however, Mary Beth decided we couldn't go yet since we hadn't had lunch, so we headed farther south, to the Plaza. I complained a little but I really didn't mind. Just seeing his neighborhood had made my throat go dry and itchy.

We ate and hung out at the Plaza, looking in store windows, trying on clothes we couldn't afford. Finally, Mary Beth said we'd better get going, and we headed back up to Harrison Street.

We found the address quickly. It was a three-story, dark red brick apartment building, run-down looking, with an overflowing Dumpster on the side, and two yellowing plastic chairs sitting on the front lawn. We opened the door, and I swallowed hard when I saw Henry Norris printed neatly on a white card above the middle of the six buzzers.

Mary Beth rang the buzzer. No one answered so she rang again. Still no answer, so she rang the buzzer on the left, underneath the card that said Landlord.

A woman in a purple housecoat and silver-sequined slippers opened the door. She looked us over without any expression. "Who're you looking for?"

Mary Beth said, "Henry Norris. I see his name here, but he doesn't answer his buzzer. Do you have any idea when he might return? We're sorry to bother you, but we've come a long way, and we can't wait too long."

"I wish I knew. He lit out of here two weeks ago without so

much as a good-bye. He didn't owe me no back rent, but he left the place in an awful state. My nephew came over last week and took one look and told me he'd have to give it at least two coats of paint before I can advertise. In the meantime, I'm losing money, and I can barely make ends meet as it is. So I'm not real happy with Henry Norris right now. Are you related?"

"Yes," Mary Beth said. "We're his daughters."

She looked us up and down again, but she didn't say anything. I figured she was waiting for us to go, but I wasn't about to do that. This was as close as I'd come to him for five years.

"I want to see the apartment," I said quickly.

The landlady shrugged, but Mary Beth shook her head.

"Come on," I said, grabbing my sister's arm. "Maybe there's a new address or something. It'll only take a minute. Please. We can't just leave without trying."

"Okay, okay." She turned to the landlady. "If it's not too much trouble."

The woman shrugged again. "Maybe you can figure something out from the mess he left behind."

We walked up one flight of narrow, creaking stairs. "It's up here," the landlady said, pulling a ring of keys from her housecoat pocket. "Be careful," she added, looking at me. "This place ain't no playground."

She opened the door. "I'll be downstairs. Let me know when you've finished so I can lock up."

It was a one-room apartment. Over on the left was the living room area, with a small green couch, an old TV with bent rabbit-ears antenna, and a wobbly, wood-veneer coffee table. The kitchen area was in the back corner, with a plastic tabletop and two metal chairs with sticky brown rubber cushions. The bedroom area was by the window and was the smallest of all, just a three-drawer dresser and a twin bed that came out of a closet. The landlady was right, it was a mess, but I hardly noticed the trash even though a couple of times I had to kick away crumpled paper and old cans. I didn't really pay attention to the smell, either, although it reeked of spoiled food. It was the walls I noticed. They were covered with words, filled with big square letters. Someone—it took me a minute to realize it must have been Dad—had actually written on almost every available inch of the walls with a thick black pen. On the wall behind the couch, he'd written "EVERY MORNING" in large print, and then underneath a list numbered from one to fifteen. Many of the words were smeared and illegible, but I made out:

Brush Teeth
Wash Face
Bowl of Cereal Juice Coffee
Bus #9 leaves from corner at 7:42
Pack lunch FIRST!
Get three quarters from drawer for bus there, three quarters more for bus home: total of six quarters needed.
Coat! KEYS!!!
Lock apartment door

Lists like this covered every wall in the place. There was a list for every evening over by the pullout bed, with instructions like "eat dinner," "lock the door," "wash out underwear for the next day." There was a list for each day of the week: Tuesday's list, in the bathroom, included taking the trash to the Dumpster outside; Saturday's longer list, by the kitchen table, included going to the Laundromat and the corner grocery store. There was another list right by the refrigerator of things to buy at the store (which seemed senseless to me until I decided he must have copied this one down on paper before he went to do his shopping). There were even reminders for specific days over by the door, such as "December 17th: Library Books Due. Library Closes at exactly 7:30," and "November 8th, 10:30 A.M., plant physical. Shower in morning first."

There were so many words, so many lists, and I moved from wall to wall like a spider, taking it all in. I couldn't stop reading, even though my mind was becoming numb and my eyes were aching from the strain of trying to read as the room grew shadowy in the early dusk of February. I kept looking for something that would make sense of it, something that would explain the why of all these words. Only after more than an hour, when I'd seen all the walls and read every legible word, did I finally fall back, bone-tired, on the couch by Mary Beth.

Her eyes were closed, and her head was laid back, but I knew she wasn't asleep because her teeth were pressed down, biting her bottom lip. I told her I was ready, and she stood up without saying anything and walked downstairs.

The landlady was cooking spaghetti when we knocked on the door. The garlic smell was so heavy it made me feel a little sick to my stomach. When she opened the door, she asked us if we'd found what we were looking for and Mary Beth nodded. Then Mary Beth opened her purse and pulled out two twenty-dollar bills. "It's not much, but it'll help pay for the paint at least. I'm really sorry about your trouble, and thanks again for letting us go up there."

The woman smiled warmly for the first time. "That's awfully good of you. It's just too bad you didn't catch him. Hold on. I've got something for the little girl."

She brought out a bruised apple and put it in my hand.

"You're probably hungry by now. You all take care of yourselves. If I see Henry Norris again, I'll be sure and tell him you were here."

We walked to the car in the darkness. Mary Beth started down the street and twisted the radio dial until she found the rock station playing "Tuesday Afternoon." She started humming along like nothing had happened and maybe I wanted to believe her, at least for a while. Or maybe I was just exhausted. Before the song ended, I sank into sleep and I didn't wake up until we were at O'Fallon, about ninety miles from home.

It took me a moment to remember where we were, why we were in the car at ten o'clock on Saturday night. As I looked out the window at the big green highway signs telling me the number of miles to places I'd never heard of and places I'd probably never go, I felt calm and grateful for the night that could hide everything from me and make the highway seem like all there was in the world.

When Mary Beth realized I was awake, she said she wanted to talk to me, and turned down the radio. I braced myself for whatever she would say.

"You know, I bet you can tell an awful lot about a person from the songs they sing. I don't mean if they're in love, it's a happy song; if they've broken up, a he-done-me-wrong song. I mean something else. Something in the brain maybe, that lets the music slip past all the things you think you know, and wish you believed, to what you really are." She glanced at me. "It's kind of strange, don't you think? Those same words would be ignored if someone tried to just say them to you, but when they're in the music, it's different—you can't help but open up. And then you start singing them, too, and it's like your voice is telling you something you still don't know, but need to. Like you're stuck on a particular song and you can't get it out of your head for a reason."

I was more than a little confused. Of course I expected her to talk about Dad. "Did this happen to you?"

"Sure, lots of times, but I'm talking in general here." She moved into the right lane. "I'm saying if you looked at the songs people keep singing, you might find out something important about them." She shrugged. "Oh, not every song. But a lot of times, the person could be figured out by the song, kind of like dream interpreting. You know how they say if you dream about a house, you're dreaming about yourself. Well, I'll bet if you're singing certain songs, it's the same way, and you could work out a method to figure out what it all means."

I didn't know about dream interpreting, but before I could ask, she said, "Here, let me try it out on you. Tell me the last song you couldn't stop humming, that you kept going back to whenever your mind wasn't busy with something else."

The only song I could think of was "Blue Bayou." It was on the radio when I woke up.

"Okay," she said, "but let's say you got stuck on it, and two weeks or even ten years from now, sometimes, all alone, you were still hearing it. Don't you think that would be important? Like your mind was still in the car in a way, trying to make sense of everything that happened on this trip, but maybe you wouldn't remember anymore where you were when you heard it, and why it kept playing in your head. So instead of just singing it, you decide to think about it. And then you know something about yourself, something the song was trying to tell you."

"Like what?"

"Well, it depends. You'd have to think about how you felt when you sang it. Do you want to cry? Or are you more angry? Or are you just repeating the words, numbly, without feeling anything? But this isn't a real example. Tell me a song you've actually gotten stuck on."

"I don't have one," I said, pulling at the bottom of my sweater.

"Oh sure you do."

"I can't think of one right now."

"Come on, Lee. Try."

"I am."

"Well, try harder. This is important."

I was too tired to try harder, and when she kept pressuring me, I started to cry.

She touched my shoulder and said, "poor baby," "oh sweetie, it's all right"—but now that I'd let myself start, it wasn't so easy to quit. She grabbed a napkin from the dashboard, and kept patting me while I blew my nose several times. When a station wagon behind us started honking because we were going so slow, she yelled, "We're a little busy here," but she put both hands back on the wheel and accelerated.

Ten miles down the road, when I was still sniffing and coughing, she said, "Okay, I know what you're thinking. You're thinking it was your fault that Dad left. It's not true. Trust me, honey. You had nothing to do with it."

I was so surprised that I stopped crying and stared at her. She was right, although I wouldn't call what I was doing thinking. There were no words that went with this feeling. It was just cold emptiness, a blind panic. Like I'd somehow let go of my father, and he'd fallen through the earth.

I hadn't felt this way since I was so little. I'd forgotten I'd ever felt this way, actually—until Mary Beth reminded me. "You used to say all the time that you'd lost Daddy." Her voice was airless. "Like he was your favorite doll."

She pulled onto the exit for Tainer. Neither of us spoke for a moment. Finally I said, "Is something wrong with him?"

Mary Beth exhaled loudly. "Did I ever tell you about Dad and me watching *The Wizard of Oz* together?"

"No."

"It was kind of a big deal. Every year when it came on, Dad and I would sit together on the old couch, glued to the set, grabbing handfuls of popcorn. Okay, well, one year when I was about twelve and you were just a baby, Dad and I sat down to watch the movie. You were in your crib sleeping. Mom was gone somewhere, I don't remember where. I didn't think anything was wrong until Dorothy was halfway through singing 'Somewhere Over the Rainbow,' and Dad got up and walked outside. I called him back, told him not to miss the tornado part, but he didn't answer, so when the commercial came, I ran out to get him. He was sitting on the porch swing in front of the old house, but he wasn't swinging. He had his head down and his face in his hands.

"He'd already lost his job. I could see the For Sale sign planted in our front yard. When I asked him what was wrong, he raised his head, but he stared off at the sky instead of looking at me. Then he lifted his hands, palms up, above his shoulders, like he was apologizing to the moon, and said something so strange I'll never forget it. He said, 'There's no somewhere for me. No place far enough away. Because no matter where I go, I'll always be there.'"

She paused and rubbed her forehead. "We moved and things got worse and worse. I don't know. I guess I always hoped he'd be better off; maybe that he'd even find his own rainbow someday."

I heard how sad her voice was, and I was trying to think of something to say to all this. But then she shrugged off her mood—and the topic—by claiming she was so tired she was starting to babble. "I've driven almost six hundred miles now." She pointed at the odometer and smiled a half smile. "Me, who doesn't even like to drive to the grocery store."

Yet the next morning, she didn't sleep in like she'd said she was going to. I woke up to find her sitting at the kitchen table, downing her second pot of coffee and scribbling lines from songs on a notepad. She was so excited about her song-interpreting idea that she'd already called a friend from the diner to come over and test it out.

"I really think this could work, Leeann." She was still staring at the notepad but her voice sounded strangely urgent. "I think I have to try."

"Then you should," I said, and she looked up at me and smiled.

She did her first chart about an hour later while I was lying on my bed, reading a book for school. Later that night, she told me this was her "calling." I agreed with that, too.

I was ten years old; I wanted to please her. From the very beginning, I helped her make notes on the charts, helped her pick out her business cards, and listened to her talk about songs for hours—even though I didn't really believe in song reading. I didn't disbelieve, I just didn't really understand the idea well enough to decide. Until it happened to me, that is.

It was maybe two months after we came back from Kansas City. Mary Beth was at work, and I was sitting at the Laundromat, watching the dryers spin around, when all of a sudden, I remembered very clearly coming here with my dad.

I was five years old and Mom was in the hospital for her gallbladder. It wasn't serious, but she had to stay in the hospital for a week, and Dad and I were on our own to get ready for the beginning of kindergarten. The night before he helped me pack my lunch and lace my new shoes, but when I went to get dressed that morning, I realized I had nothing to wear. All my clothes were in the hamper, we'd forgotten to do the laundry.

I told Dad this, and he fell apart. He started crying and grabbing up the laundry. I tried to tell him I'd just wear something dirty, but he wouldn't hear of it. He hurriedly gathered up every slightly dirty thing in the house, even the bedsheets and the dusty guest towels hanging in the rings by the bathroom sink, while I grabbed my lunch box and shoes. We rushed out of the house like it was about to collapse around us and headed to the Laundromat.

I sat up on the big brown plastic table in the middle of the place, dangling my legs, watching him. I remembered how he'd adjusted his glasses on the end of his nose, straining to read the little faded tags on shirts and underwear, trying to sort everything into piles for washing. He swore whenever a tag was completely illegible or missing, and nervously tried to match these tagless items by sight with the large piles of laundry on the table. He even asked me about some of these things, one tense question after another, not waiting for my response. "Do you think these purple jeans belong with the black sock pile or the blue jeans pile? They are jeans, but they're not as light as these blue ones. Oh hell, I'll just wash them by themselves . . . How about the striped stuff—does it go all together: striped towels, shirts and underwear? Or do the shirts go with shirts and towels with towels? . . . Let me see that tag again on the red and white blouse over there."

It took him a very long time to sort the laundry. When he finally hit the start button on the last washing machine, his shoulders loosened and he breathed a heavy sigh of relief. When it was time to dry the stuff, though, he ran out of quarters.

Because the change machine on the wall was broken, we had to walk to the bank around the corner, but Dad couldn't decide whether to take our laundry, dripping wet, with us, or leave it there—he'd seen the large sign on the wall that said Do Not Leave Laundry In Dryers. This choice made him tense all over again. Only when I told him that Mom and Mary Beth did it all the time, that we'd even gone grocery shopping while the laundry was drying, did he agree to leave the clothes and go.

I never made it to school that day. I saw several school buses drive past the big glass window of the Laundromat, already taking kids home, while Dad was still busy folding our clothes into neat fabric squares. He must have completely lost track of time, because when we got home he was surprised to see Mary Beth and Mom sitting at the kitchen table. Mary Beth had been sleeping when we left—she was a senior, and high school didn't start for another week—but Mom wasn't supposed to be released from the hospital until one o'clock that afternoon. Dad was supposed to pick her up; he'd told me that over and over while we were doing the laundry, but I couldn't tell time yet so I couldn't tell him that one o'clock was long past. I found out later that Mary Beth had picked her up, after Mom had waited almost an hour for Dad and finally called home.

At first, Dad was confused. He thought Mom had gotten out early and started to ask her why. But when she interrupted him to find out how my first day of school had gone, he seemed to suddenly remember why we went to the Laundromat to begin with. He put down the laundry basket in the middle of the kitchen floor and covered his forehead with his hand. I saw the look of alarm in his eyes, the fear and confusion in his slack, open lips, and I reached out to take his arm. Before he could speak, I told Mom I had refused to go to school, that Dad had tried to get me out the door but I'd insisted on staying home and helping him with the laundry.

She started to fuss at me, but when she looked closely at Dad's face she stopped. She got up, motioned him into their bedroom, and closed the door behind them. I guess he must have told her something like the truth because she never mentioned that first day of school again.

I watched the bright colors of our clothes spinning in the dryer as I remembered all this, and I was only a little sad. Mary Beth had said if you find yourself stuck on a song, there has to be a reason—and I was amazed at how right she was.

The song was "Please Come to Boston." I didn't know where or when I'd heard it, but I'd been humming it for days, including this very afternoon in the Laundromat. And it fit amazingly well. The song was about a girl wanting a man to stop drifting and come home to her. I'd been thinking about Dad for weeks. No wonder that tune was on my mind.

I was planning to tell Mary Beth about this, but then I went home and looked up "Please Come to Boston" in her book of lyrics. All I'd known was the melody and the words of the first verse. I didn't realize that the chorus had "a man from Tennessee" and a girl who was his "number one fan."

It fit all right, but it was so embarrassingly obvious I couldn't bring myself to share it with her. The only thing that would have been worse was if the chorus said the man was from Shelbyville, Tennessee: my dad's hometown.

chapter
three

Mary Beth's song reading caught on quickly, but it wasn't until late in the summer of '81 that she became known all over Tainer. My sister called it the "summer of endless love," both because "Endless Love" was the number one song reported by her customers, and because everyone who came to her suddenly seemed to be obsessed with romance.

Maybe it was because Prince Charles had just married Diana. Maybe it was because Luke and Laura on *General Hospital* were finally getting engaged. Whatever the reason, the women who flocked to my sister that August wanted to know one of two things. Would *he* ever show up? Or was *he* here already, in the form of the ordinary guy they were seeing, the one with smelly socks and a dirty car and an irritating tendency to cry over baseball?

Tainer was a small town, but it was big compared to the tiny places around it. Most of them had one traffic light, tops, where we boasted of eleven. They had one corner with a Fina or Texaco;

we had two grocery stores, a strip mall, and a theater that could show four different movies at the same time. True, we didn't have any cool clothing stores, as my friends liked to point out, but we had a good-size JC Penney. Then too, Tainer had all the guys. Even if they didn't live here, they had to pass through. The plastic factory that employed most of the county was down on River Road. The only farm equipment place for fifty miles was a few blocks from our neighborhood, over on Twain Boulevard.

My sister's customers would often find men, but they usually lost them just as fast. The guys around here worked, but according to the women, that was about all you could say for them. It had something to do with the town's history, or so the joke went. The local legend was that Tainer was founded by a trader from back east who was heading down south on the Mississippi and got tired and just stopped. On the wall of Mr. Lucas's drugstore, he had a plaque that read Tainer. Put Up Your Feet and Stay Awhile. This used to be the town slogan. The women who came to my sister insisted it was an all too perfect description of Tainer's couch potato men.

Or as one of Mary Beth's customers put it, "I am woman, hear me roar. I am man, hear me snore."

I was used to hearing this kind of thing. One of my earliest memories was of Mom telling me how ridiculous it was that men were considered tougher. "Women give birth," Mom said, "and most men can't even stand the sight of blood." I nodded, but I was wondering what blood had to do with birth. At six, I had given up the stork theory for the much more reasonable conclusion that the baby popped out of the mom's belly button.

I was used to hearing this kind of thing, but it didn't change how I felt. I was thirteen that summer, and I knew "Endless Love" by heart, along with all the other romantic songs my sister's customers reported. I'd been imagining what love would be like for a long time. It started with my parents' honeymoon at the Lake of the Ozarks. The one and only fact I knew about the trip was that they'd bought a rocking chair from a little craft store on their way home. They strapped it to the top of their Mercury, but they didn't tie the ropes tight enough and it fell off and slammed into pieces on the highway. It was late and the road was almost deserted, luckily, because if that flying rocker had hit another car, the people inside could have been killed.

My version supplied the missing details. How she told him it was all her fault because her side of the rope was too loose, but he said no, it was his fault because he hadn't used a double knot on the back piece, and how they put their arms around each other then and said that it doesn't even make sense to talk about fault when you're in love. How they both cried, not because of their lost rocker, which they knew was only a thing even if it would be impossible to replace (it was a very special, one-of-a-kind rocker: hand carved with flowers on the slats that looked just like the roses at their wedding), but because they were so grateful no one had been hurt. Being in love is like that, they both said later. It makes you care about everyone more, almost as if you're in love with the whole world.

My deepest wish that August was for my sister to fall in love. If only she would get married like Prince Charles and Lady Diana, I would get to be a bridesmaid and wear a beautiful gown. But she hadn't even had a date for more than a year, because she was already in love—with a thirty-three-pound, two-and-a-half-year-old.

Tommy was pretty irresistible. The baby nobody wanted had grown into the cutest toddler. His skin had become a rich, golden brown and he still had those beautiful black curls. He gave the goofiest sloppy kisses and this whole-faced grin when you came in the room that made you feel like you were the most important person on the planet. He'd waddled at eighteen months, and now he could walk perfectly and talk in sentences. And he seemed to be over his biting phase, which made hanging out with him a lot more relaxing.

I didn't mind taking care of him on Saturdays so Mary Beth could meet customers downstairs in the office. I wouldn't have minded baby-sitting him in the evenings, too, except she hadn't gone out in the evenings since Tommy came to live with us.

She'd set up a permanent schedule at the diner—Monday through Friday, seven to four—so she could leave Tommy with Mrs. Green, an older woman in our neighborhood who took in four toddlers. Mrs. Green was sweet, but Mary Beth felt Tommy needed her personal touch as much as possible. "Human beings weren't born in litters, you know," she would say.

I thought what Tommy needed was a father. I knew Mary Beth could find someone if only she'd try. She'd never had trouble attracting men. Being tall and blond didn't hurt, although I knew it was something else, too. She seemed incapable of being needy. Unlike so many of her customers, she never wanted more from a guy than he wanted to give.

Whenever I asked her why she wasn't married yet, she always shrugged off the question. I might have thought she just didn't care about that part of life, but she certainly didn't sound that way talking to other women. "A man has to be more than a paycheck and fun on Saturday night," she would say. "There has to be a soul connection, an unbreakable tie to your heart that can't be confused with hope. When you find that, trust me, you'll know."

It was talk like this that helped make her an authority on relationships to her customers. They believed her when she said she was sorry but reporting lines from "Endless Love" was actually a bad sign. It was the kind of song you only sing when you're not in love, but desperately want to be. "Bette Davis Eyes," also popular that summer, was better, because it hinted at the confidence you feel when you're having a good time with a man. Best of all was something intensely personal and not current. A song associated with happiness in the past that comes back to you suddenly, seemingly out of nowhere—because you're happy again.

For one person, it could be a show tune they sang in high school; for another, a lullaby their mother used to sing as they went to bed. When Janine Thompson started seeing a new guy, her chart was filled with lines from Bing Crosby songs. Mary Beth helped her remember her sweet grandpa had always listened to Bing Crosby, so of course she should keep dating this man.

I loved listening to my sister talk about these things. After Tommy was asleep, we'd sit on the floor with the windows open and the fan blowing, updating the charts, preparing for the next Saturday. Of course if the chart was a guy's, I'd pump my sister for what he looked like. But the chart was almost never a guy's, and when it was, Mary Beth would roll her eyes as though I'd asked something as irrelevant as whether he preferred waffles or pancakes.

She herself was tired of all these romantic problems. She'd taken to groaning whenever she heard "Endless Love," and I heard her complain more than once that she wanted a chart with "some meat on it."

Rebecca Mathiessen seemed to fit the bill. She showed up in the middle of August with a list of songs that filled four charts, both sides. Her problem had nothing to do with a boyfriend, Rebecca was clear about that. Otherwise, she didn't say much, but normally that wouldn't have been a problem. Normally, my sister could figure out the trouble from the songs the customer couldn't get out of her head.

"But no one can hear this much music," my sister insisted. She was sitting at the kitchen table, making stacks of the coins she'd dumped out of her tip jar to roll up for the bank. "And why won't she tell me what lines affect her? Something's not right here."

Rebecca was an unusual customer in another way. Her family lived a full forty miles from Tainer, in a town that wasn't even a town, really, since most of the people who lived there commuted to St. Louis. St. Louis was a long commute, sixty or so miles each way, but Rebecca made the trip every morning to work at an advertising company. She thought nothing of the drive to Tainer. She told my sister that she got her card from a hairdresser who knew the owner of the beauty shop here in town, A New You.

Mary Beth wondered if Rebecca wasn't serious about the reading, but Rebecca kept saying she was. In the office, she even cried once or twice, but her tears weren't connected to the music she reported. One time Mary Beth asked if any songs upset her, and she said, "Yes, but don't put them on the list. They have nothing to do with why I'm here."

Finally, Mary Beth told Rebecca she couldn't help her if she wouldn't be honest. "There's something you're not telling me," my sister concluded. "Until you do, this reading is bound to fail."

Rebecca nodded but she didn't come forward with anything. But then the next Thursday, we got a phone call. Mary Beth was listening to The Doors (one of the groups on Rebecca's list—she was still trying) and getting dinner ready; I was playing hide-and-seek with Tommy. At the moment, he was curled up on the couch with a pillow over his face. I was looking everywhere.

Mary Beth picked up the phone and I watched spaghetti sauce drip off the spoon in her hand while she listened and then said, "Yes, of course," a little stiffly.

"Who was that?" I said.

"Rebecca's brother. He wants to come with her this week."

She was back at the oven and Tommy was yelling one, two, three. He wanted me to find him and he always forgot who was supposed to count. I said, "I bet he's in the kitchen," loudly, and followed Mary Beth. "Why would her brother come?"

"Maybe he thinks I'm ripping her off. He made a big point of telling me that Rebecca is young and very vulnerable." Mary Beth shrugged. "He sounds like a jerk, but he might be able to give me something to work with for Rebecca."

On Saturday, Mary Beth had just finished wiping up eggs from Tommy's high chair when they rang the doorbell. She ran downstairs to meet them and Tommy and I settled back to watch *Superfriends,* his favorite cartoon. But a few minutes later, there was a knock on our apartment door.

"Ms. Norris told me to wait here while she's seeing my sister." He glanced around me to where Tommy was flopped on the couch and crossed his arms. "Is it all right if I come in?"

"Sure," I said, although it wasn't. I was still in my pajamas; I hadn't even brushed my teeth yet. Why didn't Mary Beth let him stay in the office?

He walked in but he didn't sit down. When Tommy waved at him, he smiled and said, "What are you watching?"

Wrong question. Tommy could never say *Superfriends* without naming every superhero on the show, and their powers, and the colors of their suits, and just about anything else he could remember. Rebecca's brother nodded along pleasantly with no sign of what Mary Beth called The Reaction. In some people, it took the form of saying how incredibly good Tommy looked, over and over again, as though they were surprised. Others just stared like they'd never seen anyone like him before, which, as Mary Beth pointed out, was probably true. There was no one else on earth as sweet as her little boy.

"What's your name?" Tommy asked. Since this one required an answer, I was prepared to translate. Tommy tended to leave off the first letters of words and only Mary Beth, Mrs. Green and I could reliably decode "At ur ame?"

"Ben," Rebecca's brother said, and walked over to Tommy and leaned down and stuck out his hand. Tommy didn't know he was supposed to shake it. He stuck his hand out, too, but a few inches away, as though it was a special superpower greeting.

Ben laughed, and I took a good look at him. He was wearing old jeans, a baggy T-shirt, and scuffed-up tennis shoes, and his hair was pretty messy, too, although I could see why: just since he'd been here, he'd run his hand through it several times. His eyes had dark circles underneath them, like he was worried or sad, probably about Rebecca. I figured him to be twenty-five, maybe twenty-six. Almost exactly my sister's age.

He had a really noisy laugh, but I didn't mind. It seemed genuine, not at all like the way a jerk would laugh.

After a half hour or so, he and Tommy were getting along so well that I decided to get dressed and brush my teeth. When I came back, they were lining up Hot Wheels on the armrests of the couch. Tommy said they were going to have a race.

"You have to come with me first," I said.

"No."

I grabbed his hand. "Come on." I didn't want to say it with Ben there, but when Tommy kept pulling, I leaned down and whispered, "You need to be changed."

Tommy was going through a phase where he got upset if anyone mentioned his diaper. Mrs. Green thought it meant he was ready to be toilet trained; Mary Beth worried that something had happened in day care to make him self-conscious. There was no choice this time, though. The smell was the first thing I noticed when I came back into the living room.

He was getting ready for a full-scale meltdown—when Ben told him to go on. "I'll finish getting everything ready." His voice was light. "But hurry back. It's going to be exciting."

Tommy ran to his room and flopped backwards on his bed. While I was taping on the new diaper, he said he liked "en." I didn't say anything, but I was thinking the same thing myself.

I watched the race from the floor by the stereo. I was waiting for the right moment to ask my question, but finally I just blurted it out. "Do you have a favorite song?"

It was one of my sister's biggest rules: you can't trust anyone who has a favorite song. "There's too much out there to love," she explained. "Any person who can choose just one song must be deaf to the rest of them. It's like a man who likes a woman only for her looks. It's nice at first, and she feels great, but give her enough time, she'll realize she can't trust him because he's blind to the rest of her."

Ben didn't even have to think about it. He shook his head. "How could you pick between greats like Jim Morrison and John Lennon?"

By the time I heard footsteps on the stairs, I was eager to see him with my sister. Specifically, I wanted to see him stand next to my sister. He seemed about her size, but I had to make sure. She'd dated shorter guys before, but I knew she preferred someone her own height or taller.

But it wasn't Mary Beth, it was Rebecca. She told Ben that

Mary Beth was waiting for him down in the office. He stood up, and ran his hand through his hair again, this time leaving a horn of hair sticking out on the left side. When Rebecca walked across the room and sat in the window chair, he looked at her. "Aren't you coming?"

"No," she said. "Mary Beth wants to talk to you alone."

He raised his eyebrows, but he didn't object. He said thanks for the race to Tommy and laughed again as they did their goofy hand thing for good-bye.

Rebecca didn't talk much and she definitely didn't play with Tommy. She crossed and uncrossed her legs several times and kept looking at her watch. After about twenty minutes, Tommy and I were done with the cars. We went back to cartoons and munching Cheerios from the box. When I asked her if she wanted some, she said no thanks and laughed. "If I pull this off, I'm taking myself out to lunch."

I wasn't sure what she meant, but I liked hearing her laugh. It reminded me of her brother. They didn't seem alike in any other way. On the phone with Mary Beth, he'd called Rebecca "young," but she didn't look as young as he did. They both had dark brown hair, but hers was as perfect as his was messy. She was wearing a crisp beige shirt and tan miniskirt. Even her purse looked shiny and flat as a new one.

A lot of Mary Beth's customers didn't look as troubled as they were, but Rebecca didn't look troubled at all. And another thing. The Doors album cover was lying on the floor right by her chair. When she glanced in that direction, I pointed at it and said, "It's pretty good," trying to be friendly, but she just shrugged, like she had no interest in the group or the album. Ben, on the other hand, had mentioned Jim Morrison.

It was all very curious, and it got even stranger when Mary

Beth and Ben returned. He was barely in the room when Rebecca said, "I hope you're not mad, bro."

"I have a right to be, don't I?" he said.

Tommy ran over to Mary Beth and she picked him up, but she didn't say anything. Rebecca looked at Ben. "I only did it because I was worried about you."

"You're worse than Mom," he said, but he didn't sound annoyed.

"Untrue. Mom wants you to go to that old fart Dr. Baker." Rebecca smiled. "Didn't I find you someone better?"

He nodded, and shot a quick glance at Mary Beth. They were exactly the same height, I noticed. And Ben was blushing a little, which I thought was a very good sign.

But Mary Beth just looked tired. And the only thing she said when they left was she'd give her left foot for a nap.

Another customer was due in five minutes, but I fired questions at her. What was wrong with him? Could she help? Why did Rebecca pretend to be a customer? Why didn't she just say these were her brother's songs? Was he coming back by himself next week? Did he even want her help?

She looked at me. "I gather you liked him."

"Well, yeah. He was nice to Tommy. He seems to really like music."

"He does like music," she said—and then nothing. She headed to the Rubbermaid box in the kitchen where she kept the charts.

I followed her. "He seems pretty smart."

"I guess he is." She filed Rebecca's chart under M and pulled out the next customer's. "He told me he's a graduate student in neuroscience and biochemistry at Washington University. It's in St. Louis."

She turned around but she didn't look up from the chart in her hand. She walked back to the living room that way. I was surprised she didn't stumble into something.

"Come on, Mary Beth." I was right behind her. "Is he coming back? Tell me."

"Yeah," Tommy threw in, although he was throwing the couch cushions on the floor and not really listening.

"Don't let him pile them too high," Mary Beth said. She was at the apartment door, ready to go. "I don't want him falling again."

"Fine." I frowned. "Be that way."

She walked onto the landing, but before she started down the stairs, she popped her head back in. "He doesn't want to be a customer."

"Oh," I said, and exhaled.

"But he is coming back."

"When? Why?"

"Tonight," she said, and smiled just enough for me to know the answer to the why part. It was a miracle. My sister was going on a date.

chapter
four

Could a wedding be far behind? This was the question I spent hours discussing during the fall and winter of that year with my two best friends, Darlene and Denise. The Ds, as I called them, were almost as interested in Mary Beth and Ben as I was. We all thought it was just the most romantic story, every bit as good as *General Hospital*'s Luke and Laura.

Rebecca hadn't known what was wrong with Ben when she brought lists of his albums to my sister. He'd told his family he wasn't going back to grad school in September, but he wouldn't give a reason. It was Mary Beth who got out of him that he'd lost a close friend in a biking accident last spring. He'd been there; he'd held his dying friend in his arms. After that, school and careers and almost everything else didn't mean very much.

I wasn't supposed to tell anybody about this, but I had to tell the Ds. We were in eighth grade, surrounded by boys whose idea of a romantic gesture was taking the straw out of their nose. And this was the real thing. A suffering guy who fell madly in love with a woman because she helped him through a terrible tragedy.

Not that Ben ever seemed to be suffering much. If anything, from the very beginning, he seemed like the most together guy my sister had ever dated. But that just made it better. He was wounded, but he could still entertain Tommy and unstop the kitchen sink. He was sad about his friend, but not so sad that he didn't let out that noisy, happy laugh at least once every time I saw him.

He'd started spending the night with us in October, and by November, he was keeping his clothes and records at our place, rather than his parents'. But it was only temporary, Mary Beth said. She wanted him to go back to school; she kept saying his work was too important to give up now. He was working on what he called "the chemistry of depression." His research adviser had gotten a grant from a big drug company that hoped to be able to develop a pill using their results.

"Think of the people you can help," my sister kept saying. "Trust me, Ben, the work you're doing will be responsible for saving someone's life someday."

This from my sister, who always complained about doctors trying to drug away people's feelings. It had to be love.

Even Juanita Alvarez, my sister's best friend, was impressed with Mary Beth and Ben's relationship—and she never thought anybody was good enough for my sister. Juanita had had what Mary Beth called a "very hard life." She was older, forty, maybe forty-five, and she worked at the diner, too, on the graveyard shift, or as Juanita called it "the truckers, drunks and insomniacs shift." She'd been divorced twice: she referred to her two ex-husbands as "the Dumb and the Arrested." According to Mary Beth, the Arrested really had been arrested, for stealing money orders from the QuikTrip, and bouncing checks from Juanita's account, and was doing eighteen months in the county jail.

Juanita met Ben when he came to the restaurant to change a flat on Mary Beth's car. It took him almost three hours—he wasn't what you'd call mechanically inclined—but Juanita didn't hold that against him.

"You seem happy, kiddo," Juanita told my sister. Later she told me that she'd never seen Mary Beth happy like this, not in all the time they'd been friends.

Of course I wanted my sister to be happy, but still, it was a little disconcerting at times, how different she was now that Ben was around. When she first told me he was moving in, temporary or not, I was a little worried that our lives would change *too* much. Yet when I told her so, she said my fears were normal. "Any new person added to a family seems too big to fit at first, but somehow they do." She pulled her blond ponytail tighter. "It's like a new couch: at first it seems gigantic because your eyes can't quit staring at it, but after a while the rest of the room starts looking just as big and important as it did before and the couch becomes a part of the whole. You just need to give it time."

And she was right as usual. By Christmas, I felt like our new couch, Ben, was fitting in fine. He took me to the mall in his almost brand-new VW Rabbit with the cool sunroof. He volunteered to baby-sit Tommy on Saturdays, so I could spend more time with my friends. He did so much for us that Mary Beth called him her house husband, and wondered how we'd ever gotten along without him. But it was only temporary, she still insisted—and finally, he agreed. His savings were running out and he admitted he did miss his research. He would go back to school in January, but he would come back every weekend to be with us.

He left right after New Year's and he kept his promise. He came every weekend in January and February, even when he had to drive through a foot of snow. On Friday nights when we'd hear him coming up the steps, Tommy would run to the door and start jumping and trying to turn the knob. Ben had bought Tommy a thirty-gallon fish tank for Christmas, and he usually arrived holding a baggie full of water with yet another brilliantly colored fish. Tommy named them all. Aquaman, Wonderdog, Marvin and Wendy, Zan and Gleek. When he ran out of Superfriends, Ben showed him the periodic table and said that the elements would make cool names. Of course Tommy had no idea what the elements were, but he went along, even though a lot of them sounded alike in his rendering: Calcium, Potassium, and Magnesium became "seeum"; Hydrogen, Oxygen, and Nitrogen, were all just "gen."

About half the time, Ben also brought something for me. He gave me notebooks and sweatshirts and pens with the Washington University logo; he gave me punk band albums you couldn't even buy around here, which really impressed my friends.

Mary Beth told him repeatedly not to bring her anything; it was more than enough what he was doing for us. Sometimes she would put her hand on his face and whisper, "This is unbelievably sweet, you know that, don't you?" Once, when he was riding Tommy on his shoulders to the fish tank, she stopped him in the hall. "Tell me again. What rainbow did you say you came from?"

The last two weekends in March he had to stay in St. Louis and work, but they talked on the phone and wrote to each other every day. Then, the first weekend of April, he walked in the door and told Mary Beth he'd made reservations at Scalatti's, one of the fanciest restaurants in St. Louis. While she was getting dressed, he slipped me ten dollars, even though I said I didn't mind baby-sitting Tommy, I had no plans. Actually, I was supposed to meet Denise and some girls from school at McDonald's, but this was way more important. If all went well, my sister and Ben would come back engaged.

That had to be what was going on. Darlene thought so, too. I called her after Tommy went to bed to discuss. She'd been out sick for days, but she barely coughed as we went through all the evidence. Driving to St. Louis was very significant, I thought. Sure, Ben had taken Mary Beth to St. Louis before, but never on a Friday night, when the drive back and forth would take hours. Scalatti's was significant, Darlene said, since everything on the menu was over twenty-five bucks. Nobody went to Scalatti's unless they had something very big to celebrate, she was sure. I asked her if she'd ever been there and she said no, but her parents had when they spent the weekend in St. Louis on their twentieth wedding anniversary.

Ben wasn't wearing a suit, but he was very dressed up for him: pressed khakis, a button-down shirt and tie—even the scuffed tennis shoes didn't weaken the effect. Mary Beth had on her burgundy dress with the little flowers and her best black pumps. She even fixed her hair into long yellow rings, although she said it probably wouldn't last through dinner. Her hair was so straight.

And he'd paid me to baby-sit Tommy. He'd never done that before. It had to mean something, I said, and Darlene agreed.

The big question was: did he have something in his pocket? Darlene laughed hysterically when she asked this, although I knew she meant a ring.

"How would I know?" I was lying on the floor in the kitchen. The chairs were too uncomfortable for what was already a long conversation.

"Please, Leeann. Don't you think a guy acts different if he has a couple thousand dollars of diamond in his pants?"

"Acts different how?"

"Make sure it's still there." More laughter. "Touches his tuna while he's at it."

"Gross, Darlene."

"Come on, they all do it," she said, still laughing and now coughing. "It's their favorite thing other than sex."

When she barked out that she had to get a drink and dropped the phone, I found myself thinking about a night a few months ago when I got up to go to the bathroom and saw Mary Beth and Ben sprawled out on the couch. I tried to hurry, but by the time I was on my way back, he had her shirt pulled up and his face against her breasts. She was telling him to wait until they got in bed so the kids wouldn't see, but he said he couldn't wait another minute.

"I have to have you," he panted. "If I don't have you now, I'm going to die."

I ducked into the kitchen so I wouldn't embarrass them and stood in the dark, the floor tile freezing against my feet, until she grabbed his hand and pulled him into their room. They hadn't closed the door yet, and as I rushed by, I saw her skirt drop to the floor and heard him gasp, "You're so gorgeous. God, I want you so much I can't breathe."

I ran into my room, my face radiating heat in the cold air of our apartment. Later though, I decided it was kind of cool that they were so passionate. It was just part of being in love.

"You know that song 'Whip It' is about this." Darlene was recovered, and still on the same topic. "Lots of songs are about guys doing—"

"Who cares?"

"Okay, but ask your sister, she'll tell you I'm right." She paused and took a drink. "So what do you think is happening? Do you think he'll ask before dinner or after?"

I was relieved to be back on track. "Before is better."

"Yeah. Before, over champagne. And on his knees. He has to be on his knees or it doesn't count."

"I'm sure he will be." Ben was a floor person. He was always squatting or kneeling or sitting on the rug with his feet crossed over his legs like in yoga. I took a deep breath. "I wonder how he'll say it."

"How he'll say it? What can he say other than will you marry me?"

"Maybe he'll recite a poem," I said. "One he wrote just for her."

"Does he write poems?"

"No, I guess not."

Right then and there, I decided the man I married would have to write poems. They wouldn't have to be good, really, just expressive. Like a song lyric that catches you and stays with you for days and days.

I was still thinking about this when Darlene's father told her she had to hang up now. I moved to the couch, planning to watch TV, but instead I found myself staring at the ceiling, wondering what my first boyfriend would be like. Even if he couldn't write poems, it could still work, I decided, as long as he could recite poetry and really feel the words.

I must have fallen asleep, because the next thing I knew, I heard Mom's voice telling me to wake up and go to bed.

I saw the burgundy dress with all the flowers, but still I didn't get that it was my sister until she leaned down and touched my face. Mom wasn't really the touching type. Even when I was little, she rarely touched me unless I was hurt or sick.

I wasn't even fully awake, but I knew something was wrong. Mary Beth only sounded like Mom when she was very depressed. And Ben wasn't with her. His absence filled the room like a cold blast of wind.

"What happened?" I said, sitting up.

When she didn't answer, I snapped on the lamp and looked at

her. Her face was unreadable but her eyes were lined with red, like she'd been crying for hours. But this was impossible. My sister hadn't cried since we found out about Mom.

"Where's Ben? Is he all right?"

"He's fine," she said, in that same flat depressed voice.

She didn't speak for what felt like minutes. I flashed to how nervous Ben had seemed, standing in his pressed khakis and yellow tie, waiting for my sister to get dressed. At the time I thought it was cute that he was so distracted he couldn't pay attention to Tommy, couldn't even remember the name of Tommy's favorite goldfish, the one that was named after him.

"These things happen," she finally said, looking at her lap. "You can't always predict what—"

"I can't believe it!" I was gulping back my own tears. "Are you saying he broke up with you?"

She nodded weakly.

"It's not fair!"

"I know, honey. But really, fair has nothing to do with it. People can't help how they feel." She glanced at me and back at her lap. Her voice was a whisper. "I just hope you don't blame Ben too much."

"What about his stuff?" It was stupid, but I was afraid to ask anything else. Her chin was trembling like she might break down any minute.

"He wants me to send it to him." She exhaled. "UPS, insured."

That did it. I jumped up to the album cabinet by the stereo and grabbed a record from Ben's shelf and smashed it against my knee. The cover was still on: it didn't snap in half; it didn't even crack. Before I could smash it again, my sister was there, holding my wrist.

"Stop," she whispered.

"I hate him!"

"No, you don't." She swallowed and her voice got thick. "He's been good to you." She ran her hand over her eyes. "He did care about you and Tommy, I really believe that."

I dropped the record and threw my arms around her. "He cared about you, too. He must have. He did, I know he did."

When she didn't respond, I said, "Maybe he'll realize he's made a mistake. You know, like the guys always do in the songs."

She laughed, a weak laugh but better than nothing. So I kept it up. I lowered my voice to sound like a guy's, knelt down and grabbed her foot, and sang the first verse of "Baby Come Back." Then I went through a few lines from "Miss You," while pretending to collapse in grief. I got back up and belted out all I could remember of "I'm Sorry," clutching my heart like the pain was overwhelming.

It was working, she was laughing—until she turned toward the kitchen, where the bouquet of dried lilies and violets Ben had given her when they first started dating was sitting in an empty wine bottle on our table. She mumbled that she had to check on Tommy and disappeared down the hall. I sat very still until I was sure she wasn't coming back; then I picked up Ben's album from the floor. It was Talking Heads, a group he'd introduced me to, a group I liked, but still I took off the cover, and scratched her name across the grooves of Side Two with a ballpoint pen.

I'd already put the scratched record back when I remembered the ten-dollar bill he'd given me in the pocket of my jeans. I ripped it up and slid the pieces in the cover before stuffing the album back on the shelf.

•　　•　　•

If Ben had just hurt my sister, I think I would have gotten over it soon enough. But there was something else at stake here. Something that kept upsetting me every time I thought about it for months.

It was back in December, when he was still living with us. Weekdays, Mary Beth would go to work and Tommy would stay at Mrs. Green's until she picked him up at four-thirty. Ben had offered to take care of him, but Mary Beth said no. She wanted him to spend the time reading and researching. She was still trying to motivate him to get back to his own science work. When I got home from school, he'd be lying on the couch, sometimes with a chemistry journal but just as often with nothing. (He was thinking a lot in those days, but Mary Beth said that was good, too. He had a lot to think about after what had happened to his friend.) But he always sat up and said hi and asked how my day was, usual things. And then we had a routine. We'd go into the kitchen for a snack, usually potato chips and dip, and head back into the living room to watch TV.

Ben was funny about the TV. He'd never owned one before; he said his parents had been opposed to television while he was growing up, and he hadn't thought of buying one in college or grad school. I thought this meant he'd only want PBS or the After-School Special, but I was way off. He was so TV starved that he was happy watching anything now, no matter how awful.

I was a little TV starved myself, since my sister always insisted on the stereo. Ben liked to joke that we had to get our TV fix before MB came home. (MB was his pet name for her. I thought it was sweet, even if it did sound like a nuclear weapon.)

Most of the time we just sat there and watched, but occasionally we'd talk through the commercials. If he'd had a good day reading, he'd bring up some point or another, although I usually couldn't follow it. Mary Beth loved to hear him talk about his brain chemistry stuff, but I thought he was more confusing than the worst junior high teacher. Sometimes he told me about his family. Just little comments, like his dad was a college professor. His mom didn't believe in serving dessert. His sister Rebecca used to date a golf fanatic.

I made little comments, too, about school and my friends. Rarely about the family, because he knew the family already, that is Tommy and Mary Beth. One time I told him that Linda, Tommy's birth mother, had given us a letter for when Tommy was older, but the letter didn't say I'm sorry for giving you up or I loved you or anything normal, but just went on and on about all the troubles she'd had. She even wrote a paragraph about how men were scum, which Ben agreed was a pretty lousy thing for a mother to tell a son.

The topic of my mother came up one night when Mary Beth called to say she'd be late. She told Ben she was picking up Tommy and heading to the cemetery, to put a Christmas wreath by Mom's grave. He offered to go with her, but she said she wouldn't be long. When he hung up, he said he was sorry; he should have put me on with my sister, since I would obviously want to go.

"Not really," I blurted. "I mean, it's okay."

He sat back down on the floor next to the coffee table. "Why not?"

"It's kind of complicated," I said. I was on the couch. *The Rockford Files* had gone to commercial. I had no excuse not to look at him.

"Give it a try." He tilted his head to the left in that sympathetic way he had, and smiled. "I like complicated."

I said okay, but I really didn't plan to tell him much. I started with the little fact that I hated the cemetery, and then I said that

Mary Beth didn't mind it; plus, she and Mom were a lot closer, and then he asked why they were closer, and I found myself blabbing about the two phases of our family: Before, which I knew almost nothing about, but had heard contained a nice house and a swing set and a father who worked and a mom who stayed home; and After, which I also knew very little about, except that it started when I was a baby after Dad lost his job and we moved to this apartment on top of Agnes's house and Mom got her job at the insurance company.

"When I was a kid, she worked constantly." I grabbed another potato chip. "That's a big difference. She had a lot more time to spend with Mary Beth."

"Makes sense," Ben said.

"Plus, Mary Beth is more like her. I mean, she isn't really like Mom, but she's a lot more like her than I am."

"MB told me your mother was a very strong woman."

"True," I said, although strong wasn't exactly the word to describe Mom. She'd grown up in an orphanage outside town. It was closed by the time I was born, and she never talked about it, or about her parents. She always said, "I care about them just as much as they cared about me."

One of my earliest memories was the time she slammed her hand in the car door when we were leaving Kroger. Her hand looked as purple and swollen as a fetal pig, but Mom not only didn't cry, she wouldn't let me say a word of comfort. "I wasn't paying attention," she said, through clenched teeth. "I got what I deserved."

I remember I had a huge wad of gum in my mouth, and as I watched her try to bend her crushed fingers over the steering wheel, I sucked in my breath and accidentally swallowed it. I'd been told you weren't supposed to swallow gum, and all the way home, I wondered if it would get stuck in my stomach or even kill me. I never thought of asking Mom. I was afraid she'd say I deserved it, too.

"But she wasn't mean or anything," I said to Ben, and laughed. "I don't know why I used to be a little scared of her."

It was out of my mouth before I could stop myself, but it was true—I used to be afraid of my own mother. I'd never told this to anyone. Not any of my friends and definitely not Mary Beth.

My sister was our mom's biggest fan and most loyal defender. One time when I just hinted that maybe Mom didn't relate that well to me because she had me later in life and I was obviously an accident, my sister said I was way, way off. Mom loved me to pieces, she insisted. Mom would have given her life for me without pausing for a second.

Later it hit me that she hadn't denied I was an accident.

I expected to feel terrible now that I'd blabbed my big secret to Ben, but it was just the opposite. The relief was so strong, it was all through my body, like I'd finally confessed to a murder. Afterwards, I was on such a roll, I didn't even try to stop myself. When Ben asked what my dad was like, I volunteered the whole story of going to his apartment, and how depressing it was, but later when I remembered the Laundromat, how much better I felt because I knew I'd loved my father. That was very important to me, I said. Knowing I'd loved him, even if he was kind of nuts.

The Rockford Files was over and so was some game show, but I was getting to a big point. I could feel it coming as I spoke, even though I didn't know what it was. It was the strangest thing, how much of this was news to me, too. It was like my voice was telling my brain what I really thought.

"I've wondered a lot what happened between my mom and dad. Like, why did he leave and was she sad about it? I'm thinking maybe she wasn't. You know, cause she hated weakness."

"I see what you mean," Ben said quietly.

"It wasn't her fault, though. It's like Mary Beth says, people can only be who they are. Even if she kicked him out, she couldn't help it I guess."

I was picking my thumbnail, vigorously, because I'd just realized that last part wasn't true. It couldn't be true, because Mom had stayed married to Dad. Why would you stay married to a man—and continue to wear your wedding ring—if you wanted him to leave you?

Which meant the big point, the thing that was coming next, wasn't true, either. But I heard myself saying it anyway. I heard myself say that maybe my mom didn't relate to me very well because I reminded her of my dad.

"In what way?" Ben said. A perfectly normal question, but it convinced me for sure I had no idea what I was talking about. I didn't look like Dad, and I certainly didn't act like him. We had nothing in common, as far as I knew.

I paused for a moment; then I sat up straight. "I think this theory lacks substantiation."

It was what Ben always said when he didn't agree with some science article. I figured he'd start laughing and he did. But when I tried to tell him that everything I'd said was probably crap, he shook his head. "Even unsubstantiated theories usually have a grain of truth in them, Leeann."

"Maybe," I said, but I feigned a sudden interest in the TV. Mary Beth and Tommy were due home any minute, and I was feeling both embarrassed and really anxious. Of course he'd have to tell my sister about this conversation—why hadn't I thought of this before? Even if I asked him not to, it would just backfire and make him more convinced that he should, for my sake.

I spent the next few days in a nervous fog, but by the weekend, I was okay again. As strange as it seemed, Ben obviously hadn't mentioned our talk to Mary Beth, because she never mentioned it to me. Maybe he just assumed she already knew all this. Or maybe—and this was what I liked to think—he understood that I wanted this to be kept strictly private. This could even be the point of sharing something big, I thought: that after you did, the other person really understood you.

Ben and I never had another discussion about my parents. Within days it was Christmas, and then he went back to school, and when he came on the weekends, there was always so much to do with Tommy and Mary Beth. But still, I was sure something had changed between us, and I convinced myself he thought so, too. When he would bring me an album, I would listen carefully to every word, in case he'd picked this one because there was a message in it for me.

I never found the message, but I was still looking when he left. And then it all suddenly fit together: the reason he'd never mentioned the topic again and the reason he hadn't told my sister about it and the reason he hadn't sent me a message. He wasn't all that interested. He was just being nice, the same way he'd been nice to Tommy. He'd probably forgotten my heartfelt revelation the same way he'd forgotten the name of Tommy's favorite goldfish.

By the time I found out how wrong I was, I'd let what happened with Ben develop into a full-blown betrayal. Sometimes I even thought he'd tricked me into talking about my parents, just like he'd obviously tricked my sister into believing they had a future together. I hated myself for trusting him, but I hated him more for being someone you couldn't trust. A typical man, as my sister's customers would say. Only nice when they need you. Incapable of really caring about you. Always ready to leave you without warning, without even saying good-bye.

chapter five

The summer of endless love was long gone. It was 1982, and I called this the summer of tainted love. The song "Tainted Love" wasn't all that popular with Mary Beth's customers, but it was very popular with my friends. We played the record constantly; it expressed how we felt now. Ben had been gone for three months; we knew he wasn't coming back. We no longer believed Luke and Laura would stay together. We didn't even know if Charles and Diana would last, although Denise claimed they couldn't get divorced even if they hated each other. It was against the rules for royalty.

Tainted love: the theme of the summer, maybe even of the whole town.

These days, it seemed like everyone who came to my sister was nursing a heartbreak. In the space of only a few months, Mary Beth had discovered affairs between near strangers, and babies born whose daddies didn't know them, and hatreds so intense friends hadn't spoken in years. Compared to all this hidden agony, Rose driving Clyde's truck through the window of his place that Saturday in June was almost a relief.

If there was anyone left in Tainer who hadn't heard of Mary Beth, Song Reader, they had to hear after what Rose did. For a week, there was police tape around Clyde's tobacco store, smack in the heart of downtown. And Rose worked afternoons at the Photomat. She loved to lean out the window of her little booth, and tell yet another person her story and the moral: if only she'd listened to Mary Beth, she'd have known that Clyde was no damn good.

When Rose asked Mary Beth for a stack of her song reader cards to hand out with the picture envelopes, my sister complied. It was her calling, she reminded me. She had to make herself available to anyone who needed her.

Mary Beth had reacted to losing Ben by working ten times harder than before. Every week now she took on new customers, sometimes at the astonishing rate of five or six at a time. As soon as she got home from the diner, she snapped on the stereo, and until Tommy went to bed it was turned up loud enough so she could hear it while she made dinner and played with him. After he was asleep, she kept it on but lowered the volume and did whatever she had to do in the living room—sort laundry, pay bills, sew a button back on—pausing every once in a while to make notes on one of her charts. We were never in her car without the radio playing. FM was the one thing she'd insisted on, not power steering, not air-conditioning, even though it was pushing ninety degrees when she traded in her old Buick for a used Ford at the Deals on Wheels over on Twain Boulevard.

She was still working out the details of her theory that music and memory were related. She'd gotten a new idea after she did Nicole Lowrey's reading last March. Whenever I saw her scribbling thoughts in her notebook, I remembered how excited she'd been about telling Ben the idea—and that she never got the chance. It made me hate him even more.

When Nicole first came to my sister, she was unhappy but she didn't know why. For the first few weeks, her chart was no help: lots of sixties' songs, which my sister knew was pretty standard for somebody in their thirties like Nicole. One of Mary Beth's first observations when she started her readings was that for most people, the songs they hear in high school stick with them the longest, but that a lot of times, when they hear the songs later they don't mean what they did originally. "Everything's new then and the music gets attached to all of it," she told me. "Even if you heard a song right when your boyfriend was dumping you, when you hear it later, it doesn't make you feel sad, it makes you feel that newness. That's why oldies stations are so popular, they cheer people up." She laughed. "They make you think you're in high school again and that high school was actually fun."

Mary Beth thought a song from high school was only impor-tant if it was reported for several weeks in a row, and Nicole didn't have any of these. But Nicole was desperate, and finally, Mary Beth suggested she make a note of *every* bit of music that came into her mind—phrases, lines, commercial jingles, any-thing. Even if it seemed totally meaningless. Even if it passed through her mind so quickly she wasn't sure it was a real song.

The very next Saturday, my sister uncovered the source of Nicole's trouble. The key was a phrase, "hope you know it, baby," that came into Nicole's mind several times. Nicole could hear the melody of those five words, but that was all. When she hummed it to Mary Beth, though, my sister recognized the song immediately. It was an old R&B tune called "Didn't I Blow Your Mind." She got out her lyric book, and when she recited two lines from the first verse, Nicole leaned back in her chair and just stared at my sister. The lines were about someone laughing while another person cried—and this had just happened to Nicole last week. But she'd convinced herself it didn't matter. Her boyfriend Jeff said she was being too touchy. He wasn't laughing at her, he was just laughing. And she was always crying over nothing, wasn't she?

The music was trying to tell her how she really felt about the way Jeff treated her. When my sister told me about it, her voice was full of wonder. "Somewhere in Nicole's brain every word of that song was still stored. And so the phrase was like a message from her unconscious coming to help her."

"Is she going to break up with him?"

"I don't know. But even if she doesn't, she knows what's going on now." Mary Beth tapped her fingernail on the chart. "That's what the song did for her. It revealed her to herself."

After her success with Nicole, my sister set about collecting evidence that even very small phrases from songs can be messages from the unconscious. But she still wasn't satisfied. She was looking for the one customer who would pull it all together. A customer who had even less knowledge about their problem than Nicole had had. A customer whose mind used music to tell them the deepest truths about themselves that they could not have known otherwise.

And then, in early July, she found Holly Kramer.

Holly had gotten Mary Beth's card from Rose, and she'd called my sister the very same night. She was in bad shape. She wasn't sleeping, she wasn't eating much, she'd lost all interest in her husband—meaning sex of course, but Mary Beth wouldn't say that around me. Worst of all, she claimed she had no songs now and never had.

"Why call a song reader?" I asked.

"Good question," my sister said. "I guess because she's already tried a shrink and pills and even a psychic."

After Holly's first appointment that Saturday, Mary Beth told me it was going to be a really difficult case. "Having no songs is like having no dreams. It only happens when your mind is shutting down. Hiding from something."

She was making pizza rolls for Tommy. He'd been cranky all day, and now he was in his room, throwing toys out of his toy box. She stuck the pan in the oven and I looked at her. "What could it be?"

She yelled for Tommy to come in the kitchen. "It's hard to tell. Holly really didn't say all that much. When I asked her whether she felt sad, she said no, she just didn't see the point of life."

I tried to imagine feeling this way, but I couldn't. I was feeling restless that summer. If anything, I wanted more life.

Tommy ran in and Mary Beth picked him up. "I'm seeing her tomorrow," she said. "Just for a little while." She nuzzled Tommy's neck. "I gave her an assignment to listen to the radio for four hours this afternoon. Find out if anything sticks with her."

I was very surprised; Mary Beth never saw customers on Sunday. I didn't mind baby-sitting Tommy again, but I wasn't sure I liked the idea of my sister changing her routine for this Holly Kramer person, whoever she was. We didn't know her, really. Until a few days ago, we'd never even heard of her.

We certainly heard about her plenty after that. Some days it seemed like Mary Beth would wake up and talk about Holly and come home from work ready to talk about her again. Even though the radio assignment worked, Mary Beth had no idea why Holly picked the songs she did. And there were only two: the Rolling Stones's "Angie" and Gordon Lightfoot's "If You Could Read My Mind." We had the Rolling Stones album and Mary Beth tracked down the other one on a used LP at the Trading Post. "They're both sad, that's for sure," she said. "And there's something in that Lightfoot thing I can't put my finger on."

When Holly mentioned the line she kept hearing, Mary Beth was even more puzzled. It was from the Gordon Lightfoot, about feeling like a ghost that no one can see, and Holly reported it for three weeks straight. The third week, Holly was sobbing a little on the machine and I wanted to put a C by the line, but Mary Beth thought Holly was more angry than sad. "Listen to the way she's spitting out 'ghost.' That isn't crying, that's hatred."

It was a mystery though, since Holly said she was happy with her husband and Mary Beth believed her. She'd met Holly's husband Danny: a sweet, boring guy who worked hard for his family and coached Little League on the weekends. I suggested perhaps a previous boyfriend but Mary Beth said, "No one in love is that angry with a man from the past unless he's around again—and Holly says no one new or old has come into her life lately." I kept going, I said maybe it's her kids, and Mary Beth frowned. "Leeann, when you have kids you'll realize how ridiculous that is."

Whatever the problem was, I was getting tired of it. I was used to Mary Beth fixing people and sending them on their way. Then too, I was completely sick of that Lightfoot song. I was fourteen now, and painfully aware that a lot of the songs Mary Beth's customers reported were totally uncool. The Police were cool. The Cars were cool. Queen, Tom Petty, John Cougar: all fine. But Gordon Lightfoot was like Barry Manilow or Olivia Newton-John: if you were ever caught listening to that stuff, you'd be ruined.

It was the first week of August and we were in the middle of a heat wave that scorched grass and melted pavement from Boise to Oklahoma City. Everyone wanted it to rain, even the kids talked about it. Every day the temperature reached a hundred or more, and the humidity never went below ninety percent. How could it go on like this much longer? At night our place was so hot that Mary Beth worried about Tommy getting heat sick. She put the biggest fan we had right by his bed, but he still kept getting up, crying that his sheets felt "sticky." After she settled him back, she'd sit by the breezeless back window, listening to "If You Could Read My Mind," over and over. Sometimes I sat with her, but usually I was on the phone with one of the Ds. Darlene had landed herself a boyfriend, an older guy named Greg, and she was trying to set me up with his friend Jason so we could double-date. Denise was being reassured that *if* I went with them, it would be merely a fact-finding mission, to see if this Greg was as bad as we feared.

We'd heard he had a bad temper. Of course he also had a car and a job and the money to take Darlene out on real dates.

When Jason finally called on Friday afternoon, I said yes before he'd even told me what movie we were going to see. Of course I still wanted a boyfriend. Even tainted love sounded better than sitting home, eating too many potato chips, and watching *Saturday Night Live*.

Plus, the movie theater would be air-conditioned.

When I told Mary Beth about the date, I made her promise to be done with all her customers by three o'clock on Saturday. I needed time to prepare. And I reminded her of that promise that morning—but when three o'clock came, she was still downstairs in her office with who else but Holly.

I waited until almost four, partly because I didn't want to

bother them, but mainly because I didn't want to walk around downstairs with Tommy and risk running into our landlady Agnes. She loved to speculate about Tommy's background, never with Mary Beth though, only with me. So far she'd guessed that he was African, Puerto Rican, Jamaican, Greek, and Egyptian. Usually I didn't say anything, but the last time I said, "Hey, I think you're right. He's really a pharaoh!"

Luckily before we hit the bottom step, Mary Beth and Holly were out of the office and headed to the front door. I grabbed Tommy's hand and we made it to the porch in time to see Holly getting in her blue Chevy truck. In all the times she'd been here, I'd only caught glimpses of her. Most of Mary Beth's customers came upstairs at some point—to get a drink or use the bathroom or just say hey to me and Tommy—but Holly never did. My sister said she was shy, and she certainly looked it. She was a good ten years older than Mary Beth, but she had the slumped-over shoulders and downcast eyes of an awkward kid. She wore jeans and a T-shirt, no makeup, no heels, no jewelry that I could see. The overall impression you had looking at her was of someone trying hard not to make any impression at all. She was skinny, she was pale, she was in every way forgettable, except for her hair. It was thick and shiny and the most beautiful red, and it came all the way down her back, much longer than mine and even longer than my sister's.

Mary Beth was walking slowly, clearly exhausted, but I didn't care. I was tapping my foot on the porch and pointing at my wristwatch.

"Oh, my God, I completely forgot!"

"You sure did."

"I'm sorry, sweetie. I'll make it up to you, I promise."

I told her it wasn't necessary, but she insisted. First, she said she had to get me something brand new to wear—to build confidence. I told her there wasn't time, but we hopped in her Ford and hurried to Penney's, even though it was so hot Mary Beth could barely hold the steering wheel and Tommy was in a bad mood because I'd been too distracted to put him down for a nap. He darted around opening and closing the dressing room doors while I tried on shirt after shirt, finally settling on a soft black jersey with a scoop neck and cap sleeves. Mary Beth said it made me look sophisticated. "Which you are, of course," she said, standing behind me in the mirror and smiling.

When we got home, she gave me a little packet of expensive shampoo that had come in the mail, stapled to a coupon. After I washed and blow-dried my hair, she brushed it and then twisted the front locks into perfect little braids. She had me sit right by the fan, so I wouldn't sweat on my new shirt. When I was all ready, she went into the back of her closet and pulled out a dusty shoe box. Inside were what she called her "magic shoes."

Tommy said they were "sparkly." They were shiny red with little straps around the ankles. I looked at her, wondering why I'd never seen them before.

"Wear these shoes," she said. "They will give you your center. If you forget who you are, look straight down at the shoes—they will remind you that you are Leeann Norris, a wonderful girl, with a home full of people who love you."

"Full of people?" I glanced in the hall mirror to see if the makeup stick was still doing its job—hiding my new, angry zit. "Last time I looked there was just Tommy and you."

"And Big Bird!" Tommy said. He was holding his stuffed Big Bird and pulling the voice cord over and over.

"And Big Bird." I smiled at Tommy. He'd insisted on wearing a shirt that didn't really fit anymore. He was three and a half now, but he still had his baby fat tummy. It was so cute on him, but it made me suck in my own stomach. I was always afraid of being fat, but so was everyone else, even Denise, who wore a size four.

"Very funny, Leeann," Mary Beth said. "You get my point, don't you?"

Jason was already downstairs, ringing the doorbell. I told her yes and I was grateful for the shoes, even though they were so big I had to keep my toes curled down all night to keep them from falling off. And I convinced myself that maybe they were magic later, when Jason gave me my very first kiss and it wasn't even awkward. The talking part on the way to the movie had been tough, since Jason and I didn't really have anything in common—and Darlene was too busy smiling at Greg to do more than glance in the backseat—but the kissing part during the movie was actually pretty good. I wasn't worried that there was something wrong with my breath or my lips or anything else. I had the magic shoes, and I was all right.

We were in Greg's Camaro, driving away from the theater, when Greg said we were going up to the river bluffs. I shot a look at Darlene, but she didn't say a word. The bluffs were the big make-out place, that much I knew, but what guys like Greg and Jason considered making out, I wasn't sure.

"I have to call my sister first," I said. It was almost eleven, and I'd told Mary Beth I'd be home by then. Greg pulled into the next gas station. The phone booth was so bright and hot I felt dizzy.

When I told Mary Beth what was going on, she paused for a long minute. "Tell them you have to come home."

"Are you sure?" I said.

"Tell them I'm in a very bad mood and you'll be in trouble if you don't."

I let out a long, deep breath. It was as close as I could come to thanking her.

Greg grumbled about having to drop me off, but Jason didn't complain. As I got out of the car, he said he'd call me. I wasn't sure if he meant it, but I wasn't sure if I cared, either. I'd had my first date, that was the important thing. In one day, I had changed into someone who dated boys rather than just whispering their names and letting out sighs.

When I walked in the door, Mary Beth grabbed my hand and pulled me into the kitchen. It was time to eat ice cream and talk, she said. An occasion like this should always be capped off with a Nutty Buddy.

I smiled and wondered for the hundredth time how Ben could have left her. She was always so good at knowing what mattered to other people and reflecting it back so it seemed both the most natural thing in the world and as particular and special as their birthday.

I'd given her the highlights of the date; I was down to the bottom of the cone, when it hit me that our stereo wasn't on for the first time in weeks. I asked my sister what happened with Holly.

"She had a real tough time today." Mary Beth was still licking the top of her Nutty Buddy. "But I think she's going to be all right now."

I looked at her, surprised. "You mean you figured it out?"

"No, Holly did."

She always said this. It was one of her biggest beliefs: that she was only a guide. She could ask the right questions and interpret the music, but the customer had to do the real work of accepting what the music was trying to reveal.

"I should have known what was going on," she continued. "Looking back now, I see all kinds of clues. She kept mentioning her dad at the weirdest times."

"Her dad?"

"That's who she felt like a ghost around." She was down to her cone now, too, and she was wiping nuts from the table onto a paper towel. "You know, in the song."

"Didn't you tell me Holly's father is George, the hardware store guy?"

She nodded.

"And he owns that store?" I sounded irritated, and I was suddenly. "He owns that store, and probably lives on the hill just like Holly?"

The hill was a neighborhood on the west side of Tainer that was home to most of the richer people in town, including the mayor. Very few of Mary Beth's customers were hill people. She said they usually saw shrinks for their problems, not song readers.

"What are you getting at?" She was holding the crumbled-up paper towel, but she hadn't moved to the trash.

"Holly's dad was there when she was growing up. They had piles of money." I paused, but I couldn't stop myself. "I just don't see what *she* could possibly have to bitch about."

"There's a lot to life you don't know about yet." Mary Beth's voice was soft, but I rolled my eyes. "I'm serious, Lee. Trust me, there are worse things than being left. Much worse."

"Yeah, sure," I said, but I turned away from her because I had a feeling I did know what she meant and I felt a little sick. We knew Holly's father George—he'd sold us the child-proofing web for Tommy's window. He was a loud, big-faced, blustery man who told jokes no one thought were funny. At least my sister didn't. I didn't really understand most of them.

He seemed harmless enough, though. He seemed like any other old guy.

"That's Tommy," she said, and stood up. It was thundering, the way it did almost every night, but there was never any rain. Once the sound woke him up, he remembered how hot he was and started yelling for my sister.

Usually it took her a while to settle him, but this time she was back in only a minute—with Tommy right next to her. He was blinking and rubbing his eyes but he was wearing his getting-away-with-something grin.

I looked at him. "What do you think you're doing, you little goof?"

"Mama says I get to sleep in her bed." He climbed up to the chair with his booster seat. Mary Beth was getting his apple juice box from the refrigerator.

"Why? Is something wrong with yours?"

"It's sticky!" he said, and grinned wider because he knew I'd laugh. I'd just told him this morning that sticky and sweaty weren't the same thing.

We were still sitting at the table when the rain started. It was very sudden: one minute there was nothing, and the next we were running around checking windows, talking about how hard it was coming down as it pounded against trees and rattled the metal gutters.

It was after midnight and Mary Beth told Tommy they had to get to bed, rain or no rain. "You should come in my room, too," she said to me. "We can move the big fan in there, and listen to the storm and cuddle." She smiled. "That way if we lose power, we'll be together."

I started to say no, but I realized I didn't want to be alone yet. I couldn't stop thinking about Holly and her dad. That wasn't tainted love, it was disgusting. It even made me feel weird about kissing Jason, although I knew that didn't make sense.

I threw on my sleep shorts and T-shirt and crawled in with them. Within just a few minutes, Tommy was snoring softly, one arm around Mary Beth and the other one thrown across my stomach.

"Can I ask you a question?" I whispered, turning my head in her direction.

"Sure, sweetie."

I gulped. "How could anybody do that? I mean, to their own daughter?"

"I don't know," she said softly. "I'd like to believe that something happened to him to make him that way. But then whoever hurt him must have been hurt, too, and it just keeps going." She exhaled and rubbed her eyes. "All this suffering, passed from generation to generation, but where did it begin? With God?"

The lightning was so bright it lit up the room for a second. I could see her blond hair streaming over the pillow and her face looking straight up at the ceiling. "Maybe it was God. When He threw Adam and Eve out of their beautiful garden just because they made a mistake, and even though they cried with loneliness for Him, He would never let them back home."

"Did that really happen?" Our family rarely went to church, and my Bible knowledge was pretty weak. All I remembered from the Eden story was a talking snake, a bad apple, and two naked people in fig leaves.

"Oh, honey." I could hear the gentle laugh in her voice. "I don't know what I'd do without you."

She reached over Tommy and touched my shoulder. We listened to the storm for a few minutes before I remembered the other thing I wanted to ask her.

"Those magic shoes of yours." Somehow I knew this wasn't a question she'd want to hear, but I had to know. "Where did you get them?"

"Oh, you can't buy them anymore. The store they came from has been closed for almost ten years. Remember the old W. T. Grants over on—"

"No, I'm talking about who gave them to you."

She sounded surprised. "How did you know someone did?"

"It was Dad, wasn't it?" I was thinking about the day we drove to Kansas City and the story she told me on the way home about her and Dad watching *The Wizard of Oz,* year after year.

She let go of my shoulder before she whispered, "Yes." My eyes had adjusted to the darkness and I could see her put her arms around herself.

"You still miss him?" Now I was surprised, but I shouldn't have been. Why wouldn't she miss Dad? He was her father, too.

"Of course I do. . . . I think it's the price the heart pays."

I was hoping she would say something else, but if she did I didn't hear it. I woke up the next morning still in her bed, with Tommy's foot against my nose.

It rained all that day. The next day it was still pouring. By the third day, people were getting nervous, listening for the emergency sirens, ready to help out with sandbagging. But the Mississippi didn't go over its banks that time. As suddenly as it began, the rain just stopped, leaving behind only a few flooded basements and a cool spell that brought everyone back outside.

Naturally, my sister thought it was a sign. I heard her tell Holly it was like the sky opened up because she had opened up, finally.

Holly had dropped by our place to give Mary Beth her payment: a five-hundred dollar check (the most my sister had ever made) and a violet afghan with a silver star in the center that reflected in the sun like a real jewel. The card with the check was a basic thank-you from the drugstore with phony-looking daisies, but Holly had written "To Mary Beth, who saved my life," under the verse, and she kissed my sister when she gave it to her.

She was still a little slumped over, but she was wearing nice white pants and a green blouse and even a necklace and pearl earrings. And she was very friendly. She asked me how my date went and whether I was looking forward to school; she asked me and Tommy whether we'd ever played Pac-Man. "My kids love Pac-Man," she said. "I tried it yesterday and I have to say, it's certainly addictive."

When she stood up to leave, she had tears in her eyes, but this was pretty normal. A lot of Mary Beth's customers choked up a little when their reading was finished.

"You know you can come see me anytime," Mary Beth said, hugging her and smiling. "I'm always here for a follow-up."

Holly nodded and whispered another thanks and then she was gone. Within a few days, we'd stopped talking about her, although I still thought of her sometimes whenever I glanced at her afghan hung on the wall by our stereo.

The afghan was beautiful but that's not why we framed it. Poor Holly, it turned out she didn't really know how to knit. After she left that day, my sister took one look at it and said there were threads you don't dare touch for fear of unraveling it all.

chapter
six

I'm trying to remember if I ever fought with Mary Beth before that Sunday at the end of November, my freshman year. It seems like we must have had arguments, but when I try to remember them, I keep coming up empty-handed. Even before Mom died, when we could still turn on each other in the casual way of families who think they have forever, I don't recall anything but how close we were. But maybe this just shows how huge that fight in November felt to me—that it was capable of blocking out all the other fights, and dividing our relationship into a before and after.

It started when I decided to go to the annual crafts fair down by the river. Mary Beth and Tommy were supposed to go with me, but then they didn't, I don't remember why. I didn't mind riding my bicycle. It wasn't bad for November, fifty degrees, and the trip was downhill for the most part. Getting home would be another story, but by then I would have what I wanted, what I'd been saving for since I heard they were going to have a glass-blower at the fair.

I loved those delicate little figures. So far, I'd collected an elephant, a dolphin, two unicorns, and a blue angel. I'd saved up thirty dollars and I was hoping to get at least one new piece, maybe two. My goal was to cover my windowsill with them, so the sun could refract through the glass onto my bedspread and my floor, spraying light everywhere.

The fair was about twenty minutes away by bike. The glassblowing demonstration was at the end of a row of craft booths, past the quilts and the pipes, the jewelry and the clay pots. A small crowd had gathered to watch the glassblower. He was making what looked to be a harp, but I couldn't see much beyond the flash of the propane torch. I'd just put down my kickstand and started moving closer when I felt a hand on my shoulder and heard a woman's voice say, "Leeann?"

I turned around, and came face to face with Rebecca. I hadn't laid eyes on her since last Christmas, when all of us went to Ben's parents' house for dinner, but I had no trouble remembering who she was. She still had that flat purse, and her red wool jacket was as stylish as something out of a magazine.

Her smile was so friendly it was a little disconcerting. And she fired loud, friendly questions at me: who did I come with, what did I think of the fair, had I ever seen glassblowing before, did I like it. My answers were as short as I could manage. Then she pointed to a man standing across from us, in front of the candle booth. She said he was her new boyfriend, Andrew. "We're looking for a present for his mother. She's fond of crafts."

He had on one of those sweaters with the polo player logo. He looked like a short, plump Michael Douglas.

"So," she said lightly, "how is Mary Beth?"

"Just fine."

"That's good to hear." She paused. "I always liked your sister. I was very sorry it didn't work out."

"How about Ben?" I said, after a moment. I felt like I had to know, even if it was going to upset me. If he was engaged or married already, I'd just have to deal with it.

"I wouldn't say he's fine." She smiled but it was forced. "Of course he hasn't had a tremendous amount of experience with women. I suppose that makes all this much harder for him."

I blinked at her.

"I've told him repeatedly that he has to move on." She glanced in Andrew's direction and lowered her voice. "Even if you don't find The One, you distract yourself. It's part of the game."

I was having trouble keeping up. "Are you saying Ben is upset?"

"I suppose anyone would be under the circumstances. I don't blame Mary Beth, although I'll confess that initially, I found it difficult not to. It's one thing to be afraid of commitment, but it's another thing to get so involved and then back away. Of course he could have misread her, but knowing my brother, it's unlikely. He's always been very cautious. Typical scientist."

The glassblower had finished the piece and the crowd was clapping. I was standing as close to Rebecca as I could, but people kept walking by, making it hard to follow what she was saying.

"Granted your sister is very pretty, but I don't think that explains it. I consider myself attractive, and yet none of the men I've dated have asked me to marry them."

"What?"

"I'm just saying that normally a man doesn't ask, unless he's been given reason to believe the answer will be yes." Rebecca stood up straight and smiled. "But as I said, I don't blame Mary Beth anymore. And perhaps there were reasons none of us are privy to." She looked over at Andrew. "I really should get back."

I was more than ready for her to go. I needed to be alone, to digest all this, but before she walked away, I thought to ask, "Do you know if he bought her an engagement ring?"

"My poor big bro." She sighed loudly. "He still has it. It's sitting on a shelf in his apartment, right next to her picture and the letters she sent him. I call it the Mary Beth Norris shrine, not that he finds that very amusing."

I mumbled some kind of good-bye and was on my bike before she finished telling me to say hello to my sister. I nodded and stomped on the pedal, and in minutes, I was flying along Main Street so fast that I felt the wind stinging my cheeks.

All the way home, I kept reminding myself there had to be an explanation. No way could this be true. Mary Beth loved Ben, she said so herself. She still loved him, I was sure of it. His letters were in her top drawer, wrapped in tinfoil, in case of a fire, just like Tommy's adoption papers. And she still had a picture of him, stuck in the frame of her bedroom mirror. I'd wanted to tear it up many times but she obviously didn't feel the same way or she wouldn't have kept it there.

I was so out of breath when I walked in our apartment that she rushed over to see if I was all right. Tommy had just gone down for his nap, and I could tell she'd been working. Her fingers were stained with ink from writing on the charts.

"Sit down, sweetie," she said, leading me by the elbow to the couch. "Your face is on fire."

I leaned back into the couch and waited a moment, but that was all. It never occurred to me not to blurt out exactly what happened. Later, I would wish I'd handled it differently. Tricked her into some kind of revelation, rather than handing her everything I had, so she could change it all around until it seemed like nothing.

At first, I thought she was very upset. She was so quiet. She was blinking furiously, especially when I got to the shrine part. And her lips were quivering a little. I saw them with my own eyes.

But then she said, "Rebecca is such a gossip."

"What?"

"She's always making up things about other people." Mary Beth shrugged. "I think she believes other people exist just to entertain her."

"But she really seemed like she was telling the truth."

"Of course she did. She does this all the time."

"Then he didn't ask you to marry—"

She waved her hand. "Rebecca is obsessed with marriage. Ben told me she's been reading *Brides* magazine since she was nine."

She launched into her usual speech about how sad it was that so many women feel they can't live without a man. I knew it by heart, but I didn't see what it had to do with what we were talking about. Before I could ask her, she stuck her finger in the air, like she was getting to a grand conclusion. "Women like Rebecca always turn breakups into tragedies. It's the way they see the world: coupled and happy, or alone and miserable."

"But you were sad when you and Ben broke up."

"Yes, I was. I was also very sad when Mom died."

"Huh?"

"Bad things happen. This is reality, Lee, not a soap opera."

I was speechless with confusion. She moved a strand of my hair out of my eyes—and tried to change the topic to the fair. She wanted to know if I got to see the glassblowing at least, before Rebecca started up with all her *gossip*.

I told her I was thirsty, and got up and went into the kitchen for a drink of water. When I came back, she was messing with the stereo. The record player needle was dirty, she said. At least she hoped it was that, because she couldn't buy a new needle on Sunday and she had a lot of records to listen to.

"Nancy Lyle called again. You know that pretty brunette who works at the Kroger?"

I stared at her back. She blew on the needle again.

"Nancy said she's had bad insomnia for the last month, and while she's lying awake, she always hears certain songs. But she doesn't have any idea why. And she's totally exhausted, poor thing. She wants me to help her so she doesn't have to take sleeping pills. She said they make her so groggy it's hard to get up and fix breakfast for her kids."

Mary Beth stood up and walked to the shelves. While she thumbed through the records, she talked about Nancy's songs. All oldies and most not so goodies. The only one we even had was Henry Mancini. Nancy said she didn't know why she was hearing that old stuff.

My sister had the Henry Mancini in her hand. It was from Dad's old record collection. She said she wanted to get some listening in before Tommy woke up. She'd promised to take him to the park, so he could do his favorite thing: slide down the big slide. Now that he was almost four, he could do it all by himself. He was as proud of that as I had been about starting high school.

My water glass was empty but I hadn't set it down. I hadn't moved since I walked back into the living room.

"Are you ever going to tell me what really happened?"

My voice was a whisper, but she shrugged. "I don't know what else there is to say. I fell in love with a man and we didn't end up happily ever after. It was sad, like I said. It still makes me sad, as I think you know." She gave me a sideways glance before turning back to the stereo. A moment later, the Henry Mancini orchestra was filling the room with "Moon River."

I flopped down on the couch and watched her as she scribbled notes. I'd heard this song before, but it had been so long ago that I couldn't remember most of the words. It was about the Mississippi, Mary Beth said. Then she joked that we crossed the river in style all the time, just like in the song—whenever we went to the outlet stores in Illinois in her Ford.

I might have let her get away with it. I was already tired of the topic, and part of me knew it was none of my business anyway. If the phone hadn't rung right then, maybe we would have spent the next hour talking about "Moon River" and Nancy Lyle and who knows what else. Maybe I wouldn't have made the mistakes I did.

But the phone did ring, and it was Kyle Downey—even though I was sure he hadn't meant it when he said he was going to call me this weekend. He was a junior and a big deal on the basketball team. He was also considered one of the cutest guys in school.

Why he'd even started talking to me was a mystery. Darlene said it was because he liked me, but Denise thought he just wanted to copy my math homework. I was the only freshman in the advanced algebra and trig, full of juniors and sophomores. I thought Denise was probably right, but after I told him I didn't believe in cheating, he was still stopping me after class and in the halls. It flickered across my mind that it was something else about me that attracted him, even though I always wore loose shirts and usually a jacket, too, no matter how warm the school got. I hated my breasts. I would have given anything to be a nice normal B cup like my sister and Darlene and Denise and everybody except Harriet Wheeler, who smoked and dyed her hair purple and was rumored to have sex with guys with tattoos.

The real miracle was that Kyle didn't just call to talk; he called to ask me to the homecoming dance. I told him yes without hesitating; I figured Mary Beth would be happy for me. She knew how bad I felt about having zero dates since Jason last summer. She also knew that I'd felt like an oddball ever since the beginning of freshman year, when the principal decided my test scores were so good he had to put me in the honors program, with all the other geeks.

She knew everything I knew, so naturally I assumed she'd see it the same way I did. I wasn't thinking about the other things I'd told her, including that Kyle had tried to look at my math homework. "He doesn't sound very smart," she'd said, and I'd agreed. Even his looks weren't that great, in my opinion. All those muscles, but such vacant eyes. And his smile was so cocky. "Why would you want to go out with a cheater?" she continued, and I'd said I didn't want to go out with him, which was true—then. As desperate as I was for a boyfriend, I'd learned enough from Mary Beth's customers to know when women went out with guys they couldn't respect, they ended up not respecting themselves.

But this was the homecoming dance. A once-in-a-lifetime opportunity, I felt. And like I told my sister, I wouldn't have to keep seeing him. I could show up and impress everybody and have him take me home. Simple as that.

"I heard you on the phone, honey. You didn't even sound like yourself."

"I was a little nervous. So what?"

"Come on, Lee, I know what jocks are like. You have to be careful with guys like that. They're used to a lot of attention, and they think they deserve whatever they want."

"So I'll be careful."

"It's not a good idea. I'm sorry, but you're only a freshman, honey. You have lots of years to go to dances." She clapped her hands together, like we were finished with the topic.

"Are you saying I can't go?" I didn't try to hide my surprise. She'd never told me no before, but then again, she'd never had to. Normally, her disapproval was enough for me to decide not to do whatever it was she disapproved of.

"I can't believe you really want to." She paused and looked at me. "This guy is not your type, you know that as well as—"

"But are you saying I can't?"

"Okay, then yes. This boy is a cheater and a drinker. I don't want you in any car with him, not even his fabulous Honda Prelude."

I'd forgotten that I'd told her about his car and the keg parties he and his friends were known for. For a split second, I considered that she was right, but a second later, I found myself feeling furious. How dare she tell me what to do?

"You don't even know him. This is so unfair!"

"I know you, and I know you have no business with a guy like that."

"What's that supposed to mean?"

"You're an honor roll student, Lee. You need to be with somebody smart."

"Somebody smart?" I hissed. "You mean like Ben?"

"Is that what this is about?" She walked across the room. The record was over but there was a crackling in the speakers. She snapped off the stereo and spun around to face me. "You're mad at me because it didn't work out with Ben? Well, I'm sorry, honey, but the world can be a very hard place. We don't always get what we want."

I could almost hear Mom. It was one of her favorite sayings, that the world is a hard place, and you have to be hard to survive it. I'd never heard my sister say this, though. Actually, it was Mary Beth who took me aside when I was about six, to whisper that even if the world was hard, it was a friendly hard, like the calloused touch of an old man's fingers. A beautiful hard, she said, like the most magnificent diamond, given by a prince whose love for his princess was so strong it could never be broken.

We were always talking about princesses back then. She'd told me about Cinderella, and when I asked her if it was a true story, she said no, but it was still true. "It's what everybody dreams about. A love so grand it can change your life."

She was eighteen. With her long blond hair and perfect pink skin, I thought she looked exactly like a princess should look. "And what people dream about," she'd said, touching my cheek, "comes from the deepest place inside them. The place where lies never reach. The truest place of all."

It had been a long time since I believed in fairy tales, but still, I hated that she said the world was hard. Even if it was true, it made me feel like my heart was shriveling up inside my chest. It made the room seem smaller and dirtier. It made everything seem dusted gray with hopelessness.

"There's nothing wrong with *Bride's* magazine," I said. I'd never read it, but I shot her a look of defiance. "There's nothing wrong with wanting to fall in love."

"Honey, I didn't say there—"

"It's not silly!"

It was finally starting to hit me that everything Rebecca said was true. Of course my sister had dumped Ben: why hadn't I suspected this before? She'd dumped every guy she'd ever dated. Nick and James. Chris and Scott. Even the one who took her to the prom, the one whose name I couldn't remember, who brought her violets each and every time he came over. Never roses, because he knew Mary Beth didn't care for roses.

And come to think of it, I'd liked them all. Not as much as Ben, but well enough. They were all nice guys, but she threw them away as easily as trashing a scratched-up record.

"Did you care about Ben at all?"

"Of course I did." Her voice was strangely hollow, but she was smiling because Tommy had just woken up. He walked across the room and was hanging on her leg. She picked him up and nuzzled his neck.

"Park," Tommy muttered into her hair.

"I have to take him to the bathroom," she said. I shrugged and slumped down on the couch.

As they walked down the hall, I heard her say that they'd leave for the park very soon, but first she had to talk to Leeann, because Leeann was upset. "Why?" he asked. More of a whine than a question, but Mary Beth answered. She asked if he remembered Ben, and then she said that Leeann was missing Ben today, pretty bad.

His little hug of comfort when they returned did nothing to erase how angry I was. I knew what was coming. I could feel myself breathing quicker before she opened her mouth.

"There's something going on here that worries me," she said. "You're tangling up Ben with that boy Kyle, and I don't think you under—"

"This isn't about me!"

"You were hurt when he left, I know that." Her voice was so incredibly gentle, it made me want to scream. "You liked him so much, and you'd also confided in him, which had to make you feel—"

"He told you I confided in him?" I felt a blush creeping from my forehead to my neck.

"About Mom," she said, matter-of-factly. "Of course he did, honey. We were living together."

I wasn't bothered that Ben had told her. It was what I'd expected. It made sense, and it fit with what Rebecca said. He loved her; of course he told her. But I was stunned that Mary Beth had never mentioned it until now. I was stunned that she could stand there, looking so innocent, when just last summer, she'd told me she was worried because I never talked about my feelings about Mom to anyone. Had she been trying to make me admit I'd talked to Ben? Had she been trying to make me feel guilty? (If so, it had worked.)

Tommy was pulling on her shirttail, reminding her that she'd promised to take him to the park. She told him to wait, but he stomped his foot. "Now."

"All right, just tell me one thing." I stood up and faced her. "Did he ask you to marry him?"

"Rebecca shouldn't have—"

"Forget Rebecca! Just tell me: yes or no."

"But it's not that simple. There were circumstances. It was—"

"Answer me!"

"Okay, okay," she said, sounding defeated. "He did say the words 'will you marry me.' Yes. But we'd been fighting for weeks, and he was just trying to make it all go away."

"I don't remember any fights."

"Because I didn't want you involved. I was trying to protect you from my personal problems."

I was wavering, but I put my hands on my hips. "What were these fights about?"

"It doesn't matter anymore." Her voice was flat. "The truth is, he only thought he was in love with me. He didn't even know me. It never would have worked."

I felt a little afraid but mainly angry. How could she say this? I'd heard her tell Ben many times that he knew her better than any other man she'd been with. He knew about her song charts and Mom's accident and how she got Tommy. He knew she liked Diet Coke for breakfast and orange juice before bed. He knew her dress size and her favorite color and even that she liked to have two towels when she took a bath. He knew everything about her that I did.

Tommy was wailing about the slide and she said she had to go. Before she turned around, she glanced at me. "Are you satisfied now?"

I looked right in her eyes, but still I said it. I said it loud enough for Tommy to hear. "No, I'm not satisfied," I said—and then I called her a liar.

She didn't defend herself. She winced, but it was only a moment before she recovered enough to tell Tommy they were leaving and to tell me that I still couldn't go to the dance with Kyle. "It's my job to protect you," she said, "even if I am a liar."

I stomped into my room, muttering a complaint of how unfair this was, but fighting a sudden wave of panic. She and Tommy had shut the apartment door and gone down the stairs when I realized what was bothering me. I hadn't told her to drive carefully. I'd forgotten to tell her, for the first time I could remember.

I always told her. I put friends on hold to say it; I forced myself to look up from the most fascinating movie to say it, I even yelled the two words from behind the door of the bathroom, the first time I got my period and I was nervously trying to read the Tampax directions. It wasn't that I thought the words were magic, but I did believe the old saying that terrible things happen when you least expect them. So to get them not to happen, I reasoned, what you had to do was keep worrying over them. Most people could say "drive carefully" only in a snowstorm. Or late at night. Or before a long trip. But Mom's accident was in the middle of July, broad daylight, and just five miles from our house. So I had to say it all the time. I had to expect the terrible thing that most people got to forget about.

My panic subsided when I realized I was expecting it right now. Even if I hadn't told her, I was more afraid than ever something would happen to them. And I stayed a little wary, for almost two hours, until Mary Beth and Tommy were back home, safe and sound.

Then I refused to speak to her, because she wouldn't let me go to the dance. And because she'd lied. And because she was going about her business, listening to music and talking on the phone to customers as though nothing had happened.

Later that evening, I called Kyle and told him I couldn't go. It wasn't that hard, especially since Denise told me she'd heard a rumor that he was only asking me to make his real girlfriend jealous. But of course I didn't tell Mary Beth this part, and I didn't tell her that Kyle seemed even more interested in me afterwards. The next morning, he was at my locker, smiling that cocky smile but whining that I'd broken his heart. All that week, he pressured me to go, and even when the dance was over, he was still flirting with me, reminding me that I hadn't even given him a chance yet.

"Come on, Leeann," he'd say, and wink. "What's it gonna take to change your mind?" And then he'd plead with me to go to a movie or out to eat or at least let him give me a ride home.

I told him no as long as I could stand it, but then one day, I just didn't see the point. My status at school had gone up so much just from flirting with him, and I thought Darlene was right that I'd be crazy not to capitalize on this while I could. Of course Mary Beth wouldn't like it, but so what? She wasn't my mother.

I had myself convinced she'd never even have to know. She was very involved with two new customers: one with breast cancer she couldn't bring herself to tell her husband about; one with what Mary Beth called a "fear of fear." I was still updating the charts with her; actually I was doing more now, because I was older and better able to understand the process. "You're a real help to me," she would say, after I pointed out a pattern or repetition on someone's chart that she hadn't noticed. Then she would smile. "I bet someday you'll be doing readings yourself, hon."

I was flattered, but I always told her it wasn't going to happen. "I don't have the gift," I'd say, and I meant it, too. It was a gift, I knew that, because she was still as good at it as ever—except when it came to me. I was the one person she couldn't and didn't understand. Even when I sang songs that were disgustingly obvious about cheating hearts and guilty lies, she didn't guess that I was sneaking around seeing Kyle.

Later, I found out that she did notice the songs and she did think they had a meaning. She even kept track of them on a chart, and as far as I know, it's the only chart she ever got completely wrong. But it was understandable, I guess. Since it had never occurred to her that I was a liar, she had to conclude that I was singing those songs as my way of telling her, over and over again, that she was.

chapter
seven

As upset as I was, I did try to give her the benefit of the doubt. I spent an entire week jotting down every song she hummed; I thought it was a truly brilliant plan. I would present her with her own chart, and see what she would make of it. I would help her discover how she really felt about Ben.

The chart went on for pages, and she said she was impressed I'd gone to all this trouble. "It does make me feel a little like I've been spied on," she admitted, before proceeding to hand back all my hard work with a shrug. "A person can't ever read themselves, it's too dangerous."

"Come on, Mary Beth. Just take a look at it."

"I told you, I can't. It would be like being part of your own experiment."

Her using the science language she picked up from Ben just made me more determined. I stuck the pages out. "Tell me what you would say if it wasn't you."

"But it is me."

"Pretend it isn't."

I kept pushing her until she took the chart from my hand and told me she would say that the person was a song reader.

I smirked. "Thanks a lot."

"I'm serious. You think these songs are mine, Leeann?" She tapped her fingernail on the chart. "Each and every one of these is an echo in my head of somebody else's problem."

"What about 'Golden Slumbers'?"

"What about it?"

"You've been singing it as long as I can remember. It can't be a customer's."

"I used to like it, but now it belongs to whoever tells me they're hearing it."

"But nobody did report that song this week. I checked."

"What's your point?"

"Don't you remember playing it for Ben when he first moved in with us? Couldn't it be that you're humming it now because you're still trying to figure out what happened with him?"

She was so taken aback, she looked almost afraid. I was wondering how she could react so strongly to such an obvious thing when she rearranged her mouth into a dismissive smile.

"Or it could be that I'm humming it now because a customer reported it last week or the week before. Woo hoo, how strange! The songs in my mind don't get erased every week like the tape on the answering machine."

She laughed then. She actually laughed. So I gave up, and went back to what I'd been doing before I had the brilliant plan: stacking up my reasons to be angry with her until they grew as tall as Tommy's tallest block tower.

Of course she had lied to me, not once, but every time she let me keep believing it was Ben's idea to break up rather than hers.

She'd turned her back on a sweet, intelligent man who really loved her; I was positive, no matter what she said. She'd thrown away our chance to get out of Tainer, to move with Ben to some exotic new place like Seattle or New York after he finished his degree. She'd thrown away Tommy's chance to have a normal family with a dad who cared about him. And worst of all, she'd damn near ruined my fragile belief in perfect, endless love.

But I would get it back. I would believe in a wonderful future, full of possibilities—no matter how unlikely it looked.

It was the beginning of 1983, a full year and a half before the Morning in America ads, when unemployment was still terrible and people were scared of everything from Tylenol tampering to computers that would take over the world. But I was determined. I threw Tylenol into our shopping cart without hesitating; I tore off the cover from the *Time* magazine announcing that the computer was 1982's Man of the Year and hung it on my bedroom wall. I listened to Mary Beth's customers talk about automatic teller machines as though they were an evil plot, bound to lead to bar codes on our wrists and government spies who knew everything about us—and shook my head. I watched the nightly news, full of gloom and doom about everything from the farm crisis to the increasing tensions with Russia—and told myself that they were just trying to scare us. The world was about to get better; it had to be. By the time I was my sister's age, all of this stuff would be solved, and I'd live in a big apartment in a big city with a dome over everything to keep out nuclear bombs and keep the temperature at a perfect seventy-two degrees, hole or no hole in the ozone.

My optimism extended to everything, even my relationship with Kyle. I wanted to believe it was a good thing, even though almost every date ended with us parked on the cliffs by the river—and me fighting him off.

"Come on, Leeann," he would say, as he tried to pull my tights down. "I can tell you're ready."

"I'm only fourteen," I would remind him, thinking, I'm not a meat loaf. You can't look at me and tell I'm ready.

I admit, I liked making out with him. Not so much the reality, which was often awkward: our noses would bump together, out front teeth would clink, I would worry about my breath when I realized his smelled like garlic and we'd eaten the same pizza. It was the idea that pleased me, that and the knowledge I had a private life my sister knew nothing about.

She had her secrets, I had mine. Then too, who knew where this could lead? It certainly didn't seem like my great love, but maybe great loves don't seem so great in the beginning. And so what if I was often a little bored listening to him talk about basketball and his car and the next thing he was going to buy? Everyone said I was lucky and I thought so, too. At least I wasn't like my sister, who'd turned her back on men and romance and everything important in life.

Even her opinions grated on me now. For instance, her constant harping about the Maneater song. Right before winter break it had been the most popular song in the country and weeks later, it was still on the radio—and my sister was still talking about how much she detested it. Of course she had to listen to it, for customers, but she thought it was a very bad sign if a woman found herself stuck on *that* tune. "It's not only anti-female, it's one of the stupidest things I've ever heard," she said, wrinkling up her nose. "Girls chewing up boys and spitting them out? Please. Most of the girls I know barely eat in front of boys. Oh no. Can't let themselves want anything."

I knew she was right, but I wasn't in the mood to hear it. It may have been her calling to figure out what was wrong with everyone and everything, but it sure wasn't mine. I wanted upbeat, meaningless music like "I Love Rock 'n' Roll." I was for looking on the bright side, blooming where you're planted, and my favorite cliché, the one I had on my key chain: When Life Gives You Lemons, Make Lemonade.

"Don't you ever get tired of all this sadness?" I asked her one Saturday. She'd just finished a long session with Frieda Jones, a weird customer who was convinced the songs in her head were literal warnings. If Frieda heard "Don't go out tonight," she wouldn't. If she heard "I need you," she'd drive herself crazy worrying that someone needed her help and couldn't ask.

"Sure," Mary Beth said. She was peeling potatoes for stew. Her hand was moving so fast the peels seemed to be raining into the trash can. "Not half as tired as Frieda does, I bet."

"But it's not your problem."

"Yes, it is." She looked up at me, surprised. "It's mine because I understand it. Frieda has to live it, but I have to see how she feels and what she's up against. And once you know, you can't unknow."

"I'm glad I don't know then."

"You don't mean that." She blinked and turned back to her peeling. "To me, that would be hell."

"Hell?" I thought she was exaggerating.

"I'm not talking about the place filled with flames. I mean the hell the world is when cruelty doesn't have a reason. When suffering is unrelenting and unrelieved by love."

Obviously what happened with Ben had not stopped my sister from using the L word. In fact, if you'd asked her, she probably would have said she loved more people that year than at any other time in her life. Sometimes she talked about her customers as if she couldn't even see their flaws. She called Frieda, who had to weigh two hundred and fifty pounds, "fragile." She said Carol Dale had the "sweetest face," even though Carol's skin was covered in pock marks.

She was still working night and day. She had a tape deck and a Walkman now, so she could listen to her customers' songs without waking Tommy. She kept a thick yellow pad on her nightstand; half the time when I woke up to go to the bathroom, I would see her sitting cross-legged on her bed, drinking coffee and writing notes. At one-thirty in the morning. At three-fifteen. At five, even though she had to get up at five-thirty to get Tommy dressed and make it to work.

She swore she slept plenty, but I didn't see how that was possible. She had to be exhausted, but she wouldn't take a day off from the diner and she wouldn't take even an hour to get a haircut or shop for shoes with a friend. But no one seemed to see this as a problem. Even her friend Juanita accepted my sister's excuses that she had a preschooler; of course she couldn't go anywhere. A preschooler and a teenager, that is, because she threw me in, too, even though she said she wasn't worried. I heard her telling Juanita and anyone who would listen that I was going to be just fine.

"Leeann's so mature for fourteen," my sister would say. Or, "She knows what she's doing. I can't imagine her getting in trouble." Or, "She's gifted, you know. I'll bet she ends up with a scholarship to a great college."

I could have felt guilty for lying to her about Kyle (and I did, sometimes), but I also felt annoyed. Why didn't she spend time trying to understand me? Frieda Jones was important. They were all so important. What was I, chopped liver?

She was right about one thing though: I did know what I was doing. I could go with Kyle to the big party to celebrate the end of the basketball season, no problem. I was so mature, I wouldn't be bothered by the drinking, even though I didn't drink myself.

This was how I handled the issue—I claimed I'd tried alcohol *many* times and just didn't like the taste. I thought it was a brilliant solution. I congratulated myself for coming up with it, especially since Kyle seemed to understand my feelings perfectly.

The party was at a huge house in the hill section, unsupervised of course. None of my friends were there, and the other girls were all cheerleaders and jock worshippers who didn't seem to mind being either ignored or pawed or both at the same time. All the boys were either football or basketball players except for one guy, Maniac Mike, who Kyle said was only invited so the party could get "wild." I didn't know Maniac Mike, but I knew of him, everyone at River Valley did, because he was supposedly crazy enough to try anything—jump off a building, snort cocaine, destroy the teacher's lounge, you name it.

In my opinion, the party was wild enough already. Every single person was drinking; some of them were already drunk when Kyle and I arrived. I'd expected beer, but this party had a fully stocked bar with vodka and whiskey and even a blender to make margaritas.

The bartender was another basketball player, Jordan McInnery. It was his fault I started drinking, but my fault I kept going. He spiked my first Coke with rum and I took a big gulp before I realized. I choked a little, which three senior girls thought was hilarious, and so I forced myself to finish, to show them. I had the second drink when Kyle brought me back a Sprite and vodka, rather than just a Sprite like I asked for. He said it didn't taste that different, and I couldn't argue the point in front of all those people. Maybe I was already a little drunk. I know I felt warm and a lot calmer. So what if I didn't know anybody? I was sitting on Kyle's lap, laughing at Ian Reynolds belching the River Valley High fight song.

I don't know how many drinks I had altogether. It seemed like every time I finished one, Kyle was handing me another. After a few hours, I was so drunk I couldn't walk without stumbling, and he had to help me up the stairs. He said I needed to lie down and I couldn't disagree. I was feeling really dizzy and it occurred to me this might be what it felt like right before you passed out.

I didn't know whose house this was, but I knew it was their parents' bedroom when Kyle opened the door. The bed was huge with a tall oak headboard. There was a massive dresser with family pictures and powders and a weird brush shaped like a bird. And it smelled like adults. It smelled serious and stale and responsible.

Kyle closed the door and helped me to the bed. He turned off the overhead light and turned on the little lamp by the bedside table. When he started unbuttoning my shirt, I didn't cooperate but I didn't say no, either. My entire body felt heavy and strange, like it was asleep even though I wasn't. And it was like he was taking care of me, helping me get undressed and into pajamas. He seemed sweet. I might have even mumbled the word "sweet" aloud.

I don't remember him unzipping his pants. Maybe I did pass out for a moment because the next thing I knew I was being crushed by his weight and he was already trying to push himself into me.

"Hey," I said. "Hey!"

"Relax." His breath was coming in short gasps. "I know what I'm doing."

"Stop it!"

When he still didn't move, I began to struggle like mad, trying to get my elbows out from under his arms. I was thrashing my back and legs, trying to bounce him off, but he was too heavy—and too determined.

"Hold still. I can't get it in."

"I don't want to!"

"Wait," he said, moving a little to the left, and then a groan, "oh, here we go—"

I let out a scream that was so earsplitting, he jumped right off me and off the bed, stumbling to his knees, yelling "Shit!" It wasn't planned, or even part of my desire to escape—I couldn't help myself. Darlene had said the first time hurts a little, but this wasn't some pinch, this was like being cut open without an anesthetic.

He panted for a moment, then he leaned down and handed me my clothes. He mouthed, "Sorry," but I didn't say a word. The pain had sobered me up and all I wanted was to go home. When I was dressed, I told him I had to leave right now and then a lie I wished was the truth: my sister was expecting me.

On the way out, he gave a "thumbs-up" to a group of guys when he thought I wasn't looking. I heard some snickering but I didn't turn around. I grabbed my jacket off the kitchen table. A crowd of kids were watching Maniac Mike standing by the stove, stirring a pot of something that smelled awful. They were all giggling hysterically. When he saw me he said, "Want to join us in a little kitchen chemistry?" and I shook my head and moved to the door.

Kyle and I didn't say anything as we got in his car and headed down the street. The cold night air had hit me like a slap in the face—and made me wonder how on earth I could have been so stupid. I'd almost lost my virginity with a guy who didn't know my birthday or my parents' names. A guy who'd never even asked if I had a favorite song.

I had no idea how he was feeling, and I didn't particularly care. He'd almost raped me and one "sorry" wasn't going to change that, especially after his thumbs-up crap. Of course I would never go out with him again. Fighting him off at the river bluffs was bad enough, but this was damn near a crime.

"You know what you should be when you grow up, Leeann?"

His voice was all cocky, and I was taken aback, but I said "What?" before I realized I didn't want his answer.

"A nun."

I turned to look at him. He was grinning and I could see the perfect alignment of his teeth, the product of years of braces. Another benefit of his father's money, like this car and his expensive Nikes.

"A nun with giant boobs." He laughed. "What a waste."

"Shut up." My voice was a spit. "You said you were sorry. Don't say anything else or—"

"Or what?" He stuck his hand on my thigh. "You'll report me to the other nuns?"

What happened next is still unclear to me. I remember pushing him off, and I remember how mad I got when he kept putting his hand back, each time a little higher, but I don't know if the shove I gave him was the reason he strayed into the other lane. He'd been drinking, too. My sister said if the cops had been doing their job, they would have arrested him. He should have gotten a DWI. He should have been put in jail for what he did to me.

Of course she didn't know about that shove.

The other car was an ancient Chevy, pale green, with fins and a giant hood that only rippled in the crash. An old man was driving, but we didn't know that until the police showed up. The old guy wasn't hurt but he didn't move until they opened his door. Maybe he was too busy watching us.

Kyle had started yelling before we'd even skidded to a stop in the ditch. His door was dented but he forced it open and jumped out cursing and screaming about his car. The front wasn't really there anymore. The grill and the hood and the engine had all been squished together like a sandwich under a spatula.

He wasn't injured, at least, not in the accident. By the time the police arrived, his knuckles were bleeding from punching the trunk and the driver's door and a piece of the metal bumper he picked up from the street.

The underside of my chin was bleeding, but my ankle was the main problem. Kyle had a barbell under the seat and it had rolled up and hit my left leg. The throbbing pain was so sharp it brought tears to my eyes. I was out of the car, and trying to stand when I realized the queasiness in my stomach wasn't just nerves. I grabbed my hair and bent over just in time to vomit all over the gravel.

The paramedic could tell my ankle was broken just by looking at it. He also said the scratch below my chin would need stitches. He never gave me a choice about the ambulance, and he ignored all my babbling about how upset my sister would be. "It isn't that serious," he told me. "I'm sure she can handle it."

Of course he was long gone by the time she came running into the emergency room. She was a little out of breath—and a near perfect model of unreadable: flat eyes, bland expression, mouth a straight line. Even her hands refused to give away anything. They weren't clutched or wringing or even curled, but lying palms down against her side.

She was alone; she'd called our landlady Agnes to sit with Tommy. The police had already told her I was with Kyle. They'd also told her the accident took place on River Road, not a half mile from the entrance to Highway 61, and the intersection where Mom had had her accident.

I felt a rush of guilt and pity. "I'm all right," I said, and watched her eyes move from the five stitches to my ankle, purple and black and swollen to the size of a baby's head.

She sat down next to me and stroked my hair while we waited for them to do the cast. I was bracing myself for her to say I told you so about Kyle. I was bracing myself for her to yell or cry, something. Instead she was just very, very quiet. Even when I tried to apologize, she put her finger to my lips and said I wasn't to worry about anything but feeling better.

When we got home, she helped me pull my pajama top over my head without hitting my chin, and gave me extra pillows so I wouldn't be tempted to roll over and bump into the stitches or the cast. I fell asleep wondering why I'd expected her to freak out, when obviously the paramedic was right, she could handle this.

I woke up at first light of morning, suddenly aware that she was in my room, kneeling on the floor by my window. I had no idea how long she'd been there. Maybe all night.

"Mary Beth?"

"Can you see it?" she said quietly, without turning around. "See that orange streak over there? In just a few minutes, it'll fill the sky and the night will just disappear. And it always seems to happen so quickly. Like no matter how closely you watch, you can never point to the moment it changes." She leaned forward and put her hand flat on the window. Her voice sounded fragile in a way I'd never heard it before. "Sometimes I just wish it could stay like this, you know? Sometimes I wish it didn't always have to become another day."

chapter
eight

I'd only had my cast off for a few weeks when Ben's graduation announcement arrived in the mail. The envelope was creamy beige, heavy, with a seal of gold. Too important looking to just wad up and toss, though I was sure my sister wouldn't see it that way. He had finished his Ph.D., and, for reasons I couldn't fathom, his parents were inviting our family to a dinner in his honor. The restaurant was outside St. Louis, a good two hours from here. The dinner was set for a Thursday evening the second week of May: very inconvenient since Mary Beth would have to be up early on Friday for work. And Tommy would never be able to sit through it. He hated any restaurant that dared to serve food without free toys.

There were a lot of little reasons not to go—not to mention the really big reason that Mary Beth and Ben hadn't even spoken for a year. So imagine my surprise when my sister ripped out a piece of notebook paper from her pad and immediately wrote Judy Mathiessen, Ben's mother, to say she and I would be there.

"I'll have to find a baby-sitter for Tommy," she told me, "but there's lots of time." When I just stood there, staring at her, she exhaled. "Is that all right with you?"

"Sure." I wasn't going to pry or even ask what was going on— I was afraid she'd change her mind.

The Ds thought maybe they would get back together. I said maybe, though I really didn't hold out any hope for something that good.

My optimism had pretty much disappeared since the car accident. School was part of it. I wasn't surprised that Kyle had lied about what we'd done, but now I had to deal with girls shooting me sympathetic looks—since they assumed he'd dumped me after he "got what he wanted"—and boys smirking and whistling and even occasionally trying to push me in a corner and feel me up. I couldn't complain to my sister though, like I always had before. Home was the other part of the problem, and the part I was really worried about.

If only Mary Beth had punished me. Grounding me would have been easy, and so normal. Instead, she decided to focus her energies on our apartment. She called what she was doing "spring cleaning," but I'd seen spring cleaning at friends' houses, and I knew this wasn't it. For one thing, friends' mothers didn't paint the living room at two in the morning. For another, friends' mothers didn't keep going for weeks and weeks like my sister did, never satisfied, moving the couch to the left one day, and to the opposite corner the next.

Mary Beth had what seemed like a zillion projects. Stapling sheets to the fresh painted walls, because she thought it would give the kitchen "a fresher look." Taking down the old living room curtains, and then putting them back when she didn't like the bamboo shades she'd shopped for all over town. Letting

Tommy take apart those same bamboo shades, and then spending hours threading them together again, in case they would work in the bathroom or her bedroom. Covering one of Tommy's walls with cork, "for when he's older," she said. Covering his other wall with a teddy bear pattern wallpaper that was so babyish it embarrassed him.

Even when my cast was off, she wouldn't let me help her. "I love doing this," she'd say. "I'm not tired," she'd insist, when I'd wake up and find her "taking a break" from her constant song reading with her constant quest to make our apartment better. Removing all the dishes from the cabinets, to repaper the shelves. Cleaning her closet, or mine, or Tommy's, or the medicine chest. Rearranging the furniture again and again and again.

The more she did, the guiltier I felt. I was almost positive it was all my fault—especially since she only seemed to start new projects when I wasn't home. It took me a while to realize this connection, mainly because I rarely went anywhere now. But it fit perfectly. And if I was even one minute late, she'd be at it so furiously when I walked in the door that she wouldn't even remember to say hello.

She wouldn't admit she was worried about me. She said she still trusted me as much as ever. It made me feel like dirt.

The one and only time I was really late, when Darlene's car ran out of gas and we couldn't find a pay phone, my sister took all the furniture from my bedroom and moved it into the hall. When I finally got home, she was pulling up the carpet, even though below it was a hideous gray speckled floor. It turned out to be the only one of her projects that she had to pay someone to come in and change back the next day.

Ben's invitation arrived while the carpet man was still there, working on my room. Of course I wanted to go to the party—I wanted Ben to check out my sister. I wanted him to tell me what to do to make things all right again.

When the Thursday evening arrived, Mary Beth's friend Juanita picked up Tommy. I got dressed and then sat at the kitchen table, drumming my fingers, while she took a shower, washed her hair, blew it dry and brushed it a hundred strokes, painted her nails, applied her makeup, and put on a brand-new dress she'd bought at a spring sale and her best pumps. At some point I asked her if she wanted me to wrap the present but she said no, she would do it. She didn't want me to look at the map, either. She'd only gone to this restaurant once when she and Ben were dating but she insisted she remembered the way, no problem.

Our present was a leather wallet. Mary Beth said the one Ben had was unraveling at the flap. I nodded, but I wondered if she was remembering the obvious—we hadn't seen him for a year. Who's to say he didn't have a new wallet?

Even with my sister's lengthy preparations, we still would have been on time if she hadn't gotten off Highway 270 at the wrong exit. As it was, we drove into the restaurant parking lot at eight forty-one, so late I was starving and worried the eating part might be over. We rushed inside and let a waiter lead us back to the banquet room. It was bigger than I expected. There were eight or nine tables, and probably thirty-five people. The only ones I recognized other than Ben were his parents and Rebecca.

Rebecca was playing hostess. She gave air kisses to me and my sister and took our present before leading us to a table across the room from where Ben was sitting with his parents and some girl. Everyone was eating, but we'd barely sat down when a waiter arrived with plates of steaming London broil and vegetables for us, too. Ben glanced in our direction but he didn't come over to greet us. He didn't even wave.

The situation was unbearably awkward from my perspective. I was so nervous for my sister I was afraid to look at her. But she didn't seem to mind. She started eating and talking animatedly to the guy on her left, another graduate student named Gary. I heard him ask how she knew Ben and she said they were old friends.

When the toasts started, she held up her glass and smiled through all the talk of Ben's accomplishments and the funny stories about his years in grad school. She was still smiling when Ben's father stood up and said that Ben was twenty-seven years old now, high time he started his life. "In my day," Ben's dad continued, "we had families at your age. What do you think, Catherine?" Ben's dad smiled at the girl sitting next to Ben. "How long's it going to be before you and Benjamin are ready to settle down?"

I glanced at Rebecca as if her face could tell me how this happened. What about that shrine to my sister? The pathetic Ben, who couldn't get over Mary Beth?

This Catherine person had reddish brown hair, a little button kind of nose, big brown eyes. She looked cute in a bookish way. "What a question," she said, but she laughed with Ben's father before leaning over and giving Ben a quick kiss.

I counted backwards to November, when I ran into Rebecca at the crafts fair. Seven months. A lifetime ago. Before I started dating Kyle, before we had the accident. Before my sister became so incomprehensible that I had no idea what she was thinking or feeling or even why she came here tonight.

The toasts weren't even over when Mary Beth stood up. She whispered, "Stay here," and made her exit as gracefully as possible—considering that she was damn near running. I figured she was going to the bathroom and of course I was going to follow. I had to make sure she was all right.

She wasn't in the ladies' room. I checked the hall by the pay phones; I even went out to the parking lot, to see if she was sitting in the Ford. I had a moment of cold white panic that she'd simply vanished before I remembered I hadn't gone the other way down the hall. There were three banquet rooms; one of them was empty and half dark—and that's where she was.

I didn't see Ben until I was already in the room. He must have walked in a second before I did, because Mary Beth was just beginning to congratulate him when he cut her off.

"What are you doing here?" His voice was clipped and angry; I'd never heard him sound like this. I stepped into the shadows behind the busboy station. My breath was coming in short, nervous gasps and I was messing with the scar under my chin again. It was a tic I'd developed since the accident.

"Well, your mom invited me." She paused, but he just stared at her. "And of course I wanted you to know how proud I am." She patted his shoulder. "I knew you could do it, Ben. I just think it's so great that you'll be out there, doing your research. I'll bet I'll be reading about you in the paper before long with some important discovery."

Her voice was a hundred percent sincere. No one listening to her could doubt that she really cared about Ben's work. It was kind of impressive, actually, to think that she could still feel this way even though they weren't together anymore.

Ben, however, was not impressed.

"Oh right. Now I remember. Mary Beth Norris, hurt, yet always the generous spirit right up until the end. Tell me, am I supposed to see this as noble?"

"I'm not sure what you mean."

"You talked me into going back to finish the Ph.D. You saved me, just like you saved all the rest of them." He faked a bow. "Thank you very much."

Mary Beth's voice was hollow. "Please don't be this way, Ben."

"All right, how should I be? Should I tell you how beautiful you look?" He stepped back and moved his head in an exaggerated motion up and down. "A new dress, isn't it? Very nice. Very—"

"Ben, I—"

"Don't you want to hear that? Or should I tell you how it's been for me for the last year, wondering how the hell this could have happened?" He lowered his voice to a hiss. "Maybe I should tell you how much I wish I'd never met you?"

He spun on his heel to go, and that's when my sister started crying. The sound was as soft as a kitten mewing, but I heard it and Ben did, too. He turned back to her, but he didn't pull her into his arms until she muttered "Catherine." The babble that followed was as blatantly jealous as a child whose friend has a better toy. And of course it softened Ben; he obviously still cared about my sister. The shock for me was how obvious it was that she still loved him.

"Everything is such a mess," Mary Beth cried.

"I can't argue with that."

"How did this happen?"

"You threw me out, remember?"

The anger was leaving his voice, but Mary Beth was still crying. After a while, he put his hand under her chin and lifted her face to his. It looked like she kissed him first, but it might have been the other way around. It was hard to tell from my corner. I felt a little bad watching them, but I couldn't make myself stop.

They were holding each other close now, pressed together like soaked fabric against skin. And their kissing was going on and on, like they'd forgotten where they were. In between kisses, they mumbled words like "want" and "need," "baby" and "miss." The whole thing was about as romantic as I could imagine. It made me feel a little sorry for myself, because no boy cared about me this way, and as far as I could see, no boy ever would. Mainly though, it made me feel a wave of calm that was so much like being tired I had to stifle a yawn. Even if I never knew why they broke up, if they got back together, it wouldn't matter. The world would make sense again. My sister would be like she was before.

I was just wondering whether Ben would come home with us tonight—and what he would think of all the improvements around our place—when we heard a woman's voice. Catherine was walking down the hallway, calling for him.

It was Mary Beth who pulled away, not Ben. Mary Beth who stood up straight, took a few steps back. And when Catherine came inside, Mary Beth stuck her hand out, asked questions about where she worked, where she lived. Mary Beth even told Catherine she was lucky to have Ben.

I thought for sure it had to be an act. Ben must have thought so, too, because after Catherine left the room—apparently satisfied her boyfriend wasn't about to be stolen—he reached for my sister. And Mary Beth stepped back again.

"This is embarrassing, isn't it?" She put her arms around herself. "Coming here, getting between you and the woman you're with now."

"What?" His voice was airless.

"I shouldn't have come." Mary Beth spoke slowly, as if she was convincing herself as well as Ben. "It was a mistake. I lost myself before, and I'm very sorry for that."

"You can't be serious," he sputtered. "Lost yourself?" He was running his hands through his hair. "Don't you mean you remembered what you've been denying all this time—that you and I were happy?"

I stepped out of my corner, desperate to hear how she would explain this. But all she did was whisper, "Maybe some people don't deserve happiness."

He looked every bit as confused as I felt, but he didn't argue with her. That long night at Scalatti's must have taught him it was useless to try. When he spoke a moment later, his voice wasn't even all that angry, although I figured he had to be. I knew I would be.

"For the record, I don't think you lost yourself just now." He cleared his throat. "That was you and this is . . . God knows."

She didn't say anything. He stared at her for a moment, and then turned to leave.

Before I could move back into the shadows, he spotted me. I started to make an excuse for intruding, but he shook his head, and motioned me over to where he was standing by the door. "I want you to have my phone number in Philadelphia." He reached into his wallet, pulled out an old receipt, and wrote his number on the back. I noticed the wallet wasn't unraveling. "Here," he said, pressing the scrap of paper into my hand. "Call me if you need anything. Promise?"

I looked at him, but I couldn't say yes. My sister had walked up behind me. I could feel her breath on the back of my hair.

He glanced over my head at Mary Beth. "For the record, I still don't think I did anything wrong. I know you do, but I will never understand why." He paused and his voice cracked a little. "And I don't wish I hadn't met you. How could I ever wish that?"

Then he was gone, and Mary Beth and I rushed out of the restaurant and into the car without saying good-bye to anyone. She started the Ford and we were back on the road. She was sitting up very straight; her eyes looked directly ahead. We'd only gone a few miles when she apologized for taking me to the dinner. "It really wasn't fair to make you deal with all this. I wanted you to come because I knew you missed Ben. I am glad he gave you his phone number. I told you he really liked you."

"I won't call him." I was thinking about their conversation, and his claim he didn't do anything wrong. What were they talking about? Could there be a reason she dumped him after all? Even a reason why she was acting so completely weird?

We'd been on the road for about an hour when she suddenly said, "He's going to be all right, honey."

We were in the middle of nowhere; Mary Beth had tuned in a radio station from Lexington, Kentucky. The song playing was, "Baker Street." The moon was so low in the sky, it looked like we could drive to it.

Her voice startled me, but she was right, I had been thinking about Ben. It was just hitting me that he was moving to Philadelphia. It was so far away, at least a thousand miles if I remembered my geography. It wasn't even in the same time zone.

"I know," I said lightly, reminding myself that if he had done something to her, I couldn't possibly miss him.

The next day, I decided I had to know, once and for all.

I came home from school and I didn't even get a soda or a snack before I went into Mary Beth's bedroom and opened the top dresser drawer and took out his letters. Most had been written before they broke up, while he was away at school, because they'd agreed to keep their daily phone conversations down to ten minutes to save on long distance. A few had come since that horrible night at Scalatti's.

My family was in trouble, that was my justification for invading her privacy. As I was taking off the tinfoil from the letter pile, it occurred to me that I might feel worse afterwards, but it was a price I was willing to pay. At least I wouldn't feel as confused as I was feeling now.

Unfortunately, I was wrong. I felt much more confused after I read the letters, and the enormity of what my sister had done hit me like a blow. It was one thousand four hundred and eighty-five days by my calculations, which were, if anything, giving her the benefit of the doubt. One thousand four hundred and eighty-five days, at least, of her knowing where our father was and not telling me.

Later, Mary Beth would explain that she had had to track Dad down to get him to sign some papers, since he and Mom were still legally married when Mom had her car accident, and the insurance company kept refusing to release the money from Mom's life insurance policy. But no, she never thought of telling me, even though this was only a month or two after that day we spent looking for him in Kansas City. Actually, if we hadn't gone to Kansas City that day, she never would have found him, she admitted as much. But she didn't thank me for writing all those letters to Dad's relatives. And she didn't thank Ben, either, for telling her she shouldn't be keeping this big secret from me.

This was the sign I used to look for that he really had cared when I told him things I'd never told anyone about my parents. The letters made it clear he'd discussed my feelings with Mary Beth many times. "Don't you think she has a right to know where he is?" he wrote in a letter from February. "I understand your desire to protect her, but he is her father, too." And then in early March: "I still don't see what you're accomplishing by keeping her from making contact. Even if you're right that he won't respond, she may feel better knowing she made the effort."

It wasn't an argument yet. These same letters were filled with expressions of love and plans for their future. In a way, what to do about Dad was just part of those plans. Ben wondered if Mary Beth would be comfortable moving across the country without trying to see Dad one more time. "California is a long way from

Little Rock," he wrote. "Most of the good labs are a long way from Little Rock."

From which I gathered that Dad was in Little Rock now. A lot of the information I got had to be teased out of what Ben said—until I got to the after-Scalatti's letters. The very first one contained the crucial fact that Ben had driven the three hundred and fifty-one miles from St. Louis to Little Rock to see Dad. He'd done it without Mary Beth because she couldn't get off work and he could—his spring break. He did have to delay some experiment but he didn't mind. This was more important than his work. We were more important: his new family.

I couldn't tell from the letters whether he'd discussed the possibility of such a trip with her, but my sense was he had. And she'd told him not to do it. But he did it anyway, because he thought Dad might be mentally ill, and rather than sending him money from Mom's life insurance from time to time, Mary Beth should try to get him treatment.

To say she didn't appreciate his opinion is an understatement.

"Ill does not mean crazy," he wrote, more than once. "I don't know why you can't see that.

"I only wanted to see if I could help him," he continued. "I thought you of all people would understand. I still can't believe you said this means I don't really love you. Why the hell else would I do it?"

There were only a few letters after that Scalatti's dinner, and they were all Ben expressing how upset he was. The most interesting letter was probably the last one in the stack. It was dated June of last year, and I remembered it coming, but Mary Beth had told me it was just another question about some of his stuff he couldn't find.

First, he went on about how hurt he was that Mary Beth

wouldn't write him or return his phone calls. Then he accused her of being a "control freak," who was afraid to let anyone get close to her. "I'm sure you'll disagree, point to your friends and customers as evidence that you're not afraid. Sorry, but that's just bullshit. You and I both know that taking care of other people can be a means of avoiding your own problems." Then he told her that she was in denial about Dad. And her version of reality was naive: "Not in all ways, of course. But God help the person who dares to question you." He even threw in that her song reading was hypocritical. "Family problems are your specialty, except when it's your own goddamn family."

Finally, he wrote, "I thought I understood you, but it seems I was very wrong. Of course this is no surprise, is it? It's part of your self-image. You understand everyone, but no one can possibly understand you."

My hands were trembling as I put this letter on top and wrapped them back in foil. Nervous is too mild to describe what I felt, it was more like shaken to the core.

I told myself I was just angry with her for lying about Dad. I told myself I'd feel differently once I talked to her, once I gave her a chance to explain. Ben was wrong, he had to be. Sure, Mary Beth was acting a little strange lately, but she was the wisest person in town; everybody said so. She couldn't be a "control freak," who was "afraid to let anyone get close to her." It just wasn't possible.

All I needed was to hear her explanation. Of course she would have a reason for all this.

I waited until we were in the kitchen that night to ask her. She was getting ready to fry chicken; I was sitting at the table, helping Tommy finish coloring in a picture of a bunch of zoo animals Mary Beth had drawn for him. I picked this moment because I knew we wouldn't be interrupted. The hour between six and seven was the only hour left in the evening that she wasn't available for her customers. Of course the phone still rang, but she always let the answering machine pick up. She called it our family's sacred time. Even her house projects always had to wait during that hour.

I expected her to be upset that I'd looked at her letters, but I figured she'd get over it quickly enough and apologize to me. After all, I was the injured party here, the one who'd been lied to. But no sooner were the words out of my mouth than her hands dropped to her sides and she blinked at me as though she didn't recognize her own sister anymore. "God," she gasped, "how could you?"

Even Tommy could tell something was very wrong. He pointed his chubby finger at me. "You're in big trouble."

"I was only trying to help you," I said quickly. "I was worried. I didn't know what else to do."

Her voice was so insistent, it was staccato. "I do not need your help."

"I think you do," I began. The phone was ringing, but I could talk over it, I did it all the time. Except this time, when she picked it up on the second ring. I could tell from the sudden shift of her voice—she sounded so calm and cool, like nothing could ever upset her—that it was a customer.

"Right now is fine," she said, before she hung up. I was staring a hole right through her as she walked back to the stove. When she didn't say a word, I asked her if she'd just told a customer to come over now.

"No, I told her I'd come and get her." Mary Beth's voice was sharp like the popping of the grease in the pan. "Her car's in the shop, and it's urgent. We'll have to finish this conversation later."

It took all my concentration to absorb this news and I was going out of the lines, messing up the elephant's tail. Tommy took the crayon out of my hand and told me not to scribble.

"Is that all right with you?" she said, finally.

I hesitated for a moment. "Well, no. I mean, I really need to talk to you. And it seems kind of weird that right when I bring this up, you decide to break your rule and—"

She spun around. "Weird how?"

When I didn't answer, she walked over and sat down across from me at the table. Her eyes were narrow and her breath was coming out in short, angry bursts. Tommy took this moment to escape into the living room. I leaned back in my chair, wishing he'd asked me to come with him.

"Do you think my song reading is hypocritical, Leeann?" She was rubbing her temples like she had a headache. "You read what Ben said about me. Do you think he's right?"

I wasn't sure what the answer was, but then I glanced in her eyes and saw it: a self-doubt I'd never seen before, a pain I'd noticed the first time the night of my accident but had a feeling had been there for a very long time. I didn't hesitate, I told her absolutely not. "Ben doesn't know what he's talking about. It's like he must not get how gifted you are."

She touched my hand lightly with her fingertips. "Thanks, baby," she said, and exhaled. "I knew I could count on you."

When she got up to turn the chicken over, she apologized for getting so mad. "You shouldn't have gone through my things. But I guess I understand why you did." And then she changed the subject to the customer who was expecting her any second, whose music all had to do with—ironically enough—the fight she was having with her older sister Laurie.

I decided to let the topic of Dad wait. I'd waited years to

know where he was; I could wait awhile longer. For now, I would just do what Mary Beth wanted me to do. Cut up Tommy's chicken. Stir the corn. Make sure he drank his milk. Wrap up the leftovers for her to eat later tonight.

I was trying to make up for all the lying I'd done and the worry I'd caused her, but that wasn't all. Something bad was happening to my family, I could feel it, and I was determined to keep it from getting any worse. Even if my sister was wrong about Dad and Ben and a hundred other things, she was still here, frying chicken and remembering Tommy's milk and always wearing her seat belt, no matter how short the trip. And tonight she would be here, like always, maybe rearranging the furniture, but also making sure we weren't coughing or sick, always standing ready to defend us from strange noises or imagined intruders with the old baseball bat she kept under her bed.

Mom was dead, Dad was a vague memory, and Ben was a thousand miles away now. Ben was gone, and there was nothing I could do to get him back. My sister was here, it was just that simple. My sister was my family.

chapter
nine

All that summer, I hung around the house, helping Mary Beth. Summer was always her busiest season, and that one was downright crazy with all the customers she'd taken on in the last year. Every time we turned on the answering machine, it seemed like they all had new songs to report, new lines that were keeping them awake, tossing in their beds. Mary Beth said it was the sun's fault, for making people remember what it was like to be a kid wishing for swims in the lake and ice-cream cones and other things you could just reach out and have.

No hour could be kept sacred for our family anymore, but Tommy didn't seem to mind. Mary Beth did what she could, grabbing him up and spinning him around to the music whenever she had a spare moment, making notes in his room so she could help him run his trains. Also he loved having all these people around, especially when the customers brought their children along. The kids would hang out and play with Tommy while Mary Beth was with their moms down in the office. I didn't mind either, even though of course I had to baby-sit all those extra kids.

It was the summer of '83, and the number one song on the radio was "Every Breath You Take." A creepy song, my sister said, and I nodded though I was spending most of my time doing just what the guy in the song did—though I knew *my* motives were good. I was always watching Mary Beth, trying to figure out if she was really all right. She'd given up on the home improvements at the beginning of June, finally, but she still didn't seem exactly herself. There was a fragility about her now, a sense when you looked at her that she'd been hurt so many times, the slightest disappointment might topple her again. At least that was my fear, which was why as curious as I was about Dad, I vowed not to bring up the topic until I was sure she was ready. Of course I was hoping she'd bring it up herself sometime. She knew I'd read the letters; she had to figure I'd be dying to talk about it.

I made it until the middle of July before I finally broke down.

At least I picked a good time. It was a Tuesday evening, Tommy was in bed, and Mary Beth was in a great mood because one of her customers, Irene Danston, had just called with the happy news that she was leaving her husband, Jack. According to Mary Beth, Jack kept Irene a virtual prisoner at home, refusing to allow her to get a job or go to night school, refusing to let her question any of his decisions. Mary Beth had been working with Irene for two years to get her the courage to do this (Irene's very first song she reported to my sister was a country tune about escaping from a guy), and now, it was finally happening. Mary Beth had been smiling ever since she hung up the phone.

I was sitting on the couch, pretending to read, when I glanced up and asked if we could talk about something. She put down the chart in her hand. "Of course, honey."

"Can I turn the music off?" The song was too upbeat for my mood.

"Sure," she said, and I did. When I sat back down, I picked the window chair, so I could have some distance to make my point.

I planned to ease into the topic, but I was too anxious to do it. I reminded her that I knew she knew where Dad was, since I'd read her letters, which of course was wrong and I'd never do again, etcetera. (I didn't want a lecture, even though it wasn't true, what I told her about never doing it again. I'd already gone through the whole place looking for Dad's address, to no avail.)

She looked at me and calmly repeated her explanation of why she'd had to find him: that life insurance business. And she threw in that the money had sure come in handy for bills in the last few months.

I knew she was talking about the hospital bills for what happened to me. Kyle's auto insurance should have covered it, except, as it turned out, Kyle didn't have auto insurance. His dad had taken him off the family's policy—and absolutely forbidden him to drive—as punishment for getting bad grades. My sister had been round and round with Kyle's parents, who were petitioning the insurance company, and still promised to pay for everything, one way or another, eventually. But Mary Beth couldn't wait. Tommy was having those ear infections again, and he was going to need tubes inserted and more visits with the specialists. We had to be the family who always paid on time, since we didn't have health insurance.

As I looked down at my hands, I wondered if I'd ever stop feeling guilty about this. The guilt was like the scar under my chin: I had touched it so often in the last few months, secretly, shamefully, and always with a sense of embarrassment that I couldn't just leave it alone and go on with my life.

Finally, I took a breath. "Okay, well, the thing is I really want to know where Dad is." Then, before she could interrupt, "I just want to write to him. Maybe he'll write back this time, even if he is ill or whatever you want to call it."

As soon as the words were out of my mouth, I knew it was the wrong thing to say. She held up her hand like a crossing guard, palm out, and her voice became almost too gentle, angry gentle if there is such a thing. "Dad is not ill, Leeann. You have to trust me on this. He has problems, yes, but he is not crazy. No matter what some people have to say about it."

"Okay," I said slowly, glancing in her eyes. "Then why didn't you tell me you knew where he is? Why don't you want me to write him?"

"Oh, Lee," she said, leaning back, "it's so complicated." She paused for a minute and twisted her fingers in the spaces of the afghan on the couch until it looked like she was wearing rings. "Remember when we were at the cemetery? Remember what we talked about?"

I remembered being at the cemetery, but I wasn't sure which time she was referring to. We'd been there a lot that summer, starting with Memorial Day, when we spent all morning arranging flowers at Mom's grave, and at least once a week since. It was the one place Mary Beth always seemed relaxed, so I went with her without complaining for a change. The last time was just two days ago, on Sunday, when she decided we should have a picnic even though it was so hot the ham was limp and the cheese turned plastic and Tommy's little friend Jonah didn't understand why we had to eat at this place where there were no swings or slides or water of any kind, not even a wading pool.

Tommy wasn't fazed. He was used to the cemetery; he'd been coming here since he was a toddler. All those times I told Mary Beth I couldn't handle going, Tommy was too young to say yes or no. He knew all the graves in the vicinity of Mom's, and though he couldn't always read the names, he could recite the numbers like statistics from baseball cards. 1-9-0-2, 1-9-6-4. That is, Clarence J. Sutter, 1902–1964. Husband of Ida P. Sutter, who was buried right next to him, and as Tommy told his friend Jonah, was so newly dead she probably wasn't even rotted all the way.

At four and a half, Tommy's idea of death sounded a lot like a sci-fi movie. The body was like a mechanical shell you threw off when you went to heaven. Heaven was like another planet, but better, where you could have all the candy you wanted. Cemeteries were like portals from heaven to earth, where the dead people could still see you. And that's why we came here all the time. So his grandma could see what a big boy he was getting to be.

Jonah's mother told us later that Tommy's explanation must have made an impression since Jonah came home upset that he didn't have his own dead relatives to visit. It would have been funnier if Mary Beth had laughed, too.

We'd been at the cemetery plenty, but we'd never talked about Dad there. We didn't talk about much at all there that I could remember.

The phone was ringing, but before Mary Beth got up to answer it, she reminded me of a comment she'd made last Sunday about Mom maybe being better off now. She didn't mean because Mom was in a more sophisticated version of Tommy's heaven with all the candy, but because Mom was finally free from all her suffering.

It was the kind of thing you usually say when someone dies

after a long, painful illness, but I knew what Mary Beth was getting at. And it wasn't just how hard Mom had to work to support
us or how alone she was after Dad left; it was a deeper unhappiness that was always with her, maybe all the way back to when
she was a kid in the children's home. When Mary Beth got off the
phone though, I told her the truth: I had no idea what that comment about Mom at the cemetery had to do with me writing to
Dad now.

She inhaled. "The last few years of her life, Mom wanted so
badly to believe that things happen for a reason. It wasn't her
nature to think that way." Mary Beth smiled a wry smile.
"Punishment she believed in, but never grace."

My sister wasn't looking at me; she was staring out the back
window. The wind was blowing. The moon was shining big and
yellow through the flickering leaves, and maybe she thought, like
I did, that the moon looked lonely, because she stood up and
shut the curtains before she said, "Do you think we're better off
now?"

"Better off?" I had a hunch what she was asking, but I
couldn't believe it.

"I'm saying if things happen for a reason, are we better off
without Mom?"

"No," I said firmly. It was the only possible answer. It was
what she was waiting to hear.

"Okay. Now what if God told us we could have her home,
but she was happier where she was. How could we drag her back
here anyway?"

I paused until I thought I got it. "Are you saying Dad might
be better off where he is?"

"I don't know. I have no way to know that, Lee. But neither
do you, and I doubt you've even thought about it."

She had me there. I crossed my arms tightly, and willed myself not to mess with my chin.

"Isn't it possible that someone who's been gone for more than nine years wants to stay gone?" She looked at me and her voice grew soft. "Isn't it possible that's why he'd already disappeared when we got to Kansas City? Because even though he was happy to get your letter, he didn't want to be found?"

Before I could answer, the phone rang again. It was Irene Danston, who was losing her nerve about leaving Jack, and so of course Mary Beth had to talk to her, and of course Mary Beth had to offer her our couch, just for a few nights, until she decided where to go. As I helped Mary Beth make up the couch, we talked about what we'd do if Jack dared to show up here. We were being silly, bragging about how tough we were with our punches and kicks. When Irene came, she joked that we could be like *Charlie's Angels,* with Mary Beth as Farrah Fawcett and me as Kate Jackson and her as Tanya Roberts, the one season replacement everyone forgot as soon as the show got canceled.

By the time I went to bed that night, I was so confused I felt like even wanting to contact Dad made me a little like Jack Danston. If Dad wanted to be gone, what choice did I have but to respect that?

But my respect got me no closer to the truth. This was what I kept coming back to, as the summer went on and Mary Beth and I sat together night after night, doing the charts, talking about her customers. It was too ironic: me knowing the secrets of half our town, while my own father remained this huge mystery.

And I'd always hated mysteries. Every week, I would beg my sister to turn down the stereo so I could watch my favorite TV program: the one where Arthur C. Clarke showed that some famous mystery—the Bermuda Triangle or a man who claimed to have lived a past life during the Civil War or a Christian whose hands bleed like Jesus' every Easter—was really perfectly reasonable, explained by some scientific principle or another, and so not really a mystery at all. I loved hearing that there were pockets of methane gas in the Bermuda Triangle and not space aliens; that the man with the past life had found all those details about the Civil War in diaries he'd read so long ago he'd forgotten them; that the brain could actually make that old woman's hands bleed just because she believed in Jesus so strongly. I loved the idea that confusion didn't just feel like a headache; it was just as capable of being cured.

All I wanted was a little truth. Of course I'd thought about asking Ben; I must have fingered that slip of paper with his phone number on it a hundred times. But summer was almost over when I found myself standing in the kitchen, holding the phone.

My hands were shaking a little, but I kept reminding myself of his claim that he went to see Dad because he thought he could help him. Even if it made Mary Beth mad, it touched me more than anything Ben had ever said or done. I'd seen Dad's apartment, all those lists he made on the walls. Whether he was crazy or not, he needed someone's help.

It was Saturday morning but Mary Beth wasn't seeing customers because it was Labor Day weekend; she and Tommy were at a welcome open house for his kindergarten class. Ben answered on the second ring and was surprised, to put it mildly. After I said my name, he repeated it, lifting his voice like it was a question, like he couldn't believe it was really me.

"Is something wrong?" he said quickly.

"Oh no. Everything's fine."

"Mary Beth is all right?"

"Yeah." It was closer to true than a "no" would have been. She did seem fine now. Sometimes I even wondered if I'd imagined the problems last spring. After all, our house did look a lot better. What was wrong with fixing the place up?

"How about you?" I asked lightly. "Are you doing okay?"

"My work is coming along. Same old story. Work, come home to an empty apartment, go back to work. Not much else."

"Cool," I said idiotically. My foot was thumping against the table as it hit me that Catherine person hadn't moved to Philadelphia with him. I wasn't very surprised. "I mean, it's cool that your work is going good. Not the other part."

He laughed a little. "Thanks, Leeann," he said, before asking the usual questions: was I ready to start sophomore year, what was I taking, that type of thing. I kept my answers as short as possible.

I heard him take a drink of something. "It's good to hear from you." His voice was cheerful now. "My phone rarely rings. I don't know anybody in town yet. Of course, I'm not here much. I'm usually in the lab."

I listened halfheartedly while he told me about Philadelphia, his apartment, his lab supervisor. I was getting anxious to get to the point; this was long distance, twenty-five cents a minute.

Finally, I just blurted it out. "Ben, I know you saw my dad."

"Mary Beth told you?" He sounded incredulous.

"No. I found one of your letters and sort of accidentally read it." I waited but he didn't say anything. "Well, I was just curious . . . when you saw him, how was he?"

He cleared his throat. "I gather Mary Beth isn't home right now."

"Right."

"And she has no idea you're calling me?"

"Right," I said again, softer.

"Leeann, I'd like to talk about this with you." He inhaled deeply. "I'd like to answer all your questions. Tell you whatever you want to know."

I slumped back in my chair, not trying to hide the disappointment in my voice. "But you're not going to."

"I'm in an awkward position. Your sister made it very clear that she does not want me to do this. I feel as though I have to honor her wishes, even if I disagree with them."

"Which you do, right?" I was getting annoyed. "Completely and totally. To the point where you said she was 'naive' and 'out of touch with reality.' "

"That one letter you read was damn comprehensive, wasn't it?" He let out a short laugh.

I was surprised to realize he wasn't mad even though it was his writing I'd snooped through. Maybe I would have been grateful, if I hadn't felt so frustrated.

"Okay. Don't tell me about the visit. But can you at least tell me his address? Or his phone number? I know he lives in Little Rock now, but where? I called the operator and she said there's no listing."

"He doesn't have a phone." Ben was silent for a while. "Have you tried asking your sister about this? Perhaps you can persuade her to—"

"But what about the address? For chrissakes, you have to remember that, you went there."

He cleared his throat again. "It would be so much better if Mary Beth told you all this. Surely you can see that."

I could, but I wasn't in the mood to admit it. "I have to go, but will you at least tell me one thing." I took a breath. "Just tell me if he's okay."

Since Ben was a big believer in being honest, I knew he

wouldn't say yes unless it was true. And he didn't. He paused and when he spoke again, his voice sounded pained. "I wish I could help you with this, Leeann. I really do."

"So do I," I muttered, before slamming down the phone.

After I took a shower and got dressed, I rushed out of the apartment and straight to the library. I didn't want to talk to my sister. I didn't even want to lay eyes on her.

Ben had been in the same room with my father, breathed the same air as my father, maybe even shook my father's hand. Ben could tell me what he looked like now, what kind of clothes he wore, what he did for a living, if anything. Ben could tell me what they talked about, whether it was heavy stuff or just chitchat. And since Ben had a good memory, he might even be able to give me all the specifics—the exact words. For example, he might be able to tell me if Dad had asked any casual questions about the family: Mary Beth, maybe even me. Something like, "How long is Leeann's hair now?" Or, "Does she have many friends at school?" Or even, "Is she happy?"

But Ben couldn't tell me a thing, because my sister wouldn't let him. And she wouldn't even tell my why.

I spent the day in the library, hiding from the entire mess, reading hundreds of pages of a Dickens novel. When I finally put down the book, my eyes were stinging and my neck and back were cramped, but still, I didn't want to go home. I had no choice, though. The library was closing early because of the holiday weekend and Mary Beth was expecting me. Plus, Darlene was coming over to our house for dinner. Again.

A month or so before, Darlene had decided Mary Beth was the only grown-up who'd ever understood her. This was after Mary Beth broke her rule against reading teenagers' charts and did Darlene's—only to discover the real reason why Darlene had stayed so long with her creepy boyfriend Greg. Neither of them would tell me what that reason was (Darlene said it was too personal; Mary Beth said she had to treat this one as strictly confidential, since Darlene was my friend), but whatever it was, it seemed to have worked a miracle: not only had Darlene ceased all contact with Greg, but she'd also started dating a new guy she met at The Shoe Stop at the mall.

A nice guy, Mary Beth pronounced him, when Darlene surprised us by showing up with him at dinner that Saturday night, and he helped us do dishes and sat with Tommy, building Legos afterwards. His name was Chuck; I called him Up-Chuck, but only in my mind. I couldn't believe Mary Beth liked him. He couldn't make eye contact with anyone, and his smile was so totally out of sync with the conversation. Joke. Blank expression. Illness story. Smile. You're nice. Blank expression. You're an idiot. Smile.

After he left, Darlene was standing in the kitchen, watching Mary Beth make the brownies she'd been promising Tommy for days. And gushing about Up-Chuck. "He's so sweet, isn't he? He's like no boy I've ever known."

Mary Beth laughed as she poured the batter. "He sure is, honey. And I think you deserve him after what you went through with that jerk Greg."

I was drinking a soda, sitting at the table, filling out an application to be a student tutor. I needed the money, and I liked the idea that I'd be helping people, too.

Darlene went on like this for a while, her voice becoming more and more dreamy as she sang Chuck's praises. She had on almost no makeup and her hair was straighter than I'd ever seen it. Even the clothes she was wearing were different: usually she wore a modified Jennifer Beals look, like almost every girl in school since *Flashdance,* but tonight, for Chuck, she'd worn regular jeans and a blouse without a single rip. She'd even ditched her leg warmers.

The brownies were in the oven and the two of them had moved to the living room when I overheard Darlene ask Mary Beth, "What happened with that guy you were living with? I thought he was a nice boy, too."

My sister's own friends never broached this topic with her, but Darlene was so thrilled to be chatting intimately with Mary Beth that she probably couldn't resist pushing it further. Mary Beth must have known that, too, because she didn't get mad or draw back. Instead, she shocked me completely by bitching about Ben to Darlene.

"He was nice, but he thought he knew everything," she said, and laughed. "Some guys are like that."

"He thought he knew more than *you*?" Darlene sputtered.

"It happens." Mary Beth laughed again. "Especially with men."

"But why? Because he was like this college graduate?"

"No," Mary Beth said more quietly. "It wasn't that."

I was standing in the doorway now, so I could listen better. I was relieved she'd said no, because she'd told me many times that Ben wasn't a snob about the difference in their formal education. It was one of the things she loved about him.

"Well, I'll bet it had something to do with it," Darlene said. And then she blurted out that she'd heard gossip around town last year, people saying Ben dumped Mary Beth because he was such a big brain in college and his parents were rumored to have money. "But I always told them they didn't know a thing," Darlene concluded, smiling. "I said if anybody was too good for the other person in that relationship, it was you, Mary Beth."

"Thanks, honey." Mary Beth's voice sounded weak. She'd probably heard the gossip, too, but it couldn't be pleasant to be reminded of it.

"Let's go," I said to Darlene. "I'll walk you home. I want to talk about the chemistry class I signed up for."

"What do I know about that?" Darlene said, but she stood up when I glared at her. "Okay, okay."

As soon as we got outside, I turned to her. "Why'd you tell Mary Beth all that stuff people were saying? How would you feel if you heard the same crap about you?"

"Mary Beth isn't me." It was too dark to see her expression, but I could tell from her voice she thought I was way off. "She's like so cool. She could never care what other people think."

We were walking along, but I grabbed her arm. "She's my sister. Don't you think I know her a lot better than you do?"

She jerked loose. "Are you jealous, Leeann?"

"Of course not. That's insane."

"No, it isn't. Mary Beth and I are really tight right now and you're like on your own planet." She sucked in her breath. "You're not even interested in boys anymore."

I laughed. "Well, hey, maybe I'll be a lesbian. You look pretty good."

"Ha, ha," she said. It was an old joke with us, but now her voice was horrified, as if Up-Chuck was listening.

We walked in silence for a minute. I heard a dog barking across the street. Finally she said, "Mary Beth is worried about you, you know that, right?"

"No way." I tried to make my voice sound dismissive; I didn't want Darlene to know how surprised I was. "You must have misunderstood."

"She told me that since what happened with Kyle, you haven't been happy." Darlene paused. "She even asked me last week if I could set you up with one of Chuck's friends. She thought maybe a date would cheer you up."

Darlene started talking about Chuck's friends, how nice they were, and cute, too. I wasn't paying attention, though. Where did Mary Beth come off talking to Darlene about me? And how could she possibly worry about my dates when she herself hadn't had a date in over a year?

To cut Darlene off, I hissed, "If I need a guy, I can get one, okay? I don't need you to do it for me."

"I was just trying to be nice, Norris. God, you're in a lousy mood."

"I'm going back home now."

"I thought you wanted to talk about your schedule."

"Well, I don't," I said, and turned around and started walking the other way.

All the way home, I thought of arguments to justify myself. I'd almost been raped; I was too old to date high school boys now. I'd had a scary car accident, no wonder I didn't want to go out. But mostly, I was trying to help Mary Beth—which suddenly seemed like a stupid waste of time.

It was the beginning of September. For three months, I'd done nothing but hang around the house, helping Mary Beth write down song titles and listening to her explain the meaning of pop songs, corny country western, even some commercial jingles. Songs that were garbage, really, except to the hicks around here who were so desperate they had to rely on a stupid Michael Jackson tune to tell them their own feelings.

I knew this was a snobby way to look at it but I didn't care. For the first time, I was wondering why it meant so much to me anyway. My sister's song reading—why had I always taken it so seriously? I hated palm readers, psychics, fortune-tellers; I even hated social workers and school counselors, for the most part. All of them claimed to know exactly what other people should do and most of them seemed too stupid to figure out their own lives. But Mary Beth was different, that's what I always told myself. Hers was a real, true gift.

I walked up to the front porch and slumped down on Agnes's wood rocker. The night was so quiet, I could hear the next-door neighbors arguing. Their voices were sharp and angry, but I couldn't make out the words.

"The McNallys aren't doing so well," Mary Beth whispered one morning, after we saw Mrs. McNally standing in the yard screaming at Mr. McNally as he got in his truck to go to work. My sister shook her head sadly. "I'm sure they have their reasons."

Everybody has their reasons, I thought, as I rocked back and forth, harder and harder, until the floorboards of the porch creaked and groaned under my weight. Nobody is doing so well—except my sister's customers of course. They're always fine, as long as they go along with her, do exactly what she says.

I was still angry with her for talking about my life with Darlene. I know that's why I found myself wishing, as I rocked back and forth listening to the McNallys fight, that just once she would turn out to be wrong. That Up-Chuck would turn out to be a serial killer, as long as he didn't kill Darlene. Or that Irene Danston would end up poor, lonely, and utterly miserable without her husband Jack, who wasn't such a bad guy, as it turned out, but just a little possessive.

My wishing only lasted a minute, if that. Of course it didn't cause what happened to my sister. Actually, if only wishing were that powerful, everything would have worked out fine. True, I would have messed up Mary Beth with my stupid desire to see her be wrong, but I would have fixed her, too, with all my other wishes: the hundreds of pleas to turn back time, change what happened, make her okay again.

What I didn't know that night sitting on the porch was that my sister was about to fail. I could say there was no warning, and it would be true. She was trying to help someone, the way she always had before. She was desperate to help, that was her only crime. On the other hand, I could say this had been coming for a very long time, and that would be true, too. Since Ben left at least, but probably long before.

chapter
ten

I was listening to the radio when Juanita Alvarez called me to help plan a party for Mary Beth. The song was "Sweet Dreams" by the Eurythmics. I can still hear it perfectly; I even remember what verse they were up to when I turned down the volume to answer the phone, but I have no idea what it means that I remember all this. Maybe it doesn't mean anything at all.

My sister's birthday was coming up, and Juanita wanted to have a party at her house, the last Saturday in October. She said she thought Mary Beth needed something special, but she didn't offer an explanation. I told Juanita I was glad to help, even though I wasn't really in the mood for a party. My role was pretty simple: to find a baby-sitter for Tommy (I got Denise) and go along with Juanita's lie about why we were going to her house.

Juanita had told me she was inviting a huge crowd—lots of my sister's former customers, everyone from the diner—and she wasn't exaggerating. Her living room was so full, it was impossible to move from one end to the other without knocking into someone's hand or elbow, threatening a spill of a snack plate or beer. Every waitress from the diner was there except the ones who had to work. At least twenty of Mary Beth's customers were there, some I hadn't seen in so long it took me a minute to recognize them.

Over by the couch was Heidi Dickinson, who was engaged now, and told Mary Beth she had forgotten all about that guy Don who was causing her so much trouble when she came for a song reading four years ago. Next to her, eating a piece of sausage, was Carmen Lopez, who'd just gotten promoted at the data processing job she credited Mary Beth with giving her the guts to apply for. Standing in the kitchen doorway, talking to Juanita, were Dotty and Louellen Summerton, who'd come to my sister still grieving about their brother Alvin's drowning in the Mississippi River thirty years before. From their songs, Mary Beth helped them realize that what they needed was a memorial, since Alvin's body was never found. They erected a slab on the riverbank and all their friends brought flowers. The next week, they gave Mary Beth a ceramic angel with a golden halo and blue-tipped wings. Dotty was smiling. "We know Alvin's with the angels now and that's just that."

Everywhere I looked it was the same story. Over in the corner, Twyla Kingsly and Peggy Turner, whom I'd seen crying many times at our place, were now laughing and pretending to dance along with the Hank Williams playing on the stereo. Frieda Jones, the woman who thought song lyrics were literal warnings, looked perfectly relaxed even though the song playing was "Your Cheatin' Heart." Amy and Ken Miller, who were single and desperately lonely when they each came to my sister, were sitting by the wall on hard back chairs, cooing to their three-month-old baby boy.

This party was like a celebration of Mary Beth's talent. The perfect birthday gift.

I was glad for my sister, even though I wasn't having much fun myself. I'd only been here a half hour, and I was already tired of talking to women I barely knew. It was also hard to breathe. Juanita smoked, about half the people there smoked, and the air was so thick my eyes wouldn't stop watering. After about an hour, I decided to slip outside. It was already dark, I didn't know anyone else was around when I unfolded a rusting lawn chair and sat down in the front yard. Then I heard voices coming from a truck parked on the street.

"Come on. Dad said you need this."

"It was a mistake. I'm just not up to talking to anybody."

"Please, Mom. Please try."

"I can't . . ."

I strained my eyes and saw Holly Kramer sitting in the passenger seat with her arms folded around her knees. And Maniac Mike was leaning against the door frame.

I'd always known Maniac Mike's last name was Kramer, but I'd never realized he was Holly Kramer's son.

"Yes, you can. Just go in."

"But what if—"

"If it doesn't work out, I'll take you back home. I promise."

"I don't know, Mikey."

Her voice sounded as weak and unsteady as an old lady's. I thought back to when she gave us the violet afghan with the silver star and told my sister that she'd saved her life. It felt like a long time, but it was only two summers ago.

They were both silent for a minute; finally she got out of the truck and he shut the door behind her. As they walked up the driveway, she said, "I'm so sorry. You probably had plans for tonight."

"It's no big deal," he said, touching her elbow.

"You're a sweet boy," she muttered. "I don't deserve you."

They were so close now I could smell Holly's shampoo. I wanted to just sit there, but I figured if they spotted me first, they'd be horribly embarrassed. I cleared my throat, stood up, and said hello.

She walked over and gave me a hug. "Leeann, look at you. You're all grown up."

I smiled. "Mary Beth will be so glad you came."

"Great," she said, but her voice was wavering. I glanced at Mike, standing behind her. He nodded at me before he said, "Come on, Mom. Let's go."

I followed them in. I only had on my sweater and I was getting cold. Plus, I had to find my sister. I had to tell her something was going on with Holly.

As soon as we got inside, I took a good look at Holly and realized it was even worse than I'd thought. The last time I saw her she was thin, but now the bones in her face and arms were sticking out like twisted paper clips. And her beautiful red hair. It wasn't just chopped off, it was uneven and ugly as if she'd taken a scissors to it herself.

I pushed my way through the crowd into the kitchen, where I could hear my sister laughing. The birthday cake was about to be cut. It was seven layers tall, like a wedding cake. Mary Beth was laughing about the poster-size card Juanita had stuck next to it that read, "You're not getting older, you're getting better at lying about your age."

When I finally managed to get next to her, I said I needed to talk to her, but she leaned over and whispered, "I have to do this first, honey. Juanita went to a lot of trouble."

"But Holly Kramer just got here and—"

"She did? Wow." Mary Beth stood up on her tiptoes, peering

into the living room. "Holly," she yelled. "Come here and have some cake!"

When Holly came into the kitchen, Mary Beth put her arm around her. Holly smiled. I watched them until one of the waitresses from the diner came up and started telling me a long, boring story about problems with her car; then I made an excuse to escape.

The music in the living room had gotten louder and the smoke was even worse than before. Also, I was a little nervous, I was afraid I'd run into Mike. I went back to my lawn chair, thinking I could take the cold again. But as soon as I sat down, I heard him coughing. He was sitting in the grass under the big oak tree, not six feet away.

After I said hi, he grunted what sounded like hi back, and then we both sat quietly for several minutes, staring up at the sky, pretending an intense fascination with the stars.

When he finally spoke, his voice startled me. "You heard everything, didn't you?"

I turned and saw him looking through the big front window in Juanita's living room. "No," I said slowly. "I mean, I heard you and your mom talking, but—"

"She's just having some problems. She'll be all right."

"I'm sure she will."

He paused for a moment. "My dad thinks your sister is the only person who can help my mom. That's why he wanted me to bring her here tonight." He crossed his arms and kicked the ground with the heel of his sneaker. "She's been to a doctor already. He said she was depressed again."

I thought back to what Mary Beth had told me about Holly Kramer's chart. What her father George, the hardware store guy, had done to her. But maybe it was unrelated to whatever was wrong with Holly now.

"She probably can," I said. "Mary Beth is really good at helping people."

He stood up and walked in a circle around the tree, tore off a loose branch and slapped it against the ground. "It's something with music, right? What your sister does?"

"She calls it song reading. She figures out how people feel from the songs they have in their minds."

"I've never heard of that."

I shrugged. "It's really pretty cool."

He was standing above me now; I could see his face in the light from the front window. He was in my AP English class this year, but I'd never looked at him very closely before. I realized he looked like Holly. He had the same nice, full mouth, the same odd eyes—more round than oval, with a color almost too pale to call blue—the same little dent in his chin.

"I think I'll go back in now," he said. "Get something to drink." He was almost to the door when he called back. "You want me to bring you something?"

I was so cold my fingers ached. I told him I'd come, too.

The living room had been turned into a dance floor while we were outside. The coffee table was against the wall and the braided rug was rolled up in the corner. A few couples were dancing, but mostly women were dancing in little groups, giggling and talking. I squirmed my way through the crowd into the kitchen, where a handful of people were still eating cake, but Mary Beth and Holly had disappeared.

Juanita was refilling the cooler with beer. I went over and asked her where my sister went.

"She and Holly are back in my bedroom. Just for a while."

I nodded, and turned around to find Mike, in case he was looking for his mom, but he was right there, at my elbow.

For what felt like forever, Mike and I stood in the kitchen, picking at stale crackers and warm cheese. At some point, Juanita offered me a beer and I took it, hoping it would help me get through this awkward situation. Mike seemed so nervous. Every few minutes he would glance down the hall and ask how much longer I thought it would be.

Whatever was wrong was big, I knew that when Mary Beth and Holly finally emerged and Mary Beth went straight over to Juanita to tell her she and Holly were leaving. Then she whispered something to Juanita and I saw Juanita nod and mouth, "Go."

Holly was leaning against the wall. Mike went up to talk to her and I went to Mary Beth.

"What's the deal?" I whispered.

"I can't talk about it now, honey. I have to be with Holly. You can get a ride home with somebody. Just make sure you're home by midnight, like we told Denise."

"Does that mean you won't be?" I asked, but she'd already turned away.

It was only ten o'clock, but Mike said he was taking off and asked if I wanted him to drop me home. I glanced at Juanita, who was whispering something to Peggy and Barb, then turned to him. "I guess there's no point in hanging out here."

When we got in his truck, he asked if I wanted to go to the drive-through at Taco Bell first. I said okay, though I wasn't particularly hungry. He didn't say a word then and neither did I. I was afraid to bring up what had just happened with his mom, but I couldn't think of any other topic since I barely knew him. By the time we pulled into Taco Bell, I was desperate to cut the tension.

"Hey," I said, and laughed a little. "I've always wanted to know something. Is it really true you're a maniac?"

He turned the steering wheel sharply and pulled in at the end of the line. "You believe everything you hear at River Valley?" He spun around in the seat so he was facing me. His voice was low. "All the rumors and gossip?"

"No. I was only—"

"Because it isn't true. It's just stupid kids talking who don't know anything about me or my family."

"Okay. I didn't mean—"

"It's like everybody thinks if you're different, you must be strange. Screwed up!"

"But nobody thinks you're messed up." I was a little annoyed as I thought about the crowd of kids surrounding him at the basketball party, watching and laughing at his "kitchen chemistry," whatever that meant. "They think it's cool."

He laughed a bitter laugh. "Sure they do."

We were at the speaker. He ordered a six-pack of tacos; I told him I didn't want anything but a Coke. After he got the bag of food, he turned left into a parking spot instead of back on the road. He'd already finished off the third taco when he finally spoke again. "You know how that maniac thing got started?"

"No idea." I was drinking my soda and staring out the window, watching kids walk out of Taco Bell, half hoping I'd see somebody who knew me. It wasn't a date, true, but I was sitting with a real live guy.

"You're a sophomore, right?" He didn't wait for my answer. "This was three years ago. You weren't at River Valley." He took a drink of his soda. "My mom was messed up then, too. Not as bad as now, but she acted weird a lot. Sometimes she'd cry in the middle of dinner or at the grocery store or wherever. We never knew why.

"Okay, so one afternoon, Mom came to school to pick me up.

She was supposed to drive me to the dentist. She gets out of the truck to look for me and then she just starts crying. Right in front of all the kids who were waiting for their buses. Talk about embarrassing. So I run over there and say calm down, Mom, please, but she couldn't. I take her hand and get her back to the truck, and then I jump in the truck bed and tell her to drive. And I'm back there doing handstands. She says, 'Mike, you'll be killed,' and I say, 'No, Mom, I'm fine. Just go.'

"As we pull out of the parking lot, all those kids are cheering 'cause I'm bouncing all over the place, almost slipping out of the truck, but grinning and laughing . . . And the next day, people were calling me Maniac Mike." He glanced at me before he unwrapped his fourth taco. "And I laughed at that, too."

I didn't know what to say. I was impressed with his self-knowledge—most boys seemed to have no idea why they did things, certainly no idea why they showed off. I also felt sorry for him, and especially for his mom, but I was put off by the enormous chip on his shoulder. After all, it wasn't as though he was the only kid in the world with problems. For months after Mom's car accident, almost everybody avoided me; I told Mary Beth it was as if whenever they looked at me, all they saw was The One Whose Mother Died. And as far as reputation at school was concerned, obviously I had my problems there, too. Kyle was still spreading rumors about me, maybe because his parents had refused to get his car fixed, or maybe because he was back with Amanda, his cheerleader girlfriend, and she hated my guts for "coming between them" last year. A few weeks ago, I'd even discovered my name written in permanent red marker on the back of the bleachers in the gym, along with the brilliant conclusion: "whore."

When Mike finally finished eating, he asked what I was

thinking about. I told him, "Nothing," but when he said sarcastically, "Go ahead and tell me. I'm used to being misunderstood," I couldn't hold back any longer.

"You're not the center of the universe. Believe it or not, I wasn't thinking about you at all." I crossed one foot over the other knee, and began tearing at the rubber of my tennis shoes. "I have my own things to worry about. My own life."

"Sorry," he said. I thought he meant it, until I realized he was trying not to laugh.

I turned around. "What?"

"I *am* sorry," he repeated, grinning. "It's just that it's hard to buy you having any problems. Little miss popular who only dates big jocks like the star of the basketball team." He laughed. "But I guess it's rougher than I realized, huh? Going out with morons?"

"Take me home," I whispered. "Now."

He glanced at me. "Wait. I'm sorry. It's just that your life seems so perfect and—"

"Right. I have such a perfect life. My mom is dead, my dad is gone, and me and my sister live in a tiny apartment in somebody else's house." I smirked at him, all the while reminding myself this was common knowledge; it was no big deal I'd blurted it out. "But my life is so wonderful."

He didn't say anything, but he put the truck in reverse. I let out a sigh of relief as we finally left the damn Taco Bell parking lot.

On the way to my house, Mike mentioned that he didn't know about my parents and mumbled a vague apology. I asked if we could just drop this topic and he did. It wasn't until he pulled on to my street that he said he wanted me to know why he'd assumed my life was so great.

"I don't care," I said. "Whatever you think about me is your business."

"I told you I'm sorry." He parked against the curb. "It was really stupid. But I thought you had to be happy because in English class, I can't stop staring at you." He glanced at me, and then at his hands. "Because you're so pretty."

I rolled my eyes. "Oh, please."

"No, I mean it." He grew quiet. "I think you're beautiful."

"You do?" I was unable to keep the surprise out of my voice; no one had ever said anything like this before. Kyle had praised some things about me: the individual pieces, you could call them, but it was clear he'd have been just as satisfied if I'd had a bag over my head. And in my family, it was Mary Beth who got all the attention for being attractive. My only claim to fame was "pretty eyes," which was often thrown in as an afterthought by someone who'd just complimented my sister.

He scooted over so we were sitting right next to each other in the truck. I could hear him breathing; I knew he was working up the guts to kiss me. And I was thinking I might let him, until he put his hand on my shoulder and whispered, "I think you're the sexiest girl in school."

"You jerk!" I pushed his hand off and moved until I was up against the passenger door.

"What?"

"Here you are bitching at me about believing rumors!"

"I don't know what you mean."

"Oh right. You don't know. You were at the stinking party!"

"I really don't remember—"

"Okay, but are you telling me you don't take gym? Or is it that you can't read?"

When he didn't even attempt to deny it, my face got so hot I pressed my cheek against the cold passenger window for relief. And the worst part, I could feel tears standing in my eyes.

"Leeann, listen." Mike cleared his throat. "I told you, I don't pay attention to gossip. I think it's ugly and wrong."

"Good for you." I reached for the door handle. I had to get out of this truck, now.

"I mean it. Remember that poem we read last week in English? When the guy said you should look at everything for yourself and decide what you really think. I really believe that."

He was talking about Walt Whitman's *Song of Myself.* It was one of my favorite things we'd read so far this year, although I didn't bother to argue when the Ds claimed it was long, boring, and a waste of time.

I was still holding the door handle, but I took a breath and listened as he recited parts of the poem. He'd memorized some of the really good lines, or at least the ones I thought were really good. When I asked him if it took a lot of work to remember all this, he said no. "It's a skill I have." He sounded shy, but proud. "Words stick with me." He paused for a moment. "You want another example?"

"Sure," I said, and sat back, waiting for more poetry. But instead he recited a little speech I'd given defending a short story we'd read in English class. The story was by Kafka, about a guy who purposely starves himself to death. Most of the class thought it was stupid, but I thought it was about the search for what really feeds you, what really sustains you in life.

It was the first week of class when I'd blurted this out, but Mike still remembered every word. I was blinking with surprise when I turned to look at him.

"I've had a crush on you for a while."

I felt myself blushing but I didn't turn away. And I didn't back away, a moment later, when he leaned over to kiss me.

"I'm glad I took my mom to that party," he said, when I finally said I had to go inside.

"Me, too."

"So do you want to go out next weekend?" he said slowly. "Like a date?"

"I'd like that," I said, and smiled.

"Cool." He was smiling, too. "Everything is cool now," he said, before kissing me good-bye.

As I stood shivering in Agnes's front yard, watching his truck disappear down the street, I found myself wondering what his mom and Mary Beth were doing. It was midnight. Where had they gone, anyway? But I wasn't worried. Mary Beth could fix Holly's problem, just like she had before. Everything was cool now, like Mike said. Everything was just fine.

chapter
eleven

I t wasn't my sister's gift that betrayed her. In the days and weeks
that followed, I kept coming back to this one fact. Song reading did not cause what happened.

She did Holly's chart of course. It was the first thing she tried
when they left Juanita's party. She took Holly to the diner,
begged her to eat and later, paid for the ham and eggs Holly
barely touched, while she jotted down Holly's songs on a napkin.
None of the lines had a C by them because Holly didn't cry at all.

There were only three songs, and all three were by new wave
groups: Culture Club, The Clash, Duran Duran. Music young
people liked, not women in their late thirties like Holly. Mary
Beth thought Holly was probably hearing these songs because
her kids had been listening to them. After thinking about it for
almost an hour, she had to conclude they didn't mean anything
to Holly.

But Holly needed help. She'd come to that party just to get
Mary Beth's help. So my sister decided to take Holly to a bar over

by the river. Get her loosened up enough to talk freely. Find out what was on her mind.

I thought she meant find out what her songs really were, but that wasn't it. After they drank two beers, Mary Beth decided to ask Holly what had happened when she confronted her father, George, about what he'd done to her as a kid. My sister said as soon as she asked this question, it was like Holly's feelings seeped out of her. She cried a noiseless, hopeless cry as she admitted she'd never confronted her father, never even told her husband Danny. "You're the only person in the world who knows. It's like my entire life is a lie."

Holly said she and Danny and her kids still went to her parents' house every Sunday afternoon for dinner. And every time she sat at that table, every time she smiled at her father and ate his food, she felt like another piece of her was being smashed to bits.

Before my sister told Holly what to do she thought hard about the problem for over an hour. Hard and long. And she remembered a radio show she'd heard on the topic of incest, and a magazine article she'd read. They both said the same thing: if you keep the secret, you'll never be healed. So she told Holly she had to do it. Tell her husband. Confront her parents. And then Mary Beth spent the rest of the night sitting in her Ford on the banks of the river, talking to Holly, trying to give her courage. Convincing her she could do it, and moreover, she had to do it. She wouldn't feel better unless she did.

Mary Beth got home at seven-thirty Sunday morning, just in time for Tommy to get up. She'd made him breakfast and sat with him while he watched cartoons. When I woke up at ten, she was drinking coffee and talking on the phone with Holly. Telling her again she could do this. Telling her she had to do it.

After Mary Beth hung up, she proceeded to tell me the whole story. It wasn't until she got to the magazine part that I began to feel uneasy—this was very unlike my sister to rely on a magazine article or a radio show or anything but songs—but I forced myself not to interrupt. When she was finished, she rubbed her eyes and yawned. "Jeez, I'm tired. I keep forgetting yesterday was my birthday. I think I'm getting too old to stay up all night."

Tommy ran into the kitchen. He wanted Mary Beth to be the bad-guy robot in his pretend game. I told her I would do it so she could get some sleep, but she waved her hand. "I'm okay." She smiled before she walked out of the room with Tommy. "I love being the bad guy."

I sat at the kitchen table, drinking my milk, thinking. I'd like to say I realized it was a bad idea for Holly to confront her family, but it wasn't true. Misgivings I had, sure, but they were too vague to put my finger on. And I was busy wondering how this might affect Mike. Would he have to know, and if so, how would he handle it? How would anybody handle discovering their grandpa had done that to their mom?

"By the way, who drove you home last night?" Mary Beth was back in the kitchen about fifteen minutes later. Tommy was busy lining up the robots for the next battle.

"Mike." I forced a shrug. "You know, Holly's son."

"Oh, right," she said, as she took my empty glass and sat it in the sink. "Holly adores her kids, especially Mike." Mary Beth came over and pulled the hair off my neck. Her voice was soft. "She told me last night in the bar that she feels like they're the only thing keeping her alive."

When Tommy came into the kitchen, Mary Beth picked him up and hugged him hard even though he was squirming and telling her to come on, play. "Play, play, play," she finally said, and tickled his sides. "You'd think I was another toy, rather than your mom."

I went to take a shower, did some homework, talked on the phone with Darlene, tried to call Denise, and lay on my bed and listened to my Walkman. All my usual stuff, the only difference was I spent a lot of time thinking about what I would wear tomorrow. I had to look my best when I walked into English class and saw Mike.

It was six-thirty, already pitch-black when Mary Beth asked me if I would bike to the grocery store. She said she was too tired to drive, and I said no problem. It wasn't that cold and all we needed was milk and lunch meat. I was standing in Nancy Lyle's checkout line at the Kroger, wondering if I had room in my backpack for all my impulse purchases, when I overheard Nancy whispering to Raylene Grob, the owner of the dry cleaner over on Second Avenue, who was in line in front of me. They had a lot of time to whisper, since Raylene had five kids and her cart was loaded with enough food to feed an army.

Nancy had been at the party last night, Raylene hadn't. At first, the whispering was about how bad Holly seemed at the party, and I lost interest and thumbed through a magazine, all the while thinking Mike was sure right about gossip in this town. But then I heard the words "suicide attempt" and I froze as my hands started to sweat on the shiny pages of the magazine.

"An overdose," Nancy whispered, as she picked up a package of spaghetti. Her husband Eric was an orderly in the emergency room; he'd called to tell her they were working on Holly right now. "Supposedly, she downed enough pills to knock out the entire town."

"Good Lord," Raylene mumbled.

"Her whole family is in the waiting room. George and Betty. Even the kids."

"Those poor babies."

"Yeah. Eric said the girls can't stop crying. But the boy and his dad are like stone." Nancy weighed a bag of apples and shrugged. "You know how men are."

Raylene shook her head. "Can you imagine how George and Betty must feel? Holly is the only child they really have now. Their son is in Chicago, and their other daughter is somewhere out west. They don't visit much, don't even call but twice a year, from what I've heard."

Nancy sighed. "I don't know what she could have been thinking, to do something like this. What with her family relying on her. I hate to say it, but it seems so selfish."

The whole time I was listening, I kept telling myself to be calm, don't move, don't scream. I wanted to hear it all, and we really needed that milk. But at that point, something in me just snapped and I deserted my basket and ran over to an empty aisle and right out of the store. I had to get home and tell Mary Beth.

When I walked in the door, Tommy was yelling for her from the bathtub and she was on the phone. I had a feeling she already knew. Her chin was resting on her hand like she didn't have the energy to hold her head up, her forehead was wrinkled as though she was trying hard to figure something out, and her eyes were closed like she wanted to hide from whatever she was hearing.

After she hung up, she went in to hand Tommy a new bar of soap. Then she nodded while I rushed through what Nancy said. "Yeah, Juanita just called. She found out from a nurse who stopped in at the restaurant." We were standing in the living room; Mary Beth was motionless but her eyes were darting around. Finally she said, "I have to go there. As soon as she's conscious, I have to be there for her."

I sat down on the couch and watched as Mary Beth put her coat on. "Why'd she do this? Why would anyone?"

"I guess she just couldn't go through with it."

Mary Beth looked back at me. Her eyes were lined with red and it hit me she'd been up for thirty-six hours at this point. "I think I made a big mistake," she said. "I should have offered to be there with her. Hold her hand. Then maybe she could have finally told them."

I nodded agreement. It wasn't until I'd checked Tommy's ears and washed his back, given him a towel and his favorite race car pajamas, and read him four stories, that I realized Mary Beth was assuming Holly hadn't told anyone. But of course, that had to be it. Holly had lost her nerve. And last night, Holly had been so far down, according to Mary Beth, that telling was her only hope. Obviously, Mary Beth had been right again. Holly hadn't told, and now this terrible thing had happened. What if the doctors couldn't revive her?

As soon as Tommy went to sleep, I snapped on the television; I was too on edge to do anything else. When I heard the downstairs door open about a half hour later, I figured it had to be our landlady Agnes—Mary Beth couldn't be back already. But she was, and Juanita was with her. They walked into our apartment; Juanita was standing right next to her, holding her arm. I watched, stunned, as Juanita helped my sister across the living room and placed her in the window chair like she was an invalid.

I thought Holly had to be dead. Only that could explain the look on Mary Beth's face—beyond pain, beyond numbness even, like someone had reached right into her heart and taken away every feeling she'd ever had. I felt my eyes fill with tears for Holly and for Mike and for us, too. There was nothing I could do; it was all too familiar; my mind was going back there again, back to that summer night five years before when my sister and I were sitting right here, watching the evening news with the windows open, and we heard the sound of a car pull up outside and then a car door slam. Mary Beth looked out the front window and said, "It's a cop." Then she laughed. "I wonder what Agnes is afraid of now."

Agnes called the police at least once a month, always for what she claimed were extremely dangerous situations. She'd heard a noise. She'd seen something out back. She'd received an odd phone call. She'd been positive somebody in a black car—the kind criminals drive—followed her home from the drugstore.

Both of us listened as the policeman's slow, heavy footsteps came onto Agnes's front porch. "Poor guy," Mary Beth said. "No wonder he's dreading this."

Of course the real reason Officer Spellman was walking so slowly must have been that he didn't want to tell us our mother had been killed. I don't remember exactly how he said it, but I do remember the way he kept sniffing between sentences, until my sister finally asked him if he'd taken anything for that cold. He told us it was allergies; he said he was particularly sensitive to fresh cut grass. That's when I realized the roaring I heard wasn't in my head at all: it was old Mr. Haverly two doors down, mowing his backyard.

I was back there all right, because I could hear that roaring perfectly. I glanced at my sister and Juanita, but I was too dizzy to focus on them. I leaned back on the couch and then I did this thing I used to do a lot after my mom died, where I would close my eyes and push my fingers against the lids until I could see patterns forming. I would watch the purple and orange and green swirls until my mind went blank; it was the only way I could forget about Mom's accident, the only way I could calm down.

"Are you all right, Leeann?" Juanita's voice interrupted my patterns, brought me back to now. I opened my eyes and looked at Mary Beth. She was still sitting like a zombie.

Before I could ask, Juanita told me Holly wasn't dead. She wasn't conscious yet, but she wasn't dead. She was in a coma, the doctors said maybe she'd come out of it later tonight, maybe even in an hour or so.

I exhaled loudly, feeling the relief all through my body. "Why didn't you guys stay then? Until she woke up?"

Mary Beth showed no signs of having heard the question. Juanita crooked her finger to motion me into the kitchen. As soon as we got there, she put her hands on my shoulders and whispered, "This is very hard for Mary Beth. They told her to leave. To get out."

I felt my stomach turn over. Juanita looked down at the table. "They blame her for what happened. That creep George and Betty. They have the nerve to blame Mary Beth for Holly taking them pills."

"No way!" I couldn't help yelling. "She tried to help Holly! She stayed up all night with her, trying to make her feel better and telling her—"

"I know." Juanita shook her head. "But it's gotten all screwy now. They think Mary Beth gave Holly all kinds of sicko ideas, last night and even before, when she came to her. They think Mary Beth warped Holly's mind. Made her want to kill herself."

I sat down at the kitchen table as it hit me what Juanita was saying. What must have happened. "So before Holly took those pills, she talked to her parents."

Juanita sat down, too. "Yeah," she said, grabbing her long black braid and nervously flipping it back and forth. "I don't know what she said, but whatever it was got them all pissed off at Mary Beth." Juanita paused for a moment. "Damn, it was ugly, Leeann. As soon as we walked into the ICU waiting room, George stood up and stuck out his fat finger at Mary Beth and called her a liar. Then he told her she didn't belong there since it was all her doing. Mary Beth tried to talk to Danny, you know, Holly's husband, but it was impossible 'cause George was just screaming all this shit."

Juanita inhaled. "Your sister didn't flinch; she just stood her ground and kept saying she was here to see Holly. But then Betty came over, bawling, and Mary Beth naturally felt sorry for her. When she reached out to hug her though, that woman slapped her across the face and called her a pervert." Juanita shook her head. "I would have decked her, I swear to God, if she wasn't such an old lady."

"Jesus," I mumbled.

"You damn right Jesus. This is one big-ass mess."

We sat there silently for a moment or so until we heard a noise in the living room. Mary Beth had left her chair; she was standing by the window now, and tapping her foot so loud it occurred to me the noise would wake Tommy.

I went over and tried to put my arm around her, but she shrugged me off. "I'm all right."

"I'm so sorry, Mary Beth."

"What for?" Her voice was airless; she hadn't turned around to look at me.

"For what they did to you. Holly's parents."

Mary Beth laughed harshly. "Of course they feel that way about me, right? It's obvious, isn't it? Why they would?"

"Well, yeah, maybe, but—"

She spun around and stared at me. "Is it obvious to you or not, Leeann? Think about it and tell me the truth."

I pretended I was thinking but I wasn't really; I was too confused. Finally I said, "In a way, I guess. I mean, I don't know what—"

"And so when Holly confronted them this afternoon, they probably screamed at her too, right? Told her it was a lie, and she was sick for even mentioning it." Mary Beth smacked the side of her head, hard. "Think! Isn't that exactly what you'd expect?"

I didn't want to answer; she was being so weird it scared me. I looked at Juanita for help but she shrugged and then nodded like, go ahead, humor her.

I glanced down at the floor. "I guess her dad wouldn't just admit what he did. Especially if the whole family was there, or his wife or whatever. So yeah, he'd act mad. He'd probably go off on her. That's what I'd expect."

My sister burst out laughing, but the laugh was horrible: high-pitched, squeaking—it hit my ears like a scream. Juanita went over and told her to relax; then she went into the kitchen. When she came back, she held up a glass of water to Mary Beth. "It's okay. Drink this, then we can talk about it."

She barked out no, still laughing that horrible laugh, but when Juanita moved the glass closer, Mary Beth pushed it away and it spilled down the front of Juanita's sweater. "Shit," Juanita muttered, but Mary Beth ignored her.

After a while, her laugh lost its air and become a strangled, desperate, choking sound, which scared me even more. I took a step towards her. "I don't get this, Mary Beth. It's not your fault. It's her father's fault, for being so mean."

"Right. He's a mean guy. Very mean. Terrible." Mary Beth slumped down in the window chair. She wasn't laughing anymore, but she was wringing her hands and blinking so hard she looked like she had a tic.

"I need a smoke," Juanita said. She stood up and went into the kitchen. When she returned she was holding an empty soda can and flicking ashes into it.

We were all quiet for a while. Finally, Juanita dropped her cigarette in the can and walked closer to Mary Beth. "You have to forget about George. He's an asshole. Hell, I won't set foot in his store. Not after the time he tried to feel me up when I asked him to find a Philips head screwdriver."

"He is an asshole, isn't he?" Mary Beth whispered, as she looked over and glanced into my eyes. "And anyone who isn't stupid should have expected he'd be horrible to Holly."

Then I tried desperately to backtrack. I said lots of people wouldn't expect it, because who can predict the future, and somebody who's mean can be nice later, people change after all. I babbled on and on about how tough it is to know anything about anyone until I realized Mary Beth wasn't even listening. She'd turned her face to the wall and pulled her knees up; her body was curled in a fetal position.

Juanita knelt down beside her. "Come on, Mary Beth. You can't let this bastard do this to you."

"Don't you see? Leeann sees. She understands what I did."

"Leeann just told you that you didn't do anything. It's George's fault, all of it."

"But I did." Her voice was so soft, it was hard to hear her. "I did a terrible thing. And it is my fault Holly took those pills. It will be my fault if she dies."

Juanita cursed several times before she turned to me. "Tell her that isn't true, Leeann. I don't know where she's coming up with this crap."

I glanced at the violet star in the afghan hanging on the wall and took a breath. "She thinks it's her fault because she told Holly to talk to her family."

Mary Beth shook her head. "No. It's more than that. You know it is."

I was thumbing the scar under my chin at a furious pace. I stood up and walked around the room, looking at Juanita kneeling by my sister, looking at Mary Beth staring at the wall.

And suddenly I found myself thinking about Mike sitting in the hospital right now. Scared to death his mom wouldn't make it, but putting on a stone face, according to Nancy. Because he couldn't let anybody see him cry.

"All that matters now," I said slowly, "is if Holly is okay." I was standing over by the bookcase. "So what if you made a mistake? It's too late to care about that."

"But she didn't," Juanita stammered. "What the hell are you saying?"

Mary Beth sat up straighter and looked at Juanita. "I told Holly to talk to George. I didn't think of how cruel his reaction might be. It's so obvious, but I didn't prepare her. God, I acted like all she had to do was open her mouth and everything would be fine!"

"It ain't obvious," Juanita said, but she didn't sound like she believed her own words.

"Yes, it is," Mary Beth said flatly. "And now Holly could die because of me."

"Cut it out, Mary Beth," Juanita whispered, leaning back and shaking her head.

After a moment, Mary Beth jumped up and paced back and forth. I stood very still, mesmerized by her jerky movements, listening to my breath coming in nervous gasps.

"I can't take another minute of this," my sister finally said, as she walked to her room. "I have to sleep. I have to."

As soon as she closed the door behind her, Juanita said she had to leave or she'd be late for work. She did call the hospital, though, and they said Holly's condition was unchanged.

When Juanita had her jacket on, she stood there for a moment, mumbling stuff about what a jerk George was, but how well liked he was around town. "This could get ugly." She looked at me. "If it does, your sister is going to need you to be there for her. You understand that, right?"

"I understand," I said, but of course I didn't. Not yet.

chapter twelve

The next morning she woke up at five-thirty, got up and showered, put on her uniform, fixed her hair up with the brown hair clip, woke Tommy and made him breakfast, pleaded with him to brush his teeth, begged him to hurry and get dressed, and finally, yelled to me to wake up right before they walked out the door. Same as always, the only difference was I was already awake, listening for these familiar sounds. Comforting myself with how routine it all was.

I didn't find out until I got to school that Holly was still unconscious. I overheard some girls talking about it while I was in the bathroom. One of them was Wendy Spritz, a rich kid, whose dad was a doctor. Of course Mike wasn't in school, but I still felt like defending him from all this gossip. When Wendy whispered to another girl that Mike's mom had to be nuts to do this, I burst out of the bathroom stall and told her she didn't know what she was talking about.

Wendy was a friend of mine, sort of. Mike was right in a way when he said I was popular, because almost everybody was casual friends with me. But deep down, I always knew why: because I rarely caused any trouble, rarely told anybody they were wrong.

Wendy rolled her eyes and asked what my problem was. I said, "I just think it's stupid to assume Holly Kramer was, I mean, is, nuts. You don't know what her life was like."

"What's stupid is what she did." Wendy turned back to the mirror and started combing her long blond hair. "Life is always worth living. You can't just throw it away."

"Always worth living?" I said, as I washed my hands. "What if you were in terrible pain, like had cancer?"

"But she didn't have cancer." Wendy put her hands on her hips. "You have to get your facts straight."

"Maybe her mind was in pain, did you ever think of that?"

"Whatever," she said, and turned to Megan, her best friend, and smirked. "Leeann is getting all deep on us."

"I am not getting all deep." The paper towel bin was empty and I had to wipe my hands dry on my jeans. "I'm just thinking." When they were still smirking, I couldn't resist adding, "Maybe you should try it sometime."

"Well, up yours, grump," Wendy said.

"Same to you," I muttered, as I watched them walk out. Then I stood in the bathroom until the bell rang for class: part of me wishing I'd kept my mouth shut, the other part wishing I'd kept going, tried harder, convinced them.

The rest of the day was no better. Everybody was blabbing about Mike's mom, how weird she had to be to do this. Some people threw in rumors about him, to prove he was just as weird. The only good thing: they didn't seem to know about my sister's part. When the final bell rang, I ran out of school and hopped on my bike, relieved to be away from all this gossip. Mary Beth arrived home on schedule at four-thirty, with Tommy. The evening was ordinary enough: Tommy watched some TV, Mary Beth made dinner, and I had lots of homework. Everything was all right until seven-thirty, when the first call came. Mary Beth was putting away some of Tommy's toys so I answered.

It was Dotty Summerton, and right away, I knew something was wrong. She asked for Mary Beth, but her words were clipped and angry. Within a minute of picking up, Mary Beth went pale and slumped against the wall. Her responses were mostly weak yeses and nos; once she said, "That is not true" more firmly, but then she said, "Fine." As soon as she hung up, I asked her what that was about.

She was still leaning against the wall; her face was unreadable. "Dotty doesn't want me to tell anybody I did her chart."

"Why not?"

"I don't know," Mary Beth said softly. "I only know what she said."

"Which was?"

"She was a God-fearing woman and she didn't want to be associated with something like this."

I frowned. "What does God have to do with it?"

"Don't ask me to explain," Mary Beth said, standing up straighter. "I can't talk about it right now." Then she went into Tommy's room and continued cleaning, but now she was throwing toys in the box. When Tommy told her to be careful, she stormed out of the room and told him to do it himself.

I went in to make sure he was all right.

"Mama's tired," he said. He didn't seem upset, but he wasn't cleaning. He was playing with his Legos, perhaps more intently than usual, but I figured he might as well distract himself.

The next few calls Mary Beth answered, so I didn't catch their names. But each one upset her; that was obvious from the way she acted when she hung up: nervously pacing back and forth in the kitchen, then stopping to stare at nothing for several minutes, then more pacing. By ten o'clock, when Juanita and another friend from the diner, Sherry, came by, she was lying flat on her bed, looking at the ceiling. I'd asked her over and over if she wanted to watch TV or talk; the first few times, she'd mumbled no and finally she'd whispered, "Please, Leeann, just leave me alone."

Sherry and Juanita were both in their waitress uniforms; they were due at work at eleven. But they'd been by the hospital and they had news. Not about Holly, who was still in a coma (the doctors had given up predicting when she would regain consciousness—if ever), but about George and Betty.

The way Sherry talked, Holly's parents had been holding a press conference. Of course they hadn't; we only had one newspaper here, a weekly called the *Tainer Shopping News,* which only covered decidedly unracy things like Cub Scout car washes and library fund drives. But they were "spreading the word," according to Sherry, that Holly's depression and suicide attempt were all my sister's doing. And they were accusing Mary Beth of pretending to be a shrink when all she really was was a waitress.

While Sherry was relating this to me, Juanita was in the bedroom talking to Mary Beth. I had one eye on the bedroom; so far, Mary Beth hadn't moved.

"There were like twenty people there," Sherry said. "You know, who'd come by to see how Holly was. He was standing in the middle of the hall, holding his hand against his chest." Then Sherry put her own hand on her chest and lowered her voice to imitate George. "Mary Norris pretended she could help my daughter and she brought her to this. She calls what she does 'song reading.' She convinces people she knows things about them their families don't. Then she uses these things she sees in her little crystal ball to show they should turn on their own flesh and blood."

Sherry was breathing fast, like she was upset, but also excited. I didn't blame her. She was the youngest waitress at the diner, only a few years older than me, and although she was the bearer of bad news, she was also the bearer of big news.

"He even called it black magic," Sherry continued. "Said maybe the church should investigate this blankedy blankedy song reading." She smirked. "Here he is cursing right in front of her kids and talking about the church in the same sentence."

I was concentrating so hard it hurt, trying to understand what was going on here. It was all happening so fast. Just two days ago, at the party, my sister had been surrounded by grateful customers, people who loved her, people who credited her with saving their lives. Now, the whole town was being told she was a quack, and obviously, some of those same customers were buying it. Dotty Summerton, at least. And probably those other callers, too.

Mary Beth. Mary Beth. I kept saying her name in my mind as I looked into the bedroom, hoping I would see her get up, move around, smile at Juanita, tell her it would be all right. And tell me it would be all right, that was the main thing. Tell me to go on to bed, don't worry.

But no one said go to bed and no one said don't worry. Actually, Sherry was expecting some kind of response from me. She'd stopped talking and was peering into my face, as though I had an answer for all this.

"Holly's dad is horrible," I said.

"Yeah." Sherry leaned closer and whispered, "Did he do

something to her? Is that what this is about? I overheard Betty bragging that George was always a good father, loving to all three of his kids. Incapable of doing anything like what Mary Beth said." Sherry paused. "Is it something awful? Like, you know . . ."

I told her I didn't know. I felt like I still had to keep Holly's business private, even though it didn't seem likely to stay that way. "But whatever it was," I threw in, "Mary Beth didn't make it up. Holly said what happened and my sister just listened."

I sounded confident even though I was wracking my brains to remember how it went. Of course I remembered the Gordon Lightfoot song. I also remembered Mary Beth saying Holly was the "missing piece" of her theory about music and memory, but she never told me what that meant.

"Oh no," I said, when Juanita came out of the bedroom without Mary Beth. "She won't talk to you, either?"

Juanita was frowning. "She ain't up to it, that's what she says."

"But we have to do something." I sounded like I was pleading with them and I was. They both had to work soon; I didn't want to be left here alone with my sister like this.

Juanita exhaled. "There's nothing we can do. Wait it out. And stand behind Mary Beth."

Before they left, Sherry put her hand on my arm. "Tell her we're all thinking about her. Tell her we know George is full of shit."

"Yeah, I will," I said, as I looked into her bedroom. She heard it already, I was sure. And it didn't make any difference; she still didn't move.

But she kept trying. The next day, she went to work. All that week, she went to work. And it wasn't all bad. For every phone call we got like Dotty Summerton's, we got another one from a customer who said they'd heard the gossip and thought it was crap. Mary Beth wouldn't come to the phone anymore, but I relayed all the good messages to her, with some editing. I told her the part about them believing in her, but I left out any criticism of George, knowing it would take her right back to square one: she should have known he was a jerk, and prepared Holly for how hard it would be to confront him.

The problem was, none of these messages seemed to make a bit of difference. She'd listen, but she wouldn't respond, not even with her eyes; it was like she had gone somewhere where none of this mattered. The only thing she wanted to hear was that Holly was all right. She called the hospital every evening, sometimes two or three times, to see if there was any change. I watched her face during these calls; I could tell from how lifeless it was the answer was no.

When she called on Saturday, they told her Holly had been moved to a rehab hospital about ten miles outside of town. We found out the details from Nancy Lyle, whose husband had heard that Holly was moved because there was nothing else they could do for her in the ICU. She was breathing without a ventilator, her body was basically fine. But she was still unconscious, and they feared she'd suffered major brain damage.

Nancy made a special trip to our place to tell us, and to bring us a loaf of her potato bread. She was on Mary Beth's side, not because she didn't like George, but because she thought Holly was a grown woman and responsible for her own decisions. "You didn't hold a gun to her head," she said to my sister. "You didn't hand her them pills. Nobody did."

When it became clear Mary Beth wasn't going to chat, Nancy made some excuse to leave. I was sorry to see her go. I was glad somebody was finally saying what I'd been thinking for a while. Sure, I felt very sorry for Holly, but I also felt mad at her for showing up at my sister's birthday party with all her sadness and problems. Holly was almost ten years older than Mary Beth; she should have known what to do—or not do—with her own family, no matter what my sister said.

It was eleven-thirty in the morning when Nancy left. Tommy was watching the Incredible Hulk cartoon; I was sitting on the couch with him. Mary Beth went into her bedroom. It wasn't until the show was over that I realized she'd gone back to bed.

But still, it couldn't get much worse. That's what I kept telling myself. Sure, it was weird to walk by her door and see her lying there, wide-awake, staring at the ceiling, but motionless, almost like she was in a coma, too. And sure, it was even weirder when she told Tommy I'd have to make his lunch and take him to his friend Peter's house for their afternoon play date. "Leeann's in charge, honey," she whispered. "Just do what she says."

I'd followed him into her room. "How are we going to get to Peter's?"

It was on the other side of Tainer, way too far to walk, even if it wasn't so cold you could see your breath. It was only a few days until November. The tree outside my sister's window was already stark and leafless.

She pointed to her dresser, and the car keys.

"You want me to drive?" My voice showed how surprised I was. I had my learner's permit, but I wasn't supposed to drive without an adult. If I got stopped, I might get arrested.

When she didn't answer, I picked up the keys. I prided myself on my good driving. Obviously the only solution was to avoid getting stopped.

"Is Mama sick?" Tommy said, when we were in the hall. Maybe it was my imagination his little chin was quivering. Maybe he wasn't as worried as I was.

"Yeah," I said. "But she'll be all right."

I went into the kitchen to start hot dogs for lunch. He followed me. "Does her ear hurt?"

He'd just had the operation to put the tubes back in his ears a few weeks ago. I leaned down and gave him a quick hug; then I said that was probably it before distracting him with what toys he wanted to take to Peter's house.

When we got there, Peter's mom Vicki stopped me before I could get out the door. Vicki was a high school friend of Mary Beth's and a former customer; she was also one of the nosiest people I'd ever met. She wanted to know how Mary Beth was "coping." I said fine. She wanted to know if George was upsetting my sister with all his talk. I said no. And then she hinted there was going to be trouble because she'd heard a rumor George had talked to a lawyer.

Tommy had already run off with Peter into Peter's room. I looked at Vicki. "A lawyer? For what?"

Vicki took a step closer. "Who knows? Maybe slander, since Mary Beth accused him of—"

"*She* didn't accuse him. Holly accused him."

"Well, he's saying it's the other way around. And he says it's already hurt his business and his family."

I was furious, but I forced a laugh. "Hey, maybe we'll sue him, too. For saying all this crap about Mary Beth. For ruining her business."

"Good idea," Vicki said, and then she started to tell me about her cousin who knew a good lawyer, but I cut her off before she could give me the name.

When I got in the Ford, I turned the music up and reminded myself all this was just gossip. I had other, real problems, to think about. My sister was lying in bed in the middle of a Saturday afternoon. And she wasn't sick; she wasn't even sad, at least not in any way I could recognize.

But it couldn't last much longer. I told Darlene that when I dropped by her place to explain she couldn't come to dinner tonight. I was planning to pick up Tommy from Peter's at five and take him to Burger King. I wanted to give Mary Beth some time alone.

"She's just freaked out right now," I told Darlene, who seemed almost as stricken about my sister's situation as I was. "She'll get her act together."

"If I was her, I'd blow this whole stupid town." Darlene was painting her toenails. She held up the little brush to make her point. "Why should you guys stay in this dinky shit hole anyway? It's not like you have family forcing you to."

I shrugged. "It isn't that easy. You can't just pick up and move without a job."

Even as I said this, I caught myself wishing for the hundredth time that Mary Beth and Ben had never broken up. Then we'd be in Philadelphia right now, a thousand miles away from the whole mess. Mary Beth would have Ben, who had money and a great job. And more important, I would have Ben to help me fix my sister.

But of course she wouldn't need to be fixed if we'd gone with Ben to Philadelphia. None of this would have happened.

After I picked up Tommy and took him to Burger King, I decided to take the long way home. Give Mary Beth a little more time. We were over on Fifth Street, across from the library, when I saw Mike.

He hadn't been in school all week. His empty chair in English class had been a constant reminder of everything that had gone wrong since last Saturday.

Part of me knew our date was out of the question now, part of me even knew he might be mad at my sister, just like his grandparents. But still, when his truck pulled up to the traffic light right next to our Ford, I was so relieved to see him, I couldn't help it. I smiled a little and waved.

He looked at me but only for a second. Then he turned around and stared straight at the traffic light. Immediately I turned around, too, but I glanced over at him several times, unable to believe he wasn't even going to mouth hi. The instant the light turned green, he was gone. I sat there, unable to move, until the woman behind me started honking her horn.

Tommy was kicking the dashboard.

"Don't," I snapped.

"I wish Mama picked me up. She doesn't get me a cheeseburger."

"That's what you wanted."

"I wanted chicken nuggets."

He repeated that three times; he also said again he wanted his mom with him, not me. Then I couldn't take it anymore. I started crying, but it was dark enough that Tommy didn't notice. I listened to him gripe; then he changed the subject to Peter's cool Hot Wheels, and still, the tears streamed down my face. I told myself this had to be PMS. Why should I care how Mike felt about me? I hardly knew him.

As I followed Tommy up the stairs to our apartment, my plan was to go to my room, put a tape in my Walkman, and lie on the bed. Take it easy. Try not to worry about anything. This time, if Mary Beth wouldn't get up, I'd shake her. Tell her Tommy needed her. Tell her I was going to crack up if I didn't get a break.

It took me several minutes to accept that she wasn't home. Even though she didn't come to the door when Tommy banged on it, even though the apartment was quiet and her bed was empty, I kept wandering around the kitchen, the bathroom, back to the living room, expecting to see her. She was hardly in the mood to go anywhere; plus, I had the car, where would she have been able to go?

For the first few hours, I couldn't obsess on how odd this was, I was too busy dealing with Tommy. He'd burst into angry tears as soon as he realized Mary Beth wasn't there and it took all my energy to cheer him up, getting him playing again, and later, talk him down, get him in his pajamas, keep him in bed with his eyes closed long enough to fall asleep. Of course I kept hoping Mary Beth would walk in the door any minute, explaining that she'd taken a walk or gone to the QuikTrip for a magazine or dropped by to see Mrs. Haverly down the block, who'd been laid up for several weeks since she broke her hip. It was nine-thirty by the time I began making phone calls. Juanita first, then Sherry, then everyone else I could think of. Nobody had seen or heard from my sister. Most of them sounded concerned, which only made it worse.

At midnight, I called Juanita again. She was at work and I hated to bother her, but I had to talk to someone. After I told her Mary Beth was still gone, she whispered, "Shit." Then she put me on hold for what seemed like forever.

"I'm going out looking for her." She was out of breath. "It ain't that busy here. Bobbie said she could handle it."

"But where?" I began, before I realized Juanita had already hung up.

I was dozing on the couch when the phone rang. I looked at my watch: two-fifteen.

After I told Juanita that Mary Beth still wasn't back, she said, "I drove everywhere I could think of, kiddo." Her voice was flat but I could hear the tension behind it. "All the way over to the highway, downtown, everywhere. I had to get back to help Bobbie with the after-bar crowd." She paused and I could hear the cook's bell. "Call me as soon as she gets in."

I told her I would, but by the time Mary Beth opened the door it was four forty-five. I was so tired my eyes were burning and I was way too angry with my sister to think about calling Juanita.

"Where have you been?" I sat up and glared at her. "I've been worried sick!"

She unbuttoned her coat and let it slide off her shoulders to the middle of the floor. "I went to see Holly."

"You walked to that rehab hospital? Ten miles?"

"Yeah." She looked wobbly, uneven, and then I realized why: the heel had come off her left shoe.

"But why?" I stood up and walked over to her. "And why didn't you leave us a note? Why didn't you wait for the damn car?"

"To tell her I'm sorry."

"But she's in a coma! She can't hear you!"

Mary Beth shrugged weakly. "They wouldn't let me see her anyway. They said visiting hours were over."

My sister was being so weird, I wanted to shake her. But she looked like if I even laid one finger on her, she would break into pieces right before my eyes.

"For chrissakes," I stammered, "couldn't you have called to find that out? You didn't have to walk—"

"Yeah I did. I had to go there. I had to, don't you see?"

"No, I don't see!" I heard Tommy stirring and I lowered my voice. "All I know is Tommy was bawling because you weren't here. He's a little kid, he doesn't get all this."

"Poor baby," she said, as she looked down to the hall toward his room. "It's all my fault, I know. But it hurts so bad. I can't take it. I just want to sleep. I have to sleep."

She did look exhausted. The circles under her eyes were as purple as bruises. "Okay," I said, and took a breath. "Go on. We can talk about this later I guess."

She didn't respond; she just stood there, motionless, with her hands clutched together like she was praying. Finally she said, "I thought if I just kept trying and trying, it would be all right. But it isn't all right, is it?"

"I don't know what you mean."

"I wish I could stop this." She was looking out the living room window as though she was seeing something, as though it wasn't just blackness. "I wish I could snap my fingers and everything would be fine." She looked at her hand. "But I'm too tired to snap my fingers. And even if I did, they'd still be my fingers. They'd still be mine and I'd still be me." She exhaled. "And I'm so tired of being me, you know?"

chapter
thirteen

The next day, she didn't get out of bed at all except to go to the bathroom. She ignored Tommy's crying; she ignored my pleas to help me out here, or at least let me fix her something to eat. Monday morning it was worse. She lay looking at the wall, as I yelled that she'd get fired and Tommy and I would starve to death. When she wouldn't even speak, I broke down sobbing that I wanted Mom and she said, "Me too, baby. And I've been calling her and calling her, but she just won't come."

My sister has gone crazy, I thought, as I walked away sniffing, and into Tommy's room to coax him into dressing for kindergarten. Something in her has snapped. What if she doesn't get over this? What will happen to her—and to Tommy and me?

When she didn't go to work on Tuesday either, Juanita freaked. She came over that night and harangued Mary Beth, calling her irresponsible, telling her she was being a wimp, saying she had to pull herself together. After a while, she sighed and said she would try to talk the manager at the diner into giving Mary

Beth a leave of absence, rather than firing her. When my sister didn't reply, Juanita shook her head. "It's all right. You can thank me later when you decide to get off your ass and quit feeling sorry for yourself."

I was standing in the hallway, listening. I was relieved Juanita was there, even though it made me nervous, what she was saying. She seemed so sure Mary Beth had a choice in the matter, but what if she didn't? What if she needed to see someone, like a doctor, even a shrink?

We were in the living room when I mentioned this to Juanita. I put it indirectly; I said I wondered if Mary Beth could use some help.

She took a drag of her cigarette. "You damn right she could. I've been thinking about calling him myself. But you should do it, that would be better."

She said she didn't really know him, had only seen him a couple of times. He seemed very nice, even if he was kind of an egghead. Then I realized she had misunderstood. She thought I was hinting at calling Ben.

"But what can he do? He moved to Philadelphia."

"Hell if I know," Juanita said. "Talk to her. Fly down here and kiss her. Whatever it takes."

"Yeah," I said, as it hit me this was a good idea. Maybe Ben could help. He loved Mary Beth; plus, he was an expert on depression. And Mary Beth certainly seemed depressed, or worse.

As soon as Juanita left, I picked up the phone. It was late: ten-thirty my time, eleven-thirty Philadelphia time, but I felt like I couldn't wait. My desperation had made me optimistic. Of course Ben would know what to do. Ben would solve everything.

The phone rang four times before a woman answered.

"I was trying to reach Ben Mathiessen," I explained, sure I dialed the wrong number. "I'm sorry to bother—"

"If you want to wait, he should be back any minute. He just stepped out to get some juice."

Her voice was young, confident, but a little bit sleepy. Like my call had woken her up. Like she was . . . in his bed.

I felt a blush creep from my eyebrows to my neck, and hung up quickly without saying good-bye. For a while I sat at the kitchen table, trying to convince myself I'd been too hasty—but it didn't work. Why else would a woman answer his phone at eleven-thirty? And why was I surprised? Sure, he'd said he was only working the last time I called, but I knew that couldn't last. It had been so long since Mary Beth dumped him. Even if he didn't end up with that Catherine person, he would end up with somebody eventually.

After I checked on Tommy, I decided I might as well go to bed, too. I turned on the lamp to read myself to sleep, but I couldn't concentrate. My eyes kept wandering over to the poster Ben had given me when he first moved in with Mary Beth. It was done by M.C. Escher. At first it seems like black birds flying against a white sky, but if you look closer, you see those white shapes are really birds, too, flying in the opposite direction.

Ben used the poster as an opportunity to go on and on about his favorite subject: the Complexities of the Brain. He said it's really important that you can't keep both colored birds in your mind at the same time, no matter how hard you try. He said this demonstrates perception is a lot more complicated than we think because what we see can vary even if what we're looking at doesn't change.

It was one of the few times I thought I really got what he was talking about, and I remember feeling proud I even knew someone who could think about such important things. A few weeks later, when the junior high counselor asked what I wanted to be, I didn't hesitate. A scientist, I said. I want to study nature and the brain.

But Ben was gone now. And even if he could help us, I wasn't going to ask. Not if he was involved with a new woman. Sure, my sister was screwed up, but she still had her pride. Forget about him.

Pride had become a big deal to me in the last few days. It allowed me to handle school now that Mike was back and clearly avoiding me, not even glancing at me during English class. It allowed me to go to the store and to Tommy's kindergarten, sure my sister was being gossiped about, even overhearing bits and pieces sometimes. It allowed me to answer the phone, not knowing if it would be a friendly call or another obnoxious one, maybe even a stranger who would mumble some crap about my sister being antifamily and hang up before I could reply or demand to know their name. It allowed me to let Juanita go home without asking when she was coming again, without begging her to stay awhile longer. After all, it wasn't her family that was having trouble, it was mine. And we had our pride, at least. We had our pride and nothing could take that away.

Our pride wasn't solving the problem though, and the next morning, I decided to skip school. Pride was all well and good, but what my sister needed was a whole lot more. She needed a professional.

After I dropped Tommy off at kindergarten, I went straight into the kitchen and got out the phone book. I started with the crisis section I found in the front of the yellow pages: no question, this was a crisis. First, I tried St. Margaret's Helpline, knowing it probably wasn't right, but figuring whoever answered might be able to tell me who I should be calling. It was a woman and she was busy with another call; she asked me my age and when I told her, she said dial the 800 number youth hotline. The girl who answered listened to my whole problem before she said they only dealt with runaway kids. "You need mental health. Is there a listing for that in your phone book?"

After I said no, she asked, "How about suicide prevention?"

"But my sister isn't going to kill herself," I said, as I picked at the skin around my thumbnail. "She's just really tired."

"I still say suicide prevention is the way to go. They will know who to call in your area." She paused. "You can't always tell when someone is so depressed that they'll—"

I told her I would and hung up. But I didn't, I turned on the TV. Around noon, I made grilled cheese sandwiches and took in a plate and set it on the table next to my sister's bed; then I watched a talk show while I ate mine. The topic was "The Appeal of Dangerous Men" and it was distracting for sure, especially when they brought out three so-called dangerous men: all with long hair and tattoos, but all extremely cute in a macho guy way. It was the kind of show Mary Beth would have found hilarious. One of her old boyfriends, Nick, had been a little like this, but she used to say he was dangerous only to the bathroom floor.

I had the volume up louder than necessary. I couldn't help hoping maybe if she heard, she'd get up to watch.

At least she ate some of her sandwich. Almost half, I noticed, when I finally turned the TV off and went into her room. But she didn't say a word, not even when I tried Juanita's tactic and griped at her for not thanking me for the sandwich. So I decided I had to do it. Call the suicide prevention number.

I told the guy who answered that I was worried about my sister because she wouldn't get out of bed, wouldn't talk, wouldn't work, wouldn't take care of her son. He said it sounded like she needed some help, then he cleared his throat. "Tell me, who is taking care of her son now? Is he being fed properly? Attending school?"

"Oh sure," I said, as I looked at my watch: two forty-five. I still had more than an hour before I was due to pick up Tommy. "I'm doing everything and it's fine. It's just that my sister—"

"Aren't you in school yourself?"

"Yeah. I mean, I got off early today, but I'm in school. Normally I get home around three."

Then he asked how old I was and I told him before I realized what was going on. He didn't like the idea of a teenager taking care of a little boy and a depressed woman. And he was getting ready to do something about it—I could tell from his serious tone of voice as he asked for my address.

"Of course my father helps out," I said quickly. "He does most of it. He's good with little kids."

"Your father." He exhaled. "Oh. Perhaps I should be speaking to him?"

I babbled that he was at work now, but sure, I'd have him call back later. When I hung up, my hands were trembling so hard I had to put them between my knees. I couldn't believe how close I'd come to ruining my own family. Sure, maybe the hotline guy wouldn't have done anything, but maybe he would have arranged for both Tommy and me to be deposited in some stupid foster home before the day was over. And my sister to be put in a hospital. A psych ward.

I'd prevented a disaster and was filled with relief. It wasn't until I was driving to the after-school program, to pick up Tommy, that I realized I hadn't accomplished a thing. I'd skipped my classes to solve the problem, but my sister was still in bed.

Tommy and I were still on our own. And I was dreading the evening, when I would have to take care of him.

Poor Tommy. In just days, he had become a completely different child. Mary Beth rarely spoke, but a couple of times she muttered something about what a terrible mother she'd been—usually when I was begging her to get up and deal with him. It obviously wasn't true though: he had been such a happy kid before, with her. Now he was miserable, I knew that even as I grumbled to myself about how difficult he was.

He hated the clothes I laid out for him in the morning. "They're stupid. They don't match." He hated the lunch I packed. "The potato chips were the red kind that burn my mouth. The jelly fell out of the bread." He said it was my fault his room was a mess; he even said it was my fault one of his goldfish jumped out of the tank and died on the rug. On Monday, he accused me of being late picking him up at after-school: "Mama never left me standing here all alone." Then when I came early on Tuesday, he accused me of not wanting him to have any fun. "You never let me do the blocks! You never let me do anything!"

This time, as soon as he spotted me walking into the room, he burst into tears, sobbing that I wasn't his mother, he didn't want to go with me. While the after-school teacher held him in her arms and explained that he had to go home, all the other kids were staring in my direction like they were looking for my hat and broomstick. One dark-haired girl dropped the ball she was holding to come over and ask if his mother was dead. I said no, she's just sleeping and the girl crossed her arms. "I'm eight. I know grown-ups say sleeping when they mean dead."

"Well, sometimes they say sleeping when they mean sleeping. And that's what I mean, okay?"

When she shook her head, I started to argue with her before I realized how ridiculous it was to be arguing this point with a little kid. I got Tommy's stuff from his cubbie and finally coaxed him out the door by promising to build the biggest Lego structure ever when we got home. For two hours, I sat on the floor in his messy bedroom, clicking plastic blocks together. Then I cooked a frozen pizza for his dinner. Then I played Star Wars with him for another hour, with the couch as our starship, and paper towel rolls as light sabers. But the whole time, I was thinking about that lie I'd told the hotline guy and how much I wished it was the truth. I wanted Dad here, bad. I felt like I wanted him here more than I'd ever wanted anything in my life.

Even if he was messed up, he couldn't be as bad off as Mary Beth. And maybe he could help her. After all, he was her father, too. He'd been with her through her entire childhood, even built her a jungle gym that was the envy of the neighborhood.

And if he was better off where he was, tough. Our family needed every member to get through this. My sister needed him.

It turned out to be easy to find his address now that Mary Beth was oblivious to everything. Tommy was asleep, I was cleaning up the living room, when I realized it had to be in the cedar box under her bed. The box had been Mom's. It still contained a lot of Mom's jewelry, but it also had a brown envelope on top filled with official papers: stuff from the funeral home and the cemetery and about fifteen forms relating to Mom's life insurance disbursement. Dad had signed some of these and on one, his address was sitting just as pretty as you please. Typed no less, probably by the notary whose seal made the papers official.

I didn't write him until the next night. Those forms had made me start thinking about something even more important: money. For the last few days, while I drove Tommy to school, while I sat in my classes, ignoring my teachers' discussion of biology and calculus, I'd been wracking my brains, wondering how on earth I could get a job that paid enough to pay the rent and feed us and still finish high school. But according to these papers, Mom had been insured for fifty thousand dollars. A small fortune.

I grabbed my sister's purse from the hook by the door and dumped all the contents on the coffee table. There it was: a little blue plastic-covered savings book I'd never laid eyes on. Mary Beth had withdrawn a lot over the last few years, but we still had more than twenty-nine thousand left. If I hadn't been so relieved, I would have been annoyed with her for keeping this account a secret. But instead I repeated the sum to myself, even said it aloud, traced it with my finger. Twenty-nine thousand, six hundred and eighty-five dollars. More money than I'd ever seen, more money than I could imagine having. I could make that last a long time, if need be. Mom always said I was the cheapest kid on the planet, hoarding my allowance, always sure I'd need it later for something. Before I went to bed, I made a frugal but doable monthly plan. I also wrote my first check, to Agnes, after looking through my sister's checkbook and realizing the rent was twelve days overdue.

This time when I tried to reach Dad, I wasn't a fool. I didn't write him a heartfelt letter expressing all my worries and concerns; I didn't write as me at all but as my sister. I told him there had been a problem with some paperwork but I didn't elaborate—I didn't want to confuse him. I said he had to come to Tainer immediately and I suggested the Greyhound Bus, which I'd already called and got the schedule for. I told him when to leave Little Rock: a week from Thursday at eight-fifteen A.M., and I told him I'd pick him up at the station. I forged Mary Beth's name to the letter and the hundred-dollar check I enclosed, so he could buy the ticket. Then I sent it off the next morning, on the way to school, and forgot about it.

By the cold light of day, it seemed impossible. It would never happen. He would have to work, he would ignore the letter. He'd moved again. It was too bad, sure, but then a lot of things were too bad in my family right then. By the next day, I was almost relieved. After all, I didn't know him very well. Why make the situation any more complicated than it already was?

I did tell Juanita what I'd done on Saturday, when she dropped by to give me a break from child care and take Tommy to a movie. She thought it was a good idea. I'd already told her what happened with the suicide prevention guy and she was worried that might be a common reaction if it got around that Tommy and I were pretty much on our own right now.

"Of course you all could stay with me," she said, seeming to brighten at the idea. "But it'd be better if he was here. And it might do a world of good for Mary Beth to see her dad, know what I mean?"

I was sitting across the table from her, watching her munch potato chips. She was trying not to smoke and she was downing them one after another. The stereo was playing one of Mary Beth's Elton John albums—just in case my sister was listening.

"Maybe," I said, as I wished I hadn't mentioned that I'd written Dad. It will never happen, I reminded myself. And now I'll have to feel like a fool twice: Thursday afternoon, standing at the Greyhound station, watching strangers file off the bus, and Thursday night, explaining to Juanita that Dad wasn't one of them.

I listened as she told me how much she missed her father, who'd died ten years ago. "My poppy was a good man. He worked hard all his life for us. Hell, he treated Mom like she was a queen." Juanita laughed harshly. "Mom always said she was lucky to have him. I know what she means now. The Dumb and the Arrested sure taught me."

I paused for a moment; then I asked if Mary Beth had ever mentioned why our dad left. She shook her head. "We never talked about him. She told me a lot about your mom, all good stuff." Juanita wiped her fingertips on her jeans. "Mary Beth thought your mom hung the moon, but I guess you know that, huh?"

"Yes," I said, and stood up. Tommy was anxious to go to the movie; plus, I wasn't in the mood right then to think about Mom.

When I wrote to Dad the first time, I hadn't had that conversation with Ben where I admitted I was afraid of Mom. I hadn't even admitted to myself that I thought she must have kicked out Dad. Writing to him now felt vaguely wrong, like I was choosing sides, even betraying her.

Of course it was ridiculous. Mom was dead, and Dad wasn't going to show up anyway. That letter was probably in the trash already, or on its way back to me, marked undeliverable.

By Thursday afternoon, I was so positive he wasn't coming I almost didn't go to the bus station. Even as I drove there—twenty minutes late because I got stopped by a teacher on my way out the back door of River Valley—I was telling myself that, though it was pointless to do this, at least I'd get home early, be able to snack and listen to music, enjoy a full extra hour of free time before it was time to pick up Tommy.

And then I turned the corner and saw him, standing underneath the big Greyhound sign, holding a black duffel bag, looking back and forth for someone he recognized. I knew him immediately from the photo albums I'd been studying since I sent the letter—just in case. I was so surprised, I honked and waved and would have used the Bus Only lane to get there quicker if a Greyhound guy hadn't waved me in the other direction.

"It's my father," I said. The window wasn't unrolled; the Greyhound guy couldn't hear me. "It's my father," I repeated, as I squeezed the Ford into a tiny parking spot in the second row, and flung open the door so fast it banged the car next to me.

All my thinking it would never happen had left me wide open. If his not coming had been a certainty, then his coming had to be a miracle. And how could a miracle disappoint you? How could a miracle be anything but a hundred percent good?

chapter
fourteen

He didn't look bad. I expected him to look disheveled, maybe even like a homeless person, but he was wearing a navy blue suit, a little worn at the sleeves, a little too large around the shoulders, but nice enough. His shoes were wing tips, a bit scuffed, but otherwise fine. His thick black glasses made him look intelligent, successful even—as long as you didn't notice the duct tape holding together the left side of the frame.

He didn't look bad, but he acted very odd. When I told him who I was, he didn't hug me or say how old I'd gotten to be or say he'd missed me or any of the usual father stuff. He even repeated my name like it was a question, new to him, hard to pronounce. And he kept his eyes focused on his duffel bag. Even when I said how glad I was he was here, he nodded down at the duffel bag, not me.

I led him to the Ford, the smile still frozen on my face. We'd just pulled onto Main Street when he said, as though it explained something, "I was expecting Mary Beth. Her letter didn't mention this."

I nodded idiotically, but I felt like I'd been stepped on. *This?* Meaning me?

The light turned red; I stopped at the crossing on Elm. We watched two older women cross, then another woman holding hands with a toddler in a bright purple coat. Or at least I did. He was still looking at the duffel bag, stuck between his feet now.

The silence continued right through downtown and past the baseball field. I wanted to say something to break it, but my mind had gone blank several blocks earlier, when we passed the strip mall—and Holly's father's hardware store. We'd just gotten another letter from George yesterday, ranting how Mary Beth had NO RIGHT TO DO THIS TO HIM. (He loved using capital letters.) He also threatened a lawsuit, but he got vague when he tried to describe what he would sue my sister for, as though his lawyer had already told him he didn't have a case. He didn't mention Holly's condition; he never did. I threw the letter away like any other junk mail.

We were passing River Valley when I glanced at Dad. "Do you mind if I turn on the radio?"

His only response was to lean down and move the stupid duffel bag so he could stretch his legs. So I turned it on, quietly. The song playing was a good one by Queen, but it didn't distract me. I kept wondering what was going on. Wasn't he even slightly glad to see the daughter he hadn't laid eyes on for almost ten years?

"It's supposed to get a lot colder tonight," I said lightly. The song was over and the station had cut to the news. More about the invasion of Grenada. "It might even snow."

Again, no response, even though this was the easiest topic in the world. Now I was getting irritated. Couldn't he at least try?

It was several blocks later and he still hadn't said anything when I finally blurted, "Do you even know who I am?"

My voice sounded sharper than I intended. I thought about apologizing, but before I could he answered my question—in a roundabout way. He said he'd been thinking about another day it snowed, a long time ago, when he and I had lunch with my mother at her office.

"I doubt you remember that day." His voice was soft, maybe a little embarrassed. He still wasn't looking at me. "You were so little."

"I remember," I said, and it was true, although I hadn't remembered until just this minute. But it didn't feel like a sudden revelation, that was the strange part.

I was in kindergarten, school was canceled. Dad had already dug out our old Chevy that morning, so we were ready to go. I was always happy to eat at the insurance company cafeteria. It was on the ground floor of the building, in a room with floor-to-ceiling windows across the whole back wall. And I loved having my own tray and sliding it slowly across the metal rails while I looked through the glass partition and examined all the different foods steaming in big metal tubs.

Mom didn't know we were coming on that snow day. We planned to get there early and get our food first; then when she came through the doors to sit down at twelve-thirty, we would surprise her. When Mom came through the doors with her tray, Mr. Stanley, her boss, was right next to her. They were smiling already. When she saw me waving at her from the corner of the room, they came over and sat down: Mr. Stanley next to me and Mom across from me, next to Dad.

She was in a wonderful mood. She gave me a quick hug and said she couldn't imagine a nicer surprise. Mr. Stanley told me he liked my blue dress, and told my mom I was turning out to be as cute as any child model. I knew that wasn't true, but I beamed at him as I twirled my spaghetti around and around on my fork before I took a bite, so I wouldn't get a single spot on my dress. And I was still smiling when Mr. Stanley asked me how Lilyboo was doing.

Lilyboo was my favorite stuffed bear. She was a Christmas present, and I had named her Lilyboo because she was white, and because she was afraid of ghosts and had to sleep with me. But her name was a secret. I'd only told Mom, Dad, and Mary Beth, and I'd made them promise not to tell anyone outside of the family.

The worst part was she didn't even notice how embarrassed I was. When I didn't answer, she told Mr. Stanley my teddy bear was fine and changed the topic. And she called Mr. Stanley "Will." It was all Will this and Will that for the rest of the lunch. Dad didn't say more than a few words, neither did I.

"I remember that day," I repeated, but my voice was so soft, Dad probably didn't hear me. We were almost home; the sky was getting darker. I had just pulled up to the stop sign on our block when I took a hard look at him. He seemed so shrunken and tired. His skin was pale with broken blood vessels on his cheeks and nose. His hair was gray and coarse and cut so short his ears stuck out. One of his lobes had a scab like an old shaving cut.

But he wasn't as innocent as he looked, obviously. And he wasn't going to get away with it.

"My mother was a good person," I said. I'd just pulled into Agnes's driveway, and I was staring at him, burning the truth into the side of his head—and into my own mind.

He wasn't paying attention. He was looking up at our apartment, at the window of Mary Beth's bedroom that used to be his and Mom's. "It's just as I remembered." His tone was low, shy. And were his eyes wet? "I never thought I'd see this again."

Part of me was touched but most of me wanted to shake him. For me, he couldn't manage a sustained glance, much less a tear. Why all this emotion for the stupid house?

When we got inside, I made a point of giving him a tour of the place like any other stranger. Mary Beth's door was closed, but I took him around the rest of the apartment, knowing he would see so many things he'd never seen before. The overstuffed white chair we got with Mom's bonus when I was nine. The ferns along the kitchen window I'd kept alive since grade school. The transformation of my bed from little girl pink to the clean navy plaid I'd preferred since I was twelve. The oak bookcase my sister and I found at a garage sale when I started high school. And most obviously: the toys and clothes and pictures everywhere of the grandson he'd never met and knew next to nothing about.

He did know Tommy's name. He said Mary Beth told him in one of her letters. I wondered how many letters there'd been but I didn't ask. My plan to make him see the life we'd lived without him seemed to have worked all too well. We were back in the living room; I'd offered him a seat, but he hadn't moved from where he was standing by the bookcase, still holding his duffel bag, like he was going to take off again any minute.

A decent hostess would have asked if he wanted coffee or a soda, offered him some food. But I couldn't care about playing hostess, I was too unnerved. So I plunged ahead. I pointed to Mary Beth's closed door and told him she was sick and needed help. I told him that was why he was here.

He seemed confused; he mentioned signing some papers, but I admitted that wasn't really true. And then he asked, his voice so low I could barely hear it, "She doesn't know I was coming?"

"No. But I'm sure she wants to see you."

He blinked like he was trying to adjust to this idea, but he didn't object when I told him we should go see her now. He carefully put the duffel bag down by the coffee table and followed me into her bedroom. I could hear him breathing nervously, but he kept walking, even when I stopped by her dresser. She was lying on her side, but not asleep. She was staring at the wall.

He was right next to her bed when he said her name. His voice was still shy, but there was a deeper tone, too. A rich, musical sound, hinting at a deep emotion (love?) that would have hurt my feelings if I wasn't so relieved. And the look he gave her—no doubt about it, he cared. His lips were rolled together, but his eyes were big with compassion behind those black frames. His eyes were the deepest blue and exactly like my sister's. I thought of Juanita saying it would do Mary Beth a world of good to see her father, and I was suddenly sure it was true. I'd done the right thing. It was all going to work out now.

And then she turned over and looked up at his face for a full half minute before she turned back on her side and curled into a ball.

At least she recognized him. I was sure of that, although it wasn't much comfort. He was already stepping back, adjusting his glasses.

"Come on, Mary Beth." My voice was a whine. "Don't you want to talk to Dad?"

When she didn't reply, I turned to him. "Maybe you should ask her how she feels." Lame of course, but he did it. And she said nothing.

My sister's room smelled vaguely bad, like sour milk. I'd pulled back her curtains this morning, as I did every morning, but it was too gray outside to change the mood. Dad was still messing with his glasses, shrinking into his too big navy suit. Mary Beth lay as immobile as stone.

It occurred to me again that I should wait. He'd been on a bus all morning and I hadn't even offered him the bathroom. But Tommy had to be picked up soon, and I wasn't ready to give up the hope that Dad could perform some kind of miracle so Mary Beth could save me from another evening of child care. I wanted that world of good so bad I could taste it.

I threw the clothes off the only chair in the room and dragged it over to where Dad was standing. He could sit, but he couldn't leave this room. Not until he talked to Mary Beth.

"She's been a little depressed lately," I said, and gulped. What an understatement. "I was hoping you might . . ."

Finish this sentence please. I'm the kid here, remember?

"I don't think she wants to talk to me," he said, glancing at her back.

"But it's not you. She's like this with everybody."

He cleared his throat but he didn't say anything. I put my elbows on the dresser and propped my head up with my hands. The sudden hopelessness was too heavy. The room was thick with it.

After another awkward minute of silence, my mind was wandering. It was two forty-five. School would be letting out. Darlene and Denise would be getting in somebody's car, heading to McDonald's or Taco Bell, and griping about a stupid teacher, or a hard assignment, or an unfair grade. Mike would be getting in his truck, too, but he wouldn't be thinking of these things. Maybe he'd have to hurry home to take care of his sisters or maybe he'd head over to the rehab, to see his mom. According to the gossip, he went there every day, although this fact hadn't changed his reputation. He was still Maniac Mike, who would surely do something outrageous—and cool—if he ever got over this tragedy.

I barely knew Mike but I missed him. Maybe it was going to be my fate, I thought, to be always wishing for things and people I couldn't have. It seemed so ironic: I had wished for Dad forever, and now he was here and I didn't know what to do with him.

"I tried to visit you once," I said. I wasn't sure why; it had nothing to do with anything. "In Kansas City, after Mom died."

"She was so young," he said. He wasn't looking at me or my sister, he was looking at the picture of Mom on the dresser, at my elbow. She looked good but not particularly young. Her hair was already gray.

"Mary Beth paid for the paint in your apartment." My voice was firm, maybe a little harsh. "She gave money to your landlady, even though we had to buy my coat at a thrift store."

I'd never connected the two events until I heard myself speaking. But it was true. My old coat wore out only a week or so after we got back from Kansas City. And this was before the life insurance. This was before Mary Beth even knew she would get the life insurance, since she hadn't found Dad yet.

"I'm sorry," he said, and his eyes clouded over, but it was his voice that really surprised me. The music was gone, and in its place was the anxious desperation I remembered from that day at the Laundromat, when he was trying to sort the clothes. "I wish you hadn't . . . I didn't mean for you—"

"It's okay," I said quickly.

"No." He wouldn't look up from his hands. "I never wanted you to see that."

He was talking about the walls of his old apartment, but he was also talking about something bigger. Something inside himself. Whatever was wrong with him.

"I didn't mind." I tried to catch his eye. "Really. It wasn't that bad."

"Yes, it was." He was fidgeting furiously with the ear piece of his glasses. His mouth was jerking like it was an enormous effort to get the words out. "I wanted it to be different for you. You would be safe."

I was trying to concentrate on what he was telling me, but I was distracted by Mary Beth. She was breathing quicker, her blanket was moving, breathing, too. And she wasn't looking away anymore; she had rolled over and was staring right at him.

"It doesn't matter," I said, glancing back and forth between the two of them. "You're here now and everything will be okay."

He was shrinking into his chair, twitching the frame of his glasses, making them beat against his face like the wings of a trapped fly—but she was sitting up in bed. And miracle of miracles, her eyes were as clear and focused as though these last few weeks had never happened at all.

I had no idea she was upset. Actually, I was thinking she was going to comfort him. She was a song reader after all.

"Stop!" Her voice startled me, but it was the way she looked that was really a shock. She'd jumped up on her knees, clutching the edge of the blanket. Her face was white as bone. "Please, don't do this!"

"I'm sorry." His jaw was slack, his head was hunched into his shoulders like a puppy about to be whipped. "I shouldn't have—"

"Please," she said, with a spray of spittle she didn't bother to wipe off her chin. "I can't stand it!"

"Maybe you should wait in the living room," I said to him. I was horrified at the way she was talking, but I was also embarrassed for her. Her nightgown had come unbuttoned at the top and her hair was sticking up like a madwoman's.

He nodded weakly, but he lunged out of his chair. On the way out, he stumbled over my sister's shoes and whispered another apology. I heard him pacing in the hall as I shut the door.

"God, Mary Beth." I walked over and stood in front of her, but she was so tall, even kneeling on the bed, she seemed to tower above me. "What's—"

She put her hands over her ears. "I can't listen!"

"Listen to what?" I pulled at her arm. "Come on. Tell me what's going on with you!"

She shook her head so violently it hurt to watch. But I refused to give up. Even when she collapsed on the bed in tears, begging me to leave her alone, I said I wasn't going anywhere until she told me what she was upset about.

No question, I was more than a little freaked. I could count on one hand the number of times I'd seen my sister cry. Even when Mom died, she hadn't cried this hard.

"Are you afraid of him, is that it?" I was sitting next to her, rubbing her back. I gulped hard, thinking of Holly Kramer. "Did he hurt you somehow?"

If she'd answered yes, I would have tried to believe it, even though it didn't fit with the father I remembered, and it certainly didn't fit with the cowering man pacing our hall. He was a stranger and she was my sister. I wanted her back, no matter what it cost.

But she didn't answer yes, she started babbling about Mom. Most of it was too incoherent to make out, but I heard one part perfectly. Mom said Dad ruined her life.

"What do you mean?" My hand was still rubbing her back, but my voice had become hollow, suspicious.

"Mommy was so desperate. She needed me so bad."

"Needed you for what?" I insisted, but my sister's only reply was to go on and on about how desperate Mom was. And she wanted to help Mom. Mom had such a hard life. Mom tried so hard and was the only person who had ever really loved her.

Later, I would have time to think about what this meant, but not now. Now it felt like being kicked in the gut.

"But I love you," I said, more pathetically than I intended. "Don't you know that?"

She stopped talking and I looked at her closely. Her eyes had dark circles underneath, her face was crisscrossed with creases from her pillowcase, but she still looked pretty. I remembered Ben used to say Mary Beth would look pretty in a hurricane.

I took a breath and reached for her hand. The skin was warm and soft. Her fingernails had grown long. "Tommy and I both love you. We need you so much."

I don't know what I expected, but I know I surprised myself by how angry I was when she jerked away and slumped back into her usual fetal position, closing her eyes. Most likely, she wasn't even listening when I stomped across the room so hard her perfume bottles clanked against each other on the dresser. And she made no response when I turned around and yelled, "Mom is dead, and Dad is going to live with us now. If you have a problem with that, tough shit!"

But it made me feel better to say it, whether she heard or not. It felt like a decision, even though I knew there was no real choice in the matter. I had to plead with him to stay and help until Mary Beth got better.

There was nothing for him back in Little Rock, I knew that even before he admitted it was just luck he got my letter because he was about to move again—no doubt because he'd lost another job. And I wasn't surprised to learn that beat-up black duffel bag contained every single thing he owned.

chapter
fifteen

To say things were hard is an understatement. It was a week later, on Thanksgiving, and here was my family. Dad, sitting in the window chair, presumably watching TV with Tommy but really touching his thumbs to his fingertips repeatedly, obsessively, as though he was counting his own breaths. Mary Beth, in bed as usual, but now on the bare mattress, after I'd yanked her sheets from beneath her the day before, to wash them, and she'd refused to get up when I wanted to put them back. And Tommy, poor kid, sprawled out on the floor, pouting and sucking his thumb, watching a rerun of *Trapper John*, because I told him I didn't have time to play; I had to cook dinner.

Such that it was. The turkey was more bones than meat, the stuffing was Stove Top, the mashed potatoes, instant, and the gravy from a can. And my poor frozen pumpkin pie. It was as flat as if it'd been stepped on, which it had, by Tommy, when I was trying to put the groceries away. But still, I was going to have this holiday, even if it killed me. Juanita had just called and invited herself over, and though she wouldn't have cared if we had peanut butter and jelly sandwiches, I cared. Just once, I wanted to do it right. Just once, I wanted to do the normal thing like everybody else in the U.S. of A.

Juanita claimed she was coming over to hang with us, but I knew what she really meant. She was coming over to hang with Dad. It was almost the last thing I'd expected: that Juanita would really enjoy being with my father, even though she admitted he was, as she put it, "a little screwy." She'd been over nearly every day since he arrived, and they'd had these long, involved conversations. She told him things about herself: from her childhood to her marriages to the latest letter she got from the Arrested, who was no longer arrested, as it turned out, but was still keeping his distance from Tainer, and from Juanita, which bothered her even though she knew it was a really dumb way to feel. And Dad listened and sympathized, but also talked himself, not as much, but a hell of a lot more than he ever did with me.

It was Juanita who got out of him that he felt like a burden, being here. And on Thanksgiving, after the meal was over and I was stuck washing the pile of dishes, it was Juanita that he told he would probably leave again, as soon as Mary Beth was better.

Good riddance, I thought, and I didn't even feel all that guilty as I listened to Juanita assure him he'd feel differently if he just gave it time. "Your family needs you," she said, and I nodded when she looked at me for support, though I felt the hardness inside my chest get bigger.

He'd only been here a week, and already, I had moved past the horrible disappointment to an absence of feelings so total it scared me whenever I let myself think about it. What kind of person was I if I didn't care about my own father?

Yes, I had my reasons for being annoyed. He'd taken my bedroom without even putting up a fuss, leaving me on the couch to wake up sore every morning from the busted spring in the middle cushion poking my back. He was incapable of doing housework or the dishes or even driving the car. But he tried so hard. I watched him as he went around the house, trying and failing to do things that were effortless for normal people. Cleaning Tommy's room, for instance. Only Dad would spend more than four hours sorting the Legos by color and size only to leave all the piles on the floor, where one careless kick by Tommy left them messier than before. Dusting, too. Only Dad would insist on moving every knickknack off Mom's shadowbox and then attack the tiny line of dust between the mirrors with Q-tips, but fail to do anything about the thick pile of dust all over the wood.

It was only a few days before I started telling him no, there was nothing I needed him to do. But still he tried. I would find him in the bathroom, washing out Tommy's shirts or underwear in the tub, but without any soap. I would see him in the kitchen, going through the cabinets, looking in the boxes of cereal and the sacks of flour and sugar, counting the cans of chicken noodle soup and baked beans, making sure we weren't about to run out. And if we were low on an item, he wrote it on one of his lists. Even though they seemed to embarrass him—he stuffed them into his pocket whenever he noticed me watching—he couldn't help making them. Whenever I had to go in my room to get clothes for school, I found them all over my dresser; I even found a few crammed between the mattress and box springs of my bed.

I hated going in my own room, now that he was living there.

But still, he tried so hard. Even with me. That was the worst part: knowing he realized how much he was bothering me. He apologized so often that when I closed my eyes at night, sometimes I could still hear his voice saying he was sorry. I'm so sorry, he would say, until I had to bite my lip to keep from yelling, "What the hell for?"

With Juanita though, he was so different. This was what I was thinking as I stood with my hands in the warm sudsy water, washing our plates, listening to them. With her, he was almost normal. With her, he'd never once had to apologize.

They'd moved on to the topic of my sister. Dad was worried she was getting worse, but Juanita said that wasn't true. After all, Mary Beth had taken a shower yesterday, even washed her hair. (Juanita was ignoring the fact that Mary Beth hadn't had much choice in the matter. I'd come home from school and dragged her off the bed, pushed her into the bathroom, and basically torn her nightgown off her, all the while barking threats of what would happen if she refused to clean herself up—fungus and bacteria, mainly, but also the loss of her bed to Goodwill.)

But Juanita claimed it was Dad being here that was helping. How could it not help, she insisted, when he so obviously cared?

When I told Juanita what Dad was doing for Mary Beth, I expected her to think it was a little strange and most likely useless. After all, what good could it do to sit with my sister when she gave no signs of knowing he was there? But Juanita thought it was the sweetest thing in the world, especially when I admitted he'd done it every day since he arrived, for hours.

I would come home from school and find him in the same chair I'd pulled next to her bed, looking at my sister's back, and scribbling in that notepad of his. At first, I thought he was sketching her, or at least writing something relevant to her, but now I knew it was probably just another one of his lists. I couldn't sit next to him and find out. I had homework and housework and Tommy to handle. I had bills to pay and muddy shoes to clean and lunches to pack—all the real stuff of life.

"You want more coffee?" I asked them. I wanted to empty the pot to wash it.

"No thanks, kiddo," Juanita said. "I'm jumpy enough already." She smiled at Dad. "How about you, Henry?"

He said yes, throwing in that it was good coffee. Then Juanita said I always make good coffee. As I poured him a cup, I imagined my obituary. Not loving daughter or loving sister or loving anything, just Made Good Coffee. No flowers please, but donations in her name to Maxwell House would be appreciated.

Juanita was in the middle of a long story about her basement flooding when I finished with the dishes. Dad was nodding along, tearing up his napkin in what might seem like a normal, absentminded way, if you didn't notice all the strips were exactly the same width and the same length. I was walking out of the kitchen to check on Tommy when Juanita leaned across the table and picked up the strips of the napkin, holding her palm out for the piece he still had in his hand. He gave it to her, and then, without even pausing in her story, she walked to the trash and threw it all away. Soon enough he would find something else to mess with, and eventually, Juanita would take that from him, too. She always did, but never with any fuss. Occasionally, she kidded him about his "tics" and once or twice, I heard her ask if he was even listening, but there was no accusation in her voice. I felt even more like the scum of the earth.

I was dying to get away for a while. Tommy was busy with his train. His room was so messy, there was nowhere to sit. The living room was too close to Dad and Juanita. My room was Dad's room, and out of the question. So I went down the hallway and opened her door. At least it would be quiet in there. I could think about the paper I had to write for history or call one of the Ds on her phone. Or more likely, I could do what I usually did: sit on the side of her bed and think about what was happening to me.

Dad wasn't the only one who was spending time in Mary Beth's room these days. But at least I knew it was for me, not her. At least I wasn't pretending I was helping, when all I was really doing was causing more work.

I was being unfair and I knew it. I was always unfair and believe me, I had mountains of regret. That night, for instance, I regretted everything from the dirty look I gave him when he woke me up in the morning—accidentally, when he knocked into the side of the couch on his way to the kitchen—to the sigh I let out right after dinner, when Juanita was in the bathroom and I saw him staring at me like he wanted to say something but didn't have the nerve.

Mary Beth looked better than she had in weeks. After her shower yesterday, I'd insisted she get dressed, and the gray pants and green sweater were wrinkled, but still a hell of a lot better than her faded pink nightgown. And she was facing me for a change. She was still lying in bed, staring at the wall, but it was the wall behind me.

It was comforting in a way. True, she rarely spoke, but she also didn't start counting her fingers or messing with her glasses or tearing up napkins. Even her breathing seemed calm and soothing, compared to the nervous flutter of his.

I stood up and got the afghan from the floor. I could have put her sheets on while she was in the bathroom, but I was punishing her for refusing to cooperate. Now I felt bad. At least I would cover her.

I didn't intend to lie down next to her. I told myself I was just tired. And I had to lie pretty close to her, because she was in the middle of the bed.

She smelled good, like lemon shampoo and Ivory soap. The afghan was soft and warm, and big enough to cover us both.

"You know what I wish?" I whispered, after a while. It had gotten very dark in my sister's room. The sky was cloudy: no moon, no stars. The only light was the yellow crack under her door. Juanita and Dad had turned on the TV. Tommy was with them. I heard him ask Juanita for a bowl of ice cream.

I knew she probably wasn't listening, but I had to say it. "I wish I'd never called you a liar."

It had nothing to do with what was happening now. It was a thousand years ago. It was so simple and easy compared to what was happening now.

About an hour later, I heard Juanita put Tommy to bed. Then I heard Juanita and my father talking in the living room when they turned off the TV. I heard the chain lock clink after Dad let Juanita out. I heard him moving around the apartment before he settled in my room for the night.

And still, I was lying in the dark next to my sister, listening to her breathe. Convincing myself that though it seemed like the root of all evil, it had nothing to do with what was happening now. It was so simple and easy compared to what was happening now, and it didn't cause all this, no matter how much it felt like the beginning of the end.

And there wasn't any end anyway. That was the hardest part. Days filled with drudgery and loneliness bled into nights tossing and thrashing on the couch which bled into more days and nights exactly the same. Sure, I had school, but school wasn't long enough to make a difference. School was like a comma in the middle of the long sentence that began with the stressful mornings getting Tommy out the door, and continued with the endless afternoons and evenings, taking care of him and the apartment and my father and everything.

I was keeping my grades up, but my teachers thought I looked "troubled." They kept me after class, their voices full of concern when they asked if I had any problems at home. I told them no. And I said the same thing to Darlene and Denise when they asked if I wanted to go anywhere. No, I would say, without any explanation. I said it to casual friends who called, and I said it immediately to the only guy who asked me out, Leon, one of Kyle's best friends.

Afterward, Leon mouthed "cold bitch" whenever I saw him in the halls, but I didn't really care. It was no worse than whore, and it certainly fit me better. I was cold all right. Even Juanita had taken to calling me "tough," sometimes with approval, but other times with a look that said I was taking this toughness too far. It was fine to rip up George's letters and slam the phone down when I got one of those antifamily calls, but it wasn't fine to bark orders at Tommy and my father and even her, occasionally. "You'd make a lousy supervisor," she said, and I shrugged and told her I was never going to work with other people. I would be alone and responsible to no one. I would do my work exactly as I wanted, with no one to get in the way.

My dad was listening during this conversation, but he didn't jump in. He never jumped in or objected to anything I said. I overheard Juanita telling him that he had a right to reprimand me if I was bossing him around, but he disagreed. "She barely knows me," he said. "I haven't been a father to her for years. I can't start now."

You got that right, I thought, but later, I felt angry again. What was he doing here if he wasn't willing or able to act like my father? If he wasn't willing or able to give me anything?

Mary Beth's doctor seemed to be wondering the same thing. His name was Dr. Edgar P. Dunham. He was like a hundred and he wasn't even a shrink, but he was the only doctor in the county who agreed to come to our house.

The new tough me got things done more easily. A doctor we needed and a doctor we would have, even if it took a thousand phone calls.

Dr. Dunham examined my sister, and pronounced her physically fine, but undoubtedly depressed. He thought we should take her to a hospital, but when he found out we didn't have insurance, he didn't push it. Tainer Memorial was too small to have a psychiatric ward anyway. The only choices were expensive private places or the state hospital, which wasn't so great. He agreed to check on my sister next week and the week after, as long as necessary, as long as we paid him forty-five dollars up front, each time. Juanita said it wasn't worth it, but I told him to keep coming. He gave us a prescription for a medicine which he said wouldn't work for weeks but might eventually. He also gave us free samples of protein drinks and vitamins, to keep Mary Beth from losing any more weight.

Of course it didn't hurt that he was so impressed with yours truly. He treated me like a fellow doctor, shaking my hand when he arrived and making notes as I described my sister's situation. Dad he mostly ignored, though he did raise his eyebrows whenever Dad started in on his glasses or his fingers or whatever object unfortunate enough for him to happen upon.

"Doesn't he work?" Dr. Dunham asked once. We were standing in the living room. Dad was trying to wipe a spot off the couch with a wet, disintegrating Kleenex.

I shook my head. Dad had cut out several want ads from the *Tainer Shopping News,* but so far, he'd only managed to tape them to the mirror over my dresser while he considered which one to pursue. Most of them were ridiculous anyway. How could Dad get a job delivering flowers when his driver's license had expired years ago? Or work at the counter of the bookstore when he found answering our phone impossible?

"Can you get that?" I would yell, if I was in the bathroom or up to my elbows in cracker crumbs and chicken. And he would move toward the phone, but then something always happened that kept him from picking up the receiver. Once or twice, I asked him for an explanation, but he was so embarrassed I gave up in a hurry. After a while, I stopped asking him to answer the phone, even if he was sitting right next to it.

Sometimes I thought of him like a ghost: taking up the whole room, making it impossible to think of anything else, yet unable to be touched or reached or even talked to. Other times, I was sure he was the one being haunted, and I felt pity, sure, but also disgust, like you do when someone vomits in public.

I was working hard to get over my guilt. After all, Dr. Dunham had the same reaction to my father I had. So maybe it wasn't such a bad feeling. Maybe it was even the natural response. At least that's what I was trying to convince myself—until the day my dad finally got to me.

It was a few weeks before Christmas, a Sunday. Mary Beth had been in bed for exactly five weeks; Dad had been here for three. I had Tommy's letter to Santa tucked in my purse and I was headed to the mall. Darlene was over to baby-sit—and to find out what was going on with me, but I told her I didn't have time to talk. I'd just given her instructions about Tommy's lunch and put on my coat and gloves when Dad came out of my room and shyly asked if he could go with me.

He'd never done this before, but Juanita had always been here before. Darlene was loud and giggly and a stranger to him. I said okay, but I couldn't help letting out a sigh. I hadn't done any shopping yet and I wanted to get it all over today. I didn't need him shuffling along behind me.

On the way to the mall, neither of us said a word. It was drizzling and the roads were slick; I had to concentrate. When we pulled into the parking lot, he didn't object when I suggested splitting up. "It'll be more efficient," I said, and he nodded when I told him to get the *E. T.* poster Tommy wanted as I stuck a ten-dollar bill in his hand.

I didn't expect him to succeed, but I was going to the toy store. The poster place was on the other end of the strip. By the time he tried and failed and regretted it, I could have a cart full of toys bought. And sure, I had another reason I suggested we shop separately. It was ugly, but the tough me didn't even flinch at the knowledge that I was capable of such a low-down thought. I didn't want anyone to see us together. I didn't want to deal with the stares from clerks or other customers if he started in with his fidgeting.

I did feel a momentary catch when I turned around right before I went into the toy store, and saw him trying to make his way through the crowd. He was moving slowly, but he was standing up very straight, like he was trying to summon up all his courage. From a distance, his blue suit looked as dignified as it had on the first day at the bus station, rather than the mess I knew it was. He only had three outfits, and the suit had been worn every third day since he arrived.

It was maybe two and a half hours later by the time I was done. The toy store had been mobbed and I was stressed out from navigating the cart down the aisles, not to mention the enormous checkout line. Tommy didn't want a Cabbage Patch

Kids doll like all the rest of the kids in America, but he did want a Sit'n Spin and a Snoopy Sno-Cone Machine, and a bunch of rip Cord cars and all the Masters of the Universe action figures. I'd ended up spending eighty-nine dollars, when I only planned to spend sixty. I still had the tree to buy, and replacement lights for the front window, and presents for Dad and Juanita. This whole Christmas business was wrecking my budget.

I wasn't thinking about him at all. It took me a minute to realize the people in front of JC Penney were standing in a circle for a reason, and the reason wasn't a Santa Claus ringing a Salvation Army bell. The looks on their faces were horrified but also curious, like at any freak show.

I hurried over and saw him collapsed on the sidewalk. He'd slipped on the ice, but there was something else, too, something the curious/horrified spectators were trying, and failing, to get out of him. Their questions were innocent enough. "Is something wrong?" "Can we help you?" "Can we call someone?" "Do you need a doctor?" "The police?" But their voices were more loud than comforting, because they were carefully keeping their distance from the Crazy Man.

He was sitting in a slush puddle, his face all cold white panic. His eyes looked both weirdly empty and overwhelmed by something no one else could see. And he was holding his hand against his mouth, as if pushing back a cry.

I shoved my way through the circle, dropped my bags on the ground, and knelt next to him. Whatever embarrassment I had was replaced by a sudden, fierce anger. I hated them all for staring at him. I hated them all, even if I didn't love him.

He didn't appear to be hurt. The crowd had already noticed that. Of course that made them all the more interested—and all the more sure he was crazy.

"You can go now," I said loudly, looking around the circle. There weren't really that many people. Eight or nine adults, a handful of kids. I turned back to Dad and told him we needed to get home. He dropped his hand from his mouth but he didn't speak or move.

"He sure looks strange." The speaker was a big woman with tight brown curls peeking out under an ugly orange hat. I recognized her from somewhere, but I couldn't think where. She knew who I was though, and she also knew Mary Beth. I heard her whispering to the woman next to her and I caught my sister's name—and Holly Kramer's.

"Let's go," I whispered, putting my hand on Dad's shoulder. The ground was soaking through the knees of my pants. He had to be freezing in that puddle with only the thin suit jacket.

When he still didn't move, an older, red-faced man in a parka said he was going to call an ambulance. I thought of what the siren would do to Dad. He hated loud noises. He jumped at the beep of the Phonemate.

"That isn't necessary," I said, tugging at Dad's arm. He looked so folded up and scared. I thought I could pull him to his feet, but he didn't budge. "Can't you try?" I stammered. "Please, Dad. Please try."

As his eyes darted around the circle, it struck me he already was trying. He wanted desperately to move, but he was as frozen with fear as if he were surrounded by a pack of wild animals. He hated crowds anyway. I'd heard him tell Juanita how impressive it was she could work in a restaurant. All those noises, all those people. All those demands.

And asking them to leave didn't work. Sure, some people did, but others only stepped back a few feet, and soon enough, more curious onlookers arrived. If they were gossiping, I couldn't listen. Dad was visibly trembling. And before long, he was moaning, a sound so soft it seemed involuntary: not from him, but from his throat. And the hardest part of all, he was clinging to my hand like a frightened toddler, making it impossible for me to stay separate. Making his pain mine.

It flashed across my mind that this might be all family means, after all. Knowing who belongs to you, and who you belong to.

By the time help finally arrived, my brain had gone numb from all the faces looking at us, and my own voice repeating, "It's okay," when I could do nothing to make it true. It took me a minute to realize someone was pulling Dad's other arm, but when I felt him lift, I used my shoulder and back to push him up on my side. And then we were standing, and the crowd was going away.

Because Mike was telling them to go away. He was holding up my dad and telling everyone else to move along now, like he was a cop instead of a high school kid.

He'd appeared out of nowhere. He didn't have any bags or even a coat. Later, I would find out that he was helping out in his grandfather's hardware store a few doors down. He heard the customers talking about what was going on outside. He saw his grandfather go out to look—and he heard his grandfather say it served our family right.

"I have the truck." Mike was panting a little. Dad was still unsteady on his feet. I was trying, but I wasn't keeping up with my side. "Do you want me to drive you home?"

I nodded, knowing I was abandoning the Ford, but afraid if I said no, Mike would abandon us. All I wanted was to get Dad back to our place. I could walk back to get the Ford if necessary.

I grabbed the toy bags and adjusted my shoulder underneath Dad's arm. The mall parking lot seemed enormous as the three of us hobbled along, getting in the way of cars, trying to negotiate past other shoppers. It would have been easier to leave us on the sidewalk and bring the truck around, but I didn't think of that. I couldn't think; I couldn't do anything but follow Mike.

By the time we got to the truck, a full twenty rows back, the plastic handles from the toy bags had left red streaks in my palm and my other arm was twitching from holding up Dad. Mike opened the passenger door and eased Dad into the seat. Then he stuck out his hand and I gave him mine before realizing he wanted the packages. He was going to put them in the metal storage box in the back of the truck.

I felt my face go bright red, but he didn't let go. It was awkward, but he managed to put the bags in the storage box with one hand and keep his other hand clutched in mine. His palm felt sweaty and warm. He looked bigger than he did at school, and much bigger than he had at Juanita's party. He looked older, too, but that didn't surprise me.

I slid in the middle of the front seat. When he had the truck started and in gear, he reached for my hand again, and held it tight in the space between our legs. After a moment, I took a breath and glanced at Dad.

"He's my father," I told Mike. "He came back home."

"That's good," Mike said. His voice was matter-of-fact, not a trace of sarcasm. I felt so relieved, tears came to my eyes.

Dad must have been relieved, too. Later, he would tell me he was sorry (over and over), but now he leaned back against the seat and let out a deep sigh. We weren't even halfway home when I glanced at him and saw his mouth half open, his eyes just fluttering closed.

Juanita was getting out of her Plymouth when Mike pulled up in front of our house. She offered to help Dad inside, but he didn't seem to need much help. Whatever was wrong with him had passed. He'd woken up with a start, apparently well aware of what had just happened—and thoroughly embarrassed.

We all stood on the sidewalk for an awkward moment. His eyes were looking at the ground as he thanked Mike for helping him. His voice was shy when he added that he appreciated what I'd done, too.

"No problem," I said and smiled, though I was feeling a little shy myself. Mike was moving back to the truck, ready to take me to the mall. He'd heard me tell Juanita I'd left the Ford behind. He'd probably heard me whisper it was a long story after I introduced them, and her eyebrows darted up at the name Kramer.

We were pulling away from the house and I was watching Dad and Juanita go up the porch steps when Mike said, "Is he going to be all right?"

"I think so," I said slowly. "He has some problems. I really shouldn't have left him alone."

"I'm glad I was there to help."

"Me, too." I looked out the window as we moved out of our neighborhood and on to Elm. It wasn't drizzling anymore but the sky looked dark and swollen and strangely still, the way it always does when it's about to snow. Finally I said, "I was really surprised to see you."

My voice was as light as I could manage, but still he knew what I was getting at. He admitted he had been keeping his distance, and took a breath. "I hope you understand why."

I gulped hard and stared straight at the dashboard. "Not really."

"I couldn't face you." The truck swerved a little as we turned on an icy patch. Mike waited a moment. "I knew your sister had—"

"It's not true. I don't know what they told you, but my sister tried to help your mom. That's all."

"I know." His voice was so soft I had to strain to hear him. "What I was gonna say is I knew your sister had told you what happened to my mom. Even at the party . . . I thought about it later and realized you already knew why Mom was depressed."

The car next to us was going too fast. When the light turned red, it didn't stop before spinning out, skidding into our lane. Mike had to jam on the brakes but he didn't honk. Neither of us said anything for several minutes. I wanted to hold his hand again, but he was clutching the steering wheel so tight his knuckles looked trapped in his skin.

"You know what's really stupid?" Mike shook his head. "They think I don't know. They think I was outside with my sisters when Mom told them. But I was in the hall. I heard her voice. And I heard that son of a bitch laugh and tell her she was a slut in high school, and she was just misremembering who she slept with."

"God."

"Since that day, I've heard those words a thousand times." He smirked. "That skill of mine."

"How horrible."

"And guess what my dad did? Nothing. He didn't defend her. He stood there and listened to Grandpa call Mom a slut and he didn't say a word." Mike exhaled. "None of them can face it, but I can. I know Mom was telling the truth."

We were already at the mall. He pulled into the parking lot, then drove behind the stores, past a row of big white delivery trucks, to the nest of leafless trees on the hill behind the mall before he stopped.

"Can you believe I still work for that asshole?" He turned to look at me. "I told Dad I was quitting and he begged me not to. He said we need the money for the hospital."

His jaw was clenched but his eyes were full of pain. I found myself thinking back to the night of Juanita's party. How he'd held his mom's elbow as he walked her to the door. How he'd told her it would be all right, and if it wasn't, he would take her back home.

"Oh, Mike," I whispered. "I'm so sorry."

"It doesn't matter," he said, but his voice was cracking. "My family is over now."

He started crying then: a strangled, desperate sound that was so heartbroken I had to swallow hard to keep from breaking down myself. I took off my seat belt and scooted next to him. He wiped his eyes with the back of his hand, but then he put his arms around me and pulled me so close I could feel his chest shaking against mine.

I wanted to say something to comfort him, but I knew all the usual things would only make it worse. It wasn't okay. His mom might not get well soon—or ever. And his family really might be destroyed by this. So might mine.

"It really sucks," I finally said.

"True," he said. After a moment, he leaned back and looked at me. "It really sucks," he repeated, and sniffed hard.

The snow was coming now. He kept his arm around me and we sat quietly for what felt like a long time, watching the fat flakes melt into tiny streams on the warm windshield. Finally, he said he had to go back to work, and then put the truck in gear and pulled to the front of the mall.

I had already turned to go when he put his hand on my shoulder. "Thanks, Leeann," he said, and leaned over and kissed me.

As he disappeared into the crowd heading toward the stores, I realized the snow was falling more quickly than I'd thought. The parking lot had changed. The cars had been streaked with mud, but now they were clean little hills of white.

I took off in the direction where I'd parked the Ford. The

walk was against the wind, but the flakes were soft as feathers as they fell on my cheeks and eyelashes. It was so perfect, I thought maybe it was a sign. His mom would get better. Mary Beth would, too. He'd get to quit working for his grandfather. We'd both get to look back on this time as long and horrible, but not the forever it felt like now.

I was sitting in a line of traffic, waiting to get out of the mall. I hadn't forgotten about my father, but I wasn't really thinking about him when I noticed the little white square stuck down between the Ford's passenger seat and the emergency brake. I managed to unearth it, and discovered a piece of notebook paper, folded repeatedly until it wasn't much bigger than a postage stamp. Before I even unfolded it, I knew it would be one of Dad's lists. Even though he was obsessive about making them, he was always losing them, probably because most of his pockets had holes. (When I was in a mean mood, I would wonder why he didn't put sewing up his raggedy old trousers on one of those lists.)

I was right, it was a list, but it wasn't anything like what I expected. The items were numbered one through ten but they weren't groceries to buy or chores to do (or fail at) or pointless reminders. Each one was a date, written out in longhand: month, day, year. But the month and the day were always the same; the only thing that changed was the year.

When the light turned green, I put down the paper, but still, I had to drive very slowly. It was hard to see even though I had the wipers going full blast.

The date Dad had written over and over was April 23—my birthday. And the years on his list were all the ones he'd missed, the years he'd been away from me.

chapter
sixteen

It was only two days to Christmas and I was fighting off the flu. Everyone who saw me said I looked "peaked"—not to mention the barking cough that turned people's heads in the grocery store. I made a point of laughing it off, insisting it sounded worse than it was. And I told Mike the truth: I would not get sick. It was simply a matter of will.

I had a million things to do. There was the tree to finish decorating, Tommy's presents to wrap, Christmas dinner to worry about, stocking candy, a million things. Even if Dad and I were getting along better—I hadn't told him I'd found that list, but I kept it in my purse, took it out sometimes, fingered it like a lucky charm—he couldn't handle all this. And Juanita was busy herself, working double shifts, feeding all the tired shoppers and lonely holiday drunks.

"But at least I ain't coughing like you," she said.

We were in the kitchen, making sugar cookies. Dad was having his morning coffee in his usual place: on the chair next to

Mary Beth. Tommy was destroying a circle of dough with the rolling pin.

"Check this out," Juanita said. She'd taken a knife and pushed in eyes and a mouth on the Santa's face. "At least you can tell where the head is now."

"It looks silly," Tommy said, and giggled.

Juanita shrugged. "He's supposed to be jolly."

I was covering the countertop with flour for the next batch when Juanita mentioned that she'd run into Holly's mother at the gas station on the way over. Betty was dressed for church. Juanita said Betty was always telling anyone who'd listen that she'd attended church every day since Holly went into a coma.

"But Rose Kennedy, she ain't," Juanita said. She glanced at Tommy and lowered her voice. "She can get down on her knees all she likes and it won't change that she pimped her own daughter to that bastard George."

I was taken aback by how harsh Juanita sounded. "Maybe she didn't know."

"Oh, please. Think about it. Your kid comes and tells you something like that. If you didn't know, you might be surprised and upset and a whole lot of things. You might even be mad at your kid, for bringing it up. But you'd also be just a little bit different to your husband. Even if you thought he was innocent, it would take you a day or two to get rid of all your doubts." Juanita shook her head. "I saw them at the hospital that same night. She was fussing over George and petting him like he was the baby. And she said Holly's name like this, Howleee, like the most disgusting-ass word, all curdled milk on her tongue."

Tommy was eager to start frosting. I told him the cookies were still too hot, but when he whined, Juanita told him to start mixing the food coloring in the frosting. Within seconds, his hands were covered in green, he even had a blotch on the end of his nose.

"Don't touch anything," I told him.

"I wanna show Grandpa." He held his palms out. "I look like a dragon."

I told him to call Grandpa in here, but he'd already escaped. I heard him doing his best dragon roar as he ran down the hall to Mary Beth's room.

I followed him, coaxed him back to the kitchen, helped him wash his hands. I felt flushed, though, and a little dizzy, like maybe I could use a minute to lie down. I was just going to ask Juanita if she could handle the frosting part, when she picked up her purse and said she had to run. It was almost noon and she had to get to work.

I managed to finish the cookies and decided to take a hot shower. I was still shivering when I got out, but I reminded myself I wasn't sick. I couldn't be sick because Tommy's Christmas play was this afternoon at two o'clock.

He was watching TV. I'd already told him twice to get dressed. "Don't you want to play the shepherd?" I pleaded. We'd spent hours the night before making him a cutout staff, covered with tinfoil. He was finally in his room; I was trying to reach the camera in the top cabinet when the doorbell rang.

I was a little nervous. Last night the house had been egged for the fourth time by kids playing pranks. At least I told myself it had to be kids. Juanita swore George was putting somebody up to it.

I broke into a smile when I saw Mike's face framed by the curtains in Agnes's front door. I didn't expect him today, but I was always glad to see him. He rarely had time to come over; if anything, his life was more complicated than mine. Not only did he have school and his job and his college applications to finish, he was also working hard to save his mom—with music.

When I first picked up Mary Beth's notebook a few weeks before, I was hoping to find something in it for her. She used to say music could bring you back to yourself, but all the songs I'd tried on her so far had done nothing: in fact, she usually fell asleep whenever I turned the stereo on. I read pages and pages of her notes about music and memory before it hit me this could be exactly what Mike was looking for. He was desperate for something concrete to do for his mom, and this was so simple. As long as he didn't tell his dad or his grandparents the idea came from my sister, they wouldn't object and neither would the rehab nurses.

One of Mary Beth's big principles was that specific music evoked specific memories. She'd done some reading about music therapy, this was way back, before she met Ben, and I remembered how disappointed she was that most of it was about tones and rhythms. It didn't use the crucial fact, my sister insisted, that the mind stores music better than almost anything.

Actually, it was a scrawl in the margin of one of the last pages of Mary Beth's notebook that seemed most important. "Pick only music from the happiest part of a person's past," she wrote. "Make them want their life back."

At first I was worried because I remembered that Holly only had two songs. But Mary Beth had spent hours and hours forcing her to listen to other music, and jotting down Holly's reaction. The chart was really three charts, covered back and front. Mary Beth had even asked Holly to remember when and where she first heard a song and noted that, too. So, for instance, one of the entries on the chart was "Yellow Rose of Texas," a rodeo at the Ozarks, age nine.

Mike had so many tunes to try: from when his mom was a little kid, when she fell in love, when he and his sisters were babies. And the best part was, he swore it was helping from the very first day.

His mom wasn't really in a coma, or at least not what comas are like in the movies. Her eyes would open and move around, but she didn't seem to be responding to anything. But when he started playing the music, his mom's gaze became steady and he was positive she could hear it. Even her breathing seemed to be in sync with the music. And she didn't have one seizure the entire time he was playing the records. The nurse said it was probably a coincidence, but Mike refused to believe it. A week later, when his mom still hadn't had a seizure, Mike turned a deaf ear to all the speculation about which medicine was doing the trick because he knew exactly what was helping his mom.

I knew it was helping him. Every time I talked to him now, he had news. His mom's score on some coma scale had improved. The doctor hadn't substantiated this, but Mike knew how the scale was done and he was positive they'd see it the next time they examined her. The sounds she was making were more like words, he was sure, even if no one could understand them yet.

The improvements he talked about were all pretty vague and I feared Juanita was right that it was just wishful thinking. She admired Mike for the effort, though. "He's one hell of a kid," she'd say, and then shake her head before announcing: "He's in for a world of heartbreak."

I thought about this as I looked at him while I was unlocking the door. A world of heartbreak? Then something was wrong with the world.

I had to undo three dead bolts and two chain locks. Agnes was even more paranoid now that we were having so many "pranks." I worried constantly that she was going to tell us to move, but so far she'd only grumbled that this trouble wasn't worth the rent we were paying.

"I've been at Hillcrest all night." Mike was out of breath as he stepped into Agnes's hall.

"Is something going on?"

"Yeah." He put his hands on my shoulders and exhaled. "I told my mom about you."

He was looking right at me. His eyes were round and pale and dead-on earnest.

"What do you mean?" My voice sounded afraid, and I was, suddenly. I knew he was just going to say she'd winced more at the pinch part of the coma scale or she'd breathed differently or she'd looked straight at him—but my stomach was doing little flips. It was hope, and I didn't want it. Hope and disappointment were two sides of the same coin, I'd discovered, and I had to avoid the one to avoid the other.

"Yeah." He smiled. "She thinks we'll make a cute couple."

My legs felt like rubber. Mike went with me to the stairs. We sat on the third step, crushed together to fit.

After a moment, I said, "Your mom told you that."

It wasn't a question, but he nodded.

"Her voice is a little weird right now, but the doctor said it's just because she hasn't used it in so long. She's passed all their tests so far. She knows who we are, and who she is. The only thing she doesn't know is how she got there, but the doctor said that's normal."

"Wow."

"I told her it was all your idea." He put his arm around my waist. "You told me to play the records, because you're the smartest girl in the universe."

"It was Mary Beth's idea."

He said yeah, but he obviously wasn't interested in my sister right then. Before I could even ask how this happened, he was kissing me.

"You feel warm," he said, touching my cheek. "Like a fever."

"I'm fine," I said, turning my face to kiss his hand.

After a while I thought to ask if there was any particular song that had helped his mom.

"Yeah. An old Beatles one. 'Penny Lane.' It was on that chart you gave me." He shrugged. "Your sister wrote that Mom was listening to it when I took my first step."

His cheeks looked pink so I didn't smile. I was already thinking of how pleased Mary Beth would be that it was her song reading that brought Holly out of it.

He promised to call me later from the hospital. I went upstairs and told Dad what had happened. He nodded, but he didn't seem to get how important this was. I snapped off the TV and told Tommy he had five minutes to find his shoes and get his coat on. I wandered back into Mary Beth's room, but she was facedown, snoring loudly. She slept most of the day; Dr. Dunham called it "hypersomnia," which was just a fancy way of saying she slept too much.

Right then, I didn't mind. I knew I could use some time to think about the best way to tell my sister. It wasn't enough that Holly was better. I had to make my sister believe Holly didn't blame her for anything.

As we pulled up to Tommy's school, I knew what I'd say. I'd tell my sister that Holly asked for Mary Beth. Then I'd tell my sister that Holly said three words, loudly and clearly enough for all the nurses to hear: "All is forgiven."

It was a line from one of the nineteenth-century novels I'd

read last summer. I loved the way it sounded, but I also knew forgiveness would mean more to my sister than anything. I still remembered the night Mary Beth walked ten miles to the rehab hospital just to tell Holly she was sorry.

"All is forgiven." It gave me chills just thinking about it.

Tommy's play didn't last long, and he was adorable as a shepherd. He only got to say one sentence: "Look at that big light!" but he put his whole heart in it and blinked up at the drooping cardboard as if it really was the star of Bethlehem. His bow at the end was as dignified as the second grader who played Jesus. I clapped and whistled and jumped up with all the other parents.

I was dying to get home, but Tommy begged to stay for the snacks. "It's cupcakes," he said. "Red and green ones!"

I said okay and leaned against the wall of the gym, wishing I could wait in the car. It wasn't just that I felt bad. The longer I stood there, the more questions I would get about Mary Beth.

But all that was about to change. Holly was better. Wouldn't everyone be surprised when they found out? Holly was better and soon enough, my sister would be her old self again. Maybe the two of them could hold a little press conference of their own, exposing George for what he really was. And Mike and I would be there, standing behind them, cheering them on.

This was my fantasy as I stood in the gym of Tommy's school, watching him stuff cupcake in his mouth and giggle with Peter and Jonah and some other kids. I told everyone who asked that my sister was still a little sick, but the doctor had ruled out anything serious. And she was planning a big Christmas dinner. Both ham and turkey this year, since our dad had come home.

I was so deep in my daydream I could already smell that ham baking in brown sugar. Mary Beth and Dad were in the kitchen, and Tommy and I were in the living room, watching boring parades. I was still in my pajamas, the soft ones Mary Beth had bought me. She'd already apologized for giving me such an ordinary present, but I told her I knew she hadn't had much time to shop. And pajamas were perfect anyway, since all I wanted to do was sleep. I was so tired, but Mary Beth said it was nothing to worry about. She'd give me lots of fluids and chicken soup, and I'd be fine by New Years' Eve so I could go out with Mike.

"Leeann?"

I blinked and saw Jonah's mom Elly. We'd arranged a play date for this afternoon; I'd forgotten about that. It was just about three-thirty, Tommy was supposed to go home with her, and I would pick him up at seven. It was fine with me. It gave me lots of time to talk to Mary Beth, and maybe some time to sleep, too.

When I drove up to our house, I was in such a hurry to get in I barely noticed the BMW parked across the street. I was inside, trying to get up the stairs even though my legs were aching and uncooperative, when I realized Dad was on the landing. He was hunched down, with his hands twisted together, pacing back and forth. I called his name and when he looked up I realized something was very wrong. His face had that same panicked expression it'd had at the mall.

"What are you doing out here?" I said. My eyes felt hot and itchy; the walls behind him seemed to glisten and sway. When he didn't answer, I said, "Come on," as gently as I could manage. I took his hand and led him back inside, to the couch. I was about to sit down with him when I heard what sounded like a dresser drawer opening in my sister's room.

"Is she up?" My voice was incredulous. Unless Dad had already told her about Holly, how could she be up and getting dressed? Had Holly herself called?

He shook his head and mumbled, "Him."

"Him?"

I turned to her door when I realized it was true. Someone was in my sister's room. I heard the footsteps myself. Heavy, angry, male.

It flashed through my mind that it was George, Holly's father, here to kill my sister or even all three of us. I started down the hall. Mary Beth was in there. I would protect her or die trying.

I let out a huge sigh of relief when I saw who it really was. Ben. Just Ben. Naturally I was surprised to see him, but it was pretty easy to put together what must have happened. The BMW was Rebecca's. Rebecca must have told him all the rumors about Holly and my sister.

I might have asked him what he was doing here if he'd said hello or even looked at me. And if it hadn't been so obvious what he was doing. He had a grocery bag and he was throwing underwear and pajamas from Mary Beth's drawer into it. He was packing her things.

I was still so relieved it wasn't George that I slumped down on my sister's bed and just watched him. He seemed much more grown-up. His hair was so short that if he ran his hands through it, it wouldn't leave horns sticking out like it used to. He was wearing blue wool pants and a nice, thick gray sweater. No jeans and no sneakers. I'd never seen him without sneakers. I didn't even know he owned leather shoes.

Of course he was angry, and that might have made him seem older. His voice sounded like a teacher's, except teachers never talked this way to me, only to the unruly kids, the bad ones.

"Do you have any idea what's going on here? Dammit, can't you see how she looks?"

I really wasn't sure what he was asking. Of course I could see she'd lost a lot of weight, anyone could see that. She was so weak now; whenever she had to go to the bathroom, she swayed and crawled along the wall like an invalid. I could certainly see her hair looked like a rat's nest, but I also knew how she whimpered whenever I tried to comb out the tangles.

I watched Ben remove a pair of hose from the hook of one of her bras. He threw the bra into the bag, even though she'd always hated that bra. It was the underwire type and it would really poke her now that she was so skinny.

Was he talking about her skin? It did look pretty bad, flaking around her knuckles and nail beds, but I applied that medicated lotion every chance I got. Dr. Dunham hadn't been over since his wife had a stroke, but on the phone he told me the raw sores around my sister's mouth and nose would definitely clear up after a few more days of her antibiotic.

Actually, the stuff that worried me most Ben couldn't see. She hadn't had a period since the night of Holly's party. She'd been constipated for weeks, and the Metamucil I kept putting in her juice wasn't helping. And that mole on her shoulder had a thick hair growing out of the center. I shaved it off every time she took a bath, but it bothered me because I didn't remember it being there before.

Ben used to call that mole her beauty mark.

I tried to swallow back a cough but it didn't work. It exploded in the quiet room. She moaned and rolled over and I was about to tell him he had no right to talk to me like this when he looked up and I noticed his eyes. They were puffy and pink as a wound. It hit me that I didn't know how long he'd been here. He might have been crying for several minutes or even hours before I got home.

No wonder Dad was panicking. I could still hear him roaming around the living room, like he couldn't wait to get back to his usual chair by Mary Beth.

"Why the hell didn't you call me?" Ben's voice was a hiss, but I didn't bother defending myself. Of course he was upset, but it was almost over now.

"Holly is better," I said, and sat up straighter.

"What?"

"She came out of her coma. She's awake."

He blinked as if I'd just told him I finished a paper for school.

"Don't you see? Holly Kramer is the reason Mary Beth is like this. Didn't Rebecca tell you?"

He still didn't respond. He shut the drawer and went into the bathroom. I heard him rumbling around in the medicine cabinet and then heading down the hall. I thought about following him, but I was ready to tell her. It was probably the only way to make him understand anyway.

She woke up easily. Maybe she wouldn't wake up for him, but she did for me. I moved over next to her, said her name firmly and she opened her eyes. She even made a motion to sit up, the way she always did. Expecting me to tell her to eat this or drink that or take this pill. Waiting to see what I wanted now.

Ben would be back any minute, so I had to rush the news. I told her all the good things the doctors said about Holly's condition and I was just about to get to the "All is forgiven," when he came in holding a blanket and her coat.

"You can't possibly think you're going to say a few words and she'll snap out of this?"

It did sound ridiculous the way he put it. But it wasn't ridiculous. Mary Beth herself used to say words had magic powers. Words could change the world, she insisted. We hold these truths to be self-evident. I have a dream. I love you.

I grabbed her cold hand and told her. She was looking right at me, but she couldn't have heard because her face remained expressionless. Even when I repeated "All is forgiven," all she did was yawn.

I was just getting ready to tell her again when he snapped, "This is insane."

I glanced at him and he shook his head. "She's going to a hospital. Christ, she should have been in a hospital weeks ago."

He told me to stand up and move over, so he could get her coat on her. I was still mumbling "All is forgiven," but he was already bending down, pushing her arms into the sleeves, getting ready to take her away from me.

My ears felt like they were under water suddenly. The room was changing colors, becoming bright yellow, nauseating. I could barely see Dad standing in the doorway, crossing and uncrossing his arms. He seemed so far away. My own voice sounded far away, begging Ben to leave her here. Please don't take my sister from me. Please. Please. Please.

"You're a kid, Leeann. You did your best." He stood up and gave me a quick, awkward hug. "Dammit, I shouldn't have yelled at you."

"All is forgiven," I whispered.

"Okay," he said, and exhaled. "Don't cry, honey. Okay. All is forgiven."

chapter
seventeen

It was as if that baseball bat she kept under her bed had protected Tommy and me from nightmares, too. Or maybe it was our apartment, small, more than a little run-down, but the only home either of us had ever known. We didn't cry as the movers hurried back and forth, lugging the dismantled pieces of our happiness. We'd been told it would all be put back together again once we got to Juanita's, and it wasn't untrue. Tommy got the sewing room, after Juanita stuffed her old Singer into a closet and pushed her boxes of patterns back on the shelf to fit his puzzles and board games. I got a section of the basement separated from the washer and dryer by a bedsheet hanging from a steel beam.

The very first night I heard Tommy yelling. There was no need for me to run up the wooden steps; Juanita and Dad were already there, quieting him down, offering water and the comfort of another trip to the bathroom. I heard their tired footsteps and muffled voices again and again: that night, that week, that month. In the mornings, Tommy always said he couldn't remember anything about the dreams except they were scary. I suggested monsters, ghosts, mean kids, but he said no, scarier. I wondered aloud what could be scarier than a monster even though I knew the answer. After all, my dreams didn't have monsters in them, either.

I had one of the worst nightmares only a few weeks after we moved to Juanita's. We were back in Agnes's house in the dream. The house was bigger, four floors instead of two, with a giant attic. The stairs were different: dark wood, each step wide as our kitchen table. I had to broad jump from one to the other while holding the rail tightly so I wouldn't fall through the huge cracks. I was hurrying because I thought I heard my mother yelling.

When I opened the attic door, I saw Mary Beth sitting in the middle of the room, surrounded by people I didn't know. They were staring at something on the floor. It was my old tape recorder, the one I'd thrown away when the battery box rusted, but it was shiny black again, and I heard Mom's voice coming out of it louder and clearer than when the thing was new.

A large woman with orange hair told Mary Beth it was time for her to go with them. I said she had to stay here, but then I looked around at the strangers; they were all murmuring "no" and shaking their heads. The woman grabbed my sister's arm, and all the others started grabbing her, too, pushing her toward the doorway. Mary Beth looked back at me and started crying, and I could hear Mom's voice even louder than before. I woke up with my face smashed into the pillow, gasping for breath.

There was only one window in my makeshift bedroom, a little rectangle near the ceiling, but I'd pushed my dresser against the wall so I could climb up and look out. After one of these nightmares I would sit huddled on the dresser, shivering in the stark cold of the basement, staring at the sky. That winter wasn't particularly cold, but there was a lot of snow, and the night air always seemed so still as the moonlight spilled across the blank white ground.

By day, I told myself it was a relief being here. Juanita had a much bigger place—and apparently boundless energy to glue all the cracks in our family. She took over Mary Beth's schedule at the diner so she could pick up Tommy after school. She cooked us real hot meals every night: good stuff like fajitas and roast beef stew. She hooked Dad up with a cousin of hers who ran a mail order business, and every week a big box of envelopes would arrive for him to sort and address. Dad had beautiful handwriting, and he didn't seem to mind spending the day writing down names of people he didn't know, and streets and cities he'd never see. Even when his right hand cramped up from holding a pen so long, he'd just change to his left.

Juanita said a lot of geniuses are ambidextrous. She also told me Dad had a really high IQ. I didn't ask how she knew that, but later that night, I tried writing with my left hand. The result looked worse than the scribbling of some kid in Tommy's kindergarten.

Dad turned over his weekly check to Juanita. I'd already given her our bankbook. She said she wanted to spend as little as possible of my mom's life insurance, but it would come in handy. Her house was from her first marriage and paid for, but she had four mouths to feed now. Four people to keep in toothpaste and soap and especially vitamins.

Juanita had a thing about vitamins. Every night before we all sat down to watch TV, she would call us into the kitchen and pass around the little plastic bottles. Tommy got the chewables but Dad and I had to swallow an assortment of colorful pills: calcium and zinc, super Cs, iron and magnesium, a bright red multi-B horse choker.

"They'll make up for the stuff we're missing," she would

say. She meant fruits and vegetables and iron-rich liver, of course.

I could taste those things for hours. Even when Juanita gave us cookies to take away the taste, I still had the vague vitamin flavor when the cookie was gone.

Dad took an extra pill that Juanita's doctor had prescribed for him, sight unseen. I didn't know exactly what it was for. One night when Darlene was over, she joked it was something to make him want Juanita. A love potion, or in this case, a time-released love capsule.

My sense of humor was at an all-time low. I gave Darlene my most withering look and hissed that Juanita probably heard that.

I knew it wasn't true. She was upstairs, watching television with Dad and Tommy. Darlene and I were sitting in my basement room, listening to the stereo. I had the stereo and all the records and a good portion of our furniture down there. Darlene thought I was lucky. The room was like my own apartment.

"Come on, Leeann, you know she lusts after your father. I mean, it's pretty damned obvious." Darlene shrugged. "Why not? He's not that much older than she is, and he's so freaking sweet. He's like Linus, you know? He even looks like an old Linus. All he needs is that blanket."

"People don't lust after Linus." I leaned back on my elbows and looked at a spiderweb hanging from the ceiling corner to the lightbulb. "That is so stupid, Darlene."

"Think about the choices here. Charlie Brown is bald. Pigpen stinks. Schroeder's like such an egomaniac. Who wouldn't pick Linus?"

I finally laughed then, but after she left I found myself thinking how weird it was that Darlene thought Dad was sweet. A Linus of all things. Of course she didn't get to know him until after Christmas when we moved in here. And he was so much better here. Whether it was those pills Juanita gave him or Juanita herself, he acted like a regular person most of the time. He didn't talk that much—and not at all to me—but he listened and smiled at the right moments and helped out with everything from the dishes to the snow shoveling. He certainly looked a lot more normal in the jeans and pullovers Juanita bought for him.

It did cross my mind that he was better because Mary Beth was gone. He never mentioned her name, but then nobody brought up the topic of my sister if they could help it. Even Darlene figured out not to ask how long we expected her to be in the hospital. She knew I only knew what Ben told me and that wasn't much. He'd gone back to Philadelphia, to work at his new job. He was flying home on weekends when he could, but so far, my sister had refused to see him. I acted like this was upsetting but the truth was, I thought it served him right.

Sometimes my anger at Ben was so big it literally hurt my throat to swallow it back down. It wasn't just that he'd taken her all the way up to St. Louis, miles away, to a hospital that didn't allow anyone under eighteen to visit. It wasn't that he was going about his business, doing his research, writing papers, even sleeping with that woman who'd answered his phone, I was almost positive—since she still answered often enough that I hesitated to call. (She was just a good friend, he told me, but that only made it worse. How could he sleep with someone who was just a friend? Did I know him half as well as I thought?) All of this was unnerving, but there was something even worse. His father was a psychiatrist. He'd told me his father was a college professor, and he was—a professor of psychiatry. Dr. Theodore Mathiessen. He'd even been on staff at the hospital where my sister was. This was before he became a professor, but big deal.

He still knew everybody there. He was a shrink, no two ways around it.

I felt completely cheated. I told Mike it was as if Ben just looking at our family had changed us into a bunch of nuts. It didn't make a whole lot of sense, but it wasn't nonsense, either. After all, it was Ben who told my sister Dad was mentally ill. Wasn't that the beginning of all this?

I listened to my stereo, loud, each time he called to give us an update. Juanita had hooked me up a phone line downstairs. As soon as she yelled, "It's Ben," I'd twist the volume knob before picking up the receiver.

A lot of the conversation was spent with me asking, "Huh?" and him shouting whatever I'd missed. Once he asked if I was purposely trying to drown him out.

"I know this is hard for you to deal with," he'd say.

"What?" I'd shout, even though I'd heard him.

"I just wish I had better news, honey."

He called me honey whenever he felt like it these days—no doubt because I'd cried in front of him that afternoon he took Mary Beth. I wished I hadn't done that. I wished so badly I didn't feel like crying every time he called.

"Are you doing all right?" he always asked before he hung up. And I always said I was fine, though I had to resist shouting: What will you do if I say no? Cart me away to the hospital, too?

I thought Mike would understand. After all, he knew as well as anyone how things could look one way and be another. And all those shrinks hadn't helped his mom much. When I tried to talk to him about it though, his response was maddeningly reasonable.

"Ben didn't make your sister sick," he said.

"Well, I guess your grandfather didn't make your mom do what she did."

It was meant as a low blow, but he nodded. "He didn't, it's true. Even Mom knows that."

"Yes he did!" I was so irritated I felt out of breath. "He was mean and cruel and so awful to her, she felt like she couldn't live anymore."

Mike was blinking with confusion. "Are you saying Ben was mean to your sister?"

School had just let out and we were in his truck, parked out on River Road. We'd been kissing when I brought up the topic. I already had my bra unsnapped and Mike, who was working very hard to keep his eyes on my face, seemed determined to avoid an argument.

But I was just as determined to have one.

"What if I told you your dad was crazy? Wouldn't you call that mean?"

"I don't know." He sounded distracted. He moved to kiss me again and I pulled back.

"You think my dad is crazy, don't you?"

"No."

"Well, guess what? It's true. My whole family is totally loony tunes."

"You aren't crazy."

"What makes you so sure? If my dad is and my sister is, why not me?"

"Because you're not." He put his hand on my arm. He looked like he was trying not to smile. "You couldn't be crazy even if you wanted to."

I was more relieved than I expected to be, but I said, "Like you know," before grabbing the ends of my bra and snapping it closed.

He lowered his voice, "Why are you doing this?"

"I just think it's more complicated than you seem to get. It's like all the people who think your grandfather is fine and your mom is nuts. They don't see what really happened. They don't have a clue."

He sat up straighter. "Too much sanity may be madness. And maddest of all, to see life as it is and not as it should be."

"Don Quixote," I said, and exhaled. "I remember."

"It's true. My grandfather may have driven my mom crazy, but being crazy is better than being like him. He's evil, and crazy and evil aren't the same at all."

Mike had quit working for his grandfather weeks ago, at his mom's insistence. His family wasn't even speaking to George, and tongues were wagging all over town but I turned a deaf ear. I had my own problems to deal with.

He opened up the glove compartment and pulled out a pack of cigarettes. It was his new way of dealing with stress. He pushed in the lighter and opened the window a crack. The heater was on, but it was freezing outside.

I watched him smoke for a while. When he asked if I knew what was bothering me, I mumbled no and looked away.

It was only four-thirty but the winter sun was low, the trees were throwing shadows on the ground. "Maybe you should take me back," I finally said. "I have a lot of homework."

He put the truck in gear. Neither of us talked on the drive to Juanita's. The radio was on, and I found myself thinking about Mary Beth, wondering if she had a radio in the hospital. I made a mental note to ask Ben. She had to have music. That was one of the things I'd done wrong. I'd turned on the stereo for her, but I'd snapped it off every time she fell asleep. It wasn't just that I thought she couldn't hear it, I was mad at her.

I was always mad at someone. Sometimes I wondered if being

mad could become a permanent condition, a part of my personality.

Mike pulled into Juanita's driveway, but I didn't get out. I was thinking about apologizing when he cleared his throat and said he was really disappointed.

I turned to look at him. He sighed loudly. "All day, I was hoping tonight could be it."

Of course I knew what he was referring to. We'd only discussed it a hundred times. We'd even agreed upon the place: my basement room, because his house was out of the question with his mom's private duty nurse awake all hours. The only motel for miles was a sleazy dump off the highway. The truck wasn't even a possibility. At school, people might label us Maniac and Brainiac—my new name, to rhyme with Mike's, and a lot better than cold bitch or whore, so I wasn't complaining—but we thought of ourselves as Romeo and Juliet. Romeo and Juliet would not have sex in a truck.

Part of me wanted to do it so badly, for him, and also for myself. I loved the way he looked. His body was lean and long. Gangly in a way, but elegant, too. His curly hair in my hands felt soft as clumps of cotton. When he touched me, my whole body tingled and hummed. But every time I thought about saying yes, I flashed to the hideous pain that night with Kyle. I wanted to believe that was Kyle's fault, but what if it wasn't? What if there was even something wrong with me?

"Sorry," I told him, but I took his hand and forced a smile. "I'm sure it will be soon."

"That's what you always say."

"I told you I'm sorry."

"It doesn't make sense." He paused. "Why do you need so much time anyway?"

I blinked. "I don't know what you mean."

He looked out the front window. "I don't want to sound like a jerk, but it does seem screwed up. How could you be with that moron, and you don't want to be with me?"

"You're talking about Kyle?" I shouldn't have been surprised. The whole school had to have heard the gossip. But why hadn't Mike ever mentioned this before?

"You were what, fourteen then? How can you say you're too young?"

The truth was so embarrassing; I almost wished I could just let him keep believing that Kyle and I had done it. At least that was a normal thing, mature even.

"Forget it," he said. "I'll just have to pretend all this makes sense."

"Guess so," I said, and I was out of the truck before he could say good-bye.

After dinner he called but neither of us said much. He did manage to throw in a quote: "Do not squander time, for that's the stuff life is made of." I told him it sounded like it belonged on a pillowcase—or in a Styx song. His voice was a little cold as he informed me it was Benjamin Franklin.

I wanted to tell him what really happened with Kyle. I knew it might be easier on the phone than in person, but I could hear his mom in the background. She was talking to one of his sisters, and I could feel myself getting mad again. Of course I was glad his mom was doing better but I was also intensely jealous that he had his family back while my family had become squatters.

Talk about making no sense. How could it be that Holly was happier than she'd ever been in Mike's whole life, according to him anyway, and my sister was languishing in some psych ward? Where was the fairness in that, when it was Holly's fault that my sister crashed in the first place?

Holly's fault, Ben's fault, I didn't really care, as long as it was somebody's fault. Nobody's fault was like a tornado or a lightning bolt. Nobody's fault was too close to nothing you could do and nothing you can do if it ever happens again.

After the nightly vitamin and television routine, I headed down to the basement to work on a paper for school, but I just couldn't concentrate. I ended up looking through another pile of my sister's records instead. All of Mary Beth's albums were down here, fourteen boxes total, lined against the wall opposite the window. The history of her relationship with music, that's how I thought of them, and I'd always been good at history—until now.

The movers had boxed the records in the same order they were on the shelves. They weren't arranged by artist or type of music, like most people arranged albums. They weren't even arranged by year. They were arranged by topic, like books in a library. Mary Beth used to call it a musical Dewey Decimal system.

Ben used to tease her that this was no system at all, this was chaos. At the time, I didn't have an opinion; I had my Walkman and my tapes and I rarely had to find an album. Now I knew what Ben meant. When Mike mentioned that Neil Young's *Harvest* was one of his favorite records, I decided to listen to it. But first I had to locate it, and of course it wasn't with any other Neil Young or with albums that started with H or even other folksy rock albums. It was sandwiched between the soundtrack for Oliver and a Diana Ross Greatest Hits. And there was a Bob Dylan nearby. And next to that, the Stones's first album.

I spent a long time trying to figure out what topic all these records could possibly have in common. At first I thought the problem was that there was no meaning, but then I realized there was way too much. Most of the records had a song about a parent—was that the topic? Or was it change and the passage of time? Death and loss? Love—no, it couldn't be that, since damn near every album she owned had a love song. It was the same situation with every pile of records I examined. True, I didn't know where one topic began and another one ended, but no matter how big or small the pile, I couldn't see one clear meaning.

That night I had records all over my bed, all over the floor, before I realized this wasn't helping my mood. I wasn't my sister and I never would be. It was her gift to do this: she found the meaning for people just like she did for albums. She could take a customer who had all kinds of problems—poverty and family quarrels and lost love and even illness—and point her finger at the one thing they really cared about, the one thing that, if they found it and dealt with it, would give them the strength to handle all the rest. Sometimes it was as simple as erecting a memorial for a brother dead for decades. Or even bringing home a cat or dog.

I knocked some of the records to the side and sprawled out on the bed as I wondered what my one thing was. I was so tired of the bad dreams, so tired of waking up with my jaw clenched. I loved the idea of a pet myself, but Juanita already said she was allergic to cats and dogs.

When I heard the door creak open at the top of the stairs, I was almost asleep. Dad was saying my name.

"Just a minute," I yelled. In all the weeks we'd lived at Juanita's, he'd never come down here. I jumped up with an energy that I later realized was anticipation. He was doing so much better. Maybe he finally wanted to talk to me. Not a heart-to-heart chat necessarily, but something.

I pushed aside the sheet hanging from the beam and saw him hovering over by the basement stairs. And then I knew why he was down here. He had Tommy's art smock clutched in his arms.

"Shit," I muttered. I'd forgotten all about that smock. Tommy had already gotten in trouble last week. The teacher had sent a note home asking us to *please* make sure he had a clean one for the next art class on Thursday, tomorrow. And the laundry was my job. My only job now. I picked it because it seemed like the natural thing, since I was down here anyway.

I walked over to Dad and stuck my hand out. He looked confused.

"It's all right," I said. "I know it has to be done."

He clutched it tighter. "Your light was still on." He was looking at his feet. "I didn't want to startle you." His voice was quiet as a cat's step. "I'm just going to wash this."

"I can do it."

He looked up, but not at me, at the wall behind me. His "no" was a breath. "It's late," he whispered. "You need your sleep."

"Okay then." I wasn't going to argue the point, though I was sure I wouldn't be able to sleep with him messing with laundry.

I was wrong. I heard him opening the top of the washer and turning the wash cycle knob and after that, nothing. I didn't even hear the knocking of the agitator during the spin cycle (usually loud enough to hear outside). I did wake up for a moment when he moved the smock to the dryer, but I didn't open my eyes, I just rolled over and kept dreaming. It wasn't a bad dream, for a change, or at least it didn't start out bad. Mary Beth and I were in a big field, walking and laughing. By the time I realized she was gone, I was so deep in a forest that I couldn't take a step without vines and branches cutting my legs.

Then the dream changed into one of those running dreams. I was running so fast, I thought my lungs would explode, trying to get out of that forest. I must have been whimpering or calling out because Dad came into my half of the basement. I opened my eyes to see him leaning over my bed, repeating, "It's all right."

His hand was poised in the air halfway to my face. That's what struck me. He was going to touch me, but only if he had to. Only if he couldn't bring me out of my nightmare any other way.

And that's when I started to cry, not a normal teenage cry, but the wail of a brokenhearted child. His face looked so kind whenever he looked at Juanita and Tommy. He gave a shy smile even to Darlene and Mike. But with me, he always looked nervous. With me, he looked like he wanted to escape.

Within minutes my entire body was shaking with sobs; I felt like I would never stop. I remembered when I tried to show him that list I'd found in the car, the one with all my birthdays written on it. He'd flinched like I'd showed him an overdue bill. Maybe that's the way he thought of me now. A bill he could never pay and so preferred not to see at all.

And it wasn't just Dad, of course. It was Mary Beth. Ben having that woman friend whose name I didn't even know. My friends saying I was lucky. Mike never saying he loved me. He wanted to have sex, but he hadn't said those words yet. I wasn't sure if I loved him, but I needed him to love me. If he didn't, I'd be completely alone.

Poor Dad. I can still see him standing there in the blue sweater Juanita bought him, messing with the neckline until the thick cotton finally relented and rolled forward like a pouting lip. I think it must have taken everything he had to reach across the airspace and put his arm around me, but he did it, and there was something else, too. He called me Leebee. He said, "Don't cry, Leebee," and I was so surprised I couldn't have kept crying if I'd wanted to.

It was the name he'd used when I was little. I hadn't thought of it for years. But even as he said the word, I heard the echo of the hundreds of times I'd heard it in the past. His voice had aged, but the music was still there. The music was unmistakable.

chapter
eighteen

My father took care of me when I was little. Day in, day out, from the time he lost his job when I was two months old until I started kindergarten. I'd always known this, but I'd never really thought about what it meant—until those weeks at Juanita's house, when winter was ending, and I started to remember.

At first it was just colors. Brown for the elf costume Dad had safety pinned on me when I was three or four. Bright pink, the color of my first bicycle, the one Dad taught me to ride. Creamy yellow and blue for the blanket he used to cover me with when I took my naps. Green like the leaves when he would put me up in the tree in Agnes's backyard and hold out his arms for me to jump to him.

The process of remembering felt very natural, like going back to a place you know well rather than some big revelation. I saw him opening the door when I came home from kindergarten one day, holding a windup turtle I'd lost. I could hear him singing, spinning me around in the living room, dancing to "If I Were A Rich Man." I could smell the calamine lotion he put on me when I had the chicken pox the summer I turned four. I could taste the lumpy pancakes he made on Saturday mornings.

We were alone a lot back then. Mary Beth had school and her job at the pizza parlor. Mom worked long hours as manager of homeowners' claims. Dad took care of me—and often let me get away with murder. I got to eat cake for dinner, skip my bath, crawl in bed with my clothes on. When it stormed, he even let me sleep on his lap. I remembered waking up, droopy and warm, snuggling into the old wool jacket he always wore, waiting for the noise to end.

"He missed you every minute of every day," Juanita said. We were clearing up dishes after another of her fine meals: corned beef and cabbage and brownies for dessert. "It broke his heart to leave you. He told me that himself."

"Then why did he?" I said.

"I wanted to ask him that, kiddo, but I was afraid it'd bring on one of his fits. Nina at work says them fits your daddy has are like nervous overload. Her brother used to have them. It's something in the person's wiring. It shorts out just like a light circuit."

This was one of the many explanations Juanita had proposed for what was wrong with Dad. Her other theories included a vitamin deficiency (of course), not enough sleep, something having to do with his high IQ that she couldn't exactly specify—having never known anyone who was a genius—and her favorite explanation and the one she kept coming back to: that he hadn't been loved enough to get him over all the hard parts.

A few days later, when I asked Dad if he remembered how afraid I was of thunder, he said he did.

I was sitting across from him at the table. He was addressing envelopes, as always, but I'd gotten in the habit of doing my homework up here since that night he hugged me.

"You know, I still don't like storms," I said. I looked up from my calculus book to find him smiling that shy smile.

Now that his smile was directed at me, I could see why everyone thought my dad was so sweet. It wasn't just that his face looked a hundred-percent sincere, but also the barely perceptible surprise playing around his lips, the feeling you got that his happiness was a discovery, something he'd seen in you that no one else had.

The thought crossed my mind that my mother had married him for that smile. Or maybe it was his handwriting, all loops and curls and perfectly crossed t's.

I was thinking a lot about my parents' relationship. I imagined it as a wire that stretched from the first time they looked at each other to the day he left. Even if I would never have the whole story, I had to understand the endpoints: why they got together, why they broke up. I knew from math class if you know the behavior at the endpoints, you can infer all kinds of things about the rest.

It was one of those afternoons when Dad and I were working at the kitchen table that I decided I had to know if I was even right about *when* he left. All I remembered clearly was being out with Mary Beth and coming home to find that Dad had disappeared. Mom and Mary Beth said he'd left town; they didn't say why. My secret fear was that he'd died, though I kept reminding myself that his old suitcase, the brown one with the plaid lining, was gone, too.

I was pretty sure it was late February, early March. Ten years ago, almost exactly.

Dad said that was about right. "It was a Friday." His pen didn't stop moving. "Lot of traffic going out of town."

"That's when you went to Kansas City?"

He nodded. After a long moment, he added, "I always wished I'd waited and told you good-bye."

I glanced at him, but I didn't say anything. I was dying to hear more, but I knew Dad thrived on silence like other people thrived on encouragement.

"I just hope you can forgive what I did," he finally said. His voice was a whisper. His pen had stopped moving.

"I do forgive you," I said firmly.

"I've been ashamed all these years. I thought I'd never see you again, and that's what I deserved."

I was trying to work up the nerve to say how much I'd missed him when the phone rang.

It was Ben, but before I could be annoyed, he said he had news. He'd been telling me for weeks that Mary Beth might be doing better, but not to get my hopes up. But now Mary Beth's doctor was asking to see someone from her family. Ben said this was a good sign.

The doctor's first choice was Dad, but I told Ben—after I moved to the basement phone—that I didn't think it was a very good idea.

"He gets really upset when other people are upset." I took a breath. "He's doing so much better, Ben. I don't want him to freak out again."

I heard Dad walking around, probably pouring himself another cup of coffee. He drank it all day long, from a huge mug, like water. Juanita wanted him to stop but she hadn't pressured him. She said she'd learned from her second husband, the Arrested, that pressuring men was like handing them a challenge to do worse.

"All right." Ben paused. "How about you?"

"I thought you had to be eighteen to go there."

"That's not a hard and fast rule."

"Okay," I said, thinking, now he tells me. "But I have to get to St. Louis somehow. I'm not going to drive that far with only a learner's permit."

"You're such a pragmatist, honey." He laughed gently. "I can pick you up. Don't worry about that."

"I'm not worried. I think my boyfriend will take me. I just have to ask."

My tone was a little offended, but he didn't seem to notice— nor did he ask about Mike. He gave me the details of when I needed to be there, and we agreed to talk later in the week, to confirm. He was getting ready to hang up when I realized I hadn't asked him Juanita's question.

She wanted to know Ben's opinion of what was wrong with my dad. That's how I put it, and it was true. Juanita wanted to know—not me. I didn't want to hear his son-of-a-shrink diagnosis.

"Nothing's *wrong* with him," Ben said. "If someone is mentally ill, that doesn't mean something is fundamentally wrong with them."

"Come on. If he had cancer, you'd just blurt it out."

"It's much more complicated than that."

"Now you sound like my sister."

He laughed, and that's when I realized something had changed. It was his old, noisy laugh. Maybe Mary Beth really was doing better.

"I'm not a doctor, Leeann. I have a Ph.D. in biochemistry, not medicine."

"You must have an idea. I mean, why would you say he was mentally ill if you didn't have an idea?"

"I didn't say he was, I said he could be. And yes, I think it's likely from what I've seen, but whether that illness is chemical in nature or some kind of reaction to trauma, I have no way to know."

"Reaction to trauma? Is that like a hard life?"

"Yes, I suppose you could look at it that way." His voice sounded like a smile. "It's usually more discrete, a single event we call trauma, but perhaps that's because our measurement tools aren't sophisticated enough to capture the wide-angle view."

I wasn't sure what he was talking about, so I told him I had to go. Later, when I related all this to Juanita, she repeated her conclusion that Ben was nice but a real egghead.

Mike suggested we stay the whole weekend in St. Louis rather than just drive there and come back. He had some money saved; he could pay for a really nice hotel downtown. We could go up in the Arch and see the zoo. He thought it was really weird that my family had never toured the city. I could imagine what he'd say if I'd told him we'd never been on vacation, period.

Mom never saw the point of going anywhere. Mary Beth seemed to agree. "Home," my sister once told a customer, "is that place in your mind where you see your family just like they are. If you have to put new scenery around them all the time, it's like you can't see them unless you're distracted. Like you need more color because you've already let them fade."

I told Mike I'd go for the weekend. This was as good a time as any, I figured, to do what he obviously had in mind. I was already so nervous about this session with the shrink, I wouldn't have time to be nervous about sex.

Juanita and Dad and Tommy waved us out of the driveway early Saturday morning, loaded up with gifts for my sister. Tommy had contributed a stack of his drawings going back as far as he could find, including quite a few my sister had already seen, and some that had even been former gifts. Juanita baked Mary Beth a loaf of cornbread and a dozen white chocolate chip cookies, her favorite. Dad gave her twenty dollars. He mumbled something about needing money in hospitals and I said you never know.

It took about four hours to pull up in front of the hotel. It was skyscraper tall and fancier than anything I'd ever seen. The entrance hall was all gold and chandeliers. Our room had a king-size bed, covered with a velvet bedspread and made up with three top sheets and two blankets. On the dresser, there was a basket of special soaps, shampoos, creme rinse and even new toothbrushes in clear plastic bags. The TV was hidden in a heavy brown cabinet that looked hundreds of years old.

We were on the eighteenth floor. From one window, you could see all these buildings and restaurants; from the other, the Mississippi River and the steamboats and the people swarming the walkway to the Arch. I was dying to get out there and be part of it all.

Fifteen minutes later, Mike and I were in the Arch museum, watching the movie about how the Arch was constructed, preparing ourselves to go up. We bought T-shirts for everybody in the gift shop, and stared at the weird stuffed grizzly bear in the lobby and then got in line for the tram. The metal car rattled and creaked like it would never make it, but it actually didn't seem long before the door opened at the top. Mike was holding my hand as we walked to the windows. We leaned forward and there it was: the entire city laid out before us. Mike said the streets were like an enormous spiderweb, stretching in every direction. I thought it must be the way the world looks to God.

We stayed for a half hour. I could have stayed much longer, but Mike was anxious to get back to the hotel. He wanted to order room service for lunch before Ben came to take me to the hospital. I said okay, but we'd barely walked into the room when Ben was at the door.

He'd been waiting in the lobby for us. It was still an hour earlier than we'd agreed. I introduced him to Mike, and they shook hands; then Ben crossed his arms.

"I was hoping we could go over now," he said. "Have some time before the appointment." He looked out the river window. "Do you mind?"

I said no and went into the bathroom to brush my hair and change into my carefully selected outfit. Navy skirt, blue oxford shirt—plain but serious. I put some blush on but my cheeks swallowed it.

"What time will you be back?" Mike said. He stepped forward like he wanted to kiss me. Ben said probably not until after dinnertime. I gave Mike a quick peck on the cheek and grabbed the bag of presents.

The hospital was on the west side of the city. Ben and I didn't talk on the way. The leather seats of Rebecca's BMW, the crowded streets and heavy traffic, Ben sitting next to me, it was all so unreal. I thought about my sister, who'd been here many times back when she and Ben were together. She never said anything about not feeling like herself, but I sure didn't feel like me.

The stone building was very large and shaped like an L, surrounded by trees and what would be gardens in the spring. It looked like the private hospital it was: an expensive place unless you got one of the two state-sponsored beds reserved for people without insurance, like Mary Beth did. Of course Ben's father had to be the reason she'd been bumped to the top of that list. Ben didn't tell me the details, but he did admit that his father had "helped."

It was almost seventy degrees, much warmer than usual for

the beginning of March. A lot of the patients were outside, getting air—including my sister.

She ran across the brown grass and grabbed me and hugged me and blanketed my neck with kisses. "Baby," she said. Her voice was full of tears. "Baby doll girl."

I might have been crying a little bit myself. She hadn't hugged me in a long time. I was surprised by how strong her arms felt. She could lift me up, if she wanted to. She'd gained a lot of weight, but it looked wonderful on her. Everything about her looked good. Her hair was healthy and thick and glistening yellow in the sun. Her skin was cream and strawberries, not a sign of the sores or old scabs. Even in the boring green hospital gown, you could see how curvaceous her figure had become. She stood her height, all five-feet-eleven-and-a-half inches of it. Like a princess, I thought, or even a goddess.

No wonder Ben's eyes were glued on her.

She took my hand and pulled me to one of the benches. "Tell me everything," she said, breathlessly.

"There's not much to say." I glanced at Ben. He was holding the bag of presents in one hand, his other was shoved in his pocket. He was still looking at her, but he hadn't moved.

"Ben is fine." She waved her hand like she was shooing away a fly, but when she smiled at him, her cheeks grew even pinker. "He's always here." She turned back to me. "But I haven't seen you in ages, baby. I was afraid you'd be all grown up. Thank God, you look exactly the same."

I sat up straighter. I was pretty sure I had grown to at least five-four, but compared to her I was still short. Short, with boring brown hair, and enormous cow boobs.

"I heard you have a boyfriend. You have to tell me all about him first."

I hesitated. "How did you know that?"

"A little bird told me," she said lightly.

"No, really." I was stalling, wondering how to tell her it was Holly's son.

But she already knew. Holly had told her. "I got a beautiful card from her a while back. She still says I saved her life." Mary Beth leaned closer and giggled. "That's one way to look at it I guess."

"It's true," I said quickly. "She's doing so much better now that—"

"Let's not talk about Holly. I really don't care. My lifesaving days are over." She laughed again. "The only lifesaving I'm doing now is the candy."

"Are you serious?"

"As serious as I ever am," she said with a goofy grin. "It's easier not to be serious. That's the secret." Then another laugh. "Don't say I never gave you anything."

Ben stepped forward. "I think we should go inside. Get some tea before the session." He looked at me. "You want a soda?"

"Sure."

"Okay, Mr. Boss Man," she said, standing up and frowning. But she grabbed his arm and kissed him on the ear. "Take me to your tea."

They walked in that way, with her holding his arm, leaning against him. I followed, too in a daze to even think about what all this meant.

In the cafeteria, Mary Beth asked questions about Mike and I answered them as well as I could. Some of them were a little bizarre. "Does he eat much fast food?" "Does he know how to swim?" Ben was sitting on her side and clasping her hand tightly. Whenever there was a lull in the conversation, she peered at his face like a crib sheet for what to say next. Her fingers trembled a little around her cup; I figured it was the medicine they were giving her. She didn't mention Dad or Juanita; she didn't even ask about Tommy.

By the time Ben stood up and said we needed to go now, I was so confused I wanted to run out the door and never look back. I hated everything about this place, from the stupid little plastic cups the soda came in—no cans, cans have metal lids—to the gurneys parked in the halls, straps hanging off the bars. And the other patients, with their shuffling steps and weird stares. My sister stuck out like a diamond in a mud pie.

The first surprise was that Dr. Kaplan wanted to talk to me without Mary Beth. As I watched Mary Beth and Ben walking away, I found myself remembering the day they met, when Rebecca tricked Ben into seeing my sister. I wanted to laugh when it flashed across my mind that all this was an elaborate trick, too, and I was the one with the problem.

Dr. Kaplan herself was another surprise. I was expecting a man and someone younger. She was sixty if she was a day. She had short white hair and wire-rimmed glasses. The white doctor's coat she was wearing had Martha Kaplan in blue script on the pocket.

I took a seat in a big leather chair across from her desk. She introduced herself and gave me a firm, hearty handshake, but she skipped the how-are-you, how-was-the-drive small talk.

"I've heard a lot about you," she said, and smiled very slightly. Then she thanked me for coming and told me she was sorry but she needed her notes. She took out a leather-bound book and flipped around awhile. I was trying to decide what to look at, so I wouldn't seem nervous. I settled on my panty-hosed knee.

The biggest surprise was the topic Dr. Kaplan started with. All along I'd been assuming it would be either our family or

Holly Kramer and what had happened last fall. It never crossed my mind that Dr. Kaplan would want to discuss my sister's song reading in a more general sense—especially as I didn't know anything about that compared to what Mary Beth herself knew.

Dr. Kaplan said "song reading" tentatively, as if the words were a foreign language. "This song reading," she kept saying, until I wanted to scream, as opposed to what? *That* song reading?

She asked me to trace the history, and I did, from the first chart my sister wrote to the party at Juanita's house. When she asked where I thought the idea came from, the drive home from Dad's apartment flashed through my mind, but I told her I had no idea.

"Why don't you ask my sister?"

"I have," Dr. Kaplan said, with the slight smile again. "Now I'm asking you." She paused for a moment. Her eyes were kinder than I wanted them to be. "Let me put it another way. When your sister began this song reading, did it seem out of the ordinary to you?"

"I'm not sure what you mean."

"Were you worried about her?"

"No, not at all." I slid my hands under my thighs. The desire to mess with my chin was becoming irresistible. "I thought it was cool."

"Really?" Her voice seemed skeptical.

"I still think it's cool."

"Despite what happened?"

"That wasn't song reading's fault." I was on shaky ground. "I mean, Holly didn't have any songs, that was the problem."

"But it was the same impulse, don't you think?" She didn't let me answer. "Mary Beth's impulse to help others, no matter the cost to herself?"

"It's a gift," I said. Then it hit me. "Kind of like what you do." I leaned forward to emphasize my point. "I mean, what's the difference, really? You help people, so does she."

"That's quite flattering, but I don't think gift describes what I do. Like all psychiatrists, I spent years in training. I've always had support from the hospital, colleagues to confirm or complicate my impressions." She paused. "Let me put it another way," she said again. "Did you think it odd when she adopted one of her client's children?"

"No." Though it certainly seemed odd now. Everything seemed odd. I myself was odd, dressed in this stupid blue shirt and skirt, answering these very odd questions. "I mean, she always wanted kids, and nobody else wanted Tom—"

"Always?" Dr. Kaplan smiled. "I believe she was twenty-three at the time."

"Mom had a kid at nineteen."

"And you? Do you plan to have children at nineteen? Or twenty-three?"

"No," I said slowly, and felt caught.

"Why not?"

"Because . . . I don't want kids." I wasn't sure if it was true, but I glared, triumphant.

"Ah." She looked at the wall for a moment. "I wonder if you could tell me what your sister's song reading represents to you. You said before that you think it's a good thing. Why is it good? What does it stand for in your life?"

"I don't know," I said, and sat back, waiting for the other way she would put it, or the subject change, or something, anything, to let me off the hook. But this time she stared at me, waiting, too. I let my mind wander to Mike. He was probably watching TV, or asleep facedown on the huge hotel bed.

I wanted him to hold me.

"I'm not the only person who thinks it's good," I finally said. "I could bring you a huge list of people who would say it's good. Mary Beth helps people, that's a good—"

"Do you care about these people?"

"Sort of."

"But not enough to risk your sister's health for them?"

"Of course not."

"So again, why is this song reading a good thing? From Leeann's perspective?"

"I don't know," I repeated, because I really didn't. But I felt a gnawing in the pit of my stomach. I moved my thumb over the scar under my chin, as I thought about how unfair this was. What was this woman doing in our lives? What did she know about me or my sister or our town? About anything?

"Do you know Ben's father?" I said suddenly.

"Ted Mathiessen? Why yes, I do. Why do you ask?"

I crossed my arms. "Just curious."

She paused for so long I thought I'd upset her. But I was wrong. Her voice was very gentle, her eyes were very kind, as she asked if I considered her the enemy.

"No."

"But you don't trust psychiatrists. You think they drug away people's real feelings." Dr. Kaplan smiled. "Your sister told me that, too. It was the first thing she said when she decided to talk to me."

"Well, it's true," I said, and then before I could stop myself, I told her she'd already changed my sister.

"How so?"

"She's not herself anymore." I felt like crying, thinking about it. "She seems really weird. She laughs too much."

"Would it surprise you to hear that she's not on any medication at this time?"

"But her hand was shaking."

"Perhaps she was nervous about seeing you."

I shook my head.

"She values your opinion much more than you realize. She's told me several times that she's very afraid of losing your love."

I was so stunned, I didn't know what to say. I looked at the window on the left side of her desk. I could see the back lawn of the hospital, and people moving around, but no sign of Mary Beth and Ben.

Dr. Kaplan must have taken my silence as a sign that I'd had enough of this topic, because she changed course. She wanted to review the family history, as she called it. She asked me all kinds of questions about Mom and Dad, what I remembered about them, what I thought of their relationship. I kept my answers short. It took me a while to realize the answers were adding up to something.

It was just like that day with Ben a thousand years ago, when I'd talked my way to the conclusion that Mom wanted Dad to leave, except this time I had talked myself to the reason—Mom was having an affair with her boss, that guy Will Stanley. Of course.

Dr. Kaplan was writing in her notebook, but her face was impassive, as if this was old news. She didn't even look up when she asked if I remembered how Mary Beth had reacted to our mother's affair.

I heard my sister's voice: *Mom said Dad ruined her life.*

"Mary Beth took Mom's side," I said slowly.

"And how do you feel about that?"

"I don't care."

"Ah." Dr. Kaplan took a breath. "Your sister believes that you care very much." She glanced in my eyes. "She's convinced herself that now that you know what she did for your mother, you won't love her anymore."

"That's silly," I said, but I was wondering why Mary Beth assumed I knew whatever it was she supposedly "did" for Mom. Unless she thought Dad told me. In any case, I wasn't about to tell Dr. Kaplan I still didn't know. I wanted her to talk freely with me, so maybe I could figure it out.

"Guilt can be a very powerful force," Dr. Kaplan was saying.

"I've noticed," I said, leaning forward. "I mean, my dad feels really guilty, too."

"Do you think your mother felt guilty?"

"She grew up an orphan. She had a hard life." I caught myself sounding like my sister. "She was never happy that I can remember."

Dr. Kaplan nodded. "But she didn't feel guilty, did she?"

"I don't know."

"Do you think she had a right to involve your sister in her marital problems?"

"I don't know," I repeated. *Mommy was so desperate. She needed me so bad.*

"All right. Let me ask it another way. Do you think your mother had a right to use you in the way she did?"

"She didn't use me," I sputtered.

"You've said you know she was having an affair." Dr. Kaplan was turning the pages of her notebook, but absentmindedly. Her eyes were on my face. "Why couldn't she simply have asked your father to leave?"

I forced myself not to look as massively confused as I was. "I'm not sure. Maybe she was afraid he wouldn't do it."

This was very hard to imagine, but Dr. Kaplan nodded. "He'd been the primary caregiver since you were born. Mary Beth told me that the two of you were very close. Why should he leave?"

"But he did have problems," I said, thinking of that day at the Laundromat.

"Yes, but Mary Beth told me he'd had these so-called problems for years. If your mother's motive wasn't the preservation of her affair, why did she wait so long to persuade him he was endangering you?"

I had my chin scar wedged between my thumb and finger, but I wasn't moving. I was barely breathing. I had a feeling I did know about this already. I'd been thinking about it for weeks. It was one of the stranger memories I'd had of me and Dad.

Before, this memory didn't seem important like my first day of school or my first bike—I couldn't imagine why it kept coming into my mind. We were at the mall, this was before they added the JC Penney, back when it was just a dry cleaner and a Woolworth's and an ice-cream shop. We'd already eaten our cones, mint chip for me, butter pecan for him, as usual, and we were in Woolworth's to get buttons. My coat was missing all but one button and winter wouldn't be over for another month, as Mom kept saying. I'd heard her yelling at Dad about it. She was always telling him he wasn't taking good care of me, but I didn't see it that way. I was very mature for five, Dad said so all the time. I thought of us as taking care of each other.

I had a habit of going wherever I wanted in the store. Dad always took a long time buying things; it made him really nervous. I was over in the toys when I saw my sister. She was dressed in her pizza shop red-and-white shirt and red slacks. "You're coming with me to work today," she said. She picked me up and smiled. "I asked my boss and he said he could use a good table setter like you."

I was always begging to go with her, and I was thrilled. We were already in her old VW bug, headed out of the mall, when I panicked. "What about Dad?" I crawled on my knees and looked out the back window. "We forgot about Dad!"

"Sit down," she said. "You need your seat belt."

"He'll be scared!"

"It's okay. I told him I was taking you."

I was still looking back at the Woolworth's, but she told me to sit down again before changing the topic to how busy it would be at the pizza place. Friday night and all. Good tips for waitresses and even little busgirls like me.

The sad part was, they knew he wouldn't call the police. He probably wouldn't even ask the clerks for help. He would call Mom at work. He would turn to the one person who wanted him to believe I was in danger because he wasn't watching me close enough.

At some point, Mary Beth must have called and acted like she found me. Maybe she even said I was hurt. I'd fallen in the street. Got lost in the woods behind the mall. Ended up with a stranger who hadn't harmed me—this time.

I didn't really care about the specifics; the end result was the same. Dr. Kaplan said they persuaded him, but that wasn't the word. They taught him I'd be better off without him. They conspired together to make my father go away.

Dr. Kaplan's voice brought me back to now. "You haven't answered my question. Are you all right, Leeann?"

"Yes," I told her, because it was true. I was all right. But after I excused myself to go to the bathroom, I went straight to the pay phone in the front hall and called a cab. Ten minutes later, I was sitting in the backseat, headed to the Arch. I'd left a note with the hospital intake clerk, of course. I didn't want them to worry I'd disappeared.

The Arch line was much longer than before. It was dark by the time I made it to the top, but the city looked even more beautiful lit by the green and red of tiny traffic lights, the warm yellow of restaurants and hotels, the fluorescent blue of offices being cleaned. I didn't have to wish I could be part of this someday, because I knew I would be. It only felt like my past was coming closer. The truth was, it was lost forever, leaving me even as I lived it. Except I was the one who would leave in the end, and I knew that, too. This was my future.

chapter
nineteen

When I got back to the hotel, Mike was smoking and making paper airplanes out of the hotel stationery. He already
knew something was wrong because Ben had called twice to find
out if I was okay. After I called Ben back—and told him I didn't
feel like talking—Mike and I sat on the bed, holding hands,
while I told him what I'd remembered talking to Dr. Kaplan.
When I said, "This must seem really weird to you," he reminded
me that his family wasn't exactly the Brady Bunch.

I had the whole story out without breaking down or even
shedding a tear, when Mike suddenly became curious why I
never talked about my mom.

"I don't mean what your sister and your mom did to your
dad. I'm talking about your mom as your mom. Like you and
her." He was leaning back against the velvet bedspread. We were
waiting for the room service we'd ordered—steaks and fries. It
was after eight and we were both starving. "You were nine when
she died. You must have memories of being with her as a kid."

Before I could reply, the room service guy knocked at the door. He wheeled in a little table with two covered plates and a vase with real roses in the center. Mike gave him a tip, and I said we should eat now, talk later. "It's not that interesting," I told him. "I think that's why I don't talk about it. Plus, I really don't remember very much."

He didn't object when I got up and turned on the television, thank God. The truth was, I didn't like thinking about the way I was with my mom. But I was ten when she died—not nine—and of course I remembered. I remembered all the way back to second grade.

I would wake up in the morning, vowing to keep all my feelings to myself. No matter what happened, I would not cry. I wouldn't even giggle, because sometimes giggling led to crying by a mechanism I could never really grasp. But then I would look out the window on the way to school and see a dog, for example. Always such a simple thing.

"I wish I could have a dog," I said.

"Well you can't," Mom said. Agnes wouldn't allow pets. I knew this, but I liked the feeling of wanting things even if I couldn't have them. It made the world seem bigger and brighter and more alive.

"I love dogs so much."

"You think you do, but you've never owned a dog."

"I love animals," I said, louder. "When I'm a grown-up, I'm going to be a veterinarian."

"You have no idea what you're going to be when you're grown."

"Yes I do." My eyes were starting to itch.

"I wanted to be a dancer, and I'm the assistant director of claims." She smiled, but it wasn't a happy smile; it was a just-you-wait-and-see smile. "How many kids you think put my job in their fairy tales?"

"That's you."

"That's everybody in town except the few people who figured out that work is the only thing that matters. Dreams are a dime a dozen."

I could have saved it so easily. I could have said I'd work hard to be a veterinarian and she probably would have repeated her caution that it might not happen, but her voice would be proud instead of irritated; she'd give me the nod of approval I wanted so badly. I never understood why I went the other way.

"A dog is my dream," I told her, as smugly as I could manage given the tears rolling down my face. "I'm going to name him Alfred. He'll have long, long hair but he'll be an inside dog because he doesn't like a doghouse. He likes to sleep by my bed."

And on and on, until we got to school when I said good-bye as stiffly as if she'd just shot my dog. I don't think she even noticed. I'd heard her tell one of my teachers, "Leeann cries at the drop of the hat and she'll drop the hat."

Mom had a seemingly endless list of ways to express the pointlessness of crying.

"No use crying over spilt milk."

"No use crying for the moon."

"Your tears and a quarter will just about buy a cup of coffee."

Every time I cried, she lost respect for me. Sometimes I wanted to slap myself for failing again and again.

"There's nothing wrong with crying," my sister would say, slipping me her point of view the same way she thrust coins into my hand after I'd spent my allowance. About half the time, her sympathy would start me bawling again. "Poor baby," she'd say and hug me so close, my tears would wet the front of her shirt.

She herself never cried, though. And she never criticized Mom.

"Mom is only trying to keep us from suffering the things she did."

"Mom had such a hard life."

"If you knew what Mom had been through, you'd see why she wants us to be tough."

I wasn't tough, though. I wanted to be, but I just wasn't. I was good in school and I was a nice girl, according to my teachers. I was well liked; I always got invited to birthday parties. But I wasn't tough—and I wasn't a hard worker, at least that's what Mom said. She wanted me to be more like Mary Beth, who had started her own ironing business the summer when she was only seven. I heard the story constantly growing up. Mary Beth would go to all the houses in the neighborhood, getting a dime for each shirt, a nickel for a pair of pants. She made over fifty dollars and she gave it all to Mom and Dad, to help pay for her school clothes.

At seven, I spent most of my time reading or playing pretend games. In my favorite game, I was a unicorn, prancing through the forest, my white coat gleaming in the sunlight. When people would see me, they would ask if I'd like a ribbon and I would nod my beautiful unicorn head. I had red ones and blue ones and purple ones, and I wore them around my neck as I ran around our apartment. Mary Beth bought them for me because she knew about the game.

I remember one time I asked my sister why she'd started that ironing business. I'd heard about it so many times from Mom, but I'd never heard my sister's version.

"It wasn't that big of a deal," she said, and shrugged. We were in her Volkswagen, just the two of us.

"But why did you do all that work? I mean, you hate ironing."

She laughed a little. "I guess I thought it would make Mom happy. It was worth it for that."

I wanted to make Mom happy, but I also wanted to be happy, and I had trouble reconciling the two. Making Mary Beth happy was so much easier and more fun. All I had to do was draw her a picture or find her a flower or even just tell her something I was thinking about. "I wonder why the leaves turn color." "I think when I'm grown I'll live in Canada." "I wish the people in my books were real. The nice ones anyway."

"You're such a great little girl," my sister would say, smiling. "I'm so proud of you."

I always wanted this from my mother, but maybe she just didn't have it to give.

She did try to make sure Mary Beth and I had the things she'd missed out on. I knew the story about Mom's name almost as well as the ironing story. Mom had grown up Helen Fenton, no middle name, not even an initial. When she had her first daughter, she not only wrote a middle name on the birth certificate, she called her baby by both her first name, Mary, and a shortened version of her middle name, Elizabeth. When I was born, Mom went even further, choosing a first name that was already two names combined and a big middle name, too. Mary Beth told me that Mom started out saying "Leeann Michelle" whenever she talked to me, but it was just too long a name for such a little baby, and finally she settled for Leeann.

Of course the main thing she gave us that she didn't have was a home. She gave us a place to live, food on the table, clothes for school, a warm bed at night. And I knew what a big deal that was now, watching Juanita take care of my family. I should have known before, watching Mary Beth do it all, except with Mary Beth it always looked so easy.

Sometimes I still felt tricked by how easy it seemed, living with my sister. Easy enough to be permanent.

Mike had just finished my last french fry when I asked him if we could go to sleep now.

"It's only eight forty-five." He sounded annoyed.

"Just turn the light off then. You can keep watching TV, but I'm wiped out."

He didn't say anything, but he snapped off the lamp. I went into the bathroom and put on my new extra-large Arch T-shirt and my terry cloth sleep shorts, and crawled into the other side of the king-size bed. I knew I wasn't sexy, but I didn't care. I was determined to fall asleep, so I could stop thinking about my mother.

Mike was watching some cop movie. I closed my eyes and tried to listen intently to the show, but the thoughts kept coming.

The week before Mom's car accident, I'd come down with a summer cold. That's what Mom said it was; Mary Beth said it had to be the flu because I was running a fever.

"I'm going to stay home with her." My sister was whispering.

"You don't need to do that," Mom said. They were standing in my bedroom. I had my pink bedspread pulled up to my shoulders because I was shivering. Mom came closer to the bed and peered into my face. "Will you be all right alone?"

"Yes." My voice sounded like a frog's croak; my lips felt like they were splitting with the effort of opening them. But I knew Mom liked that I rarely got sick. I had one of the best attendance records at Tainer Elementary, and I'd heard her tell my teachers that I had a "tough constitution"—I could fight off any germ.

Mary Beth leaned down and put her hand on my forehead. "The last time I took it, it was 102 and it feels worse now."

"All right. You go on, I'll call and tell my boss I won't be in. I can take the time off." After a moment, Mom pointed to the door. "Go on. You're late already."

Mary Beth leaned down and kissed me lightly on the cheek. "I'll bring you some cake." I always wanted the cake at her restaurant; it had such thick icing. Her voice sounded sweet like that icing. "Hope you feel better, honey."

She left and Mom went into the living room to watch TV. I fell asleep for a while, and when I woke up, Mom was sitting on the edge of my bed, announcing that my temperature was down.

"I do feel a little better," I said, but when I tried to lean up on one elbow, I realized I couldn't; I was still too weak.

"I told you it's just a cold." She stood up and let out a long breath. "You think you can handle being alone for a while? I really need to go in for the eleven-thirty meeting if there's any way."

I nodded; of course I could handle it. I'd been alone before when I was sick. The only thing I really hated was vomiting, but I knew what to do if it happened. Make it to the toilet, and if you don't make it, clean up your mess quickly before the nausea comes back.

It was July, and a very hot day, already pushing ninety when Mom left. I had two fans blowing on me, but when my fever started climbing again, I had to get out of my tiny room. I wandered the apartment, too dizzy to focus on anything or think about what I could do to stop this. Then the nausea started. I must have vomited half a dozen times before my sister came home. I stayed on the bathroom floor, so I wouldn't miss the toilet, and also because the tile felt cool. I knew I was really bad off because the panty hose drying on the shower bar looked like they were moving, coming alive.

My temperature was 106 when Mary Beth found me. She sponged me off with cool water, gave me Tylenol, put ice in my hands, and kept it up until my fever dropped back down to 102 and I went back to bed. Mom came home about a half hour later. They were standing in the doorway of my room when Mary Beth told her what happened. Mom didn't make any excuses for herself. She let out a curse and said she'd been wrong to leave me. "Her fever seemed like it broke, but I should have known it could go up again. I made a big mistake."

She meant it; she felt bad and she told me she was sorry several times. But a few days later, I overheard her telling my day camp counselor that I might miss more camp before the summer was over. "Leeann used to fight off everything that came around." Mom shrugged. "I don't know why she's become so sickly lately."

I'd only been sick one other time in the last year, but I didn't bother defending myself. Mom said the word "sickly" the same way she said "whiner" or "crier": with a sneer in her voice. She herself was never sick. She always said she couldn't afford to be.

Was there anything about me she did like? Lying in the king-size bed, listening to the gunfire in Mike's movie, I couldn't think of a single thing. I'd admitted to Ben that I was a little afraid of her, but I'd never even admitted to myself the other part—until now. I never felt like she loved me.

I didn't realize I was crying until Mike rolled next to me and pulled me in his arms. When he asked what was wrong, it all poured out. He listened so well it made me even sadder.

"I'm not very tough," I said, when I could catch my breath between sobs. "I try to be, but then I end up like this, a bawling mess."

I don't know how long I sobbed; it felt like forever. When I finally calmed down, I was lying against his chest, he was stroking my hair—and I decided to tell him about Kyle. I wanted him to know why I was reluctant to have sex. I told him the whole story and he was so nice about it, so nice about everything, that I decided tonight was the night; I would do what he wanted. And I was going to tell him so, but I was really tired, I had to close my eyes for a minute. The next thing I knew, it was seven-thirty in the morning and he was already up, taking a shower.

I was sitting on the bed when he came out of the bathroom. I had thrown on my jeans and sweater, but I wasn't sure what was going on.

"It's time to go home," he said. Not a question. I was so relieved; I figured he must know how anxious I was to see my father.

We were on the highway when it hit me that he hadn't said more than a few words all morning. When I asked if anything was wrong, he said no. When I asked what he was thinking about, he said nothing. After a minute I screwed up my courage and admitted, "I feel really embarrassed about last night."

"Don't worry about it," he said, and that was all. He didn't squeeze my hand or smile or even glance in my direction. So of course I felt more embarrassed.

Another fifteen minutes or so went by before I found myself blurting out, "Are we still going to the prom?"

It was a stupid question. We'd had a little argument about this on the way to St. Louis. He said we were too old for high school junk like dances; we'd been through too much. I said I wanted to go anyway; it could be fun. He'd finally agreed, since it was so important to me.

But now he said, "If you say so, but I think it will be a total waste of time."

I turned away from him and stared out the window. He lit a cigarette and cranked up the radio; the song was "Jack and Diane." I liked the song anyway, but at that moment, the line in the chorus about life going on too long seemed an almost perfect expression of how I felt. I remembered Mary Beth used to say that music could be the most loyal friend, always taking your feelings seriously but transforming them, too, making things better just by naming them and giving them a melody. The song could make you feel less alone, my sister said, and it was true— but when it ended, I was back to all my problems. Mike was upset about something, that was obvious, even if he wouldn't talk about it. My family was a mess. And I was already worried about what I would say to my dad.

We got back to Tainer about noon and he was still at church with Juanita and Tommy. (This was another thing Juanita had added into our lives. I didn't mind; I figured our family could use help from any quarter.) Instead of going downstairs to my room, I plopped down on the couch to wait. I'd decided to tell Dad as soon as they got home. I didn't want him to spend another moment feeling guilty for something he didn't do.

Juanita was there when I told him. Tommy had run into his room to play, and naturally Juanita wanted to hear about my hospital trip, too. I thought about waiting but then she was pouring Dad his coffee and she had her hand on his shoulder the way she always did and I realized she might be able to help if he took it too hard. No matter what he thought about Mom, it couldn't be easy hearing that your eldest daughter would do this to you. I worried he might even have one of his "fits" as Juanita called them, so I went very slowly.

Neither of them reacted anything like I expected.

When I was finished, Juanita said, "I got to make a phone

call," and disappeared down the hall to her bedroom. Dad was crying a little, a noiseless pitiful cry, but not for himself. Not because he'd been betrayed by his wife and his daughter.

"Poor Bethie," he said.

"You feel bad for her?" I was sputtering, but before I could say more, Juanita was already back in the kitchen.

"Come on," she said to me, "we're going on a little trip."

"Where? I just got home."

"It won't take long. Henry and I were talking about it last night and we think that doc treating your sister needs to know about this."

"About what?"

"Get in the car and I'll tell you what. You come too, Henry. I'm taking Tommy over next door to play with little Brendan."

Dad and I did as we were told. We got in Juanita's Plymouth, Dad in the passenger seat, me behind him in the back. After a moment, he said softly, "She did it for her mama."

"So?" My voice was too harsh; he stopped talking.

When Juanita got in, I asked her where she was taking us. "To the old house. The one you were born in."

"I've seen it." Mike and I had driven by once, just for curiosity. It was way on the east side of town, near Denise's house. The jungle gym Dad had built for Mary Beth was gone, but the porch swing was still there. "I don't get why we have to—"

"You never been inside have you?"

"No, but—"

"Okay then. I already called the woman who owns it and she said it's fine for us to come on over."

I sat back for a minute, impressed as always by Juanita's ability to make things happen. How did she know this woman anyway?

After a while I said, "Why exactly are we doing this?"

My voice sounded irritable but Juanita didn't seem to notice. "Mary Beth painted the walls of the basement. One summer when she was a kid. Henry told me about it a few weeks ago, and I went over to see it last week, after work."

I flashed to all the home improvements my sister had done after my car accident. No wonder she'd known how to paint already. I looked out the window and tried to imagine how this could be worth driving across town. Maybe she painted each wall a different color. Maybe she'd even put cork on one wall, like she did with Tommy's room.

Or had she painted words all over the walls. Is that what they were trying to tell me?

On the way there, Juanita talked nonstop about Mary Beth. "The kid was what? sixteen? seventeen? And here she is in this awful spot, with her mom asking her to do something like that. I'm not saying it was right, it wasn't. But I got to tell you, I feel sorry for your sister. Dammit if her whole life hasn't been people asking her for help."

"I know," Dad whispered.

"But—" I began.

"Did you know your mom didn't even want Mary Beth to go to college? Henry and I were just talking about this last night. I knew Mary Beth when she got out of high school, she was already working at the restaurant but she could have done anything. You know how smart your sister is. But your mom said she needed her here."

I thought about it for a moment and realized I'd never known Mary Beth wanted to go to college. She always talked about me going to college, but never about her. When I said, "She didn't seem to mind working at the diner," Juanita looked in the rearview mirror and frowned.

"She played the hand she had, like people always do. And once your mom died, she really didn't have no choices. She had to take care of you, and then little Tommy came along with nobody but Mary Beth to love him. But why else do you think she was so interested talking to Ben about all his big-shot science stuff? She ain't no simple little gal, your sister. I mean, hell, have you ever thought about why she started her own business doing those readings? It was so she could have something that was just hers, something where she would get to think and dream rather than wear a uniform and kiss business-suits' asses all day." Juanita sighed. "She wanted a lot of things. Everybody does I guess, but especially Mary Beth."

I didn't say anything, but I couldn't help thinking yeah, and I wanted a father growing up. I wanted to be in a normal family, where I wouldn't be lied to and used by my own sister and mother.

The house was in a subdivision of ranch homes, street after street of little boxes, mostly white or brick, a few green or brown. Juanita drove into the driveway of our old house like she owned the place, and when the woman who did own the place came to the door, Juanita greeted her like an old friend.

The woman was holding a chubby baby and there were three other kids running around, driving her crazy, the woman said, and smiled. She invited us into the living room. It was a mess, but it was a colorful mess, and the chubby baby was looking at me and opening and closing his pink hand, like he was waving hello.

"My kids love that forest," the woman was saying. "No lie, it was a big part of the reason we took this house. It seemed lucky somehow."

Forest? I thought, but Juanita nodded and Dad didn't bat an eye.

Juanita said, "Okay, I gotta run by work and make sure the weekend girls got their paychecks." She looked at Dad. "You know where it is."

"You're leaving?" I said.

"I'll be right back, kiddo." She leaned closer to me. "I think this is something your dad and you need to do alone."

It was hard to imagine how Dad and I could be alone with this woman and her kids still here, but when we got to the basement, it felt like we were all by ourselves—it felt like we were on another planet even. I heard the footsteps of the kids and the crying of the chubby baby, but they seemed as far away as a dream. All that mattered was me and my dad, looking at this wonderful thing.

The basement was the forest. This is what my sister had done. She had spent all her free time, the summer when she was eleven, almost twelve, turning the gray concrete into a kid's version of a tropical paradise. And she did it for Mom. That's what Dad said. He was standing next to me with his hands shoved in his pockets (his new habit, so he wouldn't fidget). He said Mom was depressed that summer and Mary Beth was trying to cheer her up.

"Bethie was always trying to make Helen happy." Dad cleared his throat. "From the time she was a tiny girl." He paused for a moment and lowered his head. "Helen had been saying that her life was over, she'd never see the world. So your sister gave her this."

The shock for me was that I didn't even know Mary Beth could draw. Sure, I'd seen her draw pictures for Tommy and they were always really good, but this would have been good for an adult, and it was just incredible for a kid. The colors didn't seem to have faded at all and it was so intricate, so rich in details.

There were trees covering all four walls, with moss-covered branches and dark green vines and broad fan leaves, and there were furry little animals, some brown, some gray, hanging off the vines and peeking out playfully from behind the leaves. There were birds flying all over the ceiling: some with long red tails, others with stubby dark yellow beaks, and one with a wing span as wide as my arms. There was even a waterfall in the corner, with fish leaping out between the splashes of crystal water, and turtles and frogs and a swarm of butterflies—orange, pink, blue—hovering at the water's edge.

I walked around the room slowly, several times, taking it all in, and about the third time I passed by the water, I noticed a large rock reflected in it. I turned back to the right wall, where the rock was painted, and I saw all these colors on the flat surface so I moved closer to get a better look. When I got right up to it, I started laughing, I was so surprised. Mary Beth had painted a tiny version of her whole forest on that rock: the water was there, and the animals and the trees, and even the rock itself, and the order of everything was exactly the same, in miniature. I started out thinking she'd done the rock first, as a kind of master plan for the rest, but then I decided she'd probably put it in after the whole forest was finished. Maybe she wanted to see her design in a smaller form, so that one picture in her mind could hold it all, or maybe she'd just loved it so much, when she was done, that she'd decided to paint it all over again.

When Dad heard me laughing, he laughed, too. He was walking around himself, looking and becoming more relaxed with every minute we spent in the basement. Later, I often thought Mary Beth's forest cast a kind of spell on Dad and me. We stayed down there until Juanita came back. We didn't talk about what had happened to our family or anything that was sad; we just looked at the forest and talked about how beautiful it was. Dad even hummed a little as I moved across the floor, looking up at the birds in Mary Beth's sky and smiling at the idea that those birds could fly forever just like this. They would never have to go wherever birds go when it rains; they would never have to travel hundreds of miles south to escape the bitter cold of winter. The birds could stay right there, the trees would never lose their leaves, the water would never dry up, the fish would never swim away; nothing would have to change at all, so nothing would ever die.

It had to be a spell, because as soon as we got back in Juanita's car, I realized that the summer Mary Beth was almost twelve was also the summer after I was born. Mom was depressed; Mom had said her life was over when I was what? Two months old?

"Did it work?" I asked Dad. We were waiting at a stoplight downtown.

"What do you mean?" Juanita said.

"Did it make Mom happier?"

Dad said no, but he didn't elaborate, and I didn't ask him to because he was messing with a wad of loose thread he'd pulled from the pocket of his new church pants. Juanita had already told him to stop. "You're going to ruin that pocket, Henry."

I closed my eyes and thought about what Juanita and Dad were trying to tell me by taking me to our old house. That Mary Beth would do anything for Mom. Okay, I got it, but it made no sense. It didn't help; it didn't make Mom happier. And neither did the other thing my sister did for Mom, I realized with a start. That guy Mom had the affair with, Mr. Stanley, got transferred to the home office in Chicago the summer after Dad left. I remembered this because Mom's new boss, a fat bald guy named Mr. Treecher, had a daughter Francine, the new girl in our first grade class, who had two raincoats: one the ordinary yellow slicker, and another reversible one, pink on one side, baby blue on the other.

Mom probably thought she got what she deserved. The world was hard and you had to be hard to survive it.

Or you could be crazy.

We were back at the house and Dad was hunched over the kitchen table, scribbling away on a piece of paper, making one of his lists for the first time in weeks. I sat down next to him and tried to get started on my homework, but it was useless. My mind was too busy trying to make sense of all this, though I knew that was probably useless, too. I could lay out everything I knew about my family, make lists of every memory and every fact, but like the night sky, there would still be holes, places too far away from me to make out any light.

chapter
twenty

That Ben was still in love with my sister was obvious, and not just because he was spending all his time—and going deeply in debt on his Visa—flying to St. Louis to see her every weekend. That could have been brotherly love, even a desire to help a friend in need. But if she was just a friend, he wouldn't have checked his face in the rearview mirror and stuck a breath mint in his mouth before he got out of the car. He wouldn't have closed his eyes when she kissed him, no matter how playful the kiss. He wouldn't have offered her his arm pretty much constantly, as if he was dying to touch her even for a minute.

Even though it had been two years now since she dumped him, he was still in love with her. We were sitting in a bar near Washington University, the last weekend in April, when I decided to ask him why.

It was my fourth visit to St. Louis, and the first time in my life I'd ever been in a bar. We were in a small booth across from the pool table. A Van Halen song was playing on the jukebox. We'd just come from the hospital, and Ben was leaning his head in his hands. He still had the long drive to Tainer ahead to take me home, and then back to his parents for the night, before he flew to Philadelphia tomorrow.

I liked the darkness of the place. It made it easier to say what was on my mind.

My faith in romance was at an all-time low. It had been bad enough hearing the relationship woes of Mary Beth's customers, but knowing about my own mother's affair, knowing the terrible thing she did to my dad, it was enough to make me lose hope. And Mike and I weren't doing so well, either. Since our weekend in St. Louis, he was always busy. He swore he wasn't mad about what happened—or didn't happen—that night. He said he understood. Nothing had changed, he insisted; he was just really, really busy. Too busy to come over or go out.

Tonight was the prom, and instead of being home getting my hair and nails done with all the other lucky girls, I was sitting here. It was my own fault. Mike was still willing to go, but I'd told him to forget it. I told him he was right, it was nothing but a waste of time.

Ben was on his second beer, and I was devouring a ham and cheese sandwich. I could never eat before I went to the hospital; my stomach was too jumpy. He didn't seem to mind that I asked why he loved Mary Beth, but he hadn't answered yet, either.

"You're what," he finally said, "sixteen now?"

He was guessing but he was right; I'd just turned sixteen on Monday. Juanita had covered the cake with candles and joked that I was sixteen going on a hundred. It felt true. The strain of trying to understand my sister was taking its toll. Of course I never said no when Mary Beth asked to see me, even though she was damn near impossible to talk to. Everything was funny to her now: the weather and the shows on TV and what she had for lunch and you name it. Even when I told her I'd seen the forest she painted at the old house, she laughed and said, "Oh yeah, I'm a real Pea-Ca-So. Move over Mike Angelo, here comes Mary Beth Norris. Cathedral smathedral, the basement is what's really tough. You have to paint behind both the washer and the dryer, and don't get in the way of any boxes!"

Every time I left the hospital, my mouth was sore from forcing smiles.

Ben took a big gulp of his beer. I looked at him. "I hope you're not about to say I'll get it when I'm older."

He smiled weakly. "I was considering that."

"You don't have to tell me. It's none of my business anyway."

"I'm not trying to be evasive. It's very complicated."

Two women walked by, giggling and talking, and took a long look at him. He was facing their direction, but for all the notice he took, they might have been ugly old men.

"She's beautiful, is that it?" It was another mystery: how she became prettier every time we saw her. That day she'd been wearing her own clothes, blue jeans and a violet shirt, Keds sneakers, hair pulled back in a ponytail. Nothing special, but even I had trouble looking away from her. Ben didn't try.

"She is beautiful." His voice was wistful, but after a minute he shook his head. "But no. That's not why I love her." He wiped his hand across his eyes. "Christ, I should have a ready answer. I've been asked this question constantly in the last few months. My mother, my father, Rebecca, most of my friends."

His beer was empty and he nodded when the waitress asked if he wanted another one. I was worried about him driving but I figured he needed the break.

After a while he tilted his head to the left side. "Did your sister ever tell you about Aaron?"

I was about to say no, but then I remembered. Aaron was the guy who died in the biking accident with Ben. The reason Ben was depressed when Rebecca brought him to my sister. I told him yes, and then listened while he went on and on about how brilliant Aaron was. The finest mind in the biochem department. The potential to be one of the finest scientists in the world. Something about nonredundant protein sequences, neurotransmitters, biogenic amine something or other . . . a bunch of stuff I couldn't have followed even if I'd tried, which I didn't. I was too tired.

"And he was your friend?" I finally said, hoping to move us back to the topic.

"Yes. We worked together, but he was also my friend." Ben's voice was quieter. "The best friend I'd ever had."

He paused for a while. I looked at my hands and wished I could have a beer, too.

"All right. Did Mary Beth ever tell you what she and I did on our first date?"

"No."

"When Rebecca first told me about song reading, I didn't think much of it. I was being a snob. I thought it was like astrology or tarot cards or any other bullshit. When I told your sister I wouldn't be coming back, this was in her office that first morning, she said fine. But then she said she'd never gone out with a graduate student. She was looking straight at me. Her eyes were a challenge. And then she elaborated; I believe her exact words were: 'I've never slept with a graduate student. Is it any different?'"

I was pretty shocked but I grabbed a potato chip and chewed, casually, maturely.

"What could I do?" Ben laughed a short laugh. "I was depressed but I wasn't dead. Of course I asked if she wanted to go to dinner.

"I don't remember how she got me talking about Aaron that night. I hadn't talked to anyone about it since I left school, and there I was, sitting with this gorgeous hick at some greasy spoon in the middle of the country, spilling my guts. After our dinner, we drove to the river. She was very friendly. I thought this was a prelude to—"

"I get it." I was still bristling at the word "hick."

"Right." He sat up straighter. "Leeann. Sorry, honey." He took a deep breath. "I'd already told her at dinner that I felt responsible for Aaron's death. Everyone always reassured me that I wasn't responsible, it was an accident, it was fate, it was bad luck—until your sister. She waited until we were at the river and then she said perhaps I was responsible. I thought she meant in some mystical boogeyman sense, like the tree being responsible for the squirrel climbing it, but she said no. Maybe I could have prevented my best friend's death."

"Jesus," I muttered.

"Of course I was surprised, but I wasn't angry. I'd believed this myself for so long. The truth is, it was something of a relief hearing another person say it. In the conversation that followed, Mary Beth insisted she didn't want to talk about my feelings, just the facts. Place, time of day, weather, condition of the road, and our bicycles. Was I in front or behind Aaron? Approximately how fast were we going when Aaron was hit by the motorcycle?"

Ben paused and wrapped his hand around his empty beer mug. "While I was relating all this, I found myself telling her what I'd never told anyone: that I saw the motorcycle weaving. I was behind Aaron, and I remember thinking the driver had to be drunk. We were going up a hill and I was winded. 'Stupid,' I said, under my breath. 'Stupid asshole.'"

The waitress picked up my empty plate. The bar was getting more crowded now. Several minutes passed when Ben didn't say anything. Finally I asked what happened next.

"The motorcycle slammed into Aaron. He flew off the bike and crashed into the pavement, head first. The paramedics said his neck snapped. I don't know about that. What I remember is the blood. I knew I wasn't supposed to be surprised by it—I knew the brain has fully twenty-five percent of all the blood in the human body—but I was surprised." Ben's voice was flat. "There was blood all over his face and neck, pooling in the gutter, dripping down the arms of my jacket when I tried to stop it. It was the first time in my life when I would have given anything for it all to be wrong: fluid dynamics, gravity, the irreversibility of time. All of it."

I shuddered, but I waited as long as I could stand to before reminding him, "I meant what happened with Mary Beth."

"Oh," he said. "Right. She told me she wanted to go farther down the river, and I drove until she told me to stop. That part of the road was an S, similar to the road Aaron and I had been biking on. Same forty-five-degree angle to the hill. We got out and walked for a while before she told me to fall back. Get behind her about as far as I was with Aaron. I went along; I didn't have the energy to argue. She was screaming at me, but it was impossible to hear what she was saying. Whenever a car went by, I couldn't hear her at all."

I thought I had it. "She wanted you to know that Aaron couldn't have heard you if you'd warned him about the motorcycle?"

"Yes. She was trying to prove to me that even if I'd yelled, it wouldn't have made any difference. There was nothing I could have done. But that was only part of it." He exhaled. "We were standing on the side of the road. It was pitch-black when she grabbed my arm, this woman I barely knew, and made me admit that the facts mattered. The truth mattered. Even if her little experiment wasn't valid, it was only because she didn't know how to design an experiment. But you do, she told me. 'You're a scientist,' she said. 'The real thing. And you're too smart to act like all the things you know have nothing to do with your own life.' "

"And then you felt better?"

"On the contrary. Then I felt much, much worse, but your sister was right. I was hiding in a blame that was completely irrational to keep from accepting that Aaron was dead."

After a minute, Ben said he also realized that night he'd been wrong about song reading.

"Had Mary Beth done your chart?"

"Perhaps, but it didn't matter. I thought she was the most intuitive person I'd ever met, and if she believed people expressed emotions in the songs they remembered, so did I."

It was true: Mary Beth had an astonishing ability to know how people felt. I still thought it was a gift, but Dr. Kaplan talked like it was part of the reason my sister was sick. "She needs to know that she doesn't have to continue this song reading," Dr. Kaplan told me. "That who she is, is sufficient. She doesn't have to take care of everyone to be loved."

"But she also needs to know that what she did was good," I said to Dr. Kaplan. "It was good to help all those people." Then I rattled off a quote Mike gave me about rainbows being miracles, not just the aftermath of storms. I thought it proved my point perfectly. "The storm would be like our family's problems, and the song reading is the rainbow." I crossed my arms confidently and looked at her. "Get it?"

Dr. Kaplan said it was interesting but she wasn't completely persuaded. We argued like this almost every time I saw her now. I liked her more and more.

Ben said we should probably get going. I nodded, but before I stood up I told him I was sorry about his friend.

"Thanks," he said. "And thanks for listening to me." He tilted his head to the left again, like he always did when he was feeling serious and thoughtful, a habit Mary Beth once joked would make him a hunchback by the time he was forty. I shook myself to keep from remembering the way she laughed then. A normal laugh.

"I find it very difficult to convey what your sister has meant to me. Rebecca keeps insisting I have to find someone else, ignoring how hard I've tried. My father thinks I feel responsible for Mary Beth, and if he found her a place at St. Christopher's, it would free me to move on with my life. It might have, if I wanted to be free." He smiled but his eyes were sadder than they'd been all day. "Of course they don't know her like we do, do they?"

"No," I said, letting him take my hand as we walked out of the bar and across the street, where Rebecca's car was parked. It was already dark, but I heard the catch in his voice when he thanked me again, adding the "honey" that I didn't mind anymore. None of this was his fault, of that I was sure. He and Juanita and Dr. Kaplan were like innocent bystanders to the crime that was my family.

When I got home, it was after ten; Tommy and Juanita were already in bed. Tommy had had the flu for days. Dad said his fever finally broke around suppertime. Juanita was exhausted.

"Were there any calls?" I asked Dad.

"That girlfriend of yours. Darlene."

I wanted to ask if that was all, but I knew Dad was terrified of forgetting a message and I didn't want him worrying he had. Especially since he probably hadn't. I was hoping Mike would call, but I didn't expect him to.

Dad was sitting in the recliner. The TV was on, but the volume was so low I knew he wasn't watching.

"How was Mary Beth?"

"Pretty much the same." I fell back on the couch and yawned. "Her doctor said she probably won't be out for a while."

"This must be so hard on her," he said softly. "Being away from home."

I shrugged but then I glanced at him. Juanita had made him worry beads for Easter. He had them clutched in his left hand and his thumb was rolling them, one by one.

I forced another smile. "You wouldn't believe how good she looks. I was just telling Ben, I think she may be better a lot sooner than those doctors think."

He didn't say anything, but his hand relaxed a little. After a few minutes, his hand stopped moving, and not long after that, I realized he'd fallen asleep. I wasn't surprised. He had to be tired, too, from taking care of Tommy. I knew he'd just waited up for me.

I walked over and gently took the beads, put them on the lamp table, next to his glasses, and then headed to the front porch. It was Saturday night, a warm spring night, and I was tired of thinking. I wanted to forget about Dr. Kaplan, Ben's friend Aaron and all that blood, Mary Beth's laughing at everything. I wanted to be a kid who didn't know that damn near everybody's secret was the same: that their life had been full of heartbreak.

By the time Mike pulled up in his truck, I was hunched over on the porch bench, knee-deep in self-pity. He was wearing a suit, which struck me as odd but then I remembered his new job at the condo development by the river. He was trying to save money for college now that he wouldn't have his grandfather's help. He'd said the hours were long, especially on weekends. Maybe it was true.

He sat down on the bench next to me, reached in his pocket, and handed me a letter. I couldn't make out most of it in the dim porch light but I saw the letterhead. And I saw him beaming.

I looked up and smiled. "You got in to Stanford." It was his first choice, and he almost didn't apply because he was so sure they wouldn't take him. He had great grades and test scores, but he was just a regular Joe from nowhere Missouri. That's what he always said anyway. "Oh, Mike, this is so great."

"They gave me a scholarship, too. Not all of it, but I really think I can do this."

"I'm sure you can."

He put his hands on my shoulders. "And now I think we need to go to the prom."

"What?"

"It's our last chance. In a month, I'll be done with River Valley forever."

"So? You hate River Valley."

"Come on, Leeann. I want to do this for you."

"But it's so late."

"Run in and get dressed. We'll have plenty of time to dance."

"You hate dancing."

"That was before I became a gentleman and a scholar." He smiled again. "Plus, I'm Maniac Mike. You never know what I'll try next."

I slipped inside, careful not to bang the door and wake up Dad. Fifteen minutes later, I was back on the porch wearing the only fancy dress I owned. It was an old gown of Mary Beth's; Juanita had hemmed it for me to wear to her cousin Rafael's wedding at the beginning of April. Luckily I hadn't spilled anything on it. It was pretty but not exactly right for a prom. It was deep green with a high neck and little pearl buttons, a big flouncy skirt—not a single sexy thing about it.

But Mike loved it. He said it was very Victorian, and so tonight I would be Elizabeth Barrett and he would be Robert Browning.

"Unless you want to be married." He had a corsage on the seat of the truck. He was pinning it on me. "Would you rather be Elizabeth Barrett Browning?"

I felt so happy I had to stifle a giggle. "Yes, I think I would."

"Okay then, Mrs. Browning." He did a very deep, very silly bow and held out his arm. "Shall we go?"

When we got there it wasn't quite midnight, but the River Valley parking lot was almost empty. Most people had already cut out for a party or the river bluffs or anywhere where teachers wouldn't be watching.

"All the better for us, Mrs. B," Mike said, opening the door of the truck. "We can sail across the dance floor undisturbed."

"Sail" wasn't quite the word for what we did. Mike and I had to be among the world's worst fast dancers. Slow dancing was better, mainly because we just stood and held each other while Mike recited his—that is Browning's—poetry.

"If one could have that little head of hers, painted upon a background of pure gold, such as the Tuscan's early art."

I leaned back and looked at him. "My head isn't little, is it?"

"How can you ask that? You know I dream of a red-rose tree. And which of its roses three, is the dearest rose to me?"

It actually fit pretty well with the Lionel Richie and Air Supply.

In between dances, Mike told everybody who would listen about Stanford. Only the teachers seemed to get what a huge deal it was. Mrs. Wood, our English teacher, had written one of his recommendations. She was manning the punch bowl and she damn near knocked it over, rushing around to give him a congratulatory pat on the back.

I didn't see Darlene anywhere, but I did see Kyle and Amanda. They were prom king and queen; they probably couldn't leave until it was over. When he walked by and gave me a smirky smile, I was glad Mike was looking the other way. He hated Kyle's guts now that he knew what happened to me.

But all of that was over now. This was a new night, and I was in a dream, dancing with my boy. My gangly, beautiful Robert Browning.

I only knew one poem of Elizabeth Barrett Browning's. It was very late when I finally blurted it out. The song playing was Bonnie Tyler's "Total Eclipse of the Heart," which always made me emotional. It was popular when Mary Beth got sick.

"How do I love thee?" I said, pulling him closer. "Let me count the ways. I love thee to the depth and breadth and height my soul can reach." I paused, and tried not to sound as embarrassed as I was. "Nice, isn't it? It's my newest sonnet."

"And I love thee," he said. His voice was quiet, strangely serious. "Freely, as men strive for right, purely, as they turn from praise."

I swallowed hard. "I love thee with the passion put to use in my old griefs, and with my childhood's faith."

He kissed my hair. "And I love thee with a love I seemed to lose with my lost saints."

I could feel tears standing in my eyes. It was just hitting me that he was going to California. He would be so far away from Tainer, and from me.

The song was over but I didn't want to let go of him. Finally I looked up and whispered, "I think I'm ready to stop squandering time."

He knew what I meant. His voice was very surprised. "Are you sure?"

"Pretty sure," I said, and smiled. "No, really sure."

He didn't seem as excited as I expected. Maybe he didn't believe it would actually work out this time. But twenty minutes later we were parked at our secret spot at the river bluffs. It was my idea to stay in the truck. Tommy's flu meant we couldn't go to my house, but also the truck felt like our home now. Everything important to us had happened here: from the night he drove me home from Juanita's party to the snowy afternoon he saved Dad and me at the mall and nearly everything since.

We'd barely started when I knew something was wrong. He wasn't kissing me in the passionate way he usually did; his arm around me was heavy and motionless, a duty. When I tried to move his hand to my breast, he managed to drift up to my neck. I asked if he was okay and he said yes. I asked if he wanted to talk and he said no. It wasn't until I went to unzip my dress—hoping to inspire him—that he whispered, "Stop."

He sat up straight.

"Something is wrong."

"Yeah," he said, and exhaled. "I don't think I can do this."

My face was on fire, but I crossed my arms tightly across my chest and watched him open the glove compartment. He smoked for a while, and I listened to the crickets and an owl hooting in the distance as I wondered how this could be happening.

By his second cigarette, I'd settled on the theory that he wasn't attracted to me anymore. I'd gained a few pounds since we moved to Juanita's; maybe he thought I was fat. Maybe he'd realized how dumpy I always was that night in St. Louis, when I put on that T-shirt and old terry cloth shorts. He was so tall and elegant, especially in that suit. I'd never been more attracted to him, unfortunately.

"Remember when you told me I looked like my mom?"

His voice startled me out of my self-loathing. "Sure," I said. It was after Christmas, the first time I went with him to visit her in the rehab, when she was well enough for visitors. But I couldn't imagine what it had to do with anything.

"No one else had ever said that to me. Growing up, everybody said I looked like George."

Mike never called him Grandpa anymore. Holly didn't call him Dad. He was George. Just a guy they knew. No relation.

I turned to him. The breeze had picked up and the trees were blowing, making the moonlight dance across his face. "I don't see that at all."

"Because you haven't seen the pictures." He took a long drag. "They used to show them to me. Pictures of him as a kid. They said we could have been twins." He put out the cigarette and leaned his arm on the window. After a minute he said in a harsh voice, "Old George used to talk to me about what this would be like."

"This?"

"Sex. He talked like it was so powerful, like it could turn you into a person you didn't recognize. It was one of his favorite sayings: a stiff dick has no conscience."

"God." It was still warm, but I was shivering a little.

"When we were in the hotel and you told me what Kyle did to you, I wanted to break his stupid neck. It was like Mom all over again. I couldn't believe the two people I love most were hurt by some fucking guy."

"You thought that?" My voice was soft, amazed.

"Yeah, but that wasn't the only thing. I also thought about having sex with you. And I don't mean for a minute. I mean constantly, the whole night. You were crying about your mom, and I was looking at your breasts. You were telling me how bad it hurt when that moron tried to force you, and I was imagining how you would look naked. Even when you were asleep, I was staring at you, wishing I could touch you."

He draped his arms across the steering wheel. I heard what sounded like a barge moving down the Mississippi.

It took me a minute. "Is this why you're always too busy to come over?"

"No. I mean, I have been working. But okay, yeah. I don't want to hurt you. I'd rather not see you than hurt you."

"Oh, Mike, you're not going to hurt me." I touched his arm. I was so relieved I almost laughed. "This is sweet but it's crazy. You're nothing like George or Kyle."

"How can you be sure?"

"Because they're jerks."

"Maybe I'm a jerk, too."

"Come on, they would never spend one second wondering what you're wondering right now. God, Kyle still doesn't think he did anything wrong at that party. You know that."

"True."

"And I don't care what you were thinking in St. Louis. You were nice to me. You listened and held me and it was sweet."

Then I did laugh. "The main thing is, you're not dumping me and you don't think I'm fat." I gulped. "You even said you loved me."

"Because I do." He took both my hands in his, lacing our fingers together. "I love thee with the breath, smiles, tears, of all my life."

"Well then?"

"But—"

"It's okay. We're married, remember?" I smiled. "Kiss me, you fool."

And finally he did. He kissed me and I kissed him until we were both out of breath. At some point, he pushed the seat back so we'd be more comfortable. He was sweating and I was definitely warm enough to take off my clothes when he reached for the zipper of my gown.

He told me he would take it slow. He made me promise to tell him if it hurt even a little bit. Then he whispered, "Are you afraid?"

"No," I said. It was true. His fingertips were running over me like they were touching velvet. The feeling was as intense as if I'd just discovered the existence of my skin.

The moonlight was gone now, lost in clouds, but I could still see the woods. There were fireflies blinking in the trees. "Sparks of hope," Mary Beth used to call them, when I was a little kid and she would catch them for me in Agnes's backyard. The evidence, she insisted, that things would all work out in the end.

As I felt Mike's chest rising against mine, his breath in sync with my breath, I thought the tiny flashes were just about the most beautiful thing I'd ever seen. It was the last thought I had before I became my body, all eagerness and girlish desire, wanting nothing but this.

chapter
twenty-one

My sister left St. Christopher's Hospital the third week of May. It was a Wednesday afternoon, and she checked herself out AMA: against medical advice. She had to sign a paper that said she was aware Dr. Kaplan did not feel she was ready. "But it's just so I don't sue them," she said, grinning at the nurse who'd handed her the clipboard and pen. She turned to me. "And so you don't sue them, if I walk out of here and straight off a bridge."

I carried her suitcase as we walked down the hall. She was singing a song I'd never heard. "F means I'm forever walking on. R means I got rails to move along. E-E-D is all that's left of need. O-M, omit the misery. FREEDOM, brother, is what I'm going for. FREEDOM, sister, is waiting out that door."

"What's that called?" I was just making conversation. I figured it had to be called Freedom, but she said she hadn't given it a title yet.

"You wrote it?"

"Just now," she said, and looked at her watch. "Maybe I'll call it May 16, 1:42." She shrugged. "Dr. Kaplan thinks I need to stop reading songs for other people and start writing them for myself. So I do, whenever I can remember. Well, I don't write them exactly. I think them up, but I don't care if they get saved."

"Why not?"

"It doesn't matter. There's always more."

"How many have you written so far?"

"A hundred? A thousand? I don't know. Whenever I want one, poof, it's there."

I glanced at her, trying to decide if she was serious. She seemed to be. And she didn't seem crazy or dangerous or whatever it was I was supposed to make sure she *wasn't* before I agreed to take her home.

She'd called me at seven-thirty that morning. I was getting ready for school. Juanita and Tommy were already gone; Dad was at his table, drinking coffee and arranging the envelopes. I was very surprised to hear her voice, and even more so when she told me to come get her.

"You have your license now, right?"

"Sure," I said. She'd sensed my hesitation. "Does Ben know about this?"

"No, and I don't want you to tell him. Please." She was whispering. "He's done too much for me already."

I said I wouldn't, but I didn't mean it. I also didn't mean it when I promised not to tell Dad or Juanita. As soon as I hung up, I tried to tell them all. Ben I couldn't reach. He was flying to a conference in New Mexico today. (I wondered if Mary Beth knew this. I had a feeling she did.) Juanita and Dad both had the same reaction: if she wants to come home, let's go get her.

The problem was, she'd insisted I come alone. "Just you.

You're the only one. Please, baby. Please do this for your big sis."

It was Dad who finally said I should do it. But Juanita made me promise that I would "check Mary Beth out" before we stepped one foot from that hospital. Make sure she's not too nutty. Make sure she's not gonna hurt herself. Make sure.

Was it nutty to make up a song about freedom when you're leaving a mental hospital? Not to me it wasn't. And Mary Beth had a really nice voice. Her high school chorus teacher had begged her to be in the school musicals but she was already working at the pizza place and didn't have time.

Her ditties sounded really good. She had another one for the Ford. The freedom song had a gospel sound, but this one was pure punk. "My car and me, we don't see eye to eye. I want to drive, it wants to up and die. This car is crap! The engine raps! The floorboard's got a hole. It makes me lose control . . . of . . . my shoooooooooe."

She laughed and so did I. It was fun, really. It passed the time until the Ford turned over and we were back on the road. Of course I insisted on driving. I wasn't sure if she was up to dealing with all the midday St. Louis traffic.

"So what do you think of the city?" she said, waving her hand out the window.

"I like it," I said, "but it's a little crowded."

"Where are all these people going? Do you ever wonder about that? When you look in the other cars, do you wonder what they're thinking and feeling and doing? Like that car there." She pointed at an old maroon Datsun in the left-hand lane. "Do you think that man is going to a funeral or just headed back to the office? Does he have a wife? Maybe he has two boys or five girls. Hey, pull up closer. I think he's listening to the radio. I want to know what song."

"I can't get any closer. I'm already tailgating this Chrysler."

"Fine. I don't really care anyway." She leaned back. "It's just a habit. I mean, really, why *should* I care about all these people?"

I took a quick look at her. She didn't look crazy, but she did look a little strange. The phrase that kept coming to mind was too bright. Like she was absorbing part of the sunshine. Like she might even glow once it got dark.

Of course that was a crazy thought, but it was my crazy thought, so it was okay.

"Are you hungry?" I asked.

"A little. They fed us constantly in that place, but the food was like cardboard. One time I told Ben if he didn't sneak me in some fried chicken I was going to scream. The greasier the better. I wanted it dripping off my fingers."

"Did he?"

"He brought back broiled chicken breasts and asparagus." She shrugged. "He tried, but the restaurants he goes to don't serve fried anything. It wasn't bad, though." Her voice was softer. "We sat on a blanket outside and ate lunch like we were any other couple."

"Do you want me to stop at a KFC?"

"No, but thanks, baby." She put her hand on my arm and exhaled. "You have no idea what a relief it is to be here. Just you and me, like the old days."

She grew quiet as I pulled onto the entrance for the highway. Maybe the familiar signs for Cape Girardeau and Cairo were reminding her that we were heading south, toward home.

"Tommy is going to flip out when he sees you." I smiled. "He was just telling me yesterday that his mama will be back any day now."

Actually, he told me his mama would be back by this

Saturday, and therefore, by a logic only a kid could follow, he didn't need to clean his room. "She'll sleep right here," he said, kicking his legs against his mattress. When I asked him where he would sleep, he said, "Here, too, silly!"

"I don't want to talk about Tommy yet," Mary Beth whispered. She was tapping her foot like she was hearing music. Maybe another of her songs.

Dad and Juanita were expecting a call. I'd told them I'd get to a truck stop as soon as I had Mary Beth and we were back on the road. Mike wanted a call, too. He'd dropped by to take me to school this morning right as I was leaving. I was just wondering how I'd manage all this without her knowing I'd broken my promise, when she looked at me.

"You know, Dr. Kaplan talked about you a lot. She thought I should open up to you more. Your sister loves you, she kept saying." Mary Beth was rubbing her thumb back and forth on the armrest between us. "You can trust Leeann."

"It's true." My voice didn't waver.

"That's good to know," she said, and then nothing for maybe ten miles. The car was hot and I felt my damp legs sticking to the vinyl seat. I decided if I didn't get to a phone, it would be all right. We'd be back by supper. They wouldn't have to worry for too long.

I was daydreaming about what it would be like, walking in the door with her. Especially seeing Dad and her together. What they would say to each other.

"Okay," she said softly. "I'm going to trust you, honey. So here's the thing. I don't think I can go back."

I inhaled. "That makes sense. I mean, I wouldn't want to go back to that hospital, either."

"I'm not talking about the hospital, Leeann. You know I'm not."

I could feel her eyes on me, and it was true, I did know. She was talking about Tainer. She meant she couldn't go back to our town.

I wasn't that surprised. Dr. Kaplan had hinted that Mary Beth might be better off in a new place. Facing your problems is one thing, Dr. Kaplan said, but facing an unthinking mob is another. I told her Tainer didn't have any mobs, but she said she didn't mean it literally.

I had wondered many times how my sister would deal with being home after everything that happened. The antifamily calls had stopped since we went to Juanita's, but the gossip hadn't. George made sure of that, and since he owned the only hardware store for fifty miles, he had a damn near captive audience. People still needed nuts and bolts and wood glue. People still liked hearing rumors, even if they were as bizarre as the latest: that my sister was another Reverend Moon, and Holly and her husband and kids had been brainwashed into a cult.

When I glanced at Mary Beth and noticed her hands trembling, I remembered Dr. Kaplan saying she was afraid of losing my love. It was so hard to believe. Even as a little kid, the desire to please her was one of my earliest feelings. I vividly remembered having a fit when Mom wouldn't buy me new crayons just because I needed a new violet. My old one was worn to a nub and I wanted to draw more pictures for my sister in her favorite color.

"All right," I said slowly, "let's say you did leave. Where would you go?"

"I knew you would ask that. Ben always says you're the most pragmatic person. But I'm not complaining, honey. I'm gonna need your practical side to help me plan all this. Okay, well, I could go to Philadelphia. That's what Ben wants, and I did tell him I would think about it. He has all these great plans for us:

kids, a house, the whole nine yards. But the thing is, he still thinks I'm like he is, just an all-round good person, out to save the world. If only he knew, right? Ha, ha."

She was talking so fast, I was having trouble keeping up. By the time it hit me what she meant, she'd moved on.

"So anyway last night, I went to the hospital library and studied the maps and I think I found the perfect spot. It's a small town. Cities are so dirty and mean, you know? It's still on the river. I can't imagine living anywhere without the river, can you?"

I never cared much about the river but I knew my sister did. She used to claim she could feel its presence for miles. She was the only person I knew who drove to the bluffs to look at the Mississippi instead of a boyfriend or girlfriend.

"And the best part is the name," she continued. "I just love this. Waterproof, Louisiana. I kid you not." She slapped her knee. "Don't you love that? Can't you see the postcards? Having a great time in Waterproof, wishing you were here. I could send 'em to Tainer the next time it floods. Juanita would get such a kick out of it."

I paused a moment. An eighteen wheeler was crowding me. I waved him past, and waited until he'd gone over the hill.

"What will you do for money?"

"I'm sure Waterproof has a restaurant. I'll work two jobs if I have to. I'm a hard worker. Dr. Kaplan said so, too." She let out a laugh. "I'll have you know I was the star of occupational therapy."

It made a weird kind of sense, but I suddenly felt like I had to know if all this was just crazy talk. Did Waterproof, Louisiana even exist?

"I have to go to the bathroom," I said. "We can get gas, too."

We pulled off at the next exit and into a Texaco. While Mary

Beth was pumping the gas, I went into the office and asked to look at the atlas. Sure enough, Waterproof was real and right on the Mississippi. I thought the people who named that delta town had some sense of humor.

The phone was outside, only a few feet from the car. But I didn't call them. I didn't want to lie to her, and we were already halfway home.

For the next thirty or so miles, she kept up a steady stream of talk about what it would be like to move to a brand-new place. Her brightness was more intense than ever. It was more like a vapor than a light. It seemed to fill up the whole car.

"I can come back for Tommy," she was saying. "As soon as I get work and a good place lined up. It won't take long, I'm sure. A month or two, tops."

I could see his big black eyes, hear his sweet lispy voice asking why his mama hadn't come home yet. A month or two was an infinity to a little kid. Mary Beth knew that as well as I did, or at least she used to know.

But maybe she had to do this. Maybe the only alternative was more time in the hospital, or even worse, slipping back to where she'd been last November and December.

I wanted to be supportive but I was so confused. Shouldn't I at least tell her that I would miss her? Or would that mess her up again? Dr. Kaplan had said many times that it was too much responsibility that led to my sister's breakdown. But she also said Mary Beth was afraid of losing my love.

A Camaro full of teenagers passed us. The guy in the passenger seat was staring at her, mouth open. Maybe he saw the brightness, too.

"Well, it might work," I said. It was just hitting me that this was the first time in years I'd been in the car with Mary Beth without the radio playing. No wonder our pauses seemed so loud. "Of course you'd have to call me and let me know you're all right." I forced a smile. "Let me know if Waterproof is living up to its name."

"Call you? Oh honey, you don't think I'm going without you? God, I could never leave you behind." She touched my shoulder. "Don't you remember? You're my baby princess."

I hadn't thought about this in so long, it felt like a detail of someone else's life. It was years and years ago, before Mom died, before Dad left. She was in high school; I wasn't a baby, but I was younger than Tommy. She used to hold my hand, swing it back and forth, and sing. "My little dolly, cute as can be, she wouldn't kiss any frogs. But then the prince came and took her away, oh, bring back my doll girl to me. I went across the whole wide, wide world, I found my dolly under a tree. Now it's a baby princess I see, no baby could be sweeter. My baby princess, cute as can be, no prince can take her away from me."

She'd made up the words, of course. Was this something she'd always done?

It was finally dawning on me what she had in mind here. She wanted us to go to Waterproof right now. Today, the two of us. This is why she checked herself out of the hospital. This is why she wanted me to come all by myself.

"You don't even want to go by Juanita's?" I couldn't help it; my voice sounded shocked.

"I do want to, Leeann. It's not that." She stuck her hand out the window again and after a minute or two, broke into another of her songs. It was a long and convoluted country-western about a woman who'd done things, seen things, said things—and now she had to go away. The "things" weren't specified. The part about her little boy was the only part that really got to me. Her voice sounded so beautiful and heartbroken. "Don't show me how he's grown. Don't tell me what he plays with. Don't bring him to the phone. Don't ask me to wave bye-bye. If I take just one look, I know I won't be able. To leave my little darlin'. To cut out my own heart."

I kept my face straight, eyes on the road. I was still too stunned to think of what to say to her.

When she was finished with her song, she stretched her arms out. "We do need to make one stop first."

At least I knew this was coming. I'd figured it out long before I got to St. Louis, when I realized as I left Tainer this morning that today was Mom's birthday.

The cemetery was a few miles past town; we still had a ways to go. Mary Beth used the time to reassure me that I would be okay in Louisiana. "You're gifted," she said, patting me. "You'll be fine in any school."

I'd find new friends, she insisted, of course I would. And Holly had already written her with the news that Mike was going to California for college. "I know that will be so hard for you, honey. A new start could be good for you, too."

When we got off the main road, the sun was lower in the sky, shining pink and orange on the cornfields. The cemetery was surrounded by farmland. As we drove up to the gates, I found myself remembering back to the first time we came here, when the director gave us a tour and told us his cemetery "served customers" from five counties. I was ten and I thought he meant they served food like at Mary Beth's diner. I wondered who would ever feel like eating at this place.

The last time we were here was in the fall, before Mary Beth got sick. I hadn't been here since. I hadn't even thought about coming here, unfortunately.

Mom's grave looked downright forlorn. There were weeds sprouting around the headstone. The tulips Mary Beth planted years ago had bloomed as always, but they were wilted and brown, probably because of the dry spell a few weeks ago. And the worst part, the remains of some teenagers' idea of fun were scattered around the left side of the plot: half a dozen crushed beer cans, twice as many cigarette butts, candy bar wrappers, and potato chip bags.

Mary Beth dropped to the ground and grabbed a handful of weeds, pulling so hard she took the roots with her. I knelt down, too, and started gathering up the trash. There was too much to carry, so I went to the trunk of the Ford and found an old grocery bag. I stuffed all the garbage in the bag, and then walked up the lane to the Dumpster by the caretaker's house. When I got back, Mary Beth was finished with the weeds, but she was still kneeling, staring at the headstone.

I sat down next to her. It was so quiet. The air was getting cooler, hinting at the coming night.

"I was just thinking, when we're in Louisiana, there'll be nobody to watch over her anymore." Her voice was scratchy and deep, like she was choking back a sob. "She'll be an orphan all over again."

I put my arm around my sister. She snuggled into my neck, and it felt so familiar. I remembered what it felt like to take care of her, for her body to feel as known to me as if she were my child.

We sat in silence for a while. I knew she was trying not to cry. Finally she whispered, "Why don't you feel sorry for her, Lee?"

"What?"

"Dr. Kaplan told me you don't feel sorry for her. You feel sorry for Tommy and for Dad and for me, but you never feel sorry for Mama."

Mary Beth leaned back. The brightness was still there, but focused now. It was in her eyes. Her eyes seemed like they could see right into my soul.

"I do feel sorry for her sometimes." I paused and realized I had to say it. I'd been planning to say it for weeks. I took a breath, but it didn't help. I was so nervous my voice came out like a squeak. "But I think what she did was wrong. To Dad. I think it was a terrible thing to do."

"Do you have any idea what her life was like?" Mary Beth jumped up like I'd slapped her. She walked to the big oak tree across from the grave. "Do you even know why she married him?"

"No, no one ever told me."

"Okay, I'm telling you now. She married him because she had a toothache."

"Come on, Mary Beth."

"It's true. She was right out of high school, fresh from the god-awful children's home, and working at the plastic factory. There were no benefits then. The pay was like a dollar an hour. She didn't have the money to get her impacted wisdom tooth out. She could barely afford the room she was renting and enough food to keep her from being too dizzy to stand on the assembly line."

"And Dad gave her the money?"

"Yes. He was older; he'd been working at the factory longer. He never liked buying anything, you know how he is. He had some money saved, and he slipped it to her in an envelope."

"That's sweet."

"It is sweet, but it's not a reason to get married, is it? Mom was eighteen, Leeann. Two years older than you are. She married him because she felt grateful, pure and simple."

I paused for a moment. "She never loved him?"

"Of course not. They had nothing in common except being poor. You know that as well as I do."

She was right, I did know this, but I still didn't want to hear it. I wanted to pretend Mom saw his smile, appreciated his sweetness, loved him for his gentleness. I wanted to pretend their entire marriage wasn't a lie. "Well, she should have had the guts to say so. That's what I think. She should have been honest." I was standing, too, now, working up to a sputter. "Why couldn't she have told him to leave? Why did she have to—"

"Told him to leave?" Mary Beth laughed a harsh laugh. "Do you really think Mom could have done that? You heard how she talked, all those things she said. Over and over. 'I got what I deserved.' 'I made my bed, now lie in it.' 'I can't have my cake and eat it, too.' 'If you dance, you have to pay the fiddler.' 'You reap what you sow.'"

"But it doesn't make any sense." I was trying not to yell. I was trying to remember how sick Mary Beth had been, how sick she still might be. Yet she certainly didn't seem sick. Those bright eyes were boring a hole right through me, telling me she was right about everything, the way she always was before. "Mom had an affair with that guy, Mr. Stanley. You can't say she was trying to do the right thing then."

"No, she wasn't. It's true." Mary Beth looked up at the branches of the oak tree. Her voice grew soft. "I wish you could remember her then, Lee. You know how she was, always so hard, but when she got with Will, she was like a girl. She wore pretty dresses instead of those hideous pantsuits, and she let her hair hang on her back, rather than twisting it into that ugly knot. For the first and only time in her life, she woke up smiling. She told me once if there was a heaven, it would be just like the feeling she got being with him."

"I don't want to hear this."

"She was only thirty-seven years old. Younger than Holly. Younger than a lot of my customers who never had half the responsibilities she did. Why didn't she deserve love? Why? Tell me. God, if only you could have heard her saying how bad she wanted this chance!"

Mary Beth paused but I knew there was something else she had to say. She was chewing on her bottom lip, and her eyes were darting back and forth, as if she was trying to come up with the right words. I wasn't messing with my chin scar; I wasn't trying to figure anything out. I wouldn't even say I was thinking. I don't know how it happened that I suddenly knew what it was.

"So you had to help her. You had to make him leave."

Dr. Kaplan had it wrong. Mom's happiness was the motive, but Mary Beth was the one who did it. I shouldn't have been surprised. Mom was too much a believer in punishment to risk something like this.

The only thing I didn't know was whether it was planned or just an impulse. Did my sister see me standing in Woolworth's and just grab me? Or did she work out all the details: exactly how long she'd wait before she called Mom and said she'd found me; what she would tell Dad to make sure that the guilt he always felt was sufficiently, terrifyingly magnified; how she'd handle me, even though it was very unlikely I'd cause any problems. I was such a quiet child, everybody said so. Shy and fearful, just like my father.

When I asked Mary Beth if she planned it, she said she couldn't remember. Her chin was quivering. She was looking at her hands. "I spent so long trying not to think about it, those memories are just gone."

I could feel my eyes well up, but I sniffed hard and turned to face the hill on the other side of the cemetery. The sun was so low now it seemed to be sitting on the ground. In a minute, it would disappear and the only light would be the strange brightness of Mary Beth's eyes.

"You have to understand." She was whispering. "I would have given anything to make them happy together. It's the only birthday wish I ever had. He knew she didn't love him, that's the thing. He was always apologizing to her, wishing he could be what she wanted. She would yell at him, and he was so pitiful sometimes, it would just break my heart. I thought he would be better off, I really did. It's like that song, 'Somewhere Over the Rainbow.' Poor Daddy, I thought he needed a place to go where—"

"But you let him leave thinking he hurt me. You made him think that. Jesus, what gave you the right?"

"It was a horrible thing, but it didn't feel like a right. It's always been this way. It's like people need things and I have to do something about it. I have to help them. It was like that with Mommy. She always talked like she wanted to die. Even when I was little, she would say the only thing she looked forward to was sleeping. She wished she could sleep forever, never wake up. Daddy said she didn't mean it, but I knew she did. All my life, I was just trying to keep her from leaving me."

Mary Beth was swallowing back tears, and I felt bad for her, but I had to say it, "So you picked her over him? Is that what you're telling me?"

"I know, I know. I shouldn't have done it, but Mommy was so much worse off. She couldn't even listen to music. She bought records for me and you; she even bought records for Dad, but when we tried to get her to listen to them, she couldn't relax enough to hear it. They never had music in that home she grew up in, did you know that? I used to imagine her a little girl without any songs, with nothing to relieve all her sadness. Dad's mother really loved him, but Mom had nobody. She never did."

Before I could say anything, Mary Beth reached for my hand. "We just need a new start. That's all we need." Her voice was pleading. "Can't you see it, honey? The Norris gals, doing the big town of Waterproof. Maybe we'll even get us a house there with a huge garden. White and yellow roses like we had at the old house."

I didn't pull away and I didn't interrupt while she spun the fantasy of our new life. She wanted to make it up to me, I see that now. She was still convinced that what she'd done wrong was the most important thing about her and always would be.

When she asked if I was ready to leave, I said, "I have to do something first. You can stay here. I'll be really quick."

"Sure." She squeezed my hand, but she didn't ask me where I was going. Maybe she was afraid I wasn't coming back. "You don't have to rush, though," she said, and exhaled. "There's lots of time."

But I did need to rush. I had to get to Juanita's before Tommy was in bed.

Of course I was thinking about her song, but it didn't occur to me that I was song reading. I'd forgotten that she'd predicted this. "Someday you'll be doing readings yourself, hon," she used to say, and I would say no. I don't have the gift.

No matter how many problems a customer has, you have to find the one thing they really care about, the thing that will give them the strength to handle all the rest. This is the gift, and maybe I did have it at that moment; maybe that's how I knew what had to happen next. The words she'd sung seemed like a message straight from her heart to mine, telling me how to give her back her life.

Forgiving her might take me years, but of course I wanted her to have this chance. She was my sister. She had clutched me to her, a motherless child even while my mother was alive, and called me honey and sweetie and baby princess.

Tommy was in his pajamas, and sound asleep by the time I drove back to the cemetery. I'd told Dad and Juanita that Mary Beth had to see him first, but we would all be home very soon. He felt warm and heavy as I carried him to her and put him in her arms.

She said his name and pulled him to her chest and then he opened his eyes and told her he wasn't tired before he said, "Mama!" and started laughing at his luck, to wake up and find his mother home. It was too dark to see her face, but her voice was relief mixed with something that could only be called joy. That's what I remember.

TURN THE PAGE FOR

Up Close and Personal
with Lisa Tucker

Up Close and Personal
with the Author

1. SONG READING IS SUCH AN UNUSUAL IDEA. CAN YOU TELL US HOW YOU CAME UP WITH IT?

Like most writers, I've always been fascinated with words, but growing up, we didn't have many books. We didn't even have magazines, but we always had a record player. My earliest relationship with words was through songs, and I've found that's true for a surprising number of people. The specific idea of song reading came to me about ten years ago, when I became very interested in psychology, especially how memory works. When it hit me that the songs people remember may say something about them, I decided to test the theory on my family and friends, just like Mary Beth does in the novel.

2. YOU'VE DONE SONG READING YOURSELF THEN?

Yes, but I've never made any money for it, or even received afghans and cakes like she does! Some of the charts in the book were developed from my experiences; most are invented. Of course now that I've written this novel, I'm always being asked questions about songs and I love that. When people tell me about their music—favorite songs, favorite bands, the songs they can't forget—I feel very honored. I know they are entrusting me with a little piece of their heart.

3. WHY DID YOU DECIDE TO WRITE ABOUT TWO SISTERS? DO YOU HAVE A SISTER? IS THE NOVEL IN ANY SENSE AUTOBIOGRAPHICAL?

I decided to write about two sisters because that's what the narrator, Leeann, was interested in talking about. It sounds odd, but the voice really does control a lot more of the story than I understood before I became a writer. Once I heard Leeann speaking to me, I had to follow her around, see what she would show me next. That said, I've always been interested in sisters, because I think it's such a complicated bond. The novel isn't autobiographical except to the extent that I adore my own sister and am grateful to her for believing in me and helping me understand the meaning of family.

4. *THE SONG READER* IS VERY LYRICAL, BUT IT HAS ALSO BEEN CALLED A PAGE-TURNER. WAS HAVING A STRONG STORY LINE IMPORTANT TO YOU AS A WRITER?

Yes, definitely, because the novels I love most work on many levels: they have beautiful language and memorable characters, but they also have a great plot. In graduate school I studied nineteenth-century American writers like Hawthorne and Melville—and those writers told stories! *Moby Dick* isn't just a treatise on language; it's an adventure story about a whale hunt. *The Scarlet Letter* isn't only about American history; it's also a beautiful tale of forbidden love. Some writers claim the traditional story form is dead, but I couldn't disagree more. I think we will always need new stories; they give shape and meaning to our lives.

5. THE SIGNIFICANCE OF "HOME" SEEMS TO BE A CEN-
TRAL THEME IN *THE SONG READER,* AND YET MANY OF
THE CHARACTERS' CRUCIAL REVELATIONS TAKE PLACE
AWAY FROM HOME, IN KANSAS CITY OR ST. LOUIS, IN
THE HOSPITAL OR THE CEMETERY OR EVEN IN THE CAR.
CAN YOU TALK ABOUT WHY THIS MIGHT BE AND WHAT
IT MEANS IN UNDERSTANDING THE NOVEL?

It seems to be one of the themes of American culture—that you
have to leave home to find it. *The Wizard of Oz* is probably the
best example. I think most people do find it easier to think about
their lives in a new way when they're away from their familiar set-
tings: on vacation, for example, or going off to college. Especially
if the family is very fragile, as it is for Leeann and Mary Beth, the
very act of asking certain kinds of questions might seem to put
the home at risk. What I hope is that the end of the novel finds
them with a chance at making a home that is more stable because
they have faced up to their past. I certainly wanted to give them
more family, and I think Juanita and Henry and Ben and Tommy
can be that.

6. SPEAKING OF CARS, I NOTICED MANY SCENES IN *THE
SONG READER* TAKE PLACE IN CARS. IS THIS BECAUSE
CARS HAVE RADIOS, AND SONGS?

Of course the songs are part of it, but the other part is that a car
allows people to say things to each other without having to be
face to face. It's part of the meaning of the book, this difficulty so
many people have talking about their deepest selves. If the songs
give the characters a language for what they can't say otherwise,
then the car gives them the ideal place. Plus, I love my car.
Someday I'd like to write an entire novel set in a car . . .

7. I'M FASCINATED BY THE CHARACTER HENRY. THE FIRST SCENE IN HIS APARTMENT IN KANSAS CITY HAS BEEN CALLED ONE OF THE MOST MEMORABLE IN THE BOOK. WAS IT HARD TO WRITE ABOUT SOMEONE WITH THE PROBLEMS HE HAS? DID YOU DO ANY RESEARCH ON MENTAL ILLNESS?

In some ways it was difficult to write Henry because I was determined to make him a fully rounded character rather than a stereotype of the mentally ill. I did do a lot of research on mental disorders, but in the end, I wanted Henry's condition to be a mystery to the reader so the reader would be in the same position as the people in the novel. We don't *know* what is wrong with Henry. Even if we had a label to attach we still wouldn't really *know* why he is the way he is. Today we would probably look for a biochemical explanation, but I'm still fond of Juanita's favorite reason for Henry's troubles: that he hasn't been loved enough to get him over all the hard parts.

8. THE MOTHER IS ARGUABLY THE MOST DIFFICULT CHARACTER IN THE BOOK. HOW DID YOU FEEL ABOUT HER? WAS IT HARD TO WRITE HER?

I suppose it must have been hard because I avoided writing about her until late in the revision process, when I realized Leeann had said almost nothing about her mother. It's funny, I really don't like novels that blame mothers for everything, and I certainly hope *The Song Reader* isn't interpreted that way. I feel very sorry for Helen. The harm she does to her daughters—and I think she harmed Mary Beth much more than Leeann, because Mary Beth didn't have an older sister to serve as a buffer—is due to her own terrible unhappiness with what her life has become. Some of this is her fault I guess, but fault doesn't interest me. I'm interested in compassion, and I think this is the saddest part of Helen Norris: she has no compassion for herself, and so she can't really sympathize with her daughters.

9. ONE OF YOUR REVIEWERS HAS SAID THAT EVERY PAGE OF *THE SONG READER* INSPIRES COURAGE. WHAT DO YOU THINK THIS MEANS?

Oh, I think it's such a lovely idea that my book could inspire courage in my readers. Courage is so important to me personally, and I remember when I was writing the novel, thinking about the things Leeann and Mary Beth had to deal with, and wondering if I could do as well as they did in the face of tremendous loss. I'm sure it sounds odd, but I really admire my characters for their willingness to work so hard at their lives and especially at their relationships. I suppose it's obvious by now that I have the utmost respect for the people in *The Song Reader*. I don't feel like I made them up as much as they came to me out of nowhere. For me, the writing process feels like the gift of seeing into another world.

10. CAN YOU TELL US WHAT YOUR NEXT NOVEL IS ABOUT?

It's about music again—one of my passions—but this time from the viewpoint of the performer rather than the listener. I've done some singing myself and my husband is a jazz pianist. We spent almost a year on the road playing little clubs, and the new book reflects some of those experiences. Patty Taylor, my main character, is a troubled person and a talented singer with a two-year-old boy she adores. Her child will be the motive for her success in the same way that Tommy is the motive for Mary Beth coming back to herself at the end of *The Song Reader*. Obviously, I'm not quite through with the themes of music and motherhood . . .

acknowledgments

So many people helped me along the way. Thanks are due to my brilliant agent, Marly Rusoff, who redeemed my faith in publishing, and to my wonderful editor, Amy Pierpont, and her assistant, Deirdre Dore. To all my teachers and buddies at Sewanee, Squaw Valley, and the Santa Fe Writers Conference. To the friends and fellow writers who read part or all of the manuscript: Pat Redmond, Jon Hoffman, Cheryl Nicchitta, Sara Gordon, Elly Williams, Marty Levine, Kevin Howell, Gretchen Laskas, Anne Ursu, Melisse Shapiro, and Michaela Spampinato. To family who cheered me on: Ann Cahall, Howard Tucker and the rest of the Tucker clan; Laurie's crew: Jim, Jeff and Jamie Crottinger, and my dearest girl in the world, Emily Ward. To my husband Scott, best critic and most loyal defender. To Miles, my sweet, smart, sensitive little boy, who gave me back everything. And finally for my mother-in-law, Minnie Tucker, who knew this would be published and did not live to see it. I still hear you giggling like a girl. You will always be missed.